Chaos the cat

DAVID DONDERO

David Dondero ISBN: 979-8-9886161-0-8

Book layout, art and design by David Dondero
www.davedondero.com

Please subscribe to David Dondero's Patreon for short stories, songs,
videos, and other unpublished work.:
https://www.patreon.com/davedondero

to Tate

CONTENTS

CHARACTERS

ULEE WINOOSKI: DELI WORKER

GEORGE DECARLO: ARTIST

HANS: HORSE

CHAOS: CAT

HENRY HODKEY: OWNER OF FARM

AINO: CARPENTER

ANNETTE AND SKY: POT TRIMMERS

ARAMOANA: GEORGE'S DAUGHTER

RUTH & JIMMIE AMUNDSON: CARL'S PARENTS

CARL AMUNDSON: STORE OWNER

WALTER: ASSISTANT MANAGER

HOLLY: MANAGER & BARTENDER

HECTOR: HOLLY'S BOYFRIEND/DEALER

SCHIEFELBEIN: OWNER OF FARM NEXT TO HENRY

SHERIFF RICK JOHNSON: SHERIFF OF DILLITS

DUFUR FLECK: FISH AND GAME WARDEN

BILLY JOHNSON: SON OF SHERIFF RICK JOHNSON

OTTO: MASTER GROWER

HUNTER: OTTO'S DAUGHTER

NATE: DISPENSARY MANAGER

LEO: LEGENDARY SHACK BUILDER

BECCA: FARM HAND

SIMONE: AINO'S EX GIRLFRIEND

MADGE: BILLY JOHNSON'S MOM

CAROLINA: OTTO'S WIFE

SKIP: PLANT SCIENTIST

ILF & PETROV: SKIP'S DOGS

LUKA: HENRY'S ADOPTED SON

VINCE BRODY: SOLD HENRY FARM

LEIF BRODY: SON OF VINCE

GIUSEPPE: GOLDEN GLOVES CHAMP

STANLEY: BARTENDER

MANDY: DAYTIME BARTENDER

FRANKIE: DEALER

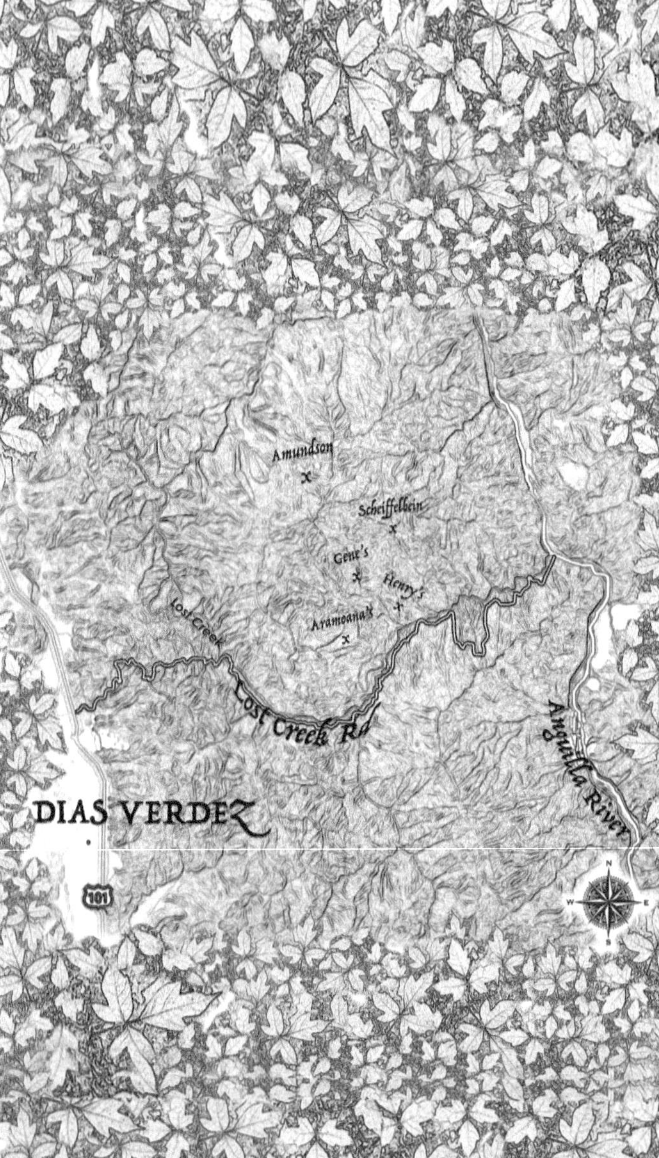

Amundson
Scheiffelbein
Gent's
Henry's
Lost Creek
Aramoana's
Lost Creek Rd
Anguilla River
DIAS VERDEZ
101

CASA DE POLLO
Lost Creek RD.
DIAS VERDEZ RV PARK
101
EZ MART
LAUNDRY MAT
HEALTH CLINIC
POST OFFICE
AMUNDSON'S GROCERY
SLINGERS
N
W
E
S

DIAS VERDEZ

WINTER

ULEE WINOOSKI

Ulee squirmed in her zero-bag, mummified and dreaming. In the dream she was driving through New Mexico with George DeCarlo. They were traveling parallel the Rio Grande close to Truth or Consequences. George was trying to distract her with a dripping ice cream cone. He held it over her cigarette, and she pushed it away.

"Come on Ulee! Don't ya want some?" goofed George.

She ashes her cigarette through the crack in the window but the burning cherry blew back into the car, lodging itself in a pile of clothes in the back seat. It turned into a small flame. George didn't see anything wrong with the situation, calmly saying, "Well, you wanted a campfire."

Some of George's paintings started to burn but Ulee couldn't stop the car. She reached for the brake pedal but it kept getting further away. She stretched and finally managed to push on it, but the pedal only amplified the volume of George's laughter.

She drove the car into the ditch, and it came to a stop in a grove of devil trees. Rushing to pull the burning clothes from the back seat only spread the fire into the sage brush. A blank canvas started to burn.

"Oh good, I'll use that one," said George.

She kept pulling out the burning clothes, but it was no use. The whole car went up in flames and she stood there while George did nothing but say, "Let it burn, Ulee."

The fire nightmare had her heart racing as she awoke in the trailer to the creaking sound of a dying live oak tree. It was covered in ice and straining from the weight. Then came a sudden crack and a thump! It shook the trailer from its resting spot. Ulee sat up and wrestled out of the zero bag. The ice was pelting the little window above the sink and sounded like popcorn. She heard a hissing sound and could smell the propane leaking.

"Dammit, I just filled that fuckin' thing," as she felt around on the floor for her headlamp.

She stepped outside barefoot into the sleet storm, nearly slipping on the ice which coated the trailer's front step. Ulee untangled the strap and slid the headlamp down over her hair then switched it on. She followed the beam of light to the tank.

A branch had landed on the tow bar and cut the propane hose. She twisted the valve shut and pulled the branch away, brushing off the snow with the sleeve of her sweater to assess the damage.

"It's not too bad, Hans. Hose was shot anyway. I think today is forty years, can you believe it? What the Christ in hell, really? Where's George? Did he come by and do this?"

She looked off to the east towards the ridgeline. "George! Show yourself! Are you there?" She continued over the crunchy ice and pulled a green apple from her sweater pocket. "Hans, I haven't forgotten you. Here you go, bud." The horse huffed as he chomped the apple and Ulee went back into the trailer.

She plugged in the kettle to boil water. The power still worked through the ice storm but appeared to be out across the street. Her pictures and magnets had fallen from the mini fridge and lay scattered on the floor. She collected them on the table of the breakfast nook, arranging them into a half moon. The magnet on the fridge had a broken thermometer, but it held up a polaroid picture of her and George that she kept for posterity. She'd talk to the picture in the morning, it was her tea time companion.

"That's not me anymore but it's certainly you, George. Every day, the ageless wonder. Is this finally my trailer? After all these years?"

Hans whinnied outside as a beam of sunlight appeared. "I still love this dilapidated shit box, George! At least it's paid for but give me the title for god's sake! Come on, gimme a sign. We gotta fix these flats and get outta here. Isn't this why we left New York? This fuckin' icy mess. You said it didn't snow in California! Liar! Oh yeah, next time. Next time it won't snow. I'll remember. It'll just ice."

Inside the trailer her breath froze as she exhaled. It left a frosty patina around the breathing hole of her sleeping bag from the night before. HWY 101 was vacant as usual at that hour. The sleet turned to snow and fell through the beams of light at the edge of the RV lot. The neon sign out front read Discover the Magic of Mendocino County, only the v, e and r were burned out.

"Disco the magic," Ulee said to the kettle as it started to boil.

She scraped the frosty window with a butter knife to get a better view of Hans. His thick winter coat had spots of brown, white and gray. Little puffs of steam came from his nostrils. Snow collected on the blanket draped over his back but began to melt away as the sun crept over the ridge.

The clouds blew over the hill giving way to blue streaks in the sky and fresh Pacific Ocean air. The humid winds came from the coastline 20 miles away as the crow flies. Ulee cracked the door and stared at the picture of her and George, the day they left New York City. She pressed a strike anywhere match into George's forehead in the photo. Then she struck the match on the zipper of her sweater and let it burn all the way to her fingertips. It was her ritual, while the frost on her sleeping bag melted into the fabric, she sipped her tea and put the photo back on the fridge.

Ulee stood six feet even, with long gray hair draping down past her waistline. A burly woman who towered over George. Her hair was straight, jet black and parted in the middle in the old photo and she resembled an Indian squaw. In the photo she wore faded overalls and the same oversized wool sweater that she currently wore, the one with an alpaca standing next to a cactus. She knitted it herself.

George was a frail man dressed in purple velvet pants and a lime green vest. He had long brown hair and sported a sunflower bandana. The two smiled in the photo like kids at Disneyland. She remembered the day they arrived in Dias Verdez. George said, "This is it! This is the place, we've finally found it!"

Dias Verdez was nestled in a valley which meant it rarely got cold enough for snow and if it did, it wouldn't last long. Usually gone by noon. The town strung along HWY 101 for about a quarter-mile, consisting of a string of random shops, close to the Mendocino-Humboldt County line. It used to be a ranching community, but pot took over in the late '60s thanks to a perfect climate for growing high-quality marijuana.

Ulee Winooski and George DeCarlo landed in Dias Verdez in January of 1970. They left New York City on a whim. She barely knew him and didn't even like men, but she liked George for some reason and wanted to escape the New York Winter. He somehow convinced her that he was a famous artist, and he definitely looked the part, but he was more like a girlfriend to her. He claimed to be a part of the Factory art crowd, but he was mostly a hanger on. George had implied that he knew Warhol and he kept a photograph of the two of them together at a party in New York. She helped George sell paintings on their trip out to California. She used the picture of George and Warhol as evidence of their connection. She talked him up to gallery owners and managed to sell several of his works for a thousand dollars each. That was a lot of money back then.

George bought a Globestar Penguin trailer, and they pulled it north to Dias Verdez. They lived a few months together at the RV park before he split. He had a lead on growing weed, and he wanted to live off the grid. So, he bought property way up in the hills, east of HWY 101. "No man's Land" Ulee stayed in town. They drifted apart after that, and he left her with the trailer. She didn't mind at all. She had a new home and she enjoyed being free from the city. She didn't want a man. She wanted enlightenment. She liked being alone.

Ulee got a job working for Amundson's Grocery shortly thereafter. A co-op store with a real community vibe. The Amundson family owned it and they were into feeding the community at a fair price. They weren't capitalists, they were hippies. Ulee clicked with their philosophy and they became like family to her until they died. In 2007, both passed away at the same time from eating poisonous mushrooms. The autopsies revealed the cause of death but many folks in town suspected foul play; due to the fact that the Amundsons were experts in finding edible mushrooms. Some even thought their son Carl had something to do with it, but no one found any proof.

Amundson's Grocery stood in the town's center which was a short stroll from the RV park. Ulee walked to work at the store six days a week and didn't own a bike or a car. She didn't need them. Ulee was the deli manager, but no longer had any friends in town. Most of them had died or moved away. She had a few old acquaintances but rarely saw them these days because they had since boycotted the store.

Longtime customers had stopped going due to their suspicion that Carl had poisoned his parents. His insane price increases didn't help. Ulee despised Carl, but she couldn't believe he would murder them. She'd known him since he was a baby. So, she kept her job but went into a shell and gave off the appearance of being lost in thought. Preoccupied from within. An easy way to cue people to leave her alone.

She rarely saw Carl and when she did, she hardly spoke to him because he had grown into a man she found repulsive. His ideology was a complete rebellion against his hippie parents. He would usually come into his office for a few hours and leave. Sometimes he wouldn't show up for weeks. It was Walter who ran the store; although he had a severe speech impediment, he was the real day-to-day guy.

She knew how to manage the place, but Carl would not allow it. Her duties changed when he took over. The coffee bar used to be the focal point but that switched to the rotisserie chicken. She'd spend the first part of the morning tying off the chickens with string to skewer them for the rotisserie machine. Carl had it installed after his parents died. He had a secret spice to apply as a dry rub to all the chickens.

This was of utmost importance. Carl had convinced himself that his chicken would spark a craze. He thought he'd become a new Colonel Sanders and use his family store to propel him to fast-food fame and fortune. It didn't catch on. Ulee used the leftover chicken for Carl's famous chicken salad sandwiches, which were only famous because Carl said they were. Most of them didn't sell and found their way to the dumpster.

Carl covered up the nature mural on the back wall of the store with a banner of himself holding a chicken with an American flag backdrop that read, "This is Poultry Paradise."

CHAOS & HENRY

I woke up inside a cat's body and I couldn't understand how I got there. I've always considered reincarnation bullshit until it happened to me.

My first memory as a cat is from a hole in a cinderblock wall behind a dumpster. My mom made a nest there. It sheltered us from the rain but not much else. I remember a man coming up and throwing a piece of chicken at us. He looked vaguely familiar, but I had just started to develop my perception. "There you go, kitties." He was a gentle human, and it became a regular thing. This giving of the chicken. As I grew into my full-size cat body, I realized I knew this man but couldn't remember his name. It was on the tip of my hairy cat tongue. He wore baggy brown pants and a green hooded sweatshirt that said KMUD. He appeared to be in his early 70s, and he wore a floppy fishing hat with round glasses, like Henry Fonda in On Golden Pond. For some reason I remember this movie. It was 1981, the last time I went into the city. How do I remember all this crap? I'm a cat, for God's sake. I liked the movie because it made me cry. I saw it at the Castro Theater in San Francisco.

The nice man who looked like Henry Fonda made it easy on my mom for a awhile. She wouldn't have to hunt for food that day or risk getting trapped in the dumpster.

She used to go inside it to scavenge for food until it turned into a trap. It scared the crap out of me the day the owner of the store locked her inside. He said "Try to get out now, you little rat!" As he closed the steel door, locking her in. I circled the dumpster all night trying to figure out a way to get her out of there.

A truck came to empty the dumpster the next day, and Mom jumped out at the last second before getting crushed. It was sweet relief when she returned with a big piece of ham in her mouth. She gave it right to me, and I could barely finish it. I was a kitten at the time.

I realized early on that I had memories from a prior life. I could read the signs behind the grocery store. I understood what "DO NOT BLOCK THE DUMPSTER" meant and I could understand what people were saying in the parking lot. I remember being a human, but I don't miss it. It was a foggy memory, but I knew I had once been a person. I remembered the car I drove, a Ford Station Wagon. In fact I parked it in this very lot. I swear I did, over there under that big tree to keep it in the shade. As I grew, the memories flooded back. Living in a cat's body sometimes frustrated me, but I found it liberating, not having to worry about clothes. I grew into a fantastic fur suit. Mostly black but with a small white patch under my chin.

The only drawback is that it requires meticulous cleaning, but I enjoy the process. Ma taught me well how to take the time to groom. It makes me feel good about myself. As a cat, it amazes me what I can climb and how I can move my body and wriggle into tight spaces. My inability to speak gets me down sometimes, because I want to talk to people again, but I never really liked talking to them when I was a human. I was an artist in my prior life but I don't see colors anymore. Only blue and gray. That's a fuckin' drag and I really struggle with it. I remember the colors, though, and I miss them.

I enjoy the solitude of being alone. Zoning out and creating things. Getting lost in the process. These days, I get plenty of that as a cat, the alone time, so it's fine by me, but when I try to create it doesn't work out how I see it in my mind. There's a physical limitation. No more opposable thumb. That's a bummer man. I can't make my paws work right. It didn't stop me from making abstract scratchings in the dirt for the sake of the art. But all of it getting washed away in the rain eventually.

I don't think my mother was a human in her prior life. She wasn't into making patterns in the dirt either. Probably some kind of bird, the way she built that nest in the wall. We got along pretty well.

Then something horrible happened when she disappeared for a few days. I couldn't understand why she would have left. The next time I saw her, she wasn't moving. The evil store owner, put what looked like a stuffed animal on the loading dock and returned inside. I went to check it out and realized it was her. I tried to wake her, but she was stiff as a board. I started to moan, and the store owner came out and yelled, "Get outta here, or you'll get the same, you little rat!" He put her in a garbage bag and threw it in the dumpster. I started growling, but he laughed and threw a rock at me. The aloneness came upon me but I shed no tears. I couldn't. I spent days in a tree by the parking lot trying to figure out what to do. I wanted to burn that store to the ground and scratch that mother fuckers eyes out.

It snowed the day after she died. I got hungry, and saw the man who looked like Henry Fonda walking into the store. He left the back window of his truck open, so I took a gamble. The truck seemed familiar to me, as if I'd been inside of it before. I darted outta the tree, ran across the parking lot, and jumped in. Prowled around the interior for awhile. The seats had burn marks, but I felt at home inside. It had a familiar smell and yes I had definitely been in it before. In fact, I've driven this vehicle.

I found a half-eaten chicken wing in a styrofoam container on the floor and scarfed it down. Then I saw the bag of chips. I remembered them; my favorite snack in my old life. So I dug in. They didn't taste the same, and they were hard for me to eat. I sat on a piece of mail, and I realized how small I was. I used to hold an envelope in my hand. I could read the address and who the recipient was. Henry Hodkey P.O. Box 1111, Dias Verdez, CA. I know that name! Hodkey! Henry Hodkey! My old friend! It was all coming back in little bits and pieces. As if I was slowly being cured of my amnesia. He was a friend of mine in my prior life. I had no idea I'd been living behind a dumpster in Dias Verdez,California and my old pal Henry was taking care of us with chicken!

The postmark on the envelope read January 2010. In my last memory as a human, I was branding an image into a piece of leather; I distinctly remember that. A bobcat. I was trying to burn the image of a bobcat into leather with a hot paperclip! I don't know what year, but I'm sure of it. Why do I think of this? It's trapped in my brain somehow.

Strange metallic discs with writing on them lay on the front seat. One read Miles Davis's Bitches Brew. Yes, I remember the great Miles Davis, but I only had vinyl records. I remembered the day Henry tried to sell me on CDs back in the 80's. He said, "These things are indestructible!" and threw one against the wall. It cracked and never played again. So, I never bought into it. I was happy with my vinyl records and the radio. I had dozens of radios, I collected them.

I was sitting there daydreaming about radios and spotted Henry heading towards the dumpster with a bag full of chicken. I watched through the windshield as he snooped around for my mother and I. He returned to the truck with a dejected look on his face.

I jumped behind the seat and hid. Henry plopped in behind the wheel. "I guess there's no chicken for the kitties today," he said. "It's alright, I'll eat it all." He cranked up the engine and the truck rumbled out. I hid deeper under the seat. A sweet, pungent smell became stronger as he drove. He'd sparked up a giant joint. Marijuana, I remember well, and it was a kind smell indeed. I tried to inhale deeply and get a contact buzz.

Henry put a CD into a slot on the dash, and the music started blaring. Ahh, it was wild horns. I watched him through the crack between the seats. He had one of those cell phones. I never got one. I refused. I didn't even have a landline. He held it in one hand, and it was glowing. It started beeping and making a vibration. Henry looked at it while holding the steering wheel with his knee, pressing a button, and talking to it.

"Wheezy, can you hear me? I got you on speakerphone. I'm in the truck."

"You made it back," she answered. "How's it goin' up there, Henry?"

"Well, the atmospheric river has finally come to Dias Verdez, but I'm still comin', rain or shine. The creek's getting pretty high."

I felt the road turn to gravel after he made a sharp turn.

"Yeah, maybe we'll have a Lake Shasta again after all this rain."

"Hey, ah, anyway, I got the seeds, and Nate's got a guy coming this week. Gonna pick him up in the city when I make the run. His name's Aino. Nate tells me he's trying to get off the sauce. Do you know him?"

"Yeah, he's kind of a drunk, but if Nate thinks he'll work out I'm sure he'll be fine"

"Yeah, I s'pose. Nate's vouching for him. Hell, I'm a drunk. Hey, ah, I might start losing you when I get to the hairpins, I just crossed over the pass."

"Okay, make sure you give me a heads-up. Lemme know your ETA. I'll have the parking spot coned off for you. Can you double up on the Strawberry Kush?"

"Oh, yeah, no worries. I got you covered." then the phone stopped working, and Henry said, "Are you there?"

He tossed the phone down on the seat and reached for a beer. I climbed up the back of the seat behind him to see through the window. He didn't notice. We drove on as the dirt road narrowed into the canyon running parallel to Lost Creek, which crossed the road about halfway to the farm. A wolf-like dog attacked the tires of the Suburban as we drove by a gate that read 'KEEP OUT!' "You wanna play that way, huh?" Henry mumbled and giggled as the dog stopped its chase in the rearview mirror.

Broken-down trailers and stripped-out cars dotted the banks of the creek. I slid back down behind the seat as the engine's rumble lulled me to sleep. The truck reminded me of a giant purring cat. Like my mom! The warmth from the engine and exhaust came up through the floorboards. I felt like a baby again.

Henry sledded the truck through the slimy parts of the road as the snow accumulated. We stopped at Lost Creek, and he stepped out to check the water flow. Henry had strung a rope across; whenever the water rose as high as the rope, the truck could not make it safely, so he'd park and wade across while holding onto the rope. Then hike the rest of the way to where he lived, about a mile and a half. But today, the water remained low enough. Henry jumped back behind the wheel, and we rolled right through.

The snow collected on the Douglas Firs, the Redwoods, and the Manzanitas. A winter wonderland. He took it easy up the rutted road to the farm, and at the split by the first gate, he stopped again.

A parked car sat idling, a Subaru Outback with San Francisco parking stickers on the rear bumper. Doctor Stetson and his wife Francine. I knew them too. They'd recently purchased a few acres of property to build a cabin.

"How you doing, Doc? You get that septic tank in yet?" Henry shouted through the drizzle.

"Pretty rocky, but we got it," replied the Doctor. "Thanks for letting us use the backhoe. I don't think I could have done that by hand. I'm doing indoor work this week, putting tile in the bathroom."

"That's a fun job," Henry said. "Hey, ah, watch that creek level with these rains. If it hits that rope, it's not safe."

"You told me, Henry. You've told me twice now. It's why I bought a Subaru. Thanks, buddy." He rolled his window up, annoyed by Henry's warning. The Doctor waved like a prince in a parade and took off toward town. From the passenger seat, his wife looked back at Henry with an impatient smirk.

Henry unlocked the first gate, pulled through, got out, and locked it again. His boots slid in the slushy mud. The truck's coil springs squeaked past an old boarded up house. It was my old place! Man, it went to hell! I wanted to ask him to stop but couldn't find the words. Figured it would be best to keep quiet. We continued to the second gate at a switchback where a smaller creek trickled through a pipe under the road. Henry rechecked his phone at the crest but couldn't make it work. Man, he's obsessed with that thing!

We drove down a nearly vertical slope of the driveway, past a shack with a dozen black and silver solar panels on the roof. Head-high fencing lined the drive on either side. The truck glided like a giant bobsled through the last slushy berm and stopped in front of a house.

I remembered the farm. I helped Henry build the

place in my prior life. How bizarre to return to it as a cat! We had nothing to do with building the original kitchen house, that dated back to the early' 6os. I sketched the design for the addition on the back of a napkin. All the cut lumber came from the property's Redwood and Doug Fir trees. We milled them on-site. The 2x4s actually measured two inches by four inches. No store-bought wood. It was a simple structure with a tall, windowed wall facing the valley, and the roof slanted back towards the hillside. The interior featured a vaulted ceiling and open space with a loft for sleeping. The memories were flooding back. A wood stove in the center of the living room heated the whole house. I modeled it after my place. Its chimney pipe rose straight through the roof. The original, smaller house now served primarily as the kitchen with another sleeping loft above the cooking area. The kitchen stove ran on propane. Three replacement tanks stood along the wall.

A garage of similar design sat adjacent, serving as a storage space for large garbage bags filled with marijuana. A broken refrigerator taped shut stood among the random garden tools that lined the back wall. A shack for firewood stood next to the garage.

The solar shack sat above the main building between a greenhouse and another leveled-off area about half the size of a football field. A battery bank fed by the solar array provided enough power to feed the main house. Twelve panels were plenty for day-to-day use, but Henry kept several portable Honda generators as backup for the harvest season.

An open field below the main house became a large vegetable garden in summer. I remember the place as if it were my own. Henry had started planting fruit trees around the field's perimeter, pear and apple mostly. He used half of the area to grow weed about seventy-five plants. He had put a compost pit and burn pile in the corner of the field furthest from the house.

Beyond the garden, past the perimeter of the tree line, a rocky cliff dropped several hundred feet into the canyon below. A remarkable view of the valley and the mountains beyond.

Above the house, beyond the solar shack, a natural spring provided water all year long, even during the driest season. The spring produced enough to keep the storage tanks full. A pipe protruded from the stones on the hillside, and the overflow pushed extra water down a relief pipe next to the house. Another smaller shack sat in disrepair in view of the garden, and yet another lay hidden further down the hill. Plastic pipes radiated off in all directions from the central point of the natural spring, and Henry had set up various pumps along these irrigation lines.

He had carved out a place to park his backhoe, work trucks, and portable wood mill in a flat area beyond the water tanks. Lean-to shelters were randomly constructed to age milled boards. Similar huts stood throughout the forest, easily visible due to the blue tarps wrapped around the lumber.

Up and over the hill from Henry's place sat the old Schieffelbein house, abandoned for many years since a group of squatters left it a shambles. Shieffelbein used to work on my cars. He was a solid mechanic but a little too much into the Grateful Dead. I remember when he stopped coming to the property because the bumpy ride aggravated his sciatica.

Further on past Schieffelbein's sat the Amundson estate. All the names and places opened up in the channels of my cat brain. Seeing Henry's name on the envelope was like turning on a switch to the memories of my old life.

It was the Amundson's grocery store downtown I was living behind with my mom. The Amundson's owned several hundred acres up the mountain behind Henry's place. They didn't have much water on their property though. I guess that was their son Carl, the guy running the store who killed my ma. I never liked that kid. That spoiled little twerp didn't deserve a single river rock.

Henry unloaded the groceries while the snowflakes grew to the size of goose feathers. I awoke with a brown leather glove on my face.

"What do we have here?" said Henry, reaching around the seat to where I lay completely asleep and dreaming. I woke to the nightmare of a giant hand clutching at me. "You're that little kitty from the store."

I went wild and clawed his face, launched off his chest, and darted as fast as I could under the house. I reacted poorly, I'll admit.

"Hey ah, after all that chicken I gave you, that's the thanks I get?" Henry crouched down to talk to me under the house. "Come on outta there. Come on, kitty."

I watched him through the latticework. He approached and bent down to get a closer look. I hissed at him and clawed at his hand as he tried to reach in. I wanted to say, fuck off, but I couldn't make my mouth work right. So, I hissed again.

Henry finally said, "Well, suit yourself," and went inside. I heard him walking around above me, so I investigated the shelter under the house. A bunch of leaves and rotten cardboard boxes. I sniffed out a dried-up alligator lizard and started gnawing at it. Flavorless, but I still ate it. I craved some more chicken, and I could hear music playing above. The snow kept falling, getting deep around the edge of the house. I didn't want to go out there. I hate snow! I heard the door open, and Henry walked off into the blizzard. So I went for it.

I bolted through the open door and froze when I hit the bright light. I had to get my bearings. I'd never been in the house as a cat before. My perspective was dramatically different. It seemed like a stadium inside. I needed a moment to see where I was and where he was. I heard him off in the distance. I jumped into the kitchen and up on the counter. There were some cheese curds on the butcher block. I snagged one and ran up the ladder into the loft.

Henry returned carrying a bundle of wood and dropped it in a pile by the stove. The house felt toasty warm. I gobbled down the cheese and stretched out in the loft.

"Did you think I wouldn't see your tracks? I see you up there." I could hear him chopping things in the kitchen below. "You're a little ball of chaos. I don't mind you staying here. Just don't shit or piss in the house."

I fell asleep. Henry was gone when I woke, so I crept out of the loft and jumped on the table by the big window. The one I helped install. It was a bitch putting that thing in, but it looks pretty damned good! I could see a headlamp moving down the hill through the snow. Where's he going, I wondered?

I searched for hiding spots and realized it's a real trick getting out of a house if you can't twist the door knob. Fuckin' hell! The piano! It would be easy to climb back there; that's a good spot to hide in a pinch. Oooh, there's a cardboard box. An easy getaway. I went back to the kitchen for a couple more nibbles. I saw a wood crate above the fridge. There were many places to hide, but then I found the chair with the cushion by the stove. That's the spot. I didn't need to hide. I curled up and fell asleep.

I woke up the next day in the same place on the chair. Henry left me alone and lay snoring on the floor by the door. I still couldn't find a way out, and I had to shit bad. I found a big plant by the picture window and figured he wouldn't notice. So, I dug a little hole in the dirt and started doing my business.

While finishing up, I noticed a shoe flying directly at me. It slapped the wall above as I leaped away.

"I told you not to shit in the house! Goddammit, not in the plant!" It surprised me to see him so angry. "Move it out now! Shoo, you little beast!"

He ushered me out the side door into the snow. I immediately regretted my decision to use his planter as a shitter. My mistake! I watched Henry from out on the slushy porch as he drank his coffee inside. I wanted a view of the place, so I climbed up on the kitchen roof and onto the main house. Smoke billowed from the chimney, and I could feel the warmth coming from the pipe. The perfect spot for a bird's-eye view of the backyard. So, I nestled in beside it and cleaned myself. Henry called to me from below.

"Hey ah, kitty, where'd you go? I have something for you. You like bacon and scrambled eggs?" I could smell food. "Come on down. I didn't mean to lose my temper. It's thick-cut bacon, not that packaged kind. Don't shit in the house again, okay?"

I jumped down and tried to apologize. I tried to explain and ask him if he recognized me but it was no use. It only came out as a string of hollow meows. Hell yeah, I like bacon and eggs. He set out a dish fit for a human. I stuffed myself and he left the door cracked, so I slipped back inside. He was messing with some scientific experiments in the corner. I went back to the chair by the wood stove and curled up.

"I'm going into the city today and I'll be back pretty late. You can't stay inside while I'm gone, so you have about another hour to relax. Then you gotta skeedattle! I recommend the woodpile. I left some cushions out there for you."

Henry picked up three red sacks that said Milwaukee Tools on the side. He pulled out a saw and a couple drills and put them on the table. Then he went out to the garage and brought back several full garbage bags. He laid them beside the table and set up a scale from the kitchen. The bags were full of weed. I watched from the chair as he weighed out little piles, sealed them in clear plastic, and stuffed them into the Milwaukee tool sacks.

"What do we have here? A pound of Strawberry Kush… Another pound of Purple Haze… Five pounds a bag, yup. This is lookin' good. Can I call you Chaos?"

I'd rather you didn't. I really don't think it's a fitting name but I understand why you might wanna call me that with my reactionary behavior. I'm not used to this new dynamic. Again, I tried to explain it to him.

"You are a talkative little guy aren't ya? What are you trying to say my friend?" asked Henry.

I can't seem to remember my own name but Chaos is not my name. I remember yours but I can't remember my own, I guess it's not that important.

"You wanna help drive, Chaos? Be my mule to the city? My cat mule." He laughed and lit up another giant joint. Man, he smokes a lot and never gets high.

"You gotta get out now, Chaos." He reached towards me. I leaped over him onto his back, clawed it, and catapulted myself out the door. I didn't like how he called me his cat mule. I taught him half of what he knows.

He closed the place up and walked off toward the Suburban. I jumped up on his back and sat on his shoulder. Oddly enough, he didn't do anything. I rode on his shoulder all the way to the truck. Like riding a two-legged horse. Now, who's the mule? I tried to laugh, but it only came out as a growl.

"Off you go, Chaos. And off I go. I'll see you later, buddy."

Yeah, whatever man.

AINO

Aino's dented trumpet was the only thing of value that he owned. He didn't have a case for the trumpet, and he'd stolen the horn from his high school band room in Proctor, Minnesota. Crammed it into his backpack with the fat end sticking out.

He spent years trying to make it in jazz bands in San Francisco. He realized his mediocre talent wouldn't take him past the dead end of the alley behind the bar where he worked. Then he lost his job. He didn't get the email about no more after-hours parties. The city was busting nightclubs. Cracking down. Aino broke the rule, and they called him in the next day. The management asked him, "Were you partying in the office last night? After hours?"

"Uh yeah, like normal. Why?"

"Don't you know the new rule? We sent out several emails to staff."

"Ah shit, I didn't see 'em. My computer's kinda fucked."

"Well, we can't let it slide. What would the rest of the staff think if we made an exception for you? Sorry, Aino. We gotta let you go."

Aino floundered around looking for shifts at other bars but nothing worked out. It wasn't about the after-hours partying. He'd already burned out of the business. His expiration number came up. Being fucked up all the time made it impossible to find another bartending gig. His bank account quickly drained, and he lived off credit cards approaching their limit. He called Nate and asked if his friend Henry still needed help on the pot farm.

"Yeah, he's still looking for someone. I told him you were a pretty good carpenter. You're a pretty good carpenter, aren't you?"

"Yeah, sure, I've done some carpentry. I don't have the tools, but I can do it. Sure."

The extent of Aino's carpentry skills amounted to a string of odd job experiences in the trades over 20 years. He bartended and waited tables at night. The music didn't pay the bills, but random hustle jobs did. Occasional piano moving, painting, roofing, carpentry, landscaping, etc. Not an expert in any of them, but capable. Given a tutorial or advice from an experienced friend.

Aino caught a bus back to San Francisco. He slept for free in the back of his broken Toyota truck inside a friend's garage off 17th and Albion. He was storing the broken down truck there but getting heat to move it.

Nate and Aino used to be roommates, and Nate was part owner of a marijuana dispensary in the Castro. That's how Nate knew Henry. Henry provided the dispensary with some of its finest weed. Nate's fingers were on the pulse of San Francisco. He had a passion for social justice and helped organize advocates for the legalization of marijuana. He saved Aino countless times with random jobs and opportunities.

From time to time, Nate worked on Henry's farm in the mountains east of Dias Verdez, especially during harvest season. He'd go up there for a weekend getaway to do trim work on the buds. They became good friends. Both are connoisseurs of beat poetry and jazz.

Aino wanted to clean up from being an alcoholic and lose his cocaine habit. Either that or he'd end up on the street or dead. He watched the homeless dudes at the 16th and Mission BART stop. Knowing he could quickly become one of them. A guy picking at his rotten foot of festering sores or the man with Vaseline tears trying to hustle up a buck, for pity's sake. An ex-pro skateboarder hocking all his freebies on the street corner. He saw himself in all of them.

Aino dangled from a frayed string about to snap. At one point, he had a good heart and soul, but it fell apart in the selfishness of his addiction. He'd reached his limit with several friends, and Nate was probably his last chance. One awful night, he fought with Nate inside the car while driving across the Bay Bridge. They came close to crashing after Aino punched Nate in the face while he drove. Something about being left out of an introduction to some pretty ladies for being too drunk and creepy. Nate forgave him and wanted to help out. No one knows why.

Nate would let Aino crash on his couch from time to time. If Aino got too drunk and didn't want to walk back to the garage to sleep in his broken truck. One night, Aino puked red wine all over Nate's brown corduroy couch. He attempted to clean it up but made the mistake of using a bleach cleaner in the middle of the night. It stained the couch permanently with pink spots of bleach and red wine. Nate had an expensive video projector propped up on some milk crates by the window. Aino drunkenly fell into it and knocked it out. It dangled from an extension cord inches from the sidewalk. Junkies grabbed at it, like fish jumping at a piece of bait, but he pulled it away from them in the nick of time.

"It works fine. Like nothing ever happened, "said Nate.

"Sorry man, I was outta my mind."

"You need to stop with the 'I'm sorry' shit! You can't handle it anymore. You only go to the dark side now."

"I know it, man, sorry."

"Well, you gotta do something. Sorry doesn't help anything. The farm will do you good. Get outta this fuckin' city for a while. Portland ain't gonna help you either. That place is designed for getting fucked up."

"I can't handle the rain anymore."

"Henry is gonna be here around noon to pick you up.

I gotta go to work. He said he'll meet you in the Safeway parking lot on Market. He can front you some money, too. He's good like that. Please don't fuck this up."

"Don't worry, man. I got this. I think I can do it."

"You gotta do it. Don't just think you can do it! Lock the doorknob when you leave."

Henry delivered to the Market Street dispensary and met Wheezy and Nate at the door. They buzzed him in.

"Glad to see you, my friend. I have something special for you." She handed him a bottle of homemade brandy. "You doubled up on that Strawberry Kush, right?

"Yes indeed."

"And this is for you, "Nate handed off a manila envelope.

Henry didn't bother to count it, but he usually got $1600 a pound. Once a week. Not a bad take for a 15 pound run. All in cash.

"I gotta go meet your friend now. Aino is the name, right? "

"Yeah, Aino, but I recommend not feeding him any brandy. I told you about the thing on the Bay Bridge."

"I can't be a camp counselor, but I won't push it on him."

"Might be best to get him to take some edibles. Here's a few for the road."

"Thank you! "Henry bowed in a prayer to Wheezy and Nate. "I gotta go. I'm 10 minutes late."

Henry pulled into the lot as Aino stood in a daze, watching skateboarders do tricks.

"Nate told me to look for the guy with the trumpet sticking out of his bag! That must be you! Aino, right?"

Aino perked up from the haze. "Yeah, Aino. Henry?"

"Nice! You travel light. Throw it in the back. I don't care where."

Henry sparked a spliff as he crept through the side streets en route to the Golden Gate Bridge.

"I don't like taking Lombard Street." said Henry. "So, I heard about what you did to Nate on the Bay Bridge. Are you gonna do that to me at the Golden Gate?"

"Ah, no. I only do that on the Bay Bridge. I mean, no. I lost control."

"Anger management. I hope you don't lose control again. Listen, man, this is a peaceful place I'm taking you to. A little slice of paradise. You'll see."

Aino stared out the window at the string of tents lining the street. Full of junkies snoozing after a fix in little nests of garbage. A shirtless man ranted and flailed his arms at an imaginary demon. Screaming into the air as they passed,

"Fuck you! Shitty fuck!

You Fuckin' Shitty Fuck Fuck!

You suck! Shitty Fuck!"

"What a lovely haiku! What happened to San Francisco? Has it always been such a shithole?"

"Blame Ronald Reagan! He's the one who closed all the mental hospitals."

"Blame it on a desire for getting loaded," whispered Aino. "A never satisfied hole."

"What'd you say?"

"Nothin' man. You know I saw a homeless guy light another guy on fire once while riding in a cab?"

"No shit?"

"The cabbie just floored it. I asked the driver if he saw what I saw, and he didn't reply. I tried to call the cops, but it rang and rang."

Henry squinted at the sun to the west as they rounded the bend approaching the Golden Gate Bridge.

"What kinda name is Aino?"

"It's Finnish."

"You're finished? What do you mean? You want to bail out already?"

"No, my name. It's Finnish. You asked me what kind

of name Aino was. My family's from Finland."

Aino had a round face, greasy, dirty blonde hair, and a bit pudgy from all the drinking. He had eczema on his hands, which made his knuckles bleed. Usually, he wore gray Ben Davis trousers and a green windbreaker. A gray flannel shirt underneath.

"Hey, ah, we gotta stop and get you some boots," said Henry. "Those dress boots aren't gonna cut it. You need some good waterproof ones for this work we're gonna be doing. What size are you?"

"Eleven, but I have no money right now. What, you don't like my fancy boots? I got 'em from the junky sidewalk sale. $5. These are Clark boots, normally about $100."

"I got it, man. It's a work expense. I can front you some money. I'll stop in Ukiah. Gotta buy groceries, too. I'll hook you up with some rain gear while I'm at it. There's gonna be a lot of rain this week. You missed the snow, though. It was beautiful. You like steak, or are you a vegan like Nate?"

"Yeah, I like steak."

"Steak it is!"

Henry relit the joint as he negotiated the winding road through the tunnels towards Marin.

"So, do you have a girlfriend or boyfriend? What's your deal, man?"

"No, that kinda fizzled out in Portland. She came to her senses."

"Sorry, bud."

"It was my own doing. Simone. She suffered from a brain injury, that's what she said when I met her. She made a full recovery, though. I guess it would take a woman with a brain injury to fall in love with a guy like me, right? "

"Sounds like a good line for a song. Do you write songs? Or just play that trumpet?"

"I play the trumpet. Or try to, at least. What about you? You gotta lady friend or a man friend?"

"My lady is the upright bass for now. Aramoana and I split years ago, but she stays down the road part-time on weekends or holidays. We're still friends. You might be doing some work over there, too. Plenty of it."

"How'd you meet up with her?"

"Her dad, George, was a friend of mine. He introduced us. He would come to our shows in San Francisco when I still played piano. Always shared his finest ganja. What a legend."

"Your weed guy?"

"Yeah, but then I became a fan of his artwork. I had no idea until I took a trip up to Dias Verdez. We got along like brothers, and then I met his daughter Aramoana."

"Interesting name, never heard that one before."

"Means pathway to the ocean. It's Maori. You know, from New Zealand?"

"Is she from New Zealand?"

"Nope, her real name's Joyce. She always hated that name, so she changed it."

"I like that better. Ever had any kids?"

"We adopted a boy."

"What's his name?"

"Luka, and no, he doesn't live on the 2nd floor." Henry smiled.

"Does he live on the farm?"

"No, he lives with Aramoana at her house in Dillits."

"How old?"

"He just turned 12."

"That's a good time to be a kid. Before all the high school bullshit."

"His main thing is skateboarding. That's the only thing that matters."

"Where'd you adopt him from?"

"He's Croatian. Came over to the States after he lost

his parents in the war. Somehow, Aramoana found this connection. He's a wonderful kid. We got pretty lucky. "

"Damn, that's fuckin' awful about his parents."

"He didn't know them. 3 months old when they died. He comes up to stay sometimes but mostly lives with Aramoana." Henry looked solemnly out the window, puffing away at his spliff. "We're still partners in raising the boy. He doesn't like comin' up to the farm, though. He's got his skateboard friends in town."

"I used to skateboard, before the ollie. The first time I saw an ollie, it was like a magic trick. Can he do ollies?"

"I have no idea. Probably."

"Are you still playing the keys?"

"Nope. I fucked up my thumb!" He held up his hand. The finger was swollen and bent in an unnatural position.

"Damn! Is that broken?"

"I don't think so, but I can't play piano right now. I've been playing the double bass instead. "

"How'd you fuck up your thumb?"

"Well, I parked the truck on a steep part of the road 'cause I was trying to get a picture of a bobcat. I forgot to put the emergency brake on, and it started rolling backward. I jumped back in the cab to grab the steering wheel; the front tire hit a rock, jerked the steering wheel over my thumb, and dislocated it. Total fluke! There's some tendon damage, I'm sure of it, so, I'm out of commission on the keys."

"It looks broken the way it's bent."

"It'll be fine; I can still move it a little. I'm getting into the double bass. "

"Ever heard of Kitten on the Keys? When you said, "out of commission on the keys, I thought of 'Kitten on the keys.'"

"Nope, doesn't ring a bell."

"You from the Midwest somewhere? "

"South Dakota."

"I can hear it."

"Where are you from? Lemme guess, Northern Wisconsin?"

"Nope, a little further west. Minnesota. Proctor. Do you know where Proctor is? West of Duluth."

"I've been to Duluth! Beautiful place. It reminds me of Astoria, Oregon. They sure do like Leif Ericksson. Isn't Bob Dylan from Duluth?

"No, Hibbing man, but I think he was born in Duluth. I was born in the same hospital, Saint Mary's."

Aino nodded off for a while, and Henry pulled into the parking lot of the GI Joe's Outdoor store.

"I'm gonna run in." Henry slinked into his rain poncho.

"You want me to come with you?"

"No, man, it's pouring. I'll be back. "

A pond formed in the parking lot. Aino sat in the Suburban feeling the shakes as he came down from his daily binge, in dire need of a drink. He knew he had to go cold turkey. It would be a rough couple of days. He nibbled on a pot cookie to take the edge off. The quiet contrast to San Francisco shocked his system. He had a hyper-awareness to the sound of the silence and the rain. With no distractions and hardly anybody around. The night fell coldly at five o'clock. He could sleep again. Sleep forever in the Suburban.

"I got ya, man," said Henry as he slid back into the driver's seat. "These are good boots and a rain suit too!"

"How much do I owe you?"

"I told you not to worry about it. It's a business expense." Henry smiled through his round glasses and winked at Aino. "We gotta make one more stop and then onward to Dias Verdez."

HWY 101 curved into the hills and turned into two lanes as it traversed another mountain pass. Henry stopped again to make a trade. He went into a health food store and came out with a couple chocolate bars and a bottle of wine.

"My friend makes this wine. It's got no name but it's a fine merlot. He crushes the grapes with his bare feet. If you don't mind, a little toe jam in your wine. Never mind, I forgot you're tryin' to dry out."

They rolled onward into Dias Verdez.

"Do you need anything? Last chance before we're outta range. Gonna fill the gas tank."

"I'm good, man."

"You sure? I won't be coming back to town for a few days."

"How's that grocery store? Amundson's?"

"Oh, No way. I don't shop at that place. Well, sometimes I shop there but I'd rather not. Only if Ulee's working."

"Why is that?"

"Carl Amundson. He's a price gauger, killer, and a greedy little bastard. I had to boycott the store."

"Is it really a 'Poultry Paradise'?" Aino gazed at the large banner draped over the store's exterior.

"That's a new one. Carl must have put that up today. "

The banner featured a cartoon chicken in a Hawaiian shirt with sunglasses on with a caption reading "Welcome to Poultry Paradise."

"It's no poultry paradise, but it's okay when fresh. It's got this weird spice on it. Cat's seem to love it. A little too heavy on the garlic salt, and I still need to understand why he got rid of the coffee bar. It used to be the best spot in town. When the Amundsons were still alive."

"Wait–did you say killer?"

"Yeah, they were poisoned. Ate poisoned mushrooms by accident. It's what Carl says. I think he did it."

"Poisoned?"

"Yeah, I think he poisoned his parents."

"And he's not in prison?"

"Well, nobody can prove it, but everybody knows it."

"Why would he poison his parents?"

"I heard something about his inheritance. They were thinking about cutting him out of the will cause some weird shit went down with a local boy."

"What kinda shit?"

"I don't know. I don't wanna get into it right now."

"They were friends of yours?"

"Yeah, they were." Henry's demeanor shifted to solemn. "It's so strange. His parents were the salt of the earth. Ruth was the epitome of a peace-loving hippie, and Jimmie, aside from his obsession with big game hunting, was a true naturalist. Back-to-the land kind of guy. They were the cornerstone of Dias Verdez. It's strange how kids rebel against their parents. Carl is the complete opposite of them. Not a nice person."

"Bummer," said Aino.

"Surprised Ulee still works there."

"Who's Ulee?"

"She's the tall lady with the gray braid. You'll see her walking down the side of the road. She is a woman of few words but should be running that place- not Carl."

"He sounds like a psycho."

"Yeah, He is a psycho. He made a big stink about me not taking off my hat during the national anthem when the World Series was on at Slingers."

"What's Slingers?"

"Slingers? It's the only bar in town.. They have music sometimes, but they don't like jazz. It's usually classic rock cover bands. I guess they have pretty good chicken fingers, hand-breaded but kinda rat farts if you ask me. Any time I've ever gone in there, I hear a racial slur. You'll see Carl's monster truck parked in the lot. Every time I come to town, I see it there. It's a big red truck with all the flag stuff, Semper Fi, and gun stickers. That dude never served in the military. He never did shit. Oh, look at that. Speak of the devil. There's his truck now. See the one taking up two parking spots? He's posted inside the bar drinking away all that family money."

As they passed, Aino stared out the window, imagining himself at the bar guzzling an ice-cold beer.

"Oh, there's no Wi-Fi at the farm, and cell service is almost nonexistent. I get two bars sometimes at the second gate. If you climb to the lookout rock, it's a lot better, or drive up the canyon to the summit. Good service up there. I think it depends on the humidity."

"My computer doesn't work anyway, so it doesn't matter. It's good that I don't get to talk to anybody. This phone is dangerous when I'm drinking.'"

"But you're not gonna be drinkin', right?"

"That's right. I almost forgot."

"You're always welcome to ride back to town with me if you need. Or borrow the car for whatever. If you get restless. I don't care. Just put gas in it. All I ever need from town is bacon, eggs, and beer. That's a quick stop, and I get that at the EZ mart, not Amundson's."

They drove past the last town lights and turned off onto Lost Creek Road.

"This is a two-beer road," joked Henry as he popped open a bottle of Sierra Nevada where the tar became gravel. "I've been drinkin' these since before the microbrew craze. But I still miss that Grain Belt from back home. I'm a sucker for cheap beer."

Aino looked queasy as he closed his eyes.

"Ooop, hold on! Coming in a little hot!" warned Henry as the truck skidded to slow down for the approaching speed bump.

"This fuckin' guy took it upon himself to put speed bumps on this road. Can you believe that? He doesn't even live here but two months out of the year. That big house right there. I'm gonna get a pickaxe and take 'em out one day. The speed bumps, not him." They passed by a walled estate. "I think it's a cartel kingpin behind those walls," said Henry.

The further they wound up into the mountains, the darker it got. The road shrunk down to one lane and was rutted from all the recent rain, forming little gullies.

"There are two ways around this mountain from here, and both roads meet at the top. So 'if you get to the fork, take it'. Just remember what Yogi Berra said. Lost Creek Road dead ends at the Anguilla River about twenty-seven miles in. Then it's wilderness all the way to I-5, about a hundred miles of nothin'. We'll go about seventeen miles past the summit and turn. "

"What about mail?"

"No mailbox, but I have a PO Box in Dias Verdez if you need it. 1111. The cops don't come out here, and neither does an ambulance. No pizza delivery. Sometimes, Fish and Game guys will be walking around. Checkin' for people stealing water. Sometimes, Search and Rescue will be prowling around searching for lost hikers. That's about it."

AINO ARRIVES

I found the perfect spot to stay out of the rain under the ledge by the water pipe. It's an excellent place to keep a lookout at the same time. I could see all the way down to the house with a clear view of the driveway and the mill. I cupped the fresh water in my paw and licked it up. Delicious and sweet. At dusk, I noticed a field mouse on the mossy rock below. I crouched into attack mode, ready to pounce on it for the kill. I like the taste of a field mouse, but my damned claw started twitching. I didn't have control of it.

I still had a nervous tick carried over from my previous life. I must have worked as a train engineer because I dreamt about it a lot. It gave me anxiety because in the dream, I'm not able to properly press the dead man's switch to keep the train running. I still pressed it every couple of seconds out of a nervous habit. Forever trained to hit that switch. It scares the mice away. My whole body was frozen, but my claw kept twitching from that dead man's switch. Dammit! The mouse darted off. Foiled again. I heard an engine sound approaching. Henry's back! It meant a good dinner that night! I scampered down through the trees and under the house. Popped out on the other side and hid behind the woodpile as the truck slid in. A small stream flowed between the firewood shack and the main house. I wanted to wait there and catch a ride on Henry's back. I heard him approaching, and I crouched further out of sight until he got his bundle and turned to walk back to the house. I leaped from the shadows and landed on his back.

Wait! I realized mid-air that it wasn't Henry! I squirmed to stop my trajectory, but it was too late. I landed on the stranger's back, and he dropped the wood and tried to swat me away. I clawed at the man with all four legs.

"Get the fuck off of me!" The man yelled and slipped in the mud. He was down and trying to find his feet but fell again. I hissed and growled. I wanted to say, "Who the fuck are you?" But I ran for the shadows.

"Henry, I got attacked by something!" Aino was standing at the door with mud covering his entire back. "There's a wild animal out there on the wood pile."

"I should've warned you. It's only Chaos."

"Chaos?"

"That's the new farm cat. He hitched a ride from Amundson's store the other day. Don't let him stay in the house. He'll shit in the plant. "

"Chaos is a fitting name."

I bolted through the door, raced past the stranger

and made a beeline for the loft.

"You're not allowed in here," said Henry with a grin.

"Hey, Chaos. Hey buddy, I'm Aino. Come here, kitty."

As he reached up and tried to touch me with his greasy hand, I hissed at him. Fuck off, man! I don't give a shit who you are! Don't you realize who I am? They don't get it, and it would be insane to try to explain it to them. Would he do that to another human? Someone he meets for the first time? Try to touch them and pet them? Do you, dear reader, as a human, want to be stroked right off the bat? By some stranger with greasy hands? I've been grooming myself for hours, and he's gonna rub his filth on me? The gall of that guy. Frumpy motherfucker!

"So far, he doesn't like to be held or touched," said Henry. "He's been keeping a distance. See, he's up there again. He won't let you pet him."

I watched them both from a distance, and that big oaf Aino plopped down in my favorite chair. Right in my spot by the wood stove.

"Gonna grill up these steaks and shred some carrots with kale for salad. Sound good to you? "asked Henry

"Sounds awesome," said Aino.

"We're gonna get started early tomorrow, rain or shine. That rain suit and boots are in the truck if you wanna go grab 'em. I wanna do a big cleanup and gather everything into piles for a dump run. Burn the pile of wood scraps when the rain stops, if it ever does. We get a short window of opportunity to burn up here in the winter.

You can sleep in the loft above the kitchen or here. Wherever you want. I sleep by the door on that mat."

Henry pointed towards a dirty foam mattress with a sleeping bag. He used a jumbo beach towel that read "The Hawaiian Islands" as an extra blanket.

"If you ever don't feel like working, just stop. It's up to you, but know it's alright if you don't want to. If you need some time. I know you may be dealing with some backlash from the bottle."

"Man, it's coming down out there," said Aino as they both stopped to listen to the pouring rain.

"Yeah, what's the song say? It never rains in California; it pours. Who was that Albert something?"

"Albert Hammond. But it's southern California not northern."

"He wrote a lot of hits for other people. 'To all the girls I've loved before, The air that I breathe.' Do you know those songs?" said Henry.

"Yeah, I love those songs; I didn't know he wrote 'em."

Aino started flipping through the records by the piano.

"You like Steve Goodman?" asked Henry.

"I haven't listened to him. What's this "The City of New Orleans"? Isn't that an Arlo Guthrie song?"

"No, that's his song. Goodman wrote it. Arlo had the hit version. Man, I thought you were mostly a jazz guy."

"I've only heard the Arlo version. I'm ignorant. Do you mind if I give it a spin? I like all kinds of music."

"No, man, you play any record you want. "

"You know I rode that train once. The Amtrak from New Orleans to Chicago. That was a wild ride. Some guy got on the train, had a guitar, and started buying everybody drinks in the smoking car. He'd just gotten out of jail. He passed out drunk and missed his stop. Lying on the floor of the smoking car in a pool of his own vomit. His false teeth were in the middle of the puddle of puke. Sleeping like a baby with bubbles coming out of his mouth. The conductor made him get up and handed him his teeth. He got off the train and left without his jacket or guitar. I remember seeing him standing on the platform in the snow, holding onto those false teeth. I wondered why he didn't put 'em back in his mouth."

"That's a guy that shouldn't drink anymore. Oh, I

gotta check out the precipitation level." Henry left out the side door and came back with a measuring tube full of rainwater. "We've had 4.2 inches since this morning.".

Henry prepared the meal, and Aino set up his sleeping bag in the loft above the wood stove in the big house.

"That's the warmest spot. Sometimes too warm," said Henry. "You'll find out. I'd offer you some brandy, but I know you're off the sauce. It's pretty good, though. Pear brandy. The same friend who made that wine."

"Yeah, no thanks, man."

Aino felt the shakes and stared at the fire in the wood stove. Imagining faces in the flames. Hypnotized by John Coltrane. He saw a little mouth in the fire singing to him, "A Love Supreme. A Love Supreme," spinning on the record player by the piano. The chills came and went. His agitation eventually faded.

"It's better than TV, isn't it? I watch the same show every night and never get bored. The fire speaks differently every time. Can I put on a Harry Potter tape? I usually listen to it to fall asleep. "

Aino was already asleep in the chair and slept there sitting up the whole night.

The fire burned down into glowing coals, and Henry polished off the bottle of brandy. He fell asleep with his boots on and the Hawaiian towel covering his head. His body lay halfway on the foamy mat by the door.

SHERIFF RICK JOHNSON EYES A BASS BOAT

Sheriff Rick Johnson drove his squad car down to Ukiah from Dillits. Official police business. He took a swig from a bottle of vodka stashed under the seat. Checked his hair in the mirror.

"You're the man! Who, me? Yeah, you." he smirked and then smiled at himself.

He unbuckled his belt below his sizable beer gut. Confident his upcoming plans would work out, he started shopping for bass boats. Expecting a law enforcement discount.

He pulled the squad car into the lot of Fisher Marine and took one last swig after a quick key bump of cocaine. He spotted what he wanted right away. A Nitro Z20 with a 225hp engine. The boat had the balls he needed to match his own. $59,530. "Wow, man. That's the one."

He closed his eyes momentarily and imagined himself darting across Clear Lake at high speed. The water, a glassy mirror. His sunglasses, a glassy mirror. People on the shore watched with envy as he went by at full throttle, wake zones be damned. The lakegoers were blown away by the speed and perfection. A couple of kids on the dock high-fived each other after catching a glimpse of Sheriff Rick Johnson in his new bass boat.

"Did you see that?! Musta been a Nitro, and that's Sheriff Rick Johnson!" said one of the boys, in awe.

He imagined himself dressed in team gear sponsored by Bass Pro Shop, a full jumpsuit with patches. The boat would get him there, where he needed to be. What he imagined himself to be. It would complete his self-image, trailer included. He believed he would pay cash for it after the Autumn mission. Hell, he could buy two. Park the other one at the hunting shack. Get another AR-15 and an extra Glock. The sky's the limit. After all, he was the law around here. All the bases were covered.

He took another key bump and checked his nose in the mirror for remnants. He relished his reflection in the plate glass window while he mosey'd towards the door. A salesman came out of the office.

"Hello, officer. What can I do for you today?"

"Well, we have reports of illegal activity in your parking lot."

"I'm not aware of any problems out there. We've never experienced any kinda break-ins or anything. "

"Hold on, chief! You see that car over there?" Sheriff Rick Johnson pointed towards any of the dozens of parked cars. "There have been reports of illegal doings in that silver sedan. Drug activity."

"Which silver sedan. Sir? There are several."

"Ha! Hang on, hang on! I'm busting your chops, buddy. I'm goofin' on ya! Just checking out the inventory. I like that Nitro Z2o!"

"You like that one, huh? That'll get ya where ya wanna go. For sure! But have you seen the limited edition?"

"No, where you got that one hidin'?"

"It's in the showroom. Let's go take a look. The Limited has a better stereo and live fishing well with the circulating water pump. It's only a couple thousand more, but it's worth every penny. If you ask me."

"I didn't ask you, but I'd say it's a better boat." Sheriff Rick Johnson followed the salesman inside and stashed his baggie in the front pocket of his sheriff pants as he walked behind.

"Here we are, sir, right in the center of the showroom where it belongs. For now, that is. I believe it belongs in the center of the lake with you behind the wheel."

"How much bud?"

"The Nitro Z2o Limited Pro Bass Boat? $64,000 even, and I'll include cooler covers."

"You guys offer any kinda law enforcement discount? We might buy a slew of these for the force, but the first one is for private use only."

"Hell yeah, we do! We back the boys in blue. I didn't know you guys patrolled the lakes. Aren't you from Dillits?"

"It's those meth labs on houseboats. We're branching out, buddy. I'm gonna be paying you a visit this autumn. I'm doing some recon work. Can you take a few grand off the price? What do ya say?"

"Well, we could probably work out a deal right now if you wanna look over some finance options?'"

"Finance? What the hell does finance mean? I'm not gonna need to finance shit, buddy. I pay cash for everything."

"If you're willing to pay cash today, I could knock off about two grand. "

"I said not today. I'm talking about November."

"Well, when you're ready, we'll cut you a deal right here at Fisher Marine. We aim to please, especially the boys in blue. We got your back."

"You sound like a commercial man. Is that your canned pitch?"

The two stood there in awkward silence. Sheriff Rick fiddled around in his pocket, looking for the baggie of blow. His heart raced as he forgot which pocket but finally found it again.

"Did you lose something?" asked the salesman.

"No, bud, I got it. Hey! I appreciate your support, boss. I'll see you in a few months. You're gonna give me a boat, right?"

"Whenever you're ready, Sheriff! And you're the boss around here, not me. Come on back, and we'll sign the paperwork."

"Hey, can I use your bathroom?"

"Absolutely, take a right at the Coke machine."

Sheriff Rick sauntered off, leaving the salesman with a confused look. He took another couple of bumps in the bathroom, stared at himself for a long time, fixing his dyed black hair, and strolled back to the squad car. He checked his 'stache in the mirror, smoothed it down, unbuckled his belt again, and put the car in gear. He peeled out of the gravel lot, spraying gravel onto the pontoon boats. He pulled another mini vodka bottle out from under the seat, gulped it down, and dialed a number on his flip phone.

"Dufur! Hey Dufus. You down at Slingers? I said, are you down at Slingers, over? "

Dufur Fleck was already at the bar and on his third drink. "Yeah, I'm here. Where do you think I'd be at the gym?"

"Don't gimme no feedback, Dufur. You owe me a drink. I've had a busy day. I'm on my way!"

"I don't owe you shit, Rick. You don't need to say 'over' either. You're talking to me on a cell phone you idiot."

Rick turned on the flashing lights of his squad car and hit the siren, flooring it into traffic as the cars pulled over to the side to let him by. He burned up HWY 101, trying to suck the last couple drops out of the mini vodka bottle. He rolled down the electric window on the passenger side and tossed it out into the ditch.

WALTER

Walter arrived every morning at 5:30 a.m. sharp. He parked his baby blue Tercel in the same spot in the Amundson's parking lot. The one furthest from the store out of respect for the customers. An extensive set of keys dangled from his belt as he waddled to the front door. A short, portly man who wore creased khaki pants and a tucked-in button-down white shirt. Amundson's Grocery embroidered on the front pocket. He wore polished black loafers and a blue Cardigan sweater with large pockets.

Walter fiddled with the keys in the dark and dropped them by accident. "D D D Damn!" he stuttered to himself and found the key amongst dozens held on a stretching cable coming from his belt. He unlocked the door and went inside to disarm the alarm. Turned on all the fluorescent lights and walked to the back of the store. He reached for the pocket-sized transistor radio inside his employee locker. The locker door had a picture of his cat taped to it. A giant Maine Coon.

KMUD community radio crackled from the tiny speaker, and he put the radio in his sweater pocket. He began his daily ritual of walking the store. Strolling every aisle and taking a mental inventory. Never having to write any of it down due to his photographic memory. The morning update chimed in on the radio.

It's gonna be a lovely day in Mendocino County. Morning fog burning off by noon with bright sunshine and a high of 61. Heads up, everybody. A procession of federal law enforcement vehicles was seen heading north on HWY 101 near Garberville. The entourage has pulled off at the Benbow Historic Inn.

Walter smiled in solidarity and thanks for the heads up. Every cannabis grower appreciated these updates. and Walter also grew weed on the side. Passing the broom closet, he grabbed a sweeper and began pushing it on his walk. It was his ritual to re-sweep the already spotless floor. Checking for dust on the registers with a white handkerchief. He propped the front door open and rolled the rack of fresh oranges out to the front entryway. By this time, it was nearly 6:oo a.m., and Ulee would be arriving.

"Happiness Runs" by Donovan came on the radio, and Walter began to sing along. He stuttered with his speech impediment but could sing along to songs without any trouble. Ulee entered the store and heard him singing.

"You sing better than Donovan, Walter!"

"Oh, G G Good M M Morning Ulee! Y y y you startled me." he looked blankly as if lost for a moment, trying to say the words correctly.

"Morning, Walter. Good to see you. The place looks good, man. You could eat off the floor in here."

Walter smiled with pride as Ulee made her way back to the deli.

CLEAN UP BEGINS

A grinding noise came from the kitchen. Henry hand-cranked the ancient coffee grinder attached to the countertop. He'd found it on the street in North Beach, San Francisco. Banging on the side to get the beans into the little slot. A tedious process. This went on for an eternity, and he giggled at the absurdity of this morning process. The whole house would shake from the dilapidated contraption.

"You want some coffee? Are you alive in there?" yelled Henry.

"Yeah, man, I'm ready. Tell me what I need to do," replied Aino.

"You need to relax, man. That's the first thing. Then we can work."

Aino put on his gear and stood in the kitchen doorway like an anxious new recruit.

"We got another six inches of rain overnight. The culvert pipe near the gate got washed down the hill. The road's impassable!"

"How can I help? I can shovel whatever."

"Don't worry. It's an easy fix. I should have cleaned out all the crap that was jammed up inside it, but I didn't get around to it. I got another culvert pipe. This is a backhoe job. Shouldn't take long."

Henry poured the ground coffee into a worn-out French press.

"Have you ever had French cowboy coffee?" He handed Aino a cup with grounds floating around in it.

"Don't worry about the grounds. A little something to nibble on."

He put a bowl of scrambled eggs and bits of bacon

on the back porch.

"There you go, Chaos. You're a lucky kitty; you got to sleep in the house last night."

I pounced over to the dish and dug in. Henry wolfed his food down and donned a rain poncho hanging on a hook by the door. He rolled a giant joint and walked off.

"I'll be back in a few."

Up the hill he went, kicking stones into the ravine the rain had formed on the driveway. He returned about a half an hour later.

"Have you seen a pen layin' around? I need that spring out of it." He switched boots to knee-high rubber ones.

"Ah, there it is," he disassembled a ballpoint pen at the table by the big picture window.

"Why are you taking apart that pen?" asked Aino.

"I need the spring for the hand controller on the backhoe. This one little spring breaks all the time. $500 repair at the shop. Insane! For a tiny spring. The same exact spring goes in a standard ballpoint pen! Crazy!"

He popped the pen spring in his pocket and walked off. Soon, the backhoe came rumbling up the hill, carrying another pipe and rolling towards the washout in the road. He dropped off the tube and started scooping buckets of gravel from the hillside, delivering them to the area. All the while puffing away on that joint, smiling like a kid at the playground.

I jumped up on the backhoe and rode along to watch. Before noon, he had that pipe replaced and filled in with fresh gravel. A precision operator.

Aino stayed at the place waiting for instructions, still dealing with his break from the bottle with occasional shakes and fits of anxiety. He put on a Joe Pass record and tried to meditate.

"Hey, ah Aino. Sorry bout the emergency. We gotta be able to get in and out of this place."

"You fixed it already? That's quick."

"Glad I had another culvert pipe. The road's working again. We won't be able to cross Lost Creek until later. Just have to wait a few hours cause it's still raging; you can hear it from the porch. That never happens. It won't take long to drop. No more rain in the forecast. You can wade across using the rope if you need to get to town. I've got a little Corolla parked in the bushes on the other side. Keys are in it."

"I don't want to go to town. I'm fine right here with Joe Pass."

"Well, take it easy. No need to rush into anything. I'm gonna have more coffee, you want one?"

"Yes, please." Aino gazed out the picture window at the fingers of fog. Imagining the trees to be bronchi in a slice of a giant lung.

"Man, he was smooth. What's this, "Here's That Rainy Day"? It was effortless for him." said Henry.

"I don't know much about Joe Pass, but I'm diggin' it," said Aino.

"After the record, I can take you around and show you where everything's at. If you're feeling ok?"

"Absolutely. I'm stoked."

The two got into Henry's other truck. A little Toyota 4x4 parked by the wood mill. Aino wore his brand-new rainsuit.

"Hey ah, we'll go to the top patch first and then work our way around to the Schieffelbein house,"

"Who's Schieffelbein?"

"Old friend of mine. He lives down in Ukiah now."

They drove onward up the muddy slope to the top of the property.

"I've got fifty raised beds up here with automatic drip lines. Those black pipes lining the ditch are all irrigation."

Raised boxes were 6' x 6' and a foot off the ground in rows along the terraced hillside. Slightly obscured by the canopy of trees.

"These ones get pretty good sunlight despite the trees, but let me take you down the hill."

The drive became a roller coaster ride, and Aino's heart raced. They crossed an open space heading towards a wall of trees. A tiny opening let them thread the needle to a nearly vertical drop down into the next patch of open field. I darted through the forest trying to keep up with them.

"This is the bottom patch. I've got sixty ladies down here. Same irrigation. It's all automatic. There are a couple dead trees I'm gonna need your help with. We'll pull them to the wood mill and turn them into boards. Have you ever worked with a Wood Mizer mill? "

Aino shook his head.

"Well, I'll show you how to do all that in the next few weeks. It's pretty easy, and it's fun. The machine does all the work."

They rolled through another nearly impassable stone pathway.

"Are you allergic to poison oak? If you are, keep your eyes open. It's everywhere out here."

They passed a house with all the windows smashed out. Broken-down vehicles were rusted into the earth and covered with vines.

"That's the Schieffelbein house."

"Are these his cars?" asked Aino, looking off at the row of VW Beetles and old Datsun pickup trucks.

"Yup, he was a mechanic. Specialized in Toyota and VW's. Obviously, right?"

Well, that's my old Datsun pickup, I chimed in.

"Oh, hey Chaos. What are you doing, following us? You're talkative today. What are you trying to say?"said Henry.

I'm trying to say, that's my pickup and that's my Woody. Oh and there's my Ford Station Wagon. He never got the electrical part I needed for that truck and now it's just junk! I climbed inside and there was a mouse nest under the seat. They all scattered and I missed my shot at an easy meal. I'll have to come back later. Good to know!

"I used to own a Super Beetle and VW van. It had one of those pancake engines. Couldn't ever figure out the electrical problem, though." said Aino

"I think that was George's Woody." said Henry.

"Damn, how did he get that thing up here?"

I drove it up here, that's how!

"Chaos loves that car. Like he's trying to talk to it," said Aino.

The car had become a permanent fixture in the landscape. I left it there because I didn't need it anymore. Schieffelbein could use it for parts, but he didn't do anything with it. I love how the weather sculpted it into the soil, and vines broke the windows. I'm watching them from the attic of the Scheiffelbein place now. Through the broken window, I can hear every word they say.

"Is he letting you use this spot for growing?"

"Yeah, we're gonna do fifty plants in his yard and another fifty across the creek on that hillside. The hill gets the most sunlight. Those are usually our biggest plants. They get to be like trees over there."

"How big do they get?"

"Fifteen feet, maybe more. "

"How much weed can you get out of one plant?"

"Couple pounds, give or take, depends. We could have a rain and get a bunch of mold. You never know. Or the deer might find a way in and have a feeding frenzy. We gotta put up some better fencing around this patch. I'll have you get on that later in the spring if you're up for it? The Amundson property is further up the hill at the top. I wouldn't recommend going up there."

"Why not?"

"Carl is paranoid. He might be drunk and try to shoot you. "

"Why is he so paranoid?"

"I don't know what his deal is. He put up that fence and doesn't want anybody going up there. Used to be I could just walk right in there. I don't see how he lives with himself."

"Do you think he really killed 'em?"

Henry didn't reply.

"Well, I'll avoid the place. How come Schieffelbein moved away?"

"Sciatica. The bumpy road was too much for him."

"Yeah, my cousin had that problem. He got addicted to painkillers. So you think he'll sell you the place?"

"I don't know. Scheiffelbein keeps changing his mind. I don't pester him. I know Carl wants to buy it, but he hates Carl. So that's not gonna happen. Carl wanted to buy my place, but Brody's only offered it to me. He won't even wave at me now. He wants it for the water but doesn't know anything about growing weed."

"Why are the windows broken? How did it get so fucked up? Look, it's Chaos up there!"

"Hey bud, what'cha doin' up there catchin' birds?"

No, watching you two loons talking bout my buddy Schieffelbein. He doesn't come back cause he's bummed about the place going to hell. Sciatica? Bullshit! It was Crazy Mary.

"These people showed up and were squatting for a couple months. I tried to run them off, but they were psychopaths. Meth heads. They trashed the place. Before they showed up, Crazy Mary had her horse living inside on the first floor. All that horse piss rotted out the floorboards."

"A horse was living in the house?"

"Yeah, Mary was Schieffelbein's girlfriend then she kinda went off the deep end. She loved that horse. So, the place no longer has a floor on the ground level. I think it was Mary that made him not wanna come back, not the sciatica."

You're damned right it was Mary.

"What happened to Crazy Mary?"

"She met some biker dude up on Spy Rock and never came back. Schieffelbein said if I fix this place, we can use it for whatever. Even live in it. Eventually, it's what I wanna do because this spot has the best view. But for now, I wanna fix up that little shack below the main house. Let's head over that way."

The shack was built on redwood stilts and sat about three feet above the ground. Perched on the cliff overlooking Lost Creek below the main house. The roof leaked for decades.

"This is the first project after we clean up the yard. I wanna move here before everybody comes to work this summer. I can't take all that noise anymore. I wanna have my own space. It's got a good skeleton."

"You can't beat the location. You'll be able to hear the creek at night."

"I want you to replace the roof, new batten board siding, demo inside and sheetrock, tongue and groove ceiling, and run a power line down from the solar shack. Use one of those Honda generators for power if you need it. I have another wood stove stashed in the solar shed. I'll move it down with the backhoe. That can be the last thing this autumn. We can burn up all the crap lying around this place. There's no need to drag it up the hill. Let's do it right there on the flat spot. I've got to reroute the overflow pipe so it stops sending the water to he backyard of the shack. It's become a swamp, and the bugs get bad here."

Aino built a blazing fire in no time and pulled all the burnable material out of the shack in a few hours. The fire burned as the sea of stars shone down on the farm.

No lights blocked the splendor of the sky.

"I'll bring the trailer down to the shack in the morning, and you can start taking the old roof off. We'll make a dump run in the afternoon," said Henry at dinner.

CHAOS AFTER DARK

On the first clear day since my arrival, I got to reaquaint myself with the area. I could see for miles at the lookout rock, which rose about 500 feet above the house. A red-tailed hawk floated on the updraft above the valley. Majestic. Then it noticed me watching and swooped in like it would tear me off the rock. I realized I was its prey. What a terrifying notion. Being twice my size, the bird could have easily picked me up and flown away. I've never been afraid of a hawk until now. I'm scared of those evil birds. Well, I guess they're not wrong; they're hungry opportunists. But those crows are the nastiest of all the birds. I went down to the compost pit after Henry dumped a chicken carcass. I had snacking on my mind, but several of those old crows came down and started pecking at my head. They nearly killed me, and I'm still recovering. Three of them went at me at once!

After some exploring, I fell asleep on a rock by the water pipe. When I woke up, I saw the mouse again. This time, my claw wasn't twitching on the imaginary switch. I flew through the air and landed with my mouth on the mouse's neck. Crunch! It was mine. A success! I devoured half of it. The head half, but I saved the tail for Henry. I've never been able to return the favor for all the food he's given me. I feel proud to finally give back. I left it on the mat by the kitchen door. I waited on the chair just in time for dinner to see his reaction. When he came back to the house, he noticed it right away.

"What's this here, Chaos? You brought me a present. Oh, you shouldn't have." He picked it up with a paper towel and brought it inside. I don't think he ate it, though. I think he threw it away. In times like these, I must think back and try to remember what I liked eating as a human. I don't remember ever eating a mouse. I certainly love them now, though.

THE DOCTOR & HIS WIFE

Lost Creek flooded in the storm. The rope and flag Henry used to warn if the water was too high had washed away. The creek rose ten feet past the rope, and you could see the debris line in the low-hanging branches. It subsided and returned to normal within a day. The trunk of the Corolla flooded, but the engine side of the car was parked higher on the slope and stayed dry.

A blanket of frost covered the forest before dawn. Aino dragged fallen branches to a new burn pile and started prying the tar sheets off the roof. He tossed them down into the trailer, and the roof was stripped clean before long.

Henry came over with the backhoe. He had a solemn look on his face and was not his normal bubbly persona.

"Hey, ah, we have a change of plans, Aino. Gonna need your help pulling a car out of the creek. They found the Doctor's Subaru downstream from the crossing; it was swept away. Aramoana found it on her morning walk."

"Anybody hurt? "

"His wife was still in the passenger seat. She didn't make it. They have yet to find the doctor. You alright with comin' down there?"

"Yeah, I'll do it. Let's go. "

Aino jumped on the backhoe, and I followed cautiously. It was a cold ride up and over the hill to Aramoana's place and down the pathway toward the creek. You could hear the chainsaws buzzing as they cleared a path to pull the vehicle out. Henry had a long cable and a mechanical winch. They looped it around the back axle and dragged it through the mud up to the path. It had taken quite a beating from being tossed every which way. All the windows broke out, and the car was full of mud.

"I warned them about the crossing man. Several times. He blew me off!" said Henry.

The rescue team proceeded to search down the creek. They found the doctor's body that afternoon about a half mile downstream. Wrapped around a tree eight feet up in the branches. Henry and Aino rode over to the crossing to find the rope had snapped and been dragged downstream by a massive log.

"They must have taken a chance 'cause the rope was gone," whispered Henry; he sparked up a joint and took a long drag. "It's a shame."

Aino stood there with a blank expression, not knowing what to say.

"I want to put that rope back in place." Henry approached the Corolla and opened the trunk. He pulled a rubber plug out of the trunk floor, and the water drained. "At least I didn't have it backed in. Even if I did, it probably would have started up anyway. These Corollas never die. Do you know that, Aino? You could park it at the bottom of the lake and pull it out a year later, and it would still crank."

Henry pulled a movable fence post from the trunk and proceeded to pound it into the ground at the riverbank. "If the water ever gets up to the base of this post, don't drive across."

ULEE & THE WIZARD PUPPY DRAGGER

Ulee smoked one cigarette a day. Her only vice. She'd light one up after work but wait until she got to the corner of the parking lot. While walking the quarter-mile trail back to the RV Park, she checked for the changes in vegetation while savoring her hand-rolled cigarette. She'd stop to meditate at the giant sage bush on the way. Always picked a piece to smell before crushing it up in her hands and slowly let it go along the path back home. Hans met her at the fence line. Same time, 3:30 p.m. She brought him an apple a day, sometimes the ones that were being thrown away because she knew Hans wouldn't mind. Sometimes, she paid for the good, fresh ones.

She noticed something wasn't right when she got back to the trailer. Someone chained a dog to the bumper. A border Collie, and it seemed well taken care of. It didn't bark as she approached; it had a collar with a Greek evil eye. She'd wondered if it was someone she knew from the store who had stopped by for a visit, but she didn't recognize the dog.

"What are you doing here, little guy?" she said before realizing someone was inside the trailer. She heard the water was running.

"Hello! Who's in there?"

The water shut off. Ulee got closer to the door that she never locked. "Hello, it's alright; I know you're in there." Someone was looking out from behind the curtains.

"Come on, man. Come out of there. Who are you?"

The person burst out of the trailer and ran around to the side to disconnect the dog leash. He wore a long brown robe with a hood and an upside-down cross. Ulee was dumbfounded. She watched the young man struggle with the leash and set it free from the bumper. He ran from the trailer, dragging the dog. It squealed as he pulled it along.

"Don't do that to your dog, you asshole!" shouted Ulee. "What the hell is wrong with you?!"

The man stopped, picked up the dog, and ran back

towards her. A little guy who didn't seem much of a physical threat. She prepared for the worst, but she thought she could take him. He ran around the back of the trailer with the dog in his arms.

"What are you doing back there, you weirdo?"

He reappeared and started walking back toward town briskly as if nothing had happened. He had come back for his wooden staff.

"You fucking whacko! You break in my place now you're returning for your wizard stick?"

He faded out of sight. Ulee went inside and found the sink wet, and the soap was used. He'd been washing himself, nothing else. He left a turquoise stone by the sink. A little keepsake in trade for use of the facilities.

"Well, I guess he wanted to clean up Hans. You think a guy could ask first. How weird is that? Are you ready for an apple?"

CARL'S WORKOUT

Carl was chubby and stood about 5'6", with male-pattern baldness. He wore sunglasses draped around his neck or backward behind his ears, and sweatshirts with the neck cut out. His favorite read, "NorCal Native," with a roaring bear in the background. He had a propensity to gain weight due to his poor diet and heavy drinking but imagined himself to be in top form. He shaved his whole body except the little hair he had left on his head. Usually, he'd work out in the garage, but sometimes, he'd pace back and forth from the house's living room, always in the nude. He'd stand before the fireplace mantle, doing curls and staring at the painting of his parents. Cursing with each repetition.

"Fuck you, hippie bitch! Fuck you, hippie bitch!"

That was his mantra. Alone in the house he grew up in. His parents were dead, and it was all his now. His own fortress. A sprawling stone home with big log beams and massive picture windows. Perched on the top of the ridge above Henry's place. His dad built it by hand. Just like he built the store downtown. Both buildings were designed and constructed by a man with tremendous drive and deep love for his family and community. In the end, they enabled Carl. They became an insulating cushion for their only son, who had no drive and no love for anyone.

"How bout this, mommy?" He threw the weight down, grabbed the rifle from the wall, and strolled out to the deck, taking a single shot into the trees. Aiming at nothing. He wanted the thrill of the explosion at his fingertips. The power of the gun gave him an erection.

He returned, put the rifle on the wall, and said, "I do what I want, mommy!" He spat at the painting and stormed out into the garage.

He rewound the tape in the boom box and pressed play. Laying back on the weight bench, he gazed at the Judas Priest poster tacked to the ceiling. The music started, and he lay there staring, fully erect.

A metal fence surrounded the home with stone pillars. Carl had it installed for extra protection after his parents died. He felt he could be robbed at any moment. Or attacked for poisoning them. He lived in an ongoing state of paranoia. He thought he would eventually shake it, but it wouldn't disappear. Carl knew what he'd done but didn't care because he knew no one could prove it. The property and the store were his now.

I followed the fence line towards the music. I'd never heard anything like that before. The singer had a growly voice and was singing something about "living after midnight." I dug the sounds, so I got closer. I know much about life after midnight, going on my nightly prowls. The giant truck was parked in the driveway, blocking the view of Carl in the garage. I kept thinking about what he did to my mother, and I wanted to claw his eyes out. I snuck up and hid behind the monster truck tire. I wanted to get back at him. Piss on his pillow or shit in his plant. I had to do something. He stood up in front of a tall mirror. Grunting.

"You got it! You got it, man! You fuckin' badass!" He flexed, and his whole flabby body turned red. His belly jiggled with every move. He attempted the pull-up bar but gave up and rewound the tape to play the song again.

I didn't wanna watch this imbecile working out anymore in his imaginary buff bod. It made me feel nauseous. The door to the house was left wide open. A prime opportunity. I took a run for it and found myself in the kitchen. A half-eaten cheeseburger lay on the counter, so I wolfed it down. Only the meat, though. Then I took a shit on the plate.

Maps were laid on a pool table in the living room with a big high ceiling and a stone fireplace. One titled "Stream Systems Declared Fully Appropriated by the State Water Board." A detailed topological map of Lost Creek with a big red 'X' on the Schieffelbein house, an 'X' on Henry's place, and a 'W' encircled at the location of the water pipe. Taxidermy stared down at me from every wall. A rattlesnake coiled in a glass jar sat on the end table beside a brown leather sofa. I clawed at the couch and prowled back out to the garage. Carl stroked himself on the weight bench and said.

"Put 'em on! Put the handcuffs on me, you bitch! I'll put 'em on you. Use your nightstick! That's right. You wanna tase me, baby? Go ahead. I can take it. I like it."

He squirmed a little and then lay there motionless as the tape ended. He took off his bandana and cleaned himself. I was under his truck, and he looked back and noticed me.

"What the fuck are you doing here?!"

I took a piss on the tire of his truck.

"I'm gonna kill you, you fuckin' little rat!"

He grabbed a rifle and aimed it at me. The first shot ricocheted off the driveway and punctured one of the tires. I could hear the hissing sound as the air gushed out. I darted back into the woods. He fired again, but the bullet whirred off into the trees. When I was safely out of there, I saw him squatting down by his truck with a flat tire. Pounding his fists in the dirt.

A PLANE CIRCLES

Aino sat on the steps of the solar shack, trying to get a chainsaw blade back on track. A small plane appeared in the distance, banking when it got near the farm. It disappeared at the ridgeline, then reappeared on the other side. It kept circling back, and Aino stood up as it approached again. It swooped in even closer, and he could see two people inside dressed in green with headphones on. One of the men held a camera out the window of the plane. Aino stood up and waved but thought, why would they fly so close and take pictures? It was a dangerous flight, especially with the crazy winds blowing up the canyon. Soon, the plane flew out of sight, and the quiet returned. Henry left for the city on his weekly delivery.

Aino planned to trim away some branches that could fall on the shack. He couldn't get the blade back on track because the saw arm warped and the chain kept slipping off every time he started it up. He clamped it with the vice and tried to bend it back into place, but it slipped when he put pressure on it. Losing his balance, he took a splinter in his wrist when he went to brace himself for the fall.

"Damn it!" The splinter stuck deep into his wrist about 2 inches. He found the needle nose pliers on the workbench and pulled it out. I was amazed by the length of the splinter and the button of blood forming at the opening of the wound. I watched from the shelf above, but he didn't notice me. He managed to get the whole thing to come out in one piece.

CARL GOES TO TOWN

Carl strained to lift the giant tire into the back of the truck and put the smaller spare on. He would have to bring it to town to get it repaired. The smaller tire made the monster truck lean drastically to one side, and he took it slowly back to Dias Verdez.

"Can you patch this thing?" Carl asked the guy at Carmello's tire place.

"It's a pretty big hole. Looks like a bullet hole. Did you get shot at?" asked Mr. Carmello.

"Yeah, I had target practice, and it ricocheted off a rock and hit the truck. It's bad luck is all. "

"I'll say. Well, I'll do a double plug and see if it holds."

"I hope so. I spent $500 each on those tires. They should be able to take a bullet for that."

The plug worked, and Carl was happy to celebrate at Slingers. He pulled his truck into the lot and parked diagonally across two spaces. To make sure no one dinged one of his doors. He assessed the stickers he'd spent hours arranging on the back window of his truck. A family of guns was his favorite. Two AR-15s, a 30-odd 6, and two handguns. He strategically placed the stickers on the driver's side to make sure everyone could see his family of guns. He had his lifetime member of the NRA sticker in the center of the window, and a Sempre Fi sticker on the bumper for some reason, even though he had never served in the military.

Sheriff Rick Johnson loafed at the bar with Dufur Fleck. Dufur worked for Fish and Game and had a curly waxed mustache. He always wore a green hat that read "California Fish and Game." He usually wore brown cargo pants and a tool belt for his cell phone, flashlight, and Leatherman multi-tool knife.

There wasn't a police station in Dias Verdez. Sheriff Rick rented a cabin by the casino after his recent divorce. He commuted to Dillits, and if anybody ever needed the police in Dias Verdez, Sheriff Rick Johnson would get the call. Usually, he ignored it because Sheriff Rick Johnson did not give a fuck.

"How's it goin', boys?" asked Carl.

"Not any better now that you're here," replied Sheriff Rick. "You want a beer?"

"Sure, thanks."

"Holly! Get us three beers on Carl's tab."

Holly rolled her eyes.

"Thanks, Carl. Twelve bucks for a rotisserie chicken? What the fuck are you thinkin', man?"

"I dropped the price after Christmas. They're $9.99 now."

"That's still too high. I get a whole rotisserie chicken for $6.99 at Safeway in Dillits."

"Well, if you wanna go all the way to Dillits, that's your choice."

"How's it goin' at the store? For real," chimed in Dufur. "Now that you scared all the locals away?"

"It's been pretty slow. I'm gonna have to let someone go."

"Well, you kinda fucked yourself by jackin' all the prices up. Ain't nobody gonna pay twelve bucks for a chicken. When are you gonna hire my son?"

"I told you I gotta let someone go first."

"Who are you gonna let go?"

"Probably Ulee."

"Ulee? She's the only reason anybody goes in there."

"Well, if all these weed-growing freaks hadn't moved in, we'd have a better tourist season. Now all we have is panhandlers and puppy draggers."

"Well, that weed paid for all the new equipment at the

Fire Station," said the volunteer fire chief, Ronny Clark.

"Well, look, I don't like this shit either, but I'm getting a new bass boat this year," said Sheriff Rick." Mark my words."

"How are you getting a new boat?"

"We got our ways."

"That's right!" said Dufur. "Operational tax."

"The gray area is the best area," laughed Rick. "Let's keep it part legal."

"What do you mean gray area?" asked Carl. "There's no gray area on the federal level."

"Well, this ain't no federal level. We hold the aces in this game."

"How are you holding any aces? You suck at poker," said Carl.

"It's not poker we're talking about Carl. Why don't we go outside for a sec and have a cig?"

Dufur, Rick, and Carl walked outside.

"We want you to be part of our bowling league. You wanna be part of our bowling league, Carl?" asked Sheriff Rick.

"Hell, I'd love to do anything with you, Rick, but where's the bowling alley? There's no bowling alley, not even in Dillits. Didn't they close it? "

"We're thinking we need a silent partner," said Rick.

"I didn't even know you guys were into bowling. Do you want me to be quiet and bowl? I can do that. I have the perfect name and slogan for our team! Team Turkey! Three Strikes, and you're in! Get it?"

"The thing is, Carl, we're not going bowling. Isn't your place above the Schieffelbein house and Henry Hodkey's?" asked Dufur.

"Yeah, it sure is. Henry's got a big operation down there. I've been trying to buy that Schieffelbein place, but he won't talk to me. I don't know what I did to him. "

"Well, it seems ole Henry's been suckin' water outta

Lost Creek. That's against the law."

"Why would he do that? They got plenty of water coming out of that spring. I don't think he's sucking any water outta the creek."

"Trust me, Carl, he's suckin' water."

"Well, if you say so, I believe you, Rick. But Dufur? I don't know. With that curly mustache, it's hard to trust."

"We got a proposal for you, Carl?" said Dufur.

"Whatever you need, I'll help, and you know it. Besides, Henry didn't even take his hat off during the national anthem. Remember that when the Giants were in the World Series?"

"Why do you give a shit about that, Carl? Shut the fuck up and listen," said Sheriff Rick.

"Sorry, Rick, my bad."

"Well, you know it's illegal to suck water out of any of those streams and tributaries? Even the smallest dried-up little creeks," said Dufur.

"Yeah, I know. I've been looking at the maps. I'm trying to find water myself, and that one little stream trickles down near the Schieffelbein house. It's off-limits, but I'm curious if I can get to that spring on Henry's side through my side of the mountain. I could drill into it. "

"You don't have a drill, man. What the fuck are you talkin' about? That would cost millions to drill through that mountain. You must be taking crazy pills," shouted Sheriff Rick.

"I just thought I could get in there pretty easy."

"Shut up, Carl. Don't fuck with that! If you're willing to run some pipe from that little creek onto the Schieffelbein property, that'll give us legal grounds for some search and seizure. In our favorite gray area of the law." said Sheriff Rick.

"Hell, I could do that!"

"All you gotta do is run about a couple hundred feet of pipe from that creek edge onto the property. Dufur will photograph it come summertime. Make sure they don't see you. I know Henry's been doing some growing out on that property. Closest to your place."

"I know. I see those plants, and it pisses me off!"

"Well, let me put your mind at ease, Carl. You put a little pipe in, and things will change real quick."

"Well, what's in it for me?"

"You know all these hippies operate on a cash basis, right? They've got so much money stashed away. We roll in and do search and seizure. If you lay the pipe for us, we'll cut you in 5 percent. We did a raid last year and found a couple hundred grand in cash. Moving in on the Schieffelbein place will put us right there at Henry's. If he doesn't have his proper credentials posted, he's fair game. Plus, I know he's growing more than he's allowed. He's selling starters to everybody. I've been taking photographs from the airplane. Propagating the whole goddamned town! You could make about 5 grand, and I'm serious." said Dufur.

"5 percent? Why not a third of it? I'm taking the risk of getting shot at?"

"Are you kidding me? Those pussy hippies aint gonna shoot you. I don't think they even got guns on the property. All you're doing is laying a little pipe." said Sheriff Rick.

"How about twenty-five?"

"10% is the max. Schieffelbein ain't gonna sell to Henry if we take down Henry. I can guarantee that. That will leave it open to you, Carl. That's incentive enough." whispered the Sheriff.

"Those guys are like best friends. I don't believe it's gonna happen," replied Carl.

"Well, believe it. Get some three-quarter-inch polyethylene and bury it in the leaves on the property. Take a photo where you put it. 10%."

"I gotcha bro," as Carl leaned in to hug Rick. "That

sounds fair."

"Easy cowboy." said the Sheriff.

He backed away and extended his arm for a fist bump.

"I get it, bro." Carl bumped his fist. "I'll see you studs later."

He strutted out all bowed up but turned before he left and said, "Oh, Holly, add 3 bucks for your tip."

She rolled her eyes and said, "Big spender, thanks a lot."

"We ain't gonna give him nothing," said Rick.

Dufur nodded in approval.

AMENDING THE SOIL

Henry set up rolling racks with steel trays in the living room. On each tray were several dozen petri dishes with pot seeds wrapped in damp paper towels. He watched over them as if they were his babies waiting to be born. Constantly pacing like a nervous father with his headlamp on. Only his proud daddy moment would feature a giant joint rather than a cigar.

Kief tumblers were set up by the piano to extract the trichomes from the leftover shake. There were bags of it after trimming the buds. He'd dump it into those spinning metal grated cylinders to extract the fine dust. The pollen with a high concentration of cannabinoids. He used kief butter for cookies and brownies. He sprinkled the powder into his morning joint. An extra kick to get the day going.

"Hey Aino. How's it going down at the shack? I might have to steal you away for a day or two."

"I got it all dried in. The roof is finished and all the siding's up."

"Cool, what's next?" asked Henry.

"I'll probably need some sheetrock pretty soon but first the insulation."

"I'll get it on the way back from the city. Can you help me turn those beds up top when I get back? I wanna start amending the soil up there, get a head start. I don't think it's gonna freeze again after Valentine's Day."

"I hope not. I like it warm man."

"Hey, ah, could you weigh out some ganja for me? Gonna leave early tomorrow morning and I'm behind."

"Of course." Aino nodded and shuffled around in his pockets. Pulling out a smooth gray stone in the shape of a heart. He moved it around in his hand then tossed it up catching it in the other. Back into the pocket it went. The gray soapstone heart he got from Simone.

"I've got a list on the table, and you know how to work the scale right? There are turkey bags on top of the fridge. Seal 'em up really good and mark 'em with the sharpie. Double up on the Strawberry Kush. Oh, the Girl Scout Cookies are twice as much as I have written down. Put the turkey bags in those Milwaukee bags under the table."

"How come you use the turkey bags?"

"They handle temperature changes pretty well and they block the smell. I mean, my truck still smells like weed so I guess it doesn't matter. It's what I've always used. Most people do."

"I'm trying to get all this kief into vials for my friend Sidney. He's making a skin cream to help eczema. "

"Eczema? I've got it bad man. It keeps me awake at night. See it on my knuckles?"

"Oh, I thought you were a brawler when I first met you cause your knuckles were all bloody."

"No, it's eczema. Does he have any of the skin cream ready?"

"Yeah. I've got some in the fridge. It doesn't look too

nice but the new stuff he's working on is gonna look like real lotion. Creamier."

"I wouldn't mind trying it."

"Sure man. It won't get you high."

Henry went to the fridge and handed Aino a brown bag with a little glass container inside. Full of an oily black lotion.

Henry watched over his vast sea of petri dishes and Aino rubbed some of the black lotion on his bleeding knuckles. He got the phone out of his bookbag.

"I'm gonna take a walk up the hill before I weigh it out. See if I can get a signal, I've got to make a call."

Lost in thought, Henry didn't even notice Aino leaving.

I followed him to the lookout rock. He sat there huddled within himself catching his breath from the long hike up. The days were getting longer, and the sun was setting after six. Time enough to watch the sunset before dinner. Aino turned on his phone and held it up in the air looking for a signal. I found a spot in the crotch of the Manzanita tree behind him. He didn't see me. He didn't even know I followed him.

"Hi Simone. It's Aino. I'm at the lookout rock. It's the only place I can get a signal around here. I hope you can hear me. I literally have to climb a mountain to talk on the phone. Look, um, I haven't drank in nearly two months. Feeling pretty good. I still love you. I can't help it. Call me back please, honey. I'm sorry for how I was. Call me, ok?"

Aino hung up but kept looking at the phone, hoping for the call back. Hoping for something, but nothing happened. He reached into his pocket and pulled out the soap stone heart, held it up to the sun, and threw it into the woods. "Oh fuck!" he said and chased after it down the embankment. He searched the slope for the stone and somehow, he found it again, grabbed hold of it and lay there in the weeds until it got dark.

He began a calming trend inside. He went through arduous internal change. The grip of alcoholism slowly loosened but not without a struggle. Especially at night when they spun records and sat by the wood stove. He watched Henry drink the brandy and sip the beer. He nearly caved several times. He'd pop the top off the brandy bottle in the kitchen and take a big whiff when Henry wasn't looking. Other times, smelling the empty beer bottles almost fulfilled the temptation. He managed to leave them alone. Weeks went by and the color started returning to his face. His pants fit a little looser and he didn't think about killing himself as much. He still thought about it nearly every day though.

Aino would walk up past the wood mill to the Schieffelbein house and back. Noticing the detail of forest growing as spring was getting closer. Distracted by the work on the shack. The repetition of movement and the tired feeling at the end of the day, which enabled him to sleep deeply. He started dreaming again. Vivid dreams for the first time in a long time. He realized he was the victim of himself. At least he knew it now.

WATER PIPE

Carl purchased the irrigation pipe, and when he got home, he didn't hesitate to put it into place. He walked down the hill to the edge of the Schieffelbein property to the spot Dufur had suggested. Uncoiled the tubing and laid it out from the creek towards the house. Running it up through a field of poison oak and out of sight. He used a shovel at the river's edge and buried the pipe but left it exposed between two boulders and took a photo of the spot. The job was done.

He returned to his house and blended some margaritas to celebrate. Checking his maps, he didn't notice the cat paws. The remnants of the cheeseburger were still there, and he put the plate in the microwave and then doused it with hot sauce. He ate the bun like a grouper swallowing its prey, chasing it down with his margarita, oblivious to the cat shit.

"Hallelujah motherfuckers!" He took off his pants and walked out to the edge of the deck, looking over the valley. Another gulp of his frozen margarita, and he let loose a stream of piss. Still feeling a lack of something inside. He needed more. He went into the house, grabbed his AR-15 machine gun, took the rest of his clothes off, and ran out into the woods.

He jumped up on logs and started firing. Squirrels and birds scattered. He laughed nervously at his arbitrary lack of control. He drained the clip of bullets but kept pulling the trigger for more. He sunk down to the ground after running out of ammo. Cursing and then crying in the fetal position.

"Did you hear those shots just now?" Aino asked. "Gunfire, right? Sounded like an automatic weapon."

"It's probably Carl," said Henry. "Glad there are trees between us and him."

"What's he shooting at?"

"I don't know. I think Carl gets off on it. Makes him feel like a big man. He's got the little guy disease."

"You know, if you can't get it in one shot, you're not a real hunter," said Aino.

"Carl's not much of a hunter. His Dad was the hunter. A bow hunter. The hardest kinda hunting if you ask me," said Henry.

"Do you like to hunt?" asked Aino.

"Not my thing. A wild turkey here and there if they mess with the garden, but check this out."

Henry beckoned Aino out to the yard. "Listen to this." Henry proceeded to make a turkey sound towards the woods, producing a "Gobble Gobble Gobble" in high pitch.

Aino looked at him like he was crazy. Henry smiled and did it again. "Gobble Gobble Gobble."

In the distance, there was a reply. "Gobble Gobble Gobble. "

"See, they talk to me."

ANNETTE & SKY

Annette and her daughter Sky arrived midafternoon in a white Volvo station wagon. Both wore black Carhartt work pants with matching black hoodies. Each had a braided ponytail dangling down the small of their back. They were both beautiful and looked Eastern European. Tall and fit, mother and daughter, nearly twins. Annette didn't look much older than her daughter. A slight wrinkle around the eyes but radiant and full of life. They were all business and got right to work. Sky wore headphones the whole time and didn't talk to anyone. They set up at the round table by the wood stove in the main room. Both had big steel bowls and were equipped with their own snippers. Sky followed her mother, and they were like a well-oiled machine. Having pounds trimmed within only a few hours.

Meanwhile, Aino and Henry were up the hill at the top patch. I did my usual thing- lay in the sun nearby. Being a cat is way better than being a human.

Henry said, "I'd like to add a couple wheelbarrows to last year's soil. One bag of peat moss, a bag of Coco coir. A couple shovels of compost and perlite. Each one of these boxes. Mix 'em up good and turn 'em over."

They hauled up the bags and laid one of each next to the raised beds. Henry hauled scoops of compost up from the yard with the backhoe. Aino sliced open the bags and dumped them into the wheelbarrow. Then he mixed in the compost and perlite. When thoroughly combined, he dumped it into the bed but first loosened up the old soil with a spade. They mixed all the beds to air out the soil, ensuring they were ready for planting in a few months. Loose drip lines for irrigation lay on the ground along the rows of boxes, ready to be placed in their proper spots.

Both of Aino's hands were blistered by the end of the day. The blisters popped and burned as the loose skin felt like hot wax on his palms. Dirt got under the skin and aggravated him even more.

Annette and Sky surprised him when he got home. Henry didn't mention they were coming to work. He had only interacted with Henry for several weeks, so he fumbled for an introduction.

"Hi, I'm ah," neither woman looked up as he attempted to introduce himself.

"Hey, I'm Aino."

He waited for a reply. The two ladies were both wearing headphones and lost in the meditation of trimming weed.

"Hello, can you hear me?" He approached the table, and Annette broke out of her trance.

"Oh, hello! You must be Aino. Henry told me all about you. Trumpet player, right?" She motioned like she was blowing a bugle.

"Yeah, a little, but I'm still a novice."

"I'll bet you play just fine," and Annette smiled flirtatiously.

Aino felt a magnate coming from her eyes even though she had 20 years on him. Instant puppy love.

"What are you doing up here? Running away from some girl?" asked Annette.

"Not exactly. I think she's running away from me."

"Sounds like she's got her directions all fouled up."

"I hope so. What's your name?"

"I'm Annette, and this is my daughter, Sky. She's lost in her work, as you can see."

Sky kept snipping away in a daze and didn't respond to any attempt at communication.

"Don't worry, she's shy, but she's nice. You have to break through the twenty-four-hour headphone shell."

Sky snapped out of it with a grimace but quickly got back on task.

"So, you come from the city? I'm from down that way. Not from there, but I lived there almost ten years."

"Where in the city?"

"The Mission. You know, the Duggins funeral parlor by the police station?"

"Oh yeah, I spent the night in that place once. We live out in the avenues."

"It's chilly out there. "

"I used to live on 16th and Mission. Before the BART was open. So, you're living it up in the sun, baby. I need to come visit you." she winked.

Aino was attracted to this lady, who was old enough to be his mom, and the feeling was mutual.

"How long are you staying?"

"We'll see how it goes. Another couple of days. I don't know. We don't plan too far out."

"Were you born in San Francisco?"

"No, honey, I came from Chicago. Summer of love. Is anybody really from California?"

Aino shrugged. He imagined riding in the Volvo with Annette, smiling beside her. Crossing the Golden Gate Bridge. Moving fast in his mind, she had returned to trimming the weed. He stood there like a zombie, staring at her. He realized the need to go wash up and broke the trance. The next time he entered the room, Annette had her headphones on and appeared to be in deep concentration.

A candle burned on the table next to a bowl of olive

oil. She'd occasionally dip the scissors in the oil to keep them lubricated and burn off the excess oil over the candle. It created a strange odor that wafted to the loft where Aino slept. The smell and the snipping sound kept him awake, so he moved to the loft above the kitchen around 2:00 a.m.

Annette said, "Don't you like the smell?" as she peered at him over her reading glasses while Aino moved his sleeping gear.

Annette and Sky occasionally rubbed their fingers together to remove the built-up tar residue from trimming. Adding to a hash ball in the middle of the table. It had grown to the size of a ping-pong ball. The result is from handling thousands of buds. Aino lay in bed and imagined Sky and Annette becoming witches. Casting a spell on him through the smoke from their scissors. Taking his mouth away so he could no longer blow on the trumpet. Laughing at him in a giant pile of miniature Christmas trees.

"We're from the city. Ha! Ha! Ha!" Flying away on their broomsticks and swooping back over the Golden Gate Bridge. "We're from the city, and we own the property! You'll never have a home in this place. There's no room left for you; there's no space. You will pay with the sadness disease. The blues will bring you down to your knees. Go back to Minnesota, Aino! Whoa! You hick from the sticks! You frump from the dump. The Mission has no place for you. California is laughing, too. There's no reason; there's nothing you can do Ha! ha! ha! "

Annette and Sky worked straight through the night until the following afternoon. They trimmed several pounds in one solid day between the two of them. At a hundred and fifty dollars a pound, a decent stack of cash for a long day's work. Aino watched through the window as they got paid in cash from the stack Henry kept in the garage refrigerator. The two women didn't appear to be tired at all. They acted as fresh as when they arrived and were gone without a goodbye.

Later, Aino found a note on the refrigerator door made out to him.

"Call me up when you get back to the city. I'd like to get to know you more. Hearts, Annette." with her number.

Aino swelled inside, realizing the dream that they were witches was only a little nightmare.

HENRY'S SUPPLIES

"I got a hundred bags of peat moss, a hundred bags of coco coir, twenty sheets of sheetrock, insulation, staples, tape, mud, trowels, sandpaper, sheetrock nails, I got it all, man. Are you ready to go to work?"

The truck and trailer were fully loaded down and parked out front.

"I can't believe you pulled that load down that crazy road and through the creek. You're the master," said Aino.

"Nothing to it but to do it, man," replied Henry.

"How was the city?"

"Every time I go to the city, I think to myself. Man, I wish I didn't have to go to the city."

"I guess I'm not missing it."

"I make my delivery, and then I get stuck in a bar. I barely got out in time before I got too drunk to drive back."

"Did you go to The Winter Fern Tavern ?"

"No, man. I usually stop at that little Irish bar right off 26th and Mission. Why can't I remember the name of the place? Shit, I'm spacing it. I've been there a thousand times. You know, well, it doesn't matter."

"They're gonna turn the block where The Winter

Fern Tavern is into a high-rise condo next year. 'Tween Post and Sutter is what I heard, "said Aino.

"It blows my mind how much people are willing to pay to live there. No wonder there's so many homeless people. It took an hour to get out of there today. Just to go two miles."

Aino said, "I remember seeing some guy wiping his ass with a baguette once. The soft part. He opened it up and left it there. It sat in the alley for months. The birds wouldn't touch it."

"Lovely story, Aino, what else you got for me?"

"Another time I saw pile of human shit on the sidewalk a few doors down. Someone stuck a syringe in the center of it and made a duct tape flag. They wrote 'true love' in black sharpie on the flag."

"That's romantic. Hey, ah, I stopped in Ukiah, got the trailer, and talked with Schieffelbein. I think he's about ready to move on to selling the property next door. So I think we'll start working on it pretty soon."

Aino unloaded the sheetrock and placed it on some boards in the garage. He brought the insulation down to the shack and started stapling it into position. It didn't take long to have it all up, and he'd begin on the sheetrock. The shack was starting to look like a pretty nice spot to live. He even started sleeping there a few nights a week. The swamp outside had dried up since Henry cut a drainage trench for the water to run out and down the hill. You could hear Lost Creek flowing below the shack. Aino paused to meditate with the stream. Blending in with the sound of the moving water.

MURAL

Ulee never claimed to be an artist, but she was. She painted the nature mural at Amundson's grocery the year after she moved to Dias Verdez. You could see the edges of it behind Carl's "This is Poultry Paradise" banner. At least it still remained underneath. One day, a customer asked, "How come they covered up the mural? It was so beautiful." Ulee shrugged it off and continued putting dry rub on the rotisserie chickens. It became another routine she didn't think twice about. She had the luxury of flying away in her mind.

The mural came out in one continuous flow. It showed the scenery surrounding the store, looking east to the mountains. If all the walls were translucent. Continuing the contour of the land without a building blocking the view. Complete with all the local wildlife. Specifically, the birds. She had an encyclopedic knowledge of them and could identify each by the sounds they made. She volunteered to make the mural when the Amundsons wondered what to do with the space. They let her do it, and fell in love with the work when she finished. It became the trademark of the store until they died.

Carl gleefully covered the mural with his banner on Ulee's day off. When Ulee saw what he had done, she wasn't surprised. It signified an ending to the good old days. Carl's statement of ownership.

Ulee hadn't picked up a brush since the mural. She hadn't done much of anything except sit still and meditate. For years, she sat, moving into decades.

SHACK COMPLETION

Aino taped off the sheetrock and mudded the seams. He used the wood planer to smooth the rough cut 1"x 6" boards. Then, he cut a notch out of each edge with a router to make the boards for a tongue and groove ceiling. It took a few days to complete with some intricate angles, but it resembled a professional job. He primed the walls and installed the trim. The shack approached completion. As nice as a hotel room. He'd installed power outlets but still had to dig the trench to bury the power line. The wood stove could wait until autumn. Aino laid on his back in the new room with the window cracked and listened to the sound of the creek flowing below the shack. He felt a sense of completion for the first time in his life. It would be a comfortable place for anyone to sleep. A peaceful retreat from the main house. Luxury living in the wilderness.

Henry started moving boxes down to the shack and, before long, filled it to the ceiling. He brought his foam mat down and put it on the floor in the corner, along with his Hawaiian towel and ancient sleeping bag.

Aino had the main house to himself for sleeping for a while. For several weeks, the two rarely spoke. I'd see Henry down at the shack in deep thought. Aino had begun cleaning up the area around Schieffelbein's house.

IN THE BLACK

Henry returned from his weekly run to the city. He walked past the shack and followed a steep trail to the creek with a backpack full of cash. He hopped the mossy stones to cross the creek and scared a ten-point buck that bounded into the forest.

Further down the creek, the land dropped into a pond with a secluded water hole surrounded by boulders. The water flowed over an outcropping of rocks. He dropped the bag, took his clothes off, and jumped into the water, deep enough to be over his head. Henry let out a "Whoop! Whoa, It's cold! Come on in Chaos!"

I'll come over when I'm ready, Henry! You're not the

boss of me. I found it entertaining watching him swim like a fool. I'd never do that. I wasn't into swimming as a human, and now it's the last thing I want to do.

Henry swam over to the edge where the backpack lay and grabbed hold of the zip-lock baggies inside. He swam to the waterfall, got under the flow of it, and disappeared. There was a little cave under the falls big enough for one person. He moved rocks around inside the chamber, pushing the baggies of cash inside an open space within. He slid back into the pond like the mountain was giving birth to him.

"I had to make a deposit at the river bank, get it? All the balance sheets are in order, and we are firmly in the black." then, splashed water at me.

Why would I want to know about your financial situation, Henry? I want to hear about something other than money. Besides, what if a giant storm washes out that little cave section. What are you gonna do then, smarty pants?

Henry sat on a stone with his feet dangling in the water. "I wish I knew what you were trying to say to me, Chaos."

The ten-point buck returned and stood staring at Henry from about fifty yards, quietly drinking from the crystal clear stream.

"How are you doing, old friend?" The buck lowered its head down to drink again. Never blinking and watching Henry. The pond became a mirror as the buck stood like a sculpture on a boulder pedastool.

LAST TRIP TO THE CITY

"Hey Henry, could I catch a ride into the city with you this week? I wanna go pick up my truck."

"Hey, ah, sure, man. I didn't know you had a truck."

"It's dead in the garage in the Mission. They want me

to get it out there. Plus, Simone is coming down from Portland."

"Who's Simone?"

"My ex, she's having an art show and playing piano."

"You gonna go?"

"I think so. I have a queasy feeling, though. Like maybe I shouldn't?"

Thursday came, and the two of them were gone before sunrise. Up and over the hill.

"Have you ever gotten pulled over with the weed in the car?"

"Several times. I got pulled over last month and kept smoking. Showed him my medical card. The cop didn't do anything."

Pea-sized hail hit the windshield as they crossed the Golden Gate Bridge.

"Where do you want me to let you off?"

"How bout Muddy Waters Coffee on Valencia? I'm gonna have the truck towed to the shop on Cesar Chavez. Well, let me out here."

Aino jumped out on the corner of 16th and Valencia and walked over to the Roxie Theater to see what was playing. Then he doubled back for a coffee. The truck came and hauled his rig away, and he saw "the Swan" handing out papers in front of Adobe Books. "Agent World," news told from a roach's perspective. Nate was at work, and Aino planned to crash on his couch that night. He found his way down to the Tenderloin. To The Winter Fern Tavern on Polk St.

"Haven't seen you in a while. I heard you guys were up north. How is it going up there?" asked Stanley.

"Paradise, man. A slice of paradise," said Aino.

"What'll you have?"

"I'm not drinking anymore."

"Oh, congratulations. So you come to a bar to not drink anymore?"

"Why would a bartender congratulate someone for not drinking anymore? If everybody didn't drink, you'd be out of a job. How bout a pint of grapefruit juice with soda water and a couple limes?'

"The hard stuff. Coming right up, my friend."

An elderly Italian man appeared in the doorway, standing in the sun, wearing a long brown trench coat. He had wild hair like Bob Dylan but graying on the sides. A face like a classic mobster from the fifties. He wore a pinstripe suit and Italian leather shoes. His purple silk shirt was untucked, coming out below the vest. In one hand was a plastic bag from Walgreens, and the other held several lottery tickets like a hand of cards as if he were getting ready to sit down at the poker table.

"Giuseppe! Giuseppe is here!" shouted Stanley as he bowed in praise to the formally dressed yet disheveled old man.

"One shot Anejo por favor. Only one shot. Not two; you pour too heavy."

"Just a shot, Giuseppe? "

"Three count shot, One, Two, Three, Yes, one shot. Only one, my friend." He said with an Italian accent." Don't do double, no heavy. I gotta keep straight for my women."

"Ok, how's that?" as Stanley handed him a precise 3-count pour.

"Perfetto!!"

"There will not be a tip! But here is the lottery ticket. If it wins, we split! Deal? "Giuseppe held out his hand with a missing ring finger. Cut off at the first knuckle, insisting Stanley shake it. "Now, pick your ticket, Stanley."

"You saw 'dis. You shake, too." Holding out his hand to Aino. Making him shake the one with the missing finger. When he shook Aino's hand, he moved the stump of the finger so Aino could feel it.

"Kinda creepy, Giuseppe," said Aino.

"What creepy? What do you mean weird? You know I'm golden gloves? Have you seen my photo? "He pulled a picture of himself from his coat pocket. It was from when he was a boxer in the 1950's. In the photo, he had slicked-back hair in the classic boxing pose.

"It's me! Golden Gloves champ. New York City 1952. The Golden Gloves champ here in the Golden State!" He held up his arms with hands clasped together like the champ. Nobody cheered in the bar.

"You're the champ, Giuseppe!" said Stanley.

"Yes, I am the champ! Wanna Dum Dum?" as he opened the bag of lollipops to show them all. "You get one anyway. "He left one in front of each of them.

A few girls entered the bar. Giuseppe swooped in.

"Hey ladies, you wanna Dum Dum?"

Aino got a text from Simone.

"Are you in town?"

"Yes, I'm at The Winter Fern Tavern on Polk Street."

"You're not drinking, are you?"

"No, I'm on the grapefruit wagon. Where are you?"

"I'm at the Edwardian Hotel on Market. You should come by before I go to the show. I wanna talk to you."

"Alright, I'll come over. "

"Thanks, Stanley, I gotta go. "

Aino left a twenty-dollar bill on the bar and walked down Polk Street towards Market. Simone waited in the hotel lobby, drinking a cup of tea. Her curly black hair pulled up into a bun, and she wore a pink frayed sweater with a flowered shirt underneath and jeans. Simone had a petite frame like a ballerina and wore a brooch of a goat on her lapel.

"Oh my god, it's good to see you, Simone!"

She smiled but didn't get up.

"Good to see you too. Let's hang out here in the lobby. I got you a tea," she said, and handed him a paper cup with a lid on it.

"Thank you, just what I needed. Are you excited for the show?"

"Yeah, I think so. I don't want to set myself up to be disappointed. So, I'm keeping low expectations. I brought the sculptures of goat skeletons."

Aino looked confused.

"The ones balancing on each other, The sparrow coming out of the top goat's mouth. Remember that one?"

"Oh yeah, I love that one! Look what I have." Aino pulled the gray stone heart out of his pocket.

"I can't believe you still have that! I didn't even know who I was when I gave it to you. It's so silly."

"I don't think it's silly." Aino looked down at the heart in the palm of his hand.

"You know it's not mine anymore, right? It's never really been. Some lady in Kansas City gave it to me. I was crazy at the time."

"Whose is it then? Whose heart is it supposed to be?"

Simone sipped her tea. "Some crazy lady's heart."

"Crazy for me?" asked Aino.

"No, just crazy." there was an awkward silence. "Look, Aino, I can't help you anymore. I'm on this healing path. The real healing."

"Well, I wanna help you. Can't we help each other?"

"You never listen."

"I'm listening to you. I've listened for years to everything. I wanna hear it all."

"You couldn't even remember my sculpture. You listen, but you don't hear anything." Simone began to tear up.

"Do you want it back? "He held up the heart.

"Why would I want it back? I want you to give me space. I want to be the one to contact you, not the other way around."

"So, I'll probably never hear from you again."

"You don't know that. Look, I am making real progress. I'm getting it all sorted out with my health. You're too much to deal with. It's a distraction from what I want to accomplish. Don't you understand?"

"I thought we could help each other out."

"You've got to help yourself. I can't do it for you. You have to do the work but haven't even started."

"I've started. Look, I've stopped drinking and doing drugs. It's a good start, don't you think? I've got fifty-seven days."

"It's more than quitting drinking. It's a good start, I'm proud of you, Aino, but you have so much to go. You don't even know."

"I always thought we could help each other along."

"I'm gonna go get ready for this thing. I'll put you on the list if you still wanna go, but it won't hurt my feelings if you don't. I understand, but I wanted to say it in person. "

Aino stared out the window at the rain on Market Street. A homeless man put his mouth on the window, pushing his tongue against it in a swirl. As if he was French kissing some imaginary friend.

"Wow, good ole San Francisco," said Aino.

"Well, I'll play piano at 8:00 p.m., but the art show starts at 7. There's hors d'oeuvres. I know you like free shit."

"Don't you even wanna know what I've been up to?"

She slipped away up the stairs to the rooms above, pretending not to hear. Aino sat for a moment, clutching the heart in his hand. Looking around the musty old lobby, he wanted to follow her up the steps, but he wasn't invited. He walked to the door and put the heart back in his pocket. His memento of melancholy. Aino stepped out into the rain on Market Street and walked to the Embarcadero. Down to the waterfront while the fog swallowed the Bay Bridge. He stood staring into the gray. Holding the heart out to the backdrop. It nearly blended in. He wondered if it could vaporize into the cloud? Wishing it would, he took a pitcher's windup and pretended to throw it out into the bay, but he couldn't let it go.

"You got five bucks? Yo, help a brother out?" came a rotten tooth voice from behind.

Aino turned, "No man, you want this thing?" as he held the heart out to the man.

"You crazy! What do I want that for? I want five bucks motherfucker! I need a beer!"

"Shit, here, man." Aino handed him a twenty-dollar bill and said, "Keep the change."

"For reals? Thank you, brother!"

Aino took a cab back to The Winter Fern Tavern and proceeded down the path to stumbling drunk again. He ran into Frankie, the dealer and bought a fifty-dollar bag of blow. He had a couple thousand in his pocket from all the work on the farm. Cash under the table. He had saved the money to fix the truck but figured, why not? The clutch was only gonna be nine hundred dollars. So, he was back at it with a bump on a key in the bathroom. Staring at the graffiti, all blending in layers of nonsense. He saw one word in the scribbled mess," Chaos." Feeling the chemical taste seep down the back of his throat. He cupped his left hand, filled it with water, and snorted it down to wash the cocaine through his sinuses. Cleaning away any evidence from his nose.

"What took you so long? "asked Stanley

"I was listening to a Swedish mix tape in the bathroom. You wanna hear it?" Aino tried to hand the baggie off under the bar.

"No, man, I'm good. "Stanley shook his head to think for a moment and then said, "Yeah, lemme give it a listen, "and reached out for it. Quickly making his way to the bathroom.

They got into countless grinded-jaw conversations that led nowhere but promised everything. Making deals that vanished into oblivion. The happy hours went by, and Aino kept tipping $20's like a high roller.

A tech guy sat at the bar and said, "Hey man, we should buy a pizza with Bitcoin. Have you ever heard of Bitcoin? 60 cents apiece. You can use it to trade, man. It's a new kinda money. Untraceable. Do you know what a blockchain is? Let's get a pizza with it! Pizzolo is taking 10 bitcoin for pizza now. I convinced him. It's an experiment," bragged the tech guy while nobody listened.

Aino pissed away hundreds of dollars by the end of happy hour.

"Man, you should put a couple hundred in Bitcoin, I'm serious!," suggested the tech guy while in the bathroom blasting another bump off of Aino's key.

"Let's get more!"

The dealer, Frankie, was still there, smiling in his tracksuit. Everybody loved him. Aino slipped him another fifty dollars, and the night raced on.

"Frankie, you gonna start taking Bitcoin?" asked Stanley.

"Hell yeah, I'll take Bitcoin. What's it at now? I hear it's going up to a dollar soon. I've already got thousands on a little thumb drive. Save it for a rainy day."

"Let's take a cab to SOMA. Simone is having an art show."

"I don't wanna go, man. Meet us later at the Lipo Lounge. Blood Bath and Beyond is playing, "said Stanley. Aino unrolled his suit jacket and put it on.

He jumped in a cab and was feeling full of life again. Jacked up on cocaine, feeling back on top. He stepped out of the cab and into the gallery. Simone had already started playing. There was a room full of affluent people and even a city judge. They were all enthralled. Aino sat down with his back to the wall by the door and looked up at the skeleton of a goat made with ceramics. Simone had sculpted a bird popping out of its mouth. She played Chopin's Nocturne in E-flat major, which morphed into something original. His heart raced, and he felt trapped inside his suit jacket.

Rain fell outside and dripped down the window of the gallery. The spitting rain of winter in San Francisco. Hanging on to the Pacific chill. Aino felt suffocated by the crowd. She finished her performance to the roar of the audience. Everyone stood up, and Aino applauded as loudly as he could, but he watched his hands clapping together in front of him. He removed his jacket and started spinning it in a circle above his head. Taking it too far. The affectionate crowd overshadowed him. He made eye contact and waved from across the room. Simone quickly turned away and continued talking with the elderly judge from the city. Trying to ignore him and his coke binge. He didn't wanna interrupt, so he stood there waiting across the room. Staring like a maniac. A gallery worker came up to him and said, "Sir, this is for patrons only. This is a ticketed event."

"I think I'm on the list. I'm sorry, I walked in late. That's my friend Simone. Simone! Hey, can you tell this lady I'm with you? "shouted Aino across the room.

People stared at him and frowned. He felt their dagger eyes, and Simone looked embarrassed by Aino's outburst. He moved towards the wine table but tripped and knocked over the display. Then grabbed several bottles and ran out the front door. He ran through the rain until he got to Market Street. Broke the top off a wine bottle on a lamppost and started chugging it down. The broken bottle cut his mouth, and he threw it into the street. Blood dripped down his chin and stained the front of his shirt.

A man on the street yelled, "What are you fuckin' doin man? You're wasting it!" Aino hailed a cab.

"To Chinatown and the LiPo Lounge"

"Dude! You alright?"

"What do you mean am I alright?'"

"You're bleeding pretty bad. You want me to take you to the hospital?" asked the cabbie.

"No, man. Fuck that! I'm good."

"There's a box of tissues back there. Don't bleed on my seats."

"Just take me to the LiPo Lounge." Aino grabbed a wad of tissues and stuck them to his bleeding mouth.

He continued late into the night. Back to an after-hours party at the 500 Club. Another bag of blow. He was blinded, and the bartender said, "Aino, you gotta go now. Your mouth is fucked up. You've had too much! You've pissed yourself."

"Fuck you! Play Joe Pass, you bastard!" screamed Aino.

The trolley bell rang from the tracks running down Market Street, and Aino woke up from his stupor on Nate's couch, not remembering how he got there. Blood from his cut lip stained the couch pillow. The same one he had puked on months before. He checked his phone. He had texted Simone. "Lovely performance. You were amazing!"

She replied, "Don't ever message me again."

He felt nauseous as the laser sun burned through the window into his eyes. The clank of the streetcar pounded through his head like a beer pitcher full of pinballs poured over a cowbell. The gray heart rested on the floor by the couch, and his pants hung out the window.

"I don't think you should come into the city anymore," said Nate, standing in the hall by the kitchen.

"What happened? Did I wreck anything?"

"Yeah, you wrecked yourself. You need to stop. This should be the last time you're not staying here again. I don't think my roommates want you to ever come back. You were ranting like a lunatic. Kicking that heart around the living room. You pissed yourself. I had to wash your pants in the sink. They're clean, you can thank me anytime. We tried to get you to go to the hospital, but you freaked out. You scared everyone. "

"I'm so sorry, Nate," sulked Aino. "Please forgive me. Again and again. Shit! I know I don't deserve it. I swear I'm done with this. No more. I'm done." He crushed his head in his hands.

"It's what you said the last time and the time before. "

"Yeah, man. You're right." He slunk down and stared at the floor.

"How's your mouth?"

"Oh shit." Aino walked to the bathroom and looked in the mirror. His lip was cut badly, and the gum was still bleeding. He rinsed with water.

"I think it needs stitches. It's gonna leave a big scar."

"You want to go to urgent care. Get a couple stitches. It might not scar so bad."

"I can't afford that, man."

"You could afford it last night, though."

"Fuck, I'm an idiot." Aino checked his pockets and realized he only had $300 left from the $2,000.

He picked up the heart. "Once I get the truck out of the garage, I have nothing left here. Simone's moving to DC. She doesn't want anything to do with me. I've gotta pick up the truck this afternoon."

"How you gonna pay for it?"

"I'll put it on a credit card."

"Sounds like Simone is moving on. Can't say I blame her. She was never with you anyway. You imagined it to be more. You know how you do that, Aino?"

"I do."

SPRING

OTTO & HUNTER

Otto sat in the leather captain's chair of a large motorhome. He towed a brand-new jeep on a car dolly while his daughter Hunter followed close behind. She drove the F-350 Ford truck. All three vehicles had matching paint jobs and vanity Texas license plates. Marine1, Marine2 and Marine3. USMC was airbrushed on one side in giant letters and Semper Fi across the other. Otto and his daughter both wore matching headsets for instant communication."

"Hunter, do you copy?

"Affirmative, Dad."

"Gonna need to pull over to replenish our fuel supply."

"10-4 dad. Copy."

Otto had a slightly effeminate build with a sinewy muscle tone. His hair was neatly groomed into a flat top crew cut greased into a part on one side. He wore khaki polyester shorts and a polo golf shirt with the USMC logo embroidered on the chest. White tube socks pulled up past his calves with scarlet and gold stripes. Nike running shoes to match.

Otto served in Vietnam and returned as a decorated war veteran after spending nearly two years in a POW camp. He learned to grow weed from his captors. Otto returned from the war with undiagnosed PTSD and a heroin habit. He managed to get clean thirty years ago and turn his life around. He became an exercise junkie instead.

His daughter Hunter was autistic, which gave her wizard-like skills in mathematics. An excellent musician and multi-instrumentalist. She resembled a young Elvis with jet-black hair combed into a pompadour. Hunter wore green corduroy pants, a jean jacket, and a western shirt. Scrappy but sweet, her eyes were a brilliant blue. In it for the adventure and future explorer of the world.

Otto's wife Carolina had died from an overdose of heroin one year after Hunter's birth. This is why Otto got clean. They had three other daughters who lived in the Houston area and were older. Otto raised Hunter after Carolina's death, but Carolina wasn't her real mother.

"I want you to pull over to the other island. I'll be over with the card in a second. We're filling all the tanks. Take all the caps off the jerry cans, too. "

"10-4 dad."

"I don't wanna see a drop spilled Hunter. Keep your eyes on it. Good work. Way to hustle!" he was only kidding around with his stern orders. Hunter played along.

"Thank you, sir!"

"You need to polish your buckle, buddy," commented Otto. "Let's get it rolling. We're at spot seventeen at the Dias Verdez RV Park."

They pulled onto HWY 101 for about a quarter mile and turned into the RV park on the north end of town. Otto hopped out of the rig and checked in with the office. Got his parking pass and a bundle of complimentary firewood. He came out waving the pass above his head like he had won the lottery.

"Let's get this thing set up and try to run up to the cabin before dark."

"Don't you wanna bring stuff up there today?" asked Hunter.

"I wanna check the road first. Let's take the Jeep and the truck, we'll drop off those jerry cans. I might leave this RV here all summer. Wouldn't it be nice to have a place to stay in town?"

"Copy."

"You can take the headset off now."

"Copy, Dad."

"Do you have to say it every time? I'm standing right in front of you."

"You're standing right in front of me."

"Yeah, right, I'm standing right in front of you."

"Copy, Dad."

Otto undid the straps from the car dolly and backed the Jeep off the trailer. Then, he took the trailer off the hitch from the RV and pushed it off to the side, pressing the self-leveling button. All the while, Hunter made dramatic gestures for parking, like flagging in a jetliner at the airport. They had a prime spot near the creek and away from the highway. Hans watched them from the fence line. Hunter tried to get the horse to come closer, but he shied away under a tree and sighed.

The old rusty trailer with flat tires sat beside their spot. It looked like it had been there for decades. Ulee peaked through the curtains at Hunter, but she didn't notice.

"Hey, come on, bud, follow me in the truck Hunter, let's go check out the cabin now."

"Copy…"

"Don't say it. Would you quit it with the 'copy' shit?"

"Copy, Dad."

Veins started popping out of Otto's neck. "Follow me."

They took it slow up, and over the hill for fear any

speck of dirt would be the kiss of death on either vehicle. Otto stopped at the summit and pulled out his phone.

"Hey Henry, how goes it, buddy? We're at the summit. We're here! We've got two vehicles. The Jeep and the white Ford truck. Just givin ya a heads up we'll be around!"

They parked at Lost Creek and the water level made it too dangerous to cross from the recent rain. Henry had reattached the rope since the doctor's demise. Otto decided not to risk bringing vehicles over until the creek went down. He got a garbage bag from the Jeep and took off his boots and pants. Hunter wadded her clothes in a ball and threw them across the creek.

"I got the garbage bag! No need to risk it, Hunter," but she was already nearly across. "That'll wake ya up, won't it!"

"It's cold, Dad!" Hunter quickly put her clothes back on.

"Thanks for not saying copy."

"Copy, Dad."

They both snickered as Otto slid his boots back on. The A-frame was only a half-mile in and up the left fork before the old abandoned house of George DeCarlo.

"I wanna open the place up and let it air out; we don't gotta stay long."

"What about all the jerrycans?"

"We'll leave the truck and come back tomorrow. Wait for the creek to go down."

The two hiked in and found the cabin as Otto had left it several months before. A few down limbs but nothing more. Dead leaves had taken over the deck. They opened all the windows to let in some fresh air, and Otto lit a fire in the wood stove.

In the early 70s, Otto built the A-frame structure with a wrap-around screened-in porch. There were bunks outside for sleeping in warmer months and bunks inside with a lovely view of the snowy peak off to the east. No frills, but the simplicity of the place opened it up to nature.

"I've decided to leave the RV in Dias Verdez. Sound okay to you?" asked Otto.

"You mean, you want me to stay in town and drive in every day. Or are you gonna stay in town too?"

"I wanna stay out here and have you stay in town. I snore too loudly, and you need your sleep. You'll have your own space in the RV."

"I'd like that, Dad."

"Let's do it then, but I'm gonna stay tonight in town. Let this place air out overnight. I wanna take you to Slingers for dinner."

"I can't go in there! Remember what happened last time?"

"Ahh, those guys are a bunch of rednecks, you can't let 'em get to you."

"I'd rather not. Better to avoid."

"Okay, I'll order food to go and we'll have a little picnic by the firepit. Wanna start walking back now?"

Hunter nodded and smiled.

LET GO

Aino paid the man at the Hernandez garage and put half on the credit card. He still had some gas money left to return to the farm. It would be a four-hour drive. His skull felt like a balloon about to pop. Checking his face in the rear-view mirror, he felt short of breath. Pressing on his swollen lip, which seeped blood. It could have used a few stitches. He put a Band-Aid on it at the gas station. His eczema spread to his eyelids, but his hand cleared up, and he assumed it was from the lotion he had gotten from Henry. The purple circles under his eyes made it look like he'd been punched in the face.

"Don't worry, the soul will grow back. It's hiding behind your spine," said a voice from within.

He tried to puke out the window while crossing the Golden Gate Bridge, but he lost it inside the car, and it dripped down the inside of the door onto the window crank.

"What if I stop here?" he thought. "Stop right now and make the jump? How long would it take to hit the water? Four, maybe five seconds?" He imagined the free fall and smacking the water like concrete. Then he saw himself coming to the surface with all the wind knocked out of him and a man in a rowboat grabbing him with a big metal hook. Fishing him out of the water like in that book Sea Wolf. Shanghaied and held captive out at sea. Still alive but now forced to be a servant for the Sea Wolf. "Maybe I'll keep driving and not jump off the bridge today."

The Toyota T100 ran like a champ as the odometer crossed the 400,000-mile mark. He'd built a loft in the back, and some damaged instruments were stored underneath. The camper shell had a broken window, and he sealed it up with a piece of plywood. The guitar had a missing tuning peg, and the trombone had a kink in its valve slide. A pile of moldy clothes lay on top of a dirty sleeping bag a cat had pissed on. He pulled over and tossed all of it in a dumpster behind the Walgreens in San Rafael. Then he sprayed the truck's interior and the back end at the Jiffy-wash, leaving the windows open to dry.

The weather turned cold again, and another frost warning was in effect. It meant the mountains would be icy that night. Dropping into the mid-twenties. He felt a chill and tried to shut the window, but the crank broke.

When he reached the Lost Creek crossing, he saw the vehicles with Texas plates and wondered who the newcomers were. He didn't risk crossing with his truck, so he parked it near the others. He took off all his clothes and rolled them up into a ball with his boots. Tossed it over to the other side and started wading through. Walking with his hands holding onto the rope. In the center of the creek, he stopped at chest deep and let the icy water flow over him. He imagined it pushing the cocaine out of his body. Washing it down the river. He held onto the rope and fully submerged in the current. He cleaned his cut lip in the icy river water. Letting his feet drift down as he held on like Superman. He turned numb and let go with one hand. Dangling on the string. Like a spaceman from an umbilical cord connecting him to the world. His voice inside said, "Let it go." But he couldn't make his hand work. Frozen to the rope. All at once it gave in and he let go. His body sunk to the bottom and drifted with the current but he didn't go far. He got tangled in the branches of a sweeper in the nearby eddy. A calmness came over him as the remaining air drained from his lungs. Somehow, he still had conciousness. A submerged branch caught him by the armpit and lodged him in its grasp while the current held him under. His legs were bouncing on the bottom like a giant fishing lure. His head tilted sideways, and the water entered his ear canal. He heard a muted voice but couldn't make out the words.

"There's a guy in the river, Dad!" yelled Hunter. You see his arm sticking up through branches?. Otto ran down the bank to the spot and grabbed a stick. He poked the body to see if he was alive.

"Hey! Hey, man! What the hell are you doing?" Otto yelled as he waded into the submerged branches. He grabbed Aino by the arm, and pulled him up.

"You alright, man? Hey! You alright?"

Aino gasped to fill his lungs again with a deep, groaning inhalation.

Hunter had waded into the creek to help. She

grabbed Aino's other arm, and they pulled him into the tall grass on the riverbank. Dazed and turning blue. He was shaking while he lay there in the nude as the temperature had already dropped into the low '30s. He flew outside of himself. Looking down at his body laying by the river facing two strangers.

"You gonna be alright, man? Do you need a lift into town? You need to go to the hospital?"

Aino didn't reply. He stood up and went to fetch his ball of clothes.

"Are you part of Henry's crew? You wanna come with us?" asked Otto.

He stood there silent like a zombie.

"What can we do for you? You gotta put your clothes on, man; you're gonna get hypothermia."

Aino picked up his clothes and started walking toward the farm. His whole body was numb from the inside out. He flew above and watched himself walk away in a trancelike state.

"Man, you gotta put your clothes on! You're gonna freeze!" yelled Otto as Aino walked away from them.

He was soon outta site.

"What can we do? Should we go after on him?" said Hunter. "Dude's fucked up."

"Do you think he's on meth or something?"said Otto.

"I don't think he's on meth. He's got good teeth. "

"Did you see his lip? Somebody must have beat the shit out of him."

"Maybe he's another squatter at the Schieffelbein house?"

"He seemed to know where he was going," said Otto. "I'll give Henry a heads-up on the dude. I'm gonna call him when we get to the summit. You still wanna go to Slingers?"

"You know I don't wanna go to Slingers!"

"OK, bud. I'll get those chicken fingers to go."

They drove back to town in the jeep and left the truck with all the jerry cans by the creek.

"You sure the dude's not gonna come back and steal our gas?" said Hunter.

"I don't think he's in the shape to steal anything. Hopefully, he can find someplace warm."

Hans eyeballed Hunter as she exited the truck and opened the RV. The horse came closer to the fence, expecting a snack.

Otto walked down to Slingers and bellied up to the bar.

"Do you have any tomato juice?" asked Otto.

"Tomato juice. Your usual. Yes, we do, Otto! Good to see you." replied Holly.

She wore tight, bedazzled jeans and a tattoo to match the logo of the band Poison but it was misspelled with two s's. "Poisson". Otto tried to joke with her about it. "What's your tattoo? Do you mean like Poisson distribution in statistics class?"

"I don't know what you're talkin' about, Otto. It's Poison. The band Poison. Do you know what you want to order?"

"How 'bout some of those homemade chicken fingers? Please, with sugar on top. Just jokin' about the sugar, sugar." He winked at Holly, and she smiled.

"You got it, Otto. You just get back?"

"Yup, pulled in today. Ready for another round."

"Glad to have you back in town."

Sheriff Rick Johnson and Dufur were at the corner of the bar. Rick whispered over to Dufur, "Fuckin' guy's back. The workout king. You'd think a real man would have a real drink."

Otto made eye contact with Rick, and Rick quickly looked away. Otto would destroy Rick if the two met in a dark alley, and Rick knew it. He ordered another beer to add to his belly and grimaced again.

"Why don't you motherfuckers play some 38 Special? Bring some life to this fuckin' place! If you don't, I will!" yelled Rick as he walked over to the jukebox and slid a dollar in the slot. The song Hold on Loosely came on. "Turn this shit up!" Rick went to the bathroom and locked himself in the back stall. Pulled out his police badge and baggy of coke. He poured a little pile out onto the star of the badge and snorted deeply.

The kitchen bell dinged, and Otto's order was in the window. Holly brought it over. "Here you go, Otto. Packed with vitamins." He gave her another wink and found his way to the door. Dufur Fleck grimaced and stared him down as he left.

"Where'd the war hero go? I wanted to buy him a real drink," blurted Sheriff Rick Johnson, returning to his perch at the bar.

"He couldn't take your manly charms," said Dufur. "I think your body language scared him away."

PORK CHOP

Hunched over and naked, Aino held his clothes in front of him while walking down the hill toward the farm. I felt the need to console him. He made a moaning sound like a chanting shaman, and his lip was bloody and swollen. I rubbed up against his ankles. I wanted to warm his feet. I circled around him a few more times, but he kept walking. So, I pounced at his legs and bounced off, landing on my back. He snapped out of the trance.

"Oh, hey, Chaos. How are you, my friend? I thought you were supposed to land on your feet?" He reached down to pet me. "You're letting me pet you? Chaos the cat?"

I haven't ever let a person scratch my back, and I

don't remember purring. Well, I did when my mom was still alive.

"Since when do you purr, Chaos?"

I jumped up on the fence post. My tail slinked around like a snake. Aino put his clothes on and stood up normally again. I don't know what came over him when he walked down the hill like a zombie. A switch flipped inside of him, and he snapped out of it. I followed him to the house, and he met Henry on the back porch.

"Welcome back, man! Damn, who beat you up?"

Aino looked shaken by the question.

"I did. That's who."

"Hey ah, Nate texted and kinda filled me in. Just remember, you're okay out here. Keep breathing, man; you're on a different path now."

"I went off the rails after seeing Simone."

"I guess you two didn't hit it off."

"Total disaster!"

"At least you know. If you need to clear your head, think about your breath from start to finish. Simple as that."

"It's easy to say."

"Yeah, easy to do too. I've got some pork chops for you, my friend. This will put some peace in your belly. And for you, Chaos! I see you slinking around."

I jumped up on the railing of the porch.

"My friend Otto and his daughter Hunter got in today."

"I think I saw them at the creek, gonna have to explain myself," whispered Aino.

"What do you gotta explain?"

"When I crossed the creek, I wanted to feel the water on me. To clean myself. I took it too far. I wanted to let go. Let the river sweep me down. It took me into the sweeper branches. Your friends pulled me outta there."

"What the hell were you thinking?" said Henry.

"I wasn't thinking. I hope I didn't scare them. Sorry man. I should thank them. They helped me out."

"Well, we all get out of our minds sometimes. Can't let it suck you down the drain. Or the creek, I should say."

"Sometimes I feel like it's inevitable."

"You still got a lifeline to hang onto, man. I hope you know it."

Aino sat in the lawn chair by the grill, and I jumped in his lap.

"I can't believe what I'm seeing," said Henry. "Are you a lap cat now, Chaos?"

I am not a lap cat! I growled.

"That's a strange noise you're making, Chaos. Are you actually trying to say something?" asked Henry.

I just clammed up.

"That was Otto and Hunter, the people I saw at the river. Is Hunter his son?" asked Aino.

"No, that's Otto's daughter."

"Oh, I thought she was a man."

"Hell of a musician!"

"Oh, yeah? What's her instrument?"

"Every instrument, she's a bit of a savant."

"How do you know them?"

"I met Otto back in the '70s. "The wizard of weed." We all bought from him back in San Francisco. He taught George and me a lot about growing weed."

"Who's George again?"

"George, George DeCarlo. You know, that abandoned house near the fork in the road. That's George's place. George is dead. He was a wonderful friend of mine. The reason I came up here. He was a genuine weirdo."

What do you mean, weirdo? I scratched the side of the chair.

"Don't scratch the chair, Chaos! Get away from there!" shouted Henry.

"Why did you leave San Francisco?"

"I got tired of living in poverty, so I got out and came up here."

"To grow weed?"

"No. I got a job working on the roads. You know we'd scrape 'em, grade 'em, and put the culverts in. Growing up in South Dakota, I know how to work all the heavy equipment. I helped build part of Lost Creek Rd. It was good pay, man, with benefits. Mendocino County benefits. Otto hooked it up for me. I started having a thing with Aramoana, George's daughter, so I moved up here."

"Where did Aramoana come from?"

"She came from New York City too, like her dad. She tracked him down. He didn't know he had a daughter. But she moved in with him. Then, he built her a place of her own."

"So, George and Otto worked together growing weed?"

"Together sometimes, but eventually, they did their own thing. George turned into a hermit towards the end."

You got that right! Peace and quiet. You people started driving me crazy.

"Chaos wants to be part of the conversation. Are you okay, buddy? What's all this meowing about?" Aino scratched Chaos's neck. "Why'd George come here?"

"I dunno. Maybe George wanted a quiet place to paint. He created a lot of artwork in the house he built. Aramoana's got all his paintings now. "

"What kind of painting, oil painting?"

"Yeah, he was a pop art guy. He knew Warhol."

"For real?"

"Yeah, man."

Hang on, I didn't know that clown. That was all bullshit.

"Is that how he got his property?"

"I don't know. George always had money. I know he

sold a lot of weed, and property was cheap back then. None of the ranchers wanted it. All the land up in the hills. George and Otto bought hundreds of acres for next to nothing. Then, Schieffelbein and the Amundson's had their hat in the ring. It's an insulated group that owns all this land up here. Until the Brody's left suddenly."

"Who are the Brody's?"

"They're the ones who sold me the farm. I was living with Aramoana. Something happened between their kid and Carl. They were all close friends, and then they all stopped talking. Next, Vince Brody's giving me an offer I can't refuse. "

"What do you mean?"

"I couldn't say no to the price. Vince came over one day and made the offer. He seemed really scared, but he wouldn't explain why. They were peace-loving Dead Heads. Haven't heard from them since."

Ole Vince was a terrible poker player. That's the only reason I got property in the first place. He didn't want to let me have any more, so he sold it to you. Fucker held a grudge over that poker game.

"Quiet down, Chaos, We're trying to talk! They must have liked you, Henry."

"Yeah, we got along well. For years, they let me use the property to grow weed. I had to pay them a percentage like sharecropping."

"I guess they just wanted out," said Aino.

"Still seems strange to me. Brody's son Leif and Carl were close. He was like Leif's big brother. He worked at the store and quit all of a sudden. A few weeks later, they moved out, and no one has heard from them."

"Glad you were able to buy the farm. It's really a sweet spot, man. When did you start growing weed?"

"I've been growing since I was 13. I grew ditch weed back in South Dakota. I didn't know any better. Then I met Otto when I got out here. You know, he's a highly decorated vet? He's got a big purple heart and expertise in high-grade sinsemilla. I call him the commando of cannabis."

"Are they from Texas?"

"Yeah, He spends half the year here and then returns to Texas in October. He's been going back and forth since the '70s."

Henry handed Aino a pork chop fresh off the grill. "Try this, my friend."

Aino smiled, "Ah, man, thank you. "

Aino tossed a piece of pork fat on the ground below me. I wolfed it down in a flash!

"See, you just gotta eat, man. Everything's gonna be alright," said Henry.

CARL'S INSECURITY CAMERAS

Carl sat in his office monitoring his employees, suspicious about thievery. How could the store be losing money? He'd recently installed security cameras and developed an obsession with watching the monitors from his office with the door locked. "Was it Ulee?" he thought. He zoomed in behind the deli counter as she applied the dry rub to the rotisserie chickens.

"I told you not to use so much!" he muttered.

He shifted over to the camera at the checkout. He recently hired Billy Johnson, the son of Sheriff Rick Johnson. A local high school football star. He zoomed in on Billy.

"You gonna listen to the coach? I'm your coach now, Billy. You're the linebacker today. Back the line, Billy." He watched Billy say, "Paper or plastic?" getting a close-up of his mouth.

"Good boy. Keep up the good work. Oh, yeah." He felt himself under the desk through his creased khaki pants.

There was a knock on his office door.

"Who's there? I'm busy here!"

"It's Ulee. Do you have a second, Carl?"

"Dammit, Ulee! Hold on!" Carl composed himself and unlocked the door. "What? I'm doing payroll. It better be important."

"Sorry to bother you. I hate to ask, but..." Ulee paused, removing her hair net.

"Well, what? Spit it out!"

Ulee looked expectantly at Carl. "Well, they're raising the rent over at the RV park, and I'm wondering if you'd be willing to give me a little boost in pay to help cover it?"

"Wait, wait, wait, wait, wait. Didn't you already get a raise? How long has it been since you had a raise?"

"Not since you took over. It used to be a yearly thing. Remember? Plus, profit sharing. That's how your mom and dad did it."

"Let's not bring them into it. This isn't a charity, this is a business, Ulee."

"I don't understand that kinda business, Carl. Don't you remember when this place was like a family? Remember how I made you those blueberry muffins every day when you were a kid? You loved those. Remember everybody hanging around the coffee station in the morning? Bringing their dogs."

"Fuckin' blueberry? Blueberry muffins don't bring home the bacon, Ulee. And coffee smells bad. I hate coffee. Chicken's the focus now."

"Coffee's what brought everybody in."

"It's my store, Ulee! I don't want those puppy draggers hangin' around asking for free refills all day."

"Puppy draggers?"

"Those hippies with their dogs. I don't want 'em coming in."

"Your parents were hippies with dogs. What happened

to you, Carl? You used to be a hippie with a dog. Do you remember? Your little dog Wooly?"

"Wooly's dead! I don't wanna talk about it. Aren't you supposed to be getting the chicken ready? Remember to go easy on the spice."

"It's already done. Can't you see it on your little video screen? See them spinning in the machine? You should go without the spice if you want my opinion. People are complaining about it."

"I don't want your opinion. It's my spice! Nobody has a dry rub like mine. Nobody! If they don't like it, fuck 'em! It's not my fault if they don't have a sophisticated pallet. It's just a matter of time before they catch on." Carl swiveled his chair, turning his back on Ulee. "It's because you put too much on! You don't know what the fuck you're doing. It's not my fault people don't like it."

Ulee could keep a cool head in most situations. But, if one person could crawl under her skin, it was Carl. "Why'd you take away the coffee station? Nobody comes in now! Your chicken is terrible, Carl! The spice ruins it. You'd be better off roasting it plain, and it's too expensive! The cats don't even like it out by the dumpster." Ulee's voice was reaching its highest level in decades. "This place is a sinking ship!"

"Cats?! Cats love my chicken. What do you know about chicken anyway? You're a vegan!"

"I'm not a vegan, Carl. I just don't eat your crappy chicken."

"Why are you giving it away to the cats? I've had about enough of this, Ulee! Are we done?"

She took a breath and attempted a nurturing tone. "I want you to think back to how your parents ran this. How smooth everything went. How vital this place is for the people of this community. It's getting worse. No one is coming in but random tourists."

"Well, I'm not my parents, and keeping a community

hang-out place is not my business model. I'm not running a cat rescue with free chicken. I run a grocery store, Ulee! And the focus is chicken! Period! Do you remember when I asked you to go light on the seasoning? Do you remember, or has your brain stopped working on that level?"

"Yes, Carl. I'm putting on half as much as I used to. Don't have a conniption fit!"

"I've been watching, and it doesn't look like it. You're dumping it on like you don't even care!"

"Well, maybe I don't," whispered Ulee.

"You should start looking for another job if you don't care about the spice-to-chicken ratio. This is a poultry paradise, and I can't have you as a weak link in the team." Carl's legs began to shake in his swivel chair.

"If you can't see my vision, I don't see where we'll go from here. How did Colonel Sanders start? Consistency Ulee! Consistency!"

"I don't know what you're talking about, Carl?"

"The Colonel started with consistency, that's how. Like putting coconut butter on after working out and seeing yourself in the mirror for the first time every day. Really seeing yourself. If you don't want to ride this train, jump off, it's your choice. It's a free country, Ulee. Take it or leave it. You gotta pull yourself up from your bootstraps."

"Isn't that impossible? Is that a joke, Carl?"

"No joke, Ulee!"

"I'm only asking for a small raise, and not sure I understand the analogy you were trying to make."

"What is an analogy? Why do you gotta use that kind of word, Ulee? $10.25 an hour is the going rate for deli workers in this town. Think twice next time you sprinkle $50 worth of seasoning on those chickens! I have a list of about twenty guys who'll replace you tomorrow with a phone call. Are we done?"

"It wasn't"

"I know what I see with my own two eyes, Ulee, and I'll be watching you." He pointed at the screen. "Now leave me alone; I gotta finish this." She closed the door, and he locked it behind her.

"Now, where were we, Billy?"

BLACK SUV

A black Escalade parked at the turn-off to Lost Creek Road. It had tinted windows with the driver's side rolled down. An elderly man sat inside wearing a striped tracksuit. He spoke with two guys on motocross bikes through the cracked tinted window as if they were getting a briefing. The window rolled up, and the two motorcyclists took off up the hill. They split at the fork but met again when the road converged at the summit. The two of them stopped while one tried to make a call. He waved his phone to the sky for a better signal. He talked for a few seconds, then gave a sign to loop back around. They took off down into the canyon at full speed. The SUV stayed in place.

Aino decided to make a dump run into town and do some laundry. He wanted to empty the trailer full of roofing material and other junk. Turn in the bottles for recycling. He liked to use the industrial-sized machines at the laundromat to wash his sleeping bag and blankets.

Henry said, "Use the old truck parked by the wood mill. Keys are in it. Turn the ignition key only halfway until the little red coil glows. It's a diesel. Then you can turn it all the way. It should kick right over. I started it up last week."

It was a '79 Dodge Power Wagon 4x4. Aino took it slowly through the creek. The tires spun in the mud at the edge but grabbed hold of the rocks on the other side.

IIc turned on KMUD, and it faded in and out of static. Fred Neil's "Little Bit of Rain" song came in clear as he emerged from the hairpin turns of the canyon.

A sedan came whipping around the corner, nearly hitting him head-on. It wasn't the car you'd typically see on Lost Creek Road. A brand-new sedan, probably a rental car. He caught a glimpse of the driver. A teenage boy who looked wide-eyed and terrified. Aino stopped the rig and got out, expecting to hear a crash from the adolescent speed demon. Then, the two dirt bikes blazed by. They were chasing after him. He listened to what sounded like gunshots coming from the direction of the chase. Aino continued to the bottom of the hill where the black Escalade parked. He couldn't see if anybody was inside because the tinted windows were rolled up. He could only speculate. Could it be that the young man driving the rental car had wronged members of the cartel, and they were chasing after him to a deadly end? They caught him and shot him, never to be seen again. The bikers returned and reported to the boss in the Escalade.

"We got 'em by the river at the end of the line. Here's the head to prove it. We gotta go back and get the car."

Aino thought about this while unloading all the junk at the dump and got $27 for the bottles at the recycling center. He threw his bedding in the washer and went across to EZ Mart to buy some beer for Henry with the recycling money.

The warm weather returned, which meant more people were hitchhiking up HWY 101. The man with the wizard stick in the long brown robe stood under a tree at the edge of the parking lot of the EZ Mart. A Border Collie lay in the shade, smiling next to him. He appeared to be in a meditative state. Another guy sat on the opposite curb with a Rottweiler tied to a short piece of rope. It barked wildly in a spiked collar. The dog had scars all over its face. Its owner had a tattoo of the Tasmanian Devil on his cheek.

He said, "Bro, you got some buds?" as Aino walked into the store. "Twenty bucks? I need a twenty, bro. My dog needs twenty, bro!"

Aino came out and the guy repeated, "Bro, twenty bro! you got any kind bud?" Aino said, "No, but you wanna beer?" The guy shook his head. "No, bro, I want buds. You know where I can get work around here?" Aino shook his head, returned to the laundromat with the beer, and put it in the truck. He put his bedding in the dryer and read the bulletin board.

There were several missing person posters. "Last seen 2/12 parked at the rest area beyond Lost Creek Rd. 32 years old. 5' 11" 170 pounds. Alex Degrosse. Van found burned at rest stop." The photo showed a skinny, bald white guy smiling and walking on a trail with hiking sticks.

"I never understood why people use those things," Aino muttered, staring at the picture.

Another read, "Missing Person: New Year's Eve, Judy Jenkins, 41. Last seen in the parking lot of the Running Rapids Casino. Upper Lake off HWY. 20." Her picture showed her smiling, giving the peace sign. Aino stared into the dryer as the minutes counted down.

"Was it you? Did you do it? Do you always talk to yourself?"

The voice from behind startled him. It was Hunter.

"Oh– hey. You scared me."

"Hi, I'm Hunter. We met at the creek yesterday. That was you, right? The naked guy?"

Aino looked puzzled. "Yeah. It was me."

"You were a blue man. My dad thought you were on acid. What were you trying to do, kill yourself or something?"

Aino went back to staring at the dryer. "It's almost

done. My mother gave me this blanket. Still works but falling apart. See how it's shredded?" He took it out and tried to fold it with the several growing holes in the patchwork.

"Man, you need a new blanket." Hunter stood there holding a sack of dirty clothes. "What happened to your mouth? Who beat you up?"

"Nobody. I tried to chug wine out of a broken bottle. Smart huh?"

"Oddly enough, I've done that before. I was careful, though. I didn't cut my lip. You really got yourself good."

"Sorry bout yesterday; I was outta my mind. I'm back to reality now."

"I'll say you were outta your mind."

Hunter put her clothes in the washer. "Fuckin' weird man. What's your name? I don't wanna keep calling you the naked blue guy."

"Aino's the name."

"Aino? Like Draino Aino?"

"Yeah. Draino Aino. That's me."

"What kinda name is that? Draino Aino?"

"It's Finnish."

"Well, now you're the only Aino I know as far as I know. Draino Aino. You know?"

They both laughed.

"I heard you were a trumpet player. You wanna play some music sometime? I'm okay on the piano. I love playing the piano over at Henry's. He always keeps it in tune."

"Won't be able to play for a while with my lip like it is."

"What about the drums?"

"I can play drums and we can get Henry on the bass.

"You know Henry has perfect pitch?" said Hunter. "The guy doesn't need a tuner. He can pick out any note from thin air and tell you what it is."

"I had no idea. Henry could be a musicologist. He knows everything about music history. Whenever I pick out a record at his place, he knows all the players, where it was recorded, and when it was recorded. All of it!"

"Yeah, he even knows what they had for lunch."

"He hurt his thumb, so he can't play guitar or piano now. He's on the bass all the time, playing along. He's good. Like a clock with rhythm."

"He's good at everything! "

"I heard you were good at everything. Every instrument! Henry was raving about you."

"Henry embellishes. I don't know what I'm doing. Having fun, though."

"It's what I wanna do. Find the fun in the music again."

"Don't you know how to have fun anymore? It's not hard, you know, having fun," said Hunter.

"I forgot, I guess."

"C'mon! Having fun is easy. Maybe we could start a band?"

"That's my dream. To be in a real band."

"Well, we gotta practice. I'll see you later. Henry invited my dad and I over for dinner. Are you gonna be there? He said he's grilling tri-tip."

"Dunno if I can eat it, with my lip like it is. I'll see ya there, though." Hunter gave him the hang loose sign and walked toward the RV park.

OFFICIAL POLICE BUSINESS

"Madge, I can't pick Billy up. Don't ask me again! I told you last Friday of the month I had surveillance in Clear Lake. No, Madge. I can't."

Sheriff Rick hung up the phone and took a left on HWY 20. heading towards Clear Lake. He stopped at the Chevron for more beer and immediately popped one open. The Sheriff got the shakes because he ran out of cocaine. He took out his flip phone and dialed a number.

"Hector, I'm on my way."

He turned down a long dirt road from the lake to several cabins. Hector swung in a chair on the front porch of the end unit. Smoking a blunt while listening to Control Machete.

"What up, Rick?"

"Two eight balls, that's what's up, Hector."

"I only give you one free; that's the deal. Right?"

"No, the new deal is two plus $500 tax."

"That's bullshit, Rick! You're gonna put me outta business!"

"I'll tell you what's bullshit is getting your shit shut down and going to jail."

Hector disappeared in the cabin and turned the music down."

"What's going on? Who's here?" asked Holly from under the covers.

Hector got close and whispered in her ear. "Fuckin' Sheriff Rick Johnson. Pendejo wants two eight balls and a $500 tax."

"Are you serious?"

"Yeah, he said he'd shut us down if we didn't give it to him."

"Well, give him that stuff with the laxative in it."

"Are we gonna pay him?"

"Fuck! I guess we gotta. There's cash in my purse from last night."

He kissed her on the cheek. "Ok, baby."

He handed the Sheriff two eight balls stashed in tape cassette cases. One Michael Bolton and the other Phil Collins.

"Why are you handing me this? I hate Michael Bolton and Phil Collins. I don't need this shit. Just gimme the coke and the cash."

"It's in the cases, man. It's how I do it now. No one will

ever suspect anything if they're watching us. We're just trading music here, that's all. Keep it on the down low. I get 'em at the thrift store. Pretty sly, huh?"

"Just gimme the baggies, motherfucker. Remember, I'm the law. You don't gotta keep this shit on the down low around me."

"Alright, alright. Take it easy, Rick."

"Now the money, motherfucker! Where's the money?"

Rick dug into one of the baggies with his key while Hector pulled a stack of twenties from his pocket and started counting.

"Thank you, Doctor Hector!" Rick took a big blast, and his eyes got wild. "What'd you cut this with? It tastes funny."

"We didn't cut it, Rick."

"That's Sheriff Rick, and I know you cut it. I like pure cocaine. Add a hundred to the tax."

"What? Come on, man. You know it's cut before we get it."

"Don't cut it again, dick weed. Gimme another hundred."

Hector returned to the cabin for more cash.

"What now?" asked Holly.

"Motherfucker wants a hundred more 'cause he said it's cut."

"Well, it is cut. Did you say it's cut?"

"I didn't say shit."

"Just play dumb. What's Rick gonna do?"

"Alright, okay."

"Rick's got an attention span of about half a second. If you would have waited, he would have forgotten he asked the question," said Holly.

"There's no more money in your purse," replied Hector.

"Check the freezer."

"There's only sixty dollars."

"Tell him we'll pay the rest later."

Hector returned to the porch, where the Sheriff waited impatiently.

"Come on, man. Cough it up! I'm gonna be late for my next appointment."

"Sorry, Rick. We only have sixty left."

"Well, I guess I can let you slide this time." Sheriff Rick paused to think for a moment. "Actually, tell Holly to give me a forty-dollar bar tab. That'll be fine."

The Sheriff peeled out in the parking lot, leaving Hector in a cloud of dust.

"I hope you crash pendejo." Hector turned the music up and sat back in the swing.

Sheriff Rick pulled into a parking spot to use the porta-potty at the boat ramp. He had to shit really bad from the laxative in the coke. "I knew it was cut, you motherfuckers." When he finished his business, he broke out the baggie and went for another blast. His hands were shaking, and he dropped it into the toilet.

"God dammit!" He pulled his flashlight from his utility belt and shined it into the hole. He saw the baggie resting on top of the soupy blue mix of shit and toilet paper. He had to get it back. But how? He returned to the squad car and foraged through the trunk. He found a coat hanger and opened it up to make a long wire with a hook. A car pulled into the boat ramp parking lot. It was a station wagon full of kids. An elderly woman exited and escorted one of the children to the porta-potty.

"Excuse me, ma'am. The porta-potty's closed."

"What do you mean it's closed? My grandson's about to have an emergency."

"Sorry. Official police business!"

The old woman scowled. "What happened? Was there a crime?"

"It's still under investigation. Please leave the area; it's not safe here. I'm gonna have to tape this off before the detectives arrive."

"Mamma, I gotta go." squirmed the young boy.

"There's a 7-Eleven just a mile down. Much cleaner. You don't wanna use this one. Trust me."

"Okay, officer. Thank you for your service."

"My pleasure, ma'am. Have a blessed day."

Sheriff Rick got back to the task at hand. He found some police tape and stretched it from signpost to signpost. Blocking the entrance to the porta-potty. He got the hanger, put a headlamp on, and began the emergency recovery operation.

He fished around for a while, and finally, the hook caught hold of the baggie. A successful mission at last. "Thank the Lord motherfuckers!"

Sheriff Rick washed the baggy off in the pump sink by the porta-potty and checked for the other eight-ball in his pocket.

"Always good to have a backup." Put the squad car in gear and burned out of the parking lot, flipping on the flashing lights and siren. Official police business.

POINT MAN

Carl walked the store and approached Billy at the register.

"You've been doing good work, Billy. Amazed at how fast you picked it up."

"Thanks, Mr. Amundson. It's pretty easy."

"Well, you do it so well, and call me Carl, Okay, Billy?" Carl approached and rubbed Billy's shoulders from behind, and Billy turned around defensively.

"I wanted to tell you I'm gonna bump your pay to $11 an hour. I like to keep quality workers around and am willing to pay for them."

"Really? Thanks, Mr. Amundson! I mean Carl."

"I was thinking. If you ever want to work out, you're welcome to come by my place. I got a weight bench in the garage. I could spot you and help you train?"

"I usually work out at the high school with my teammates. But thanks, I'll keep it in mind."

"Oh, and If you're free Sundays and wanna pick up some extra shifts in the deli, I can start putting you on the schedule."

"Isn't that Ulee's shift?"

"Don't worry about Ulee. I'm saying if you wanna change it up, challenge yourself. The offer is on the table."

"I wouldn't want to take Ulee's shift."

"She won't be available, so I need another person."

"Okay, Mr. Amundson."

"That's Carl, Billy. You're so formal. Loosen up, buddy."

"Carl. I could do a deli shift if you needed me. But only if Ulee can't do it."

"I'll put you on the schedule. Keep an eye out."

"Thanks, Carl."

Carl winked at him and squeezed his shoulder again. "You're a good kid. Keep up the good work."

Billy pulled away with a creeped-out look on his face.

"Hey, relax. If you and your buddies ever need beers, I can hook you up. I won't tell anybody. Having a shift drink is cool, but do it in the walk-in. Wanna have a beer with me in the walk-in? After your shift is over?"

"I don't drink, Carl. I'll get cut from the team."

"I respect that man. Go Dragons!" Carl gave the claw sign with his hand to support the Dillits Dragons.

He got in his truck, drove it across the street to Slingers, and parked in the handicap spot.

Sheriff Rick Johnson arrived not long after.

"Hey there, Carl, I noticed a big red truck parked in the handicapped spot outside. That's my spot! I thought I'd have to write some asshole a ticket, but then I remembered it was Carl's truck. Carl's truck with the Marine sticker, and he ain't even a Marine."

"You don't have jurisdiction to write a ticket here. Nobody writes tickets here!"

"I can start. Don't tempt me, Carl. Mr. Fake Marine."

"Look, I support our troops. Always have, and I always will. I take my hat off during the national anthem," smirked Carl.

"Gimme a Wild Turkey and a beer back; I got another $40 credit on my tab!" shouted Sheriff Rick. "Where's Holly? Sleeping it off with Hector?"

Mandy, the daytime bartender, pretended not to hear.

"How's my boy working out at the store?" he asked Carl.

"He's the best, Rick. Great kid, thanks for sending him my way."

"Mandy, you hear me?" he punched down on the bar. "We keep the lights on in this goddamn place! Don't ignore me."

"If you pay your tab. Then Holly can pay the light bill."

"Well, she got you there, Rick," slurred Dufur.

Rick slammed his drink down and nestled up to Dufur. "Hey Dufur, I think we oughta make Carl point man for our little operation at the end of the summer. What do ya say?"

"I thought he was just gonna set that pipe. I don't think we need him otherwise. I don't wanna split the money with him."

"We're not, remember? We need him on the crew. Don't you see? He doesn't know what the fuck he's doing. Supposin' something goes down. He can take the first shot, and then we can get the hell outta there. See what I mean? He could be our shield. "

Dufur looked agitated. "I don't know about Carl. He

doesn't know how to keep his mouth shut. He's gonna piss his pants if anything happens, "he whispered. The two looked at him and held their glasses up in a long-distance toast. "Well, it makes sense. If we happen to cross paths with trigger-happy meth heads. "

"So, what do you think?"

"Man, I don't know," said Dufur skeptically, shaking his head.

"Hey Carl, come over here. We got a proposal for you."

"What's up, fellas?"

"Well, we're wondering if you might wanna be part of our crew this autumn? When we go out on raids. You'd be a point man. You know what that means?"

"Is this real commando shit?"

"Yeah, man. This is the real deal. I'm talking paint your face camo kinda shit," said Sheriff Rick.

"You mean like secret law enforcement? Secret raids? Are you gonna deputize me?"

"I wouldn't go that far, Carl. Calm down! You would be part of a covert operation to enforce federal drug laws throughout Mendocino County. In fact, we want you to be the point man, but you cannot say a word about this to anyone."

"Point man? What does it mean? Why me?"

"You have the skill and the intelligence to complete our crew. It means you'll be leading us in. Cause you're a badass, Carl! We know it, and you know it. With your management experience, we think you're the right guy for our team." said Rick.

"What about a uniform? Do I get to wear a uniform?"

"Sure, you can wear a uniform. Just wear your hunting camouflage gear. No fluorescent vest or anything cause we gotta blend in. No name tags or patches. "

"I gotcha. This is great, fellas. I can't believe it. When do we start?"

"First week in September."

"I want an equal cut!"

"Hold your horses, buddy. You're green. You don't deserve an equal cut."

"I'm putting myself in danger just like you guys. Why shouldn't I get an equal cut?"

"Let's see how the first operation goes, and then we'll reassess."

"Alright, fellas. I get it. I gotta prove myself. Lemme buy the next round! Mandy! Drinks for everybody! Put it on my tab!" Carl slurped down several more Long Island iced teas. He drank so much that he passed out in his truck for several hours but managed to weave his way back home in the wee hours of the morning.

CHAOS AND THE BOBCAT

Henry filled the cups on the trays with potting soil and placed them along the wall by the front door. Poking a finger into each cup and placing a germinated seed into each hole. Starter trays were placed on the rolling racks under the grow lights. He did this all day, and by the end of the day, a couple thousand seedlings were in place. He sprayed them with a mist bottle. Bobby Troup was the soundtrack with his original version of (Get Your Kicks On) "Route 66."

I realize I'm quite content being a cat. I remember how unhappy I was as a human and how I didn't get along with most people. I liked Henry, though, and Otto, too. They were good friends of mine, but now it's not the same. They don't know who I am. It would be impossible to explain it to them. I wish I didn't have the memories of being a human. It brought back the anxiety and the blues. It doesn't last long though because my attention switches to the here and now. I find it much easier to be present as a cat.

Henry fed me everything he ate, and so did Aino. I didn't even have to go on the prowl if I didn't wanna. Nothing beats a fresh grouse or a garter snake, though. I saw more and more of them as the spring set in. I began to wander further up the mountain past the water pipe.

I wished for an honest conversation, but I lived in the memories of old times. Waking from dreams lying in the sun, feeling lonely and melancholy. I needed affection. Not some getting scratched by humans - kind of affection. I'm talking about genuine cat affection. This desire took over my entire existence.

I saw some scat on the trail by the wood mill. Definitely female scat. I don't know how I knew that, but I did. I smelled the pheromones and decided to follow them up the mountain. I found a road I'd never been on, leading to a grassy field.

There she was. The most beautiful cat I'd ever seen. I didn't know what to do? What's the protocol for being a cat? Do cat's date, or is it just, wham bam, thank you, ma'am? It's not the same as a human, that's for sure. I couldn't ask this cat if she wanted to see a movie or have a drink somewhere? I could have asked her to go to the water pipe. She was gray and brown with large paws and sideburns. Long tufts of hair came out of her cheeks. I fell in love the moment I saw her. She looked familiar. She was a wild bobcat and twice my size.

I remember why she looked so familiar. I had tried to burn her image into a piece of leather with a paper clip back when I was human. Remember how I told you about my last memory? Was I having a premonition into my future life as a cat? Holy smokes!

Suddenly, my instincts took over, and I went for it. I couldn't help myself. I tried to hump immediately, but the next thing I knew, I was caught in a whirlwind of violence. The bobcat clawed my face and tossed me around like a rag doll. She made the most terrifying sounds in the process. They became the sounds of my nightmares. The bobcat bit my neck and tore my front claw from the paw, then bit my back behind the tail. That's what did the most damage. She cut me open to my spine, and with a severely injured back, I skittered away down the hill. What a terrible date. The pain grew worse, and I limped back to the porch at the farm before collapsing by the back door.

When I awoke, I was in the sink while Henry held me down. Aino squirted warm water on the large open wound.

"He's alive! I thought we'd lost you, Chaos," said Henry, laughing with tears coming out.

"Let the water run on him, Aino. Keep flushing it out. Damn, I think I see the bone. That's the back of his spine!"

"He musta got into it with a mountain lion or coyote or something."

It was bobcat! I growled.

"I gotta stitch it up!" said Henry.

There was a mason jar with all the essentials in the cabinet. I tried to squirm away, realizing the impending surgery with no anesthesia. He found the large sewing needle and some thread. He cut off a piece and soaked it in some rubbing alcohol. Aino held me down, and Henry started giving me sutures. The pain was so intense I passed out. Henry was applying Manuka honey to the stitched-up wound when I woke up again.

"This is gonna do, Chaos. At least it's not bleeding anymore," said Henry.

Aino held me in a towel and brought me to the chair by the wood stove.

"I think he's gonna be alright."

"Well, if he doesn't get better, I can bring him to the vet in Dillits. Get some antibiotic ointment, something for animals," said Henry

Can we put Neosporin on a cat wound?" asked Aino.

"I don't see why not, but the Manuka honey should be good for now."I decided to be a celibate from then on.

LEO'S PLACE

"Let's hike down the hill before Otto and Hunter come over. I wanna show you something, Aino," said Henry.

The two walked past the newly remodeled shack. "You did good work on this, Aino."

"Thanks for letting me. It was kinda fun."

"Have you been to the swimming hole?"

"I didn't know there was a swimmin' hole."

Henry led him to a trail down the cliffside behind the shack, through some sagebrush, which dead-ended at a rocky outcropping. Henry grabbed onto a stone and swung around the edge of the cliff, finding a foothold around the blind corner. "Grab the rock and swing your leg around this boulder. There's a foothold on the other side. It's a long ledge. This is the shortcut." The stones formed natural steps downward towards the creek.

"Oh, there's poison oak everywhere. Man, I'm highly allergic."said Aino.

"Follow me up this way then." Henry traversed the cliff edge further downstream and climbed to the creekside, avoiding the poison oak.

"There's an easier trail. I'll show you on the way back." The two men stood at the precipice of the waterfall, looking down into the pond.

"It's deep right where the falls hit."

"How deep?"

"I'd go feet first. It's a narrow spot in that crease in the rocks. Probably twelve feet deep." The water was crystal clear.

"It stays nice and deep all summer. Even when the

water is down to a trickle. Let's go further down. To Leo's place."

"Who's Leo?"

"Leo Paskowski. He hid out here when Cahto Indians were the only people around these parts."

"Why?"

"He was a thief. Apparently, he was running from the law. Stole a bunch of gold from a claim in the Sierras, and they were trying to track him down."

"So, he was up here hiding out?"

"Yeah, he got away with it. Turned out he was a master carpenter," said Henry.

"T'was the old wild west."

The two came around the bend, and a structure appeared on the cliffside hanging over the river. It seemed to defy gravity. Clinging to the rocks like a tarantula made of wood. The living area resembled the body of the spider. Vines had covered it, but the ancient redwood boards were not rotting. There were toeholds in the stones for steps to access the hideout.

"He built this to blend in. He scavenged wood from the lumber mill in Dias Verdez. I don't know how he hauled it all up here. Used scrap pieces from the yard. All these pieces which make up the structure are married together. All varying sizes. He did it all with primitive hand tools. It's impressive to last over a hundred years hanging off the cliffside. I can't even fathom how he did it. Just birds living there now."

"A giant birdhouse on the cliff," said Aino.

"Gonna get Aramoana's goats out here to clear the poison oak to the swimming hole."

They walked the path, and Aino held his arms in the air to avoid the poisonous leaves. When they returned to the house, I was resting in the chair. Trying to pretend to be asleep. Otto and Hunter showed up at the same time. The house filled with humans while I lay in the chair with my back wound freshly stitched.

WELCOME BACK DINNER

"Poor Chaos got attacked by something today. Don't sit in the chair whatever you do. He's recovering," said Henry.

"Looks like he's still breathing," Otto came over and stared at me. I could smell his garlic breath. "I've never known you to allow a cat in the house."

"He's a battle cat."

"A kink in the tail, chunk missing from his ear. Yeah, that's a battle cat," said Otto.

"We've got tri-tip for dinner tonight if you don't have any dietary restrictions?" said Henry.

"I brought some BBQ seitan. Can I use the grill if you don't mind?" replied Hunter.

"No worries. Absolutely. I've got carrot and kale salad to go with it. It's good for Chaos. He'll get more when he comes back to life."

Henry put a record on. It was Desmond Dekker's album, Intensified. "Here you go, Otto!"

Otto started morphing into a chicken dance. He flapped his wings and stuck his chin in and out like Mick Jagger. Hunter looked like a lonesome cowboy with her back up against the wall. Slightly embarrassed by her father's bizarre dance. Aino tried to hit the bass chords on the piano while playing along. Trying to decipher the song.

"You thirsty?" asked Henry, handing Hunter a coconut water.

"Thanks, Henry. How did you know?"

"You've been drinking those since before you became

Elvis."

"Speaking of, can you play it?" asked Hunter.

"Of course."

Henry scanned the case and pulled out From Elvis in Memphis. When track three came up," I'll Hold You in My Heart ('Till I Can Hold You In My Arms)," the show started. Hunter became Elvis before their eyes and lip-synched the song like she was possessed by the King himself. The whole night stood still for this, and the meal was only a footnote.

"You still got it, Hunter. You are still the King!"

Hunter smiled and wiped her brow with a perfectly folded bandana she pulled from her back pocket.

"So, Henry, do you suppose I can get 300 starters this year?" asked Otto.

"I can do it for sure; why the change?"

"Price is dropping, man. We lost 15% this year and probably another next year. Colorado's killing us in Texas."

"Yeah, I know it. It's going to be recreational everywhere before long. It's why I'm growing apple and pear trees. I wanna get in on the cider craze."

"What about your bud and breakfast idea?"

"I don't know if I wanna deal with strangers always coming around? Twenty years ago, maybe, but I like it quiet now."

"I hear ya man. So Aino, are you feeling any better?"

"Yeah, man, sorry 'bout the other day. Thanks for helping me out of the river."

"You made us worried, brother."

"Well, I'm back on track."

"Your lip looks infected," said Otto.

"I think it'll be alright. I don't think I can eat the tri-tip tonight. I don't wanna split it open again."

"There's some yogurt in the fridge," said Henry. "You oughta rub some manuka honey on your lip too."

Aino nodded and disappeared into the kitchen. Otto sipped his tomato juice on the back porch, and Henry nipped his brandy. They stuffed themselves on tri-tip sandwiches. Hunter and Aino jammed in the big room. Hunter on piano and Aino on double bass. They were trying to play "Suspicious Minds," which morphed into an improvisation of chords and melodies. Aino wouldn't be able to play the trumpet for a while

HOLLY & HECTOR

"I don't know if I can do this much longer," said Hector as he pulled Holly into the hammock chair.

"Slow and steady honey. We're so close."

"That's what you said last fall. I'm tired of being on the hook with Rick. He's gonna squeeze us dry."

"Rick's not intelligent enough to do that. Plus, he's an addict. "

"Yeah, maybe he won't live much longer."

"Maybe not. Then we can make an extra $1,000 a week without throwing it away on Rick's sorry ass."

"It's kinda fun watching him self-destruct."

"I can buy the bar outright if we make it to November. Then we can quit."

"Alright, baby, November. Then, I can study coding full-time. "

"Yes, honey. It'll be easy living. So glad you don't do cocaine."

"Why would I do that? It's bad for business."

"True that. I love you, Hector."

"I love you too, Holly."

SKIP, ILF & PETROV

Skip had an elf-like appearance. Wearing beige hemp fabric pants and a matching shirt. He rarely wore shoes, and his feet were thick with calluses. He had curly brown hair, which he kept under a fabric wrap like a turban. He drove in on HWY 101 in a Volkswagen Westfalia Syncro van from the north. It had Idaho plates, but he grew up in Yellow Springs, Ohio. His parents were teachers at Antioch University. Two large Samoyed dogs slept in the back while he drove. Their names were Ilf and Petrov. Skip sipped green tea from a steel travel mug that read "Keep Tahoe Blue."

"Almost there, fellas," as the van rocked and rattled down the washboard road, passing by the vicious dog that ran at his van, barking and trying to bite the tires. This woke Ilf and Petrov, who returned fire with their barking barrage, smearing their snouts on the window and nearly clawing through the door.

"Easy guys. Petrov! Down. Ilf!"

Skip knew the road from before and negotiated the turns into the farm, finding a spot between the firewood shack and the compost pit. Mid-April bloomed on the mountainside with orange poppies. Henry worked in the greenhouse by the solar shack, attaching plastic sheeting to the hoop house.

"Skip! Good to see you, brother!"

"Likewise, my friend."

"Did you drive it straight from Moscow?"

"No, I took it easy. We camped out at Paulina Lake in Oregon. Ever been?"

"Near La Pine? With the good brown trout fishing?"

"Yeah, someone caught a twenty-eight pounder there, but I got skunked as usual. It was freezing' man. It went down to below zero. Good thing I brought Ilf and Petrov. We were snuggled up like a family of polar bears."

"Oh, you brought your dogs?" Henry was a little deflated by this. "Chaos is gonna love that. How's school been going up there?"

"I'm getting a little burned out on teaching. A lot of work for hardly any money, you know. Beginning to doubt if the adjunct professor route is worth it! I need to practice plant science. Know what I mean? Did you say chaos?"

"It's a cat. You'll see."

"Ilf and Petrov love cats."

"Not sure Chaos will feel the same."

"I never knew you to be a cat guy, Henry!"

"I'm not a cat guy. I can tolerate Chaos, though."

"How are the ladies coming along?"

"Fairly well so far, every day is a learning experience. Maybe you can teach me some more plant science, my brother."

"I would trust you to know much more than I, Henry. Especially these kinds of plants. So, do you want to clarify right off the bat? How it's gonna go this year? Then we don't gotta talk about it ever again."

"I like that method. Okay, If you stay through the end of the light deprivation harvest, I'll give you ten percent. It's about ten thousand dollars a month. It's a hell of a lot of work, as you know. I got a guy named Aino up here doing carpentry, but he's game to help. Don't feed him any booze. He's trying to stay sober. Nate's coming next week, and I'll hire one more. See how it goes. It won't cut out of your take, so don't worry. You can use a little plot up top for your own plants. Whatever experiments you want to do. Does this sound suitable? I'm open to suggestions."

"Sounds good to me, Henry."

"Are you light on dough? I can front whatever you

need, lemme know."

"I'm alright for now. Gonna take it easy this afternoon and hit it hard in the morning."

MACHINE GUN FIRE

I started sleeping on the chair outside. The nights were getting warm, and the new guy, Skip, would walk his dogs by the water pipe, so I tried to avoid the area. He never brought them to the back porch, so it became the safe zone. I woke to the sound of machine gun fire coming from up the mountain. It wasn't just one gun. It sounded like a militia having target practice. I ran into the house when Henry returned.

"Did you hear gunfire?" asked Aino.

"Yeah, I heard 'em," Henry re-lit his joint and sipped a coffee.

"Sounds like they're having military operations."

"This time of year, you never know who could be up there. I don't go up that way. It's probably just Carl and his friends."

"What friends does he have? Maybe it's the cartel guys."

"Those dudes try to keep a low profile. I don't think they'd be shooting guns. They try to keep things quiet." said Henry.

"You don't worry about the cartel dudes?" asked Aino.

"Not really. Cartel guys don't wanna bring unwanted attention. What bothers me is what they do to the land. I don't know if it's Russian mob or the Mexican cartels? They set up quick-grow operations and trash the land. They spray chemicals everywhere and then leave all their garbage behind. I wish they'd clean up after themselves."

"Have you ever gotten fucked with?"

"No, but I know people who have gotten killed

up here. Killed or robbed. There's no one to call. One cokehead cop ain't gonna protect anyone up here. It's every man for himself, I suppose."

"How come you're not packin' heat then?"

"I don't believe in it. I don't want it on the property. Bad mojo. As soon as a gun comes in, someone's bound to use it. Some of these farms have guys doing meth, carrying guns. They are a bunch of paranoid loose cannons. They might not even mean to use it, but all of a sudden, all hell breaks loose. I got a rifle, but it's only for hunting deer. But I don't even hunt deer. Never have gotten into it. I'd rather shoot pictures of the animals."

"I saw some kid driving down Lost Creek Rd. a while ago. He was driving like he was being chased. Then, two dudes on motocross bikes whizzed by like they were after him. I swear he looked scared to death. Driving a new silver sedan. Do you know that dude?"

"No, but people go missing out here all the time. Every time I go to town, there's a different missing person poster up."

"It's creepy. The machine gun fire makes me worry; what's next? Are they gonna come down and try to steal our shit?" said Aino

"Listen, I've been doing this since the eighties and never had a problem. I've heard those guns before. They're not gonna do anything."

"So, nothing's ever happened on this farm? No one's ever tried to rob you or bust you? What about the planes that keep circling? Looks like they're taking pictures."

"Those guys are clowns. Trying to justify their budgets. Schieffelbein got busted once back in the eighties. Military commando cops landed in helicopters. Part of Reagan's war on drugs. A bunch of bumbling idiots."

"He wasn't even a grower," said Aino.

"Yeah, they raided his shop. Found a bunch of poison

oak. Otto was having flashbacks for months after. It was ridiculous. I worry more about the Fish and Game to be honest. They've got free reign around here. They can go to anybody's place if they suspect them of stealing water or poaching."

"What happens then?"

"Then they set up teams and make busts. You don't see regular law enforcement around here. The state cops don't wanna go out into the wilderness and fuck with the cartels or the bikers. But they do make cash money off the pot farmers like me. We've been here all along. And I know some cops are growing it, too. Though most of those guys don't want to do the work. They'd rather make easy money by busting farmers. As it's getting closer to legal, these guys are as worried as Otto. They want it to stay illegal. They make more money off the busts. I want it to stay illegal. I make more money because it's a higher risk. Higher price per pound. Know what I mean? Otto wants more starters this year because the price is dropping. But it's not about the money, right? Or Monsanto coming in and growing GMOs on a corporate level. Putting all the small farmers out of business. No one cares about the money. Aramoana and Luka care about the money; I know that much. Sorry about the rant."

"The cidery idea sounds like a good transition."

"Speaking of, I bought a bunch of starters to plant over by the Schieffelbein house. Twenty apple trees and twenty pear trees. I wanna start making brandy, too, but today, I have a project I want you to help me with. We're gonna take down the dead Redwood and the Doug Fir trees. Remember I pointed them out? Then I'll show you how to run the wood mill."

"I'd love to learn how that works," said Aino.

"We need more sawdust for the outhouse," replied Henry.

Skip approached the house after tying up his dogs by the van.

"Morning, Skip," said Henry.

"I swear I didn't bring those machine guns with me. My dogs were trying to hide and nearly tore the back seat out of the van!"

"Oh, man. Gunfire and fireworks are torture for dogs."

"They've calmed down now. I'm gonna get started." Skip nodded and walked up toward the greenhouse. While Aino and Henry started cutting down the dead trees, Skip was happy to do his own thing. Henry quickly worked on the Redwood and the Doug fir next to it. The giant dead trees shook the ground around them as they fell.

Aino helped attach the log chain, and Henry dragged each of them into the open area with the backhoe, trimming them down into twelve-foot sections. He pulled them up the hill to the wood mill, leaving a gash on the gravel road. Placed the log sections into the wood mill's loading arm. The hydraulics did all the work from there.

The debarking process slowly turned the rounded tree into a complete square. Henry cut the boards from there. First it was 1"x 8" and 1" x 10' s and then 2" x 6" and 2"x 4"s. The boards were placed under the lean-to where Aino previously removed boards to finish the shack.

"I wanna put an addition on the solar shack," said Henry. "Getting a bunch of vinyl records, and I want a nice dry room to keep 'em in. You wanna build it with me?"

"Yeah, absolutely."

"We'll start tomorrow then. It would be good for you to build your own little spot. Knowing you're gonna be staying awhile. You can make it how you want it. "

"Thank you, Henry! You mean I can stay here long term?"

"As long as you want, man. Think of the addition as building your own home but you just gotta store my records in there. So make it how you like it. Luka might be coming for a little while this summer. Don't think I'm kicking you out of the main house, though. You can keep staying there, but I figure you'd want your own space. It gets pretty loud when the full crew is here."

SOLAR SHACK

The Solar Shack stood above the main house and was mainly a tool shed. It had a sheltered work area connecting to the greenhouse. The shack was 10' x 20' with crude built-in shelving from ceiling to floor. It served as storage for the battery bank and a full array of carpentry and landscaping tools.

Henry staked out the addition, built on a pier and beam foundation. They framed it out using fully cured wood Henry milled years before. It only took two days, and the roof took another two. Henry found vinyl windows and a pre-framed door at a builders' salvage store. They covered the floor with plywood, and Aino fully insulated the walls and used sheetrock. The ceiling was tongue and groove.

They finished the exterior in a week, and the interior trim work took another few days. It had power outlets and an overhead light but no heater. A space heater would suffice in the colder months, but a wood stove would be needed, eventually. Aino built a bunk by the window with a shelf to keep his books. Henry inherited a massive record collection from a DJ friend at KALX in Berkeley who'd recently passed away. Shelving was built to house the albums and Aino moved into the space to sleep surrounded by records.

HALF GALLON POTS

Skip amended the soil and turned the beds in patches throughout the property. At the same time, Henry transferred the starters to half-gallon pots. The seedlings grew to about five inches tall.

My back healed by late April, and I felt like my old self again. I was depressed because I realized my chances of finding love on the farm were slim to none. I wasn't about to go after another bobcat! Different types of birds started coming through with the warmer weather. The Warblers and the Grosbeaks. Poison oak became a bright green jungle.

Annette and her daughter Sky returned for another bud-trimming session. The only words Annette spoke were to Aino while he transferred his belongings to the solar shack.

"You're sleeping under those solar panels? It's gonna give you brain cancer."

"How so?" asked Aino. "What's the proof ?"

"I thought you were gonna contact me when you came to the city?"

"I had some bad luck last time. I had to leave early. Don't think I'll be going down there for a while."

"You're not missing anything. A friend of yours, came through and played the Fillmore. You know, the piano player? Spencer something? He got so drunk he fell off the stage. I called an ambulance, and we had to call the rest of the show-off. People were pissed!"

"Hope he's alright."

"A lot of pressure, I guess."

"Well, I hope sleeping in the solar shack doesn't

damage my brain. I think I'm gonna turn in. Drop by if you want."

"I'll think about it, honey. We have a lot of work to do."

Annette never visited the solar shack, but Aino didn't think she would. I watched from the water pipe as they drove out.

GUITAR BEE

Otto and Hunter walked down the hill holding a painting of a bee playing a guitar. I followed 'em back down to the house, wondering what they would try to do with my painting.

"I found a painting George made," said Otto.

"Whoa. Nice one. The guitar bee. Where'd you find it?"

"Behind a piece of plywood leaning up against the back of the A-Frame."

The painting had some mold growing on one side. It looked like a frame from a comic strip.

"Why'd he put it there?" asked Aino.

"He had dementia before he died. He thought the Feds were coming to steal his paintings, so he hid them in random places. You want this one?" asked Otto.

I did not have dementia, you liar! It was for Luka's birthday. Remember, you were hosting a BBQ! You must have dementia, not me, pal! The painting was for Luka because he liked bees and guitars, so I hid it there to surprise him at the BBQ. I outta claw your eyes out talking shit about me.

"Chaos, you are running your mouth. What the hell are you trying to say. I've never met such a talkative little kitty," said Otto, reaching down to pet me.

They never showed up at the party, Otto. Aramoana took him to San Diego and didn't say a word about it.

My grandson. Now you're telling people I had dementia! You bastard! I ran at him and clawed his shaved legs. I had a complete meltdown. He swatted me away, and I kept growling and hissing at him.

"Boy, he doesn't like you, Dad," said Hunter.

"I'll say. Not sure what I did wrong."

"You're dripping blood down the back of your legs, Dad."

"I guess he didn't like the painting. It scared him."

It's a painting for a child's room you idiot!. It's your shit-talking I don't like. I jumped up onto a boulder above them.

"You want this painting, Henry?" asked Otto.

"No, man, he probably wanted you to have it. Unless you want to sell it? It's worth a lot."

"How much is a lot?"

"$15 - 20k. That's what I heard. Don't tell Aramoana you got it. She's gonna want it back."

Fifteen K for one of my paintings? You've got to be stoned out of your mind! There's no way that painting's worth that much.

"Just keep talkin' Chaos. Tell us all about it," said Hunter.

"I think I'm gonna hang it up in the A-Frame," said Otto. "It would go well in there."

"You might wanna clean that black mold off first. You don't want that in the house," said Henry.

"Could always hang it on the porch," replied Hunter.

How about giving it to Luka next time he comes over? Wouldn't that be nice?

JUMPED IN

Carl searched for used drilling machines online in the back of Casa de Pollo, the only Mexican restaurant in Dias Verdez. He usually went there on Thursdays and sat in the same seat underneath the Don Juan painting. Always before the dinner crowd arrived. He'd set up his laptop and eat chicken fajitas at 4:30 p.m., peering at the waiter from behind his screen. He liked the waiter Enrique, the youngest son of the Gonzalez family who owned the restaurant. A debonair young musician who played music there every Thursday. He knew he wouldn't run into Sheriff Rick Johnson or Dufur Fleck because neither liked Mexican food.

On Thursday, he finished his meal and left out the side door. He drunkenly fumbled for his keys and suddenly received a thwack to the back of the head. It briefly knocked him out and brought him to the ground. Sheriff Rick Johnson put a bag over his head and handcuffed him, then, with the help of Dufur Fleck, dragged him into the back of his squad car. Carl regained consciousness as the door slammed on his leg, and he screamed in pain. The vehicle sped away while he lay in the back seat.

"Who the fuck are you?! Why are you doing this?"

"Do you wanna be part of this?" said Sheriff Rick.

"Rick?"

"Shut up, Carl!"

"What the fuck are you doing? I think you broke my leg!"

"We didn't do shit! Stop being a pussy, Carl! This is your initiation." said Rick.

Dufur sat silently in the passenger seat. The squad car headed north into Humboldt County. They came to a bridge and pulled down a narrow gravel road that curled up and under it. Dufur got out and filled a pillowcase full of rocks by the river. Sheriff Rick Johnson opened the back door of the squad car.

"Get out and take your pants off."

"I can't with handcuffs on, Rick."

Rick whacked him on the side of the head and then undid the handcuffs and slapped him again.

"Ooh, I like it," said Carl, beginning to get turned on.

"Shut up, Carl! Take all your clothes off!"

"I thought you'd never ask!" Carl stripped naked, and Dufur returned with the sack full of rocks.

"Come on, guys, this isn't funny."

Dufur swung the pillowcase at Carl and hit him on the back and then once again on his thigh. He fell to the ground, moaning. Sheriff Rick took a couple more swings at him with the bag of stones. He lay groaning on the ground.

"Get up, Carl, and put your clothes back on. Don't say a fuckin word!"

"What the hell, Rick!" Rick clobbered him again.

"I said not to say a word, Carl!"

Carl got quiet, and Dufur threw his pants at him. He struggled to put them on in the blind with the bag over his head. Dufur and Rick threw him back into the car and slammed the door. He lay on the seat motionless and started whimpering. They drove back to Dias Verdez and returned to the back of Casa De Pollo.

"Why are you crying, you pussy?"

"It hurts; I think you broke something, you bastards!"

Sheriff Rick poked him in the chest with his nightstick. "I'll break something for real if you say a goddamned thing about any of our plans, You got it?"

Carl didn't reply.

"You got it, motherfucker?!" Sheriff Rick nudged him with the stick.

"Yeah, I got it Rick."

"Get out of the car, Carl," ordered Sheriff Rick.

"Does this mean I'm in the gang? Did I make it?"

"Shut up, Carl. Meet us at Slingers."

MEET THE GOATS

"Aramoana has some work for you if you want it?" said Henry.

"What kinda work?" asked Aino.

"She wants to install new trim and baseboards around her place. The wood is already there, but you'd prime and paint it first. She wanted me to ask you."

"Sure, man. I'm into it."

"She's gonna be gone and was wondering if you could feed her goats too. It's only for a week. Oh, and you can stay there if you want."

"Sounds perfect to me."

Henry and Aino drove a mile up the road towards the crossing and took a left at the fork to Aramoana's place. The road improved the closer they got, and the driveway turned to smooth concrete. The house had the same design as Henry's but was pristine. A wooden fence surrounded a hay barn and paddock for the goats. The animals had acres to play, including a goat jungle gym with several wooden platforms connected by narrow boards and a tractor tire.

"So, what do I gotta feed them?"

"Lemme show you." They entered the paddock, and the four La Mancha goats were up on the cliff above the goat shack. Watching them intently but not wanting to give up the game they were playing with each other. Fighting it out for the top spot on the boulder.

"Hey, ya, so fill these feeders to the top with hay once a day. Aramoana put in new fencing and extended their domain, so they've got plenty to nibble on. Make sure you fill the water up. I've seen the male drink a five-gallon bucket by himself. He'll try to headbutt you but don't worry about him. The small one is the one you gotta look out for. She's the top goat, believe it or not. They will eat everything in sight if they get out. They're browsers and they love weed. Goats and deer love the same types of food. Flowers, kale, pumpkins. Man, they even eat Christmas trees."

"Christmas trees?"

"Yeah, they love 'em. They'll also eat the decal off your license plate and windshield wipers. They did mine."

"Aren't they smart as dogs?"

"Smarter. The goats work together, too. You'll see the deer hanging out with the goats. The deer can hop the fence, but the goats can't. When you get done here, I'd like you to add some chicken wire to the top of all the fencing around the patches. Last year, the deer were getting in. If we add a couple feet to the top, it should do the trick."

The goats came down the hill to say hello. Rubbing up against Henry, who pulled a handful of almonds out of his pocket.

"These are the drugs for the goats. Make sure you keep a pocket full of almonds, and they'll do anything you want. If they don't, there's a squirt bottle right there. It's their nemesis." Henry pointed to a plastic bottle hanging on a nail by the front door. "They will try to get inside the house at any cost and can quickly destroy the place. They know how to open the door, so make sure the top hook is locked."

The large male goat reared up to headbutt Aino. He stuck his knee out to block him, and then the small one followed through and headbutted him from behind, knocking him over.

"See, they're testing you out. They wanna know what

you're made of. Here's an almond. They'll start to like you after a while with each one. Don't ever strike one of these goats."

"Don't worry, man. I'll squirt them with the squirt gun."

"Oh, I got a special treat for them; hold on. They're gonna love this, watch." Henry walked over to the truck, pulled out a pink block of Himalayan rock salt the size of a car battery, and set it down in the driveway. All four goats were on it, instantly licking away.

"You were saying you're highly allergic to poison oak. I wouldn't recommend petting the goats because they're in it all day long. They love it. Aramoana used to get it bad from petting them, but she says she's immune to it now."

"How is she immune?"

"On account of drinking their milk after they've been eating it. Aramoana swears she doesn't catch it anymore."

"No shit? I should drink some."

"Well, they're not in milk anymore. Too old. Come on, I'll show you the house."

The house I built for my daughter was furnished with modern furniture, and the big room was set up like an art gallery. I was highly influenced by Frank Lloyd Wright with the furniture. I lacked concrete structure skills, so I made a simple wooden house. Dozens of my paintings hung on the wall. The abstract ones. I remember doing that one. I didn't have a title, but i'll describe it. I painted a B-52 bomber morphing into an office tower with half-pig-half rats scurrying through the doors. I was really high when I made that one. The sidewalks cracked as if the whole scene was being swallowed by a sinkhole. I had to wear jeweler's glasses to get the fine detail. I hadn't seen these paintings in a long time. I didn't know my daughter Joyce would take such good care of them. Aramoana, I mean. Still can't believe she changed her name. I didn't pick it out; her mother did, but back to the paintings. My paintings! Ahh, Hanalei Bay in Hawaii. Do you realize how many hours that painting took? The mountain range is like a dragon's back. I remember going there as a child. Henry didn't know I followed them into the house, and I enjoyed my time scoping out the gallery, but then he spotted me.

"What are you doing here, Chaos? No cats allowed! Did you ask Aramoana permission to come inside?"

I have to ask permission to come into the house I built for my daughter. Really, Henry?

"I know, meow, meow, meow. Is that all you can say?"

Don't rub it in, man.

"This is his famous one. It's that Hawaiian mountain that looks like a dragon, and all the human souls flying down to earth through its head." Henry touched the painting with his finger. "That's where all the souls get shit out," pointing at the other side of the dragon. Henry knew where I was coming from.

"It's not really Pop art. I don't know what it is," said Henry.

It's my art, not pop art. I had nothing to do with that scene, man. A bunch of garbage for rich people! Ah! My Redwood tree growing out of a cloud. What a terrible attempt at Dali. What the hell was I thinking? Below the cloud is a layer of smog and a city on fire. I loved to paint on whole sheets of plywood. Large pieces, but nobody wanted that shit. Too big, they'd say. So, I painted bottle caps out of spite. Contempt for the art world. Fuck them all. The rich and talentless. Their parents set the prices, and their uncles own the galleries. Their wealthy friends pay the price to give value to their lousy art. I resorted to refrigerator magnets, and I ducked out of the whole entire shit show. I give them Eyeballs with spiders in the pupils. They held up my daughter's postcards on the door of the fridge. Mickey Mouse fired a machine gun with bloody white gloves. All of my art flooded back into my being and I felt complete again.

Aino opinionated, "I dig his art, man. This one's bizarre," pointing at the one of a trailer and a woman floating above it.

That was Ulee, man. That was Ulee.

"You like that one, Chaos?"said Aino.

No, I never really liked it, honestly. It was mostly Ulee's idea and seemed a little self-absorbed if you ask me.

"You're a real art connoisseur, Chaos. What rating would you give it, two paws up?"

Very funny, I give it two shits in the plant.

"Yeah, he had his own thing going on."

"I don't know shit about art, but I like a lot of these."

"You can sleep anywhere in here. I'll leave you to it, brother."

Henry left Aino standing in the gallery. I bolted out of there and into the woods, feeling like I could be an artist again. So, I scratched at the dirt on the trail and made another eyeball.

RADIOS

Aino set up sawhorses in the garage of Aramoana's house and primed the trim pieces. He wanted to listen to the San Francisco Giants game. He found my old collection of radios on the shelf in the garage. The old Grundig, which read "HiFi Zauberklang" on the face. He plugged it in and found the broadcast on the AM, 680 KNBR, fading in and out. So, he tried the Nova-Tech multiband radio, which read VHF aircraft with the little airplane logo. It worked a little better, but eventually, a glowing tube inside started smoking. The signal came in waves.

Tim Lincecum, "The Freak," was on the mound, and the Giants were playing the Colorado Rockies. Static interrupted the broadcast, and Aino tried plugging in a couple of radios simultaneously. The signal waves tuned in differently for each radio, enabling him to hear the whole broadcast, filling in the static where the other wave left off. It worked for a while, so he plugged in a third and fourth one. Eventually, he had six radios going at the same time. Then they started locking into the same static wave but became an echo delay of the broadcast. Aino lay down on the garage floor, taking the gray heart out of his pocket. Threw it up towards the ceiling and caught it again. The radios were turned up loud and echoing down the canyon.

"Another strike out for The Freak!"

But then the static came back to form a deep groan. Everything shut off. Aino blew the fuse but had trouble finding the breaker box. He searched around and followed the conduit down from the solar array. Found the breaker and flipped the switch, but the static returned. Only this time, the Nova-Tech radio caught fire. Ruined after he unplugged it, he put it back on the shelf and tried to make it look like nothing happened. It's alright, Aino; those radios have seen better days.

BECCA

Becca moved from Houston to San Francisco after the first tech bubble popped in 2000. She frequented the bars of the Tenderloin and knew Aino and Nate from Donny's place. A waiflike woman with short blonde hair cut into a bob. She wanted to escape the city because her ex-boyfriend was stalking her.

Nate suggested she come to the farm for a while, and he talked it over with Henry when he came down for a delivery.

"She just needs to get away and take a breather. If it doesn't work out, I'll bring her back. She can do trim work or help with the vegetable garden. She's a quick learner. Said she doesn't need money."

"Everybody gets paid if they work, but I don't wanna deal with drama this summer." said Henry.

"No, she's cool; she's sober as far as I know. I mean, she smokes weed, but that doesn't count."

Henry gave the go-ahead, and Nate drove Becca up a few days later.

When I saw her, she reminded me of my sister. She had a similar look. I didn't feel threatened by her and jumped right up on her shoulder. She was wearing a furry pink sweater. It felt good on my paws, and I could cling to it easily. I felt an instant connection to her.

"Boy, he's a friendly little baby," said Becca.

"He's not a baby anymore. He's a seasoned battle cat!" laughed Henry. "He just recovered from a serious attack. Some creature got him pretty good. Cut his back open. Normally, he attacks people the first time he meets them, but I think he's mellowing out."

"Yeah, he clawed me pretty good when I met him," said Aino.

"Listen to him purr. Like a little motorboat."

"You can sleep wherever you feel comfortable. There's a sleeping bag and pillow up there for you. Nate tells me you like working with plants?" asked Henry.

"Yeah, I love it, but I don't know much about it. I'm here to learn."

"So, you and Nate can start by planting the vegetable garden. I've got it all tilled down there. It's ready to go. Are you guys down? I made a little map of all the seeds and placement. Here, check it out. How long are you staying, Nate?"

"Until tomorrow, but yeah, sounds awesome. I'll take

the bed above the kitchen if nobody wants it. I like that spot.

"Sounds like a plan."

Nate and Becca started planting the seeds in the vegetable garden while Aino attached chicken wire to the top of the fence. Skip rambled off to work on the other patches and had yet to make the scene. Becca enjoyed getting her hands dirty and got to work after changing into some coveralls. They had most of the garden planted by the end of the day. Beets, carrots, and greens. Scallions and turnips. Cilantro, peppers, and spinach. Various melons and cucumbers. The garden looked neat and organized by the time they were finished.

"If you want, you can be in charge of the garden?" offered Nate. "Henry is too busy with everything else. I'm sure you can trim and help with whatever you want. He pays twenty dollars an hour cash under the table."

"I said I didn't need any money."

"Henry insists on one thing, though. He doesn't wanna be considered the boss. He hates bosses."

"Well, I wanna help, but I don't need money. I love this, Nate. Thank you for bringing me here!"

"No worries, Becca. It's gonna be ok. If you get tired and you wanna get outta here, just give the word. Henry goes back once a week, but I'll be coming back up every couple of weeks. He is gonna pay you if you work. Nobody works for free here."

Becca smiled in the midday sun. I ran by her and jumped up on the fence post. The crows were lined up, but they weren't saying anything. They watched like wise old-timers, trying to figure out this new visitor to the farm.

"So glad my phone doesn't work up here. I feel calm for the first time in years," said Becca. "I think I'm gonna shave my head tomorrow."

"Why do you wanna shave your head? You have beautiful hair," said Aino.

"That's the problem. I want a fresh start. I want it off me. I wanna be free. I don't wanna be beautiful."

After a hard day's work, they all shared a meal. Nate, Aino, Henry, and Becca. Nate cooked a vegan meal of BBQ seitan sandwiches with a kale salad on the side. Beans and rice. Shredded carrots and goddess dressing. Becca and Nate drank homemade kombucha Henry had acquired from a friend in Cloverdale.

"It's got a trace of alcohol in it. Watch out, Aino!" said Henry.

It had a raspberry flavor but was pungent and spicy. Henry sipped pear brandy, but none of the others drank. They started a campfire outside in the fire pit by the back porch.

"I think there's going to be a lunar eclipse tomorrow morning. 5:00 a.m. I've never seen one. Have any of you?" asked Becca. "Where's the bathroom, by the way?"

"It's back there on the other side of the deck. Through the little swinging door," said Aino." I'll be up. I wanna see the eclipse."

"No peeing in the bucket, just poop," said Henry.

Becca looked a little terrified.

"What do you mean bucket? Where's the toilet?"

"That is the toilet," said Henry.

"Just a bucket?" asked Becca.

"There's a toilet seat. You'll see. Do you have a headlamp?"

"No, what's that?"

"There's an extra, I'll get it." Henry entered the kitchen and grabbed the one hanging from a hook by the door.

"Here, you'll need this. Press the button on top and wear it on your head like a bandana. If you go poop, put a couple scoops of sawdust on top of it. You'll see, it's self-explanatory when you get in there."

"Is there a shower here?"

"Yeah, it's past the toilet down the stone pathway. You'll see the little bamboo barrier. There's also a tub."

The shower stood next to the tub on a stone slab facing the forest with a drainpipe descending into the woods. Both hooked up to a propane water heater coming from the kitchen.

"Wow, this place is blowing my mind!" said Becca. "You guys go to bed early?"

"You'll find the longer you stay here; bedtime is usually right after sundown. I think it's time for me to turn in," said Henry.

He walked down the hill to the shack while the fire faded for the night. Aino left shortly afterward for his new spot in the solar house.

"I'm used to going to bed when the sun is coming up," said Becca.

"I'm gonna turn in, too." Nate crawled up into the loft above the kitchen.

Becca sat for a while, and I curled up in her lap. She carried me up to the loft in the living room, and I slept at the foot of her bed.

She woke up before Henry when the sky was purple on the ridge and sat on the edge of the porch in her coveralls. She started her day by cutting most of her hair into the grass.

"Hey, ah, good morning!" said Henry. "You're up early."

"Morning! I decided to give myself a haircut before work."

"Whoa, looks good! You must be a professional."

"No mirrors required," she laughed.

"You want some coffee? Eggs, bacon, the works? I usually cook the same thing every day."

"I can't resist bacon. Thank you! I'd love all of the

above."

Henry nodded and smiled behind his round glasses. "Over easy or scrambled?"

"Scrambled, please."

Nate was stirring in the loft above the kitchen.

"I've got oatmeal for you, Nate. Sorry about the bacon," as the smell wafted up to where Nate slept.

"Ah, no worries. It's a good alarm clock. I gotta get rolling soon. I'm working at the dispensary this afternoon."

Nate pulled away after breakfast and saw Skip waving goodbye from the field in the distance. Barefoot, as usual. His two white dogs by his side. Skip cooked and slept in his van. He rarely went to the house. Accompanied by his dogs and a mystery to the others.

SEXING THE PLANTS

Henry spent most of his time studying the plants in the greenhouse with his magnifying glass.

"What are you doing?" asked Becca, standing in the doorway.

"Trying to determine the sex of the plant."

"Why do you wanna know?"

"Well, the sooner the better. I need to find out who the males are and kill them immediately."

"Why do you wanna slaughter all the males? Sometimes I wanna do the same. Ha ha!"

"Before they fertilize the females. I don't want any seeds. Sinsemilla. No seeds."

"How do you know what sex they are?"

"The ladies grow a stigma at the node. It's like a hair follicle, and the males grow little pollen sacks. Once I can see, I toss em. If you wanna start transferring all those plants to the one-gallon pots, it would be a big help. You can use the soil mixture in the pile by the shed. "

"How many plants are you gonna have?" asked Becca.

"Well, hoping to get at least 500 for this farm, but half of these are starters for friends nearby. Like Otto is coming at the end of the week to get 300. There's already over a hundred ladies, as you can see." Henry nodded towards the rows of plants set out to be transferred. He'd dug a small pit and tossed the males into it, covering it up at the end of the day.

HEY GEORGE, WAS THAT YOU?

I messed with Aino by running around behind him and jumping out of sight when he'd look back. I tricked him into thinking there was a ghost in the room.

"Hey George! George DeCarlo! How's it going man? I love your paintings. I've been meaning to ask you, what do you mean by the centipede serving as a lightbulb filament? George?"

It's got no meaning, man. I meowed repeatedly. Nada!

"I'm not talking to you, Chaos. Talking to George's ghost, do you see him?"

Aino must have finally cracked. He was talking up to the rafters at some imaginary spirit in his mind. It wasn't my spirit floating around. If I could float I swear i'd be flying over Half Moon Bay right now.

"Did you really know Warhol or is it bullshit?

It's bullshit, man. Get over that hype. That crap doesn't matter. I was at the same party in New York, one time and got caught up in a group photo and all of a sudden, all my art's attached to his. I got slimed. I'm not part of that scene!

"I heard about you getting stabbed by that flying beach umbrella at the Jersey Shore. Did that really happen?"

How do you know about that? Aino heard only

silence until a loud crash came from outside. The goats knocked over one of the platforms and it fell into the fence cracking one of the boards wide enough to allow them to escape. They ran for the perennials Aramoana had planted by the door. Aino got the baggy of almonds and lured them back to the paddock."

"Good goats. Did George let you out? Hey George, did you let them out?"

Don't blame me, man. I don't control the goats. You are whacked out of your mind.

Aino finished the job and fed the goats one more time before Aramoana returned and repaired the cracked board in the fence. Still, he'd never seen her, but he left a note.

"Thanks for the extra work. Lemme know if you need anything else. Sincerely, Aino."

On his walk back to Henry's place, Aino stopped at my abandoned house. I was sitting on the propane tank watching him. He tried peeking into the windows. A red-tailed hawk fluttered away from the rooftop making a high-pitched siren sound. A call of distress. Aino walked towards me and said "Is that you, George?" The crows swooped in and distracted him. When he looked back, I was gone and I heard him yell.

"Hey George, was that you?"

TROUT BELOW THE BRIDGE

Otto and Hunter had been busy prepping the boxes and amending their soil for the entire week. They made fifty more boxes, and Otto leveled the area into terraces. Otto had a flowing spring on his property, and the storage tanks were full. He had an overflow pipe that sent the excess water down the ravine into Lost Creek, further downstream from Henry's place.

"I can't believe we knocked these out in a week. Having a hard time keeping up with you," said Otto.

"Come on, Dad, you're doing just fine. For a man in his seventies."

"Strangely, I feel younger now than I did at your age."

"When you were my age, you were a drug addict."

Otto sighed and wiped his brow with a USMC bandana. "You were born in 1980, baby."

"I know when I was born, Dad."

"It's the same year I was born. The year I got clean. "

"Oh, Dad, you know, you're pretty sweet for being such a hard ass."

"Don't tell anybody, baby."

Otto put on his running shoes and started stretching. "Gonna go for a run."

"Copy, Dad!"

He gave her a dirty look but then winked and took off down the gravel road. Hooked a right at the fork to the main road and didn't break stride running through Lost Creek which was at a trickle now. Then he hung a left to run further down the canyon. All the way to the end of the road where the creek connected to the Anguilla River, about seven miles down.

Otto climbed the rotting train trestle to the abandoned tracks above. The bridge spanned the river a few hundred yards from an old broken-down dam and a decommissioned electrical station.

Several years ago, the train tracks were warped from an earthquake and were no longer in use. Otto remembered how the quake split the irrigation pipe on his property, and a ten-inch crack formed in the yard.

Looking down into the crystal clear water, he watched the trout swimming in the calm section below the bridge. He jumped into the water feet first and lay on his back, looking up at the sky. The trout scattered into the shadows beyond the bridge, to the protection of a sunken log in the deeper water.

A man stood under the bridge, with his dog, watching Otto. The same man Ulee found cleaning up in her trailer. Dressed in his wizard robe, the wooden staff leaned against his makeshift tent. He'd made a camp under the bridge. Otto didn't notice him watching and floated onward, letting the current take him downriver.

LADIES ARE READY

Henry arranged the plants into rows according to strain. Girl Scout Cookies, Strawberry Kush, Jack Herer, and Purple Haze, among others. He completed sexing the plants, and the males were thrown into a pit next to the solar shed.

Otto wanted 300 starters, and they were ready to go. His beds were prepped, and he and Hunter drove over, pulling a trailer.

Hunter wore a green military jumpsuit with combat boots, and they seemed to be on a military mission. Otto wore a matching outfit.

"I'll be happy to get these ladies into their final homes," said Otto.

"Roger that, Dad. Why don't we grow the starters anymore?"

"I don't like coming up here so early. Wouldn't you rather stay in Texas until it warms up? Henry knows what he's doing; I taught him well."

"You are the "Wizard of weed, Dad."

"He's so neat and tidy about it. I think it's the goat pellets. They make magic in the soil."

They pulled down the steep slope and parked the truck and trailer next to the greenhouse.

"Damn, Henry! You must have over 2,000!"

The greenhouse was overflowing with plants.

"Everybody loves the ladies," added Hunter, as they started loading up the trailer.

"All of these outside the greenhouse are yours," said Henry. "If you want more goat pellets, I can hook it up after you get 'em home. Aramoana's got a stockpile, and she's not growing this year.

"Why not?" asked Otto.

"She wants to spend more time with Luka in Dillits," said Henry.

"I can always use more goat pellets. Those and my molasses are gonna make for a fantastic finish."

"How often do you use molasses?" asked Hunter.

"Every time I water until about three weeks before the harvest. Keep an eye on the soil pH as we go," said Otto.

"Make sure it's unsulphured blackstrap molasses to feed your soil microbes; sulphured will kill it," said Skip, who had just arrived. "A tablespoon per gallon keeps the rhizobacteria on track."

"Where'd you come from, Skip?" asked Otto.

"I cut through the woods. Wanted to say a quick hello. How have you been, Otto? Hunter?"

"Not too bad, man. Good to see you, Skip," said Otto.

"Hey, Skip," Hunter bowed from a distance.

"The soil up here is pretty good already. I've been doing a little more than a tablespoon and sometimes two to three," said Henry.

"Well, it shouldn't matter too much, but if you're using other nutrients, you could go on the lighter side, I suppose, "said Skip.

"How come you use the molasses?" asked Becca.

"It makes for thicker, healthier buds, wouldn't you say, Otto? It also deters parasites. Insects can't digest the sugars. Kind of like an organic insecticide. Spray it on the leaves," said Henry.

"Oh, yeah, absolutely! You probably get about 10 to

20 percent more weight in buds," said Otto. "I've tried using honey, but it didn't work as well as the blackstrap molasses. But everybody's got their own way. It's how I've grown to do it. The goat pellets are a fine addition."

"Oh, I forgot to introduce you to Becca. Otto and Hunter, this is Becca. She joined us a few days ago. Come up from San Francisco," said Henry.

"Pleasure to meet you, Becca," said Otto, as Hunter held out her hand to give a shake.

"You guys are on top of it," said Hunter to Becca.

Becca grinned and felt proud of the work she had done.

"We'll try to get some of these starters in their beds today. Later on, we'll have hamburgers and hotdogs if you feel like coming over," offered Otto.

"Sounds like a plan. I don't wanna cook tonight, and I'm heading to the city tomorrow, "replied Henry. "You game?" looking toward Becca.

She nodded with a smile.

"I'll let Aino know," said Henry.

"Thanks for the invite," said Skip. "Gonna turn in early and have dinner in the van. Rain check, though!"

"Welcome back, Skip," said Otto. Skip disappeared into the woods, heading back towards his van.

"He's got his own experiments going on up at the top patch. It'll be interesting to see what he comes up with." said Henry.

"Well, cool. Lemme know what's happenin. See y'all later. We'll eat about an hour before sundown," said Otto.

"Sounds good, brother."

They packed the trailer with the rest of the starters and slowly drove the rig back to the A-Frame.

DINNER AT OTTO'S

Becca, Aino, and Henry passed through the first gate and walked the cut-off path to the hairpin. I darted into the forest and hopped from boulder to boulder, watching them from above. They stopped at a level area with a water tank.

"This is where I'm putting the light-deprivation houses," said Henry.

"What is a light-deprivation house?" asked Becca.

"We keep some plants in hoop houses and pull tarps over them before sunset. It tricks them into budding out earlier," replied Henry.

"When should we start?"

"Round 4th of July. Dunno the exact date yet. It's easier with two people pulling the curtain and working it down over the plants."

I ran through the puddles of stagnant water inside the culvert pipe Henry installed a few months back. I came close to catching a grouse, but it ran into the rocks on the other side and escaped. I pawed at the stones and moved on. Henry grabbed a long stick from the ditch and used it as a cane.

"Don't worry, Chaos! There's gonna be plenty of food over at Otto's!"

I wondered why he thought I'd be worried about food at Otto's place. I followed along.

"How's your thumb these days, Henry?" asked Aino.

"It's all healed up. A little stiff, though."

"When are you gonna get back to playing music?" asked Becca.

"I'll never play guitar or piano the same way again." Henry lit a joint.

"Not sure I'll play the trumpet the same after cutting

my lip," said Aino.

"I think you'll be fine eventually," said Henry.

"You want some?" he asked, passing the joint to Becca.

"Sure, thanks!" She took a long drag.

Becca only weighed about 100 pounds and was half the size of Aino. She had strength and could easily handle any task on the farm.

"You're losing weight, Aino. Your beer belly's almost gone."

"Really, you think so? Five months with no booze."

"You don't always look so angry like you were at The Winter Fern Tavern. Were you always pissed off?"

"I felt like a trapped animal. Stuck behind that bar," said Aino.

"Why didn't you quit?"

"Golden handcuffs, that's why. It's hard to quit a job where you can make a hundred dollars an hour and drink for free. I was lucky to get fired because I never would have quit."

They continued up the hill past my vacant shack and took a right at the fork opposite Aramoana's house. The road narrowed, and a patch of grass grew in the median. I walked on the fresh green grass, which felt cool on my paws and stopped to rest, laying on my back and staring at the clouds. What a dreamy day it was.

The group walked on as I groomed myself and pulled a beetle from my back leg. I ate it, then chased after them towards the music coming from the A-Frame cabin.

Rows of raised beds, freshly planted with marijuana starters, sat on top of a large concrete slab. A storage tank on the hillside watered the plants by feeding automatic drip lines.

A Jeep and a truck were parked on individual slabs behind the A-Frame. Solar panels powered the house, and propane gas lines fed the kitchen. The place even had a satellite dish, but it was overgrown with poison oak and no longer worked. There were two light-deprivation hoop houses adjacent to the A-Frame.

Otto built a barbecue grill from a steel drum with handles on one side and wheels on the other. He cooked ribs, hamburgers, and hotdogs. Hunter was still at work transferring starters to the nearby beds. Most of them were completed before the day ended. Her green jumpsuit became brown, and her pompadour flopped down near her eyes.

Otto stood at the grill, poking at the meat, then closed the lid, returning to his turntable inside.

"I still can't get enough of this record," said Otto as he listened to side two of Life, Love, and Faith by Allen Toussaint. "I love this song, 'Soul Sister'." He played it again and returned to work the grill.

Otto had the dinner set up like a military mess hall. Steel trays and plates with a single spoon for each tray. A big pot of pork and beans simmered on the stove.

"Everyone gets one hot dog, one cheeseburger, and two ribs. There are two pickles per burger. One tomato slice per burger. According to my calculations, everyone can have approximately two scoops of beans," said Otto. "I have grapefruit juice, tomato juice, and water. Take your pick."

Henry grinned and took a swig from his flask. "Wow, you got it all measured out so precisely."

Otto fished a chunk of pork from the pot of beans and threw it toward me.

"There you go, Chaos!"

Hunter disappeared and came back with vegetarian options.

"We have veggie dogs and veggie burgers."

Becca raised her hand and said, "One of each, please."

Otto looked slightly upset with the additional food offering throwing off his count of fixings and said, "Suit yourself; we've got all the tasty stuff here. Help yourself."

"What brought you to the farm, Becca?" asked Hunter. "I love your hair."

"Oh, thanks! I just cut it. I needed a change of pace. Trying to reset, you know?"

Hunter understood something unspoken. "Yeah, we all need a break sometimes. Glad to see you here," and she reassuringly smiled at Becca.

SUMMER

I moved into the Schieffelbein house. Ilf and Petrov were too goddamn loud. If I came anywhere near them, they'd go nuts. They wouldn't shut up for an hour when they saw a squirrel. I know they'd kill me if they had the chance, and I wouldn't hesitate to do the same to them, but I'm no match for two dogs. I'd get a couple good scratches in, for sure. Funny, I was a dog person in my previous life.

I found a lovely place to snooze in the attic. The insulation made for a cozy place to lie down, but it got caught in my fur and took hours to clean. It's worth the peace and quiet, though. Even with the occasional machine gun fire coming from up the canyon. I'm up before dawn anyway. It's got an excellent view of the hillside from the attic, and birds fly in through the broken window. Easy prey!

One morning, I watched from the attic as a mother bear and her three cubs rolled around in the grass. Aino arrived, and they ran for their lives. He carried a post-hole digger.

"We're gonna turn this into an orchard Chaos!" he yelled. I ran up the road away from him. Becca worked in the vegetable garden at the main house, and Skip took off with the dogs. The coast was clear, so I made the rounds. Back up to the water pipe for a quick sip and cleaning. Then to the lookout rock. Alligator lizards sunned themselves and were easy pickings, but I only toyed around with them. Killed one to save for a snack later. Stashed it behind a Manzanita tree. I rarely eat leftovers, but they're there if I need them.

POISON OAK

The plants found their final homes, and the greenhouse stood empty. They were thigh-high on humans but resembled little trees to me. I hurried to the compost pit, found the remnants of a rib, and ran off with it before the crows had a chance. Surprisingly, they weren't around.

"Where have you been, Chaos?" Henry asked as I gnawed at the rib. I'd found my old familiar spot on the back porch.

"I thought you disappeared. You worry me."

I tried to reply by saying, "No, it's those fucking dogs Skip brought!" but all that came out was a meow and a growl. Why would I even try to talk to him?

Henry brought out a piece of bacon from the kitchen. "I know, those dogs scared you off, but remember, you're always welcome here. "

I snagged it from his hand and ran up to the roof, looking down at the yard as I ate. There were wooden stakes with a string running from the main house to the shack. Aino came back with some more digging tools.

"The trench needs to be at least eighteen inches deep. Follow the north side of this line. I wish we could get the backhoe here, but it's too steep," said Henry.

"Kinda wish we had done it when the soil was soft," said Aino.

"Don't think it would make much of a difference. You're gonna have roots and rocks the whole way down."

Aino looked at the line. "This is going to be a backbreaker."

"I'll be going to the city today and will return on Monday. Gonna take Luka camping in Tahoe."

He loaded up and was gone by noon. Aino got started while Becca worked in silent meditation. Weeding and watering.

Two days into the trench project, he reached the halfway point. I ran the length of it to investigate and found a big white grub the size of a human thumb. I scratched it out of the dirt and enjoyed the surprise lunch. Becca grabbed a pickaxe and joined Aino in the work.

Looking at his hands, Aino said, "Thank you for helping. At least I have calluses from before."

The strenuous work didn't bother Becca. In fact, she covered more ground than Aino.

"I feel like I can get more air into my lungs now. Passages are opening in my brain. I can't believe I'm getting paid for this, said Becca.

"Almost like doing drugs. Breathing fresh air."

"Henry should get some of those people from the city who do boot camp workouts. They can pay him to work on the farm."

She had the garden looking well-manicured and the trench nearly done. Aino started to feel some itchiness in his arms and legs. He worked in cut-off shorts without a shirt on. Staring down the length of the trench, he saw some roots sticking out of the wall and noticed poison oak running parallel. His stomach sank.

"Damn, I've got it! Poison oak!"

He had been digging through those roots all day, rubbing up against them. He wasn't using gloves. The itching reached his eyelids while his heart raced with agitation. He dropped the shovel, decided to shower immediately, and tried to scrub it off before it went into his skin. He was highly allergic. It swelled up in large patches, and the condition quickly worsened. He took a wet washcloth and covered his eyes.

"What's wrong with you?" said Becca.

"I've gotten into poison oak."

"Was wondering why you disappeared? I don't even know what it looks like."

"I got into the roots. It's all along the edge near the trench. You're not feeling itchy, are you?"

"No, I'm fine. Maybe I'm not allergic to it. Man, it's all over you!"

Aino tried to sleep in the solar shack. It got substantially worse overnight. He could barely see in the morning because his eyes were nearly swollen shut, and red splotches covered his entire body. He got in his truck and drove to the Dias Verdez health clinic. Driving and wiping his eyes with a wet washcloth. He nearly sideswiped Carl at the switchbacks.

"That drug addict almost hit me! Motherfucker!" Carl turned around to chase after him in a road rage.

As Carl revved the engine, Aino didn't notice the big truck on his tailgate. "The Bedbug Song" by Mighty Panther played on KMUD. The intensity of the itch made him oblivious to Carl following him. He squinted through the turns. He didn't realize the extra agitation the song added to the scene.

"Fucking pull over asshole!" yelled Carl while flashing his lights; Aino turned onto HWY 101, driving straight to the health clinic parking lot. When he exited his truck, Carl saw Aino's size and quickly backed off. He honked his horn and yelled, "Watch where you're going, ass-muncher!"

Aino staggered into the clinic with his entire body inflamed from itchiness. He held a wet towel over his left eye, which had swollen shut.

Carl sped off to Slingers in a huff.

Aino got a steroid injection, and the irritation subsided. Still, he had to deal with the rash for several more weeks. He drove to the coast and lay in the cold water of the Pacific Ocean for temporary relief.

ULEE GETS FIRED

Ulee punched her card to clock in for work. Another Sunday morning shift. The only difference was that Billy Johnson had already begun working behind the deli counter.

"Morning, Billy. What brings you in so early?"

"Oh, Carl put me on the schedule. Said he needed someone on Sunday mornings."

"Funny. I work every Sunday morning."

"That's what I thought. Maybe Carl wants the two of us working because it's tourist season?"

"We never needed two before."

"I don't know what's happening, but I started doing the prep work."

"Well, you got the chickens going, I see."

It threw her whole routine off, and Ulee was confused. She scrambled for something to do.

Carl slipped through the back door and into his office. He logged onto his computer and checked the security cameras.

"Good morning, Billy. Glad to see you're up so early. Ulee! I didn't put you on the schedule. Ulee, come on! Pay attention." He spoke to the monitor condescendingly.

"Billy's here, Ulee, to save the day." He switched the camera to Billy. "The shirt fits you well, my friend. Mmm. Dillit's Dragons. You're a dragon boy, aren't you? What are you, varsity this year? I like you in green and gold. Stay true to your school, Billy," he stroked himself under his desk. Then he pushed his swivel chair back towards the door and locked it. He continued to stroke away until he came. Wiping it up with a dirty deli apron.

He walked out onto the grocery store floor and approached the deli counter.

"What are you doing here, Ulee? You're not scheduled to work today."

"I work every Sunday morning, Carl."

"Check the schedule, Ulee!"

"I've worked every Sunday, going on twenty years now."

"Ulee! Did you even bother to check the schedule when you clocked in? I posted it right above the clock. Is there something wrong with your vision?"

"Are you kidding me, Carl?"

"Billy's gonna be working Sundays now."

"You never mentioned anything about this, Carl! Are you serious?"

"You should go ahead and clock out now. I'll pay you for this morning, but that's it; I only pay for scheduled hours from now on. Sorry, Ulee."

Ulee looked shell-shocked. Frozen for a few minutes but eventually started collecting her things."

"W-W-W-What hap happened U-Ulee?" asked Walter calmly in the back hall.

"Carl took me off the schedule. I just don't know."

"C-C-Carl. C-Carl did wh-what?"

"I don't know why, Walter."

Ulee left through the back door by the loading dock and walked past Carl's monster truck. Stunned and confused, she cursed under her breath.

"You evil lizard fucker!" She spit on the door handle of his truck and kicked the side. She lost control for a moment. Carl saw it on the video monitor and ran into the parking lot to confront her.

"I saw what you did! I saw it all on the security

camera! Don't bother coming back here again! I will file charges if you fucked up my truck! I'm friends with the police, remember? How about I come and kick in your trailer door? How would you like that, Ulee?"

His voice faded away as she walked towards the sage bush, trying to ignore him. She phased him out and collected herself inside her mind in meditation. Rubbed some sage in her hands and held it up to her nose. Inhaled deeply and didn't look back.

BALLOON LADY

Ulee peeked out the trailer window and saw Hunter through the tree branches out front, sitting at the nearby picnic table. She decided to introduce herself.

"How's it going over there?" yelled Ulee.

"Oh, hey. Are you talking to me?"

"Yeah, I'm Ulee. I live next door."

"I didn't know anyone was in that trailer. Hunter, by the way."

"I know. It's good to meet you again. I've known your father for years. You probably don't remember me, but we met when you were a baby. Is it okay if I join you?"

Hunter nodded and smiled.

"You look a lot like your dad, you know. Can I offer you a cup of tea?"

Hunter perked up. "Sure, that sounds lovely."

"Hold on a sec."

Ulee disappeared momentarily and returned with the tea set on a tray.

"There's a whole variety. Take your pick."

"But only one more Darjeeling, do you mind?" asked Hunter.

"Have at it!" Ulee watched Hunter closely and felt a connection.

"Thank you, Ulee. Are you okay? Have you been

crying?"

"No, it's nothing; Allergic to Coyotebrush."

"What's that? Maybe I'm allergic, too," said Hunter. "I've been sneezing like crazy. Haven't I seen you working at Amundson's?"

"Probably; usually there every day, but not anymore."

"Why not anymore?"

"I got fired today."

"Sorry, Ulee."

"It's been a long time," Ulee looked off to the field where Hans stood at the fence line.

"Maybe you're better off."

"Dunno. I didn't expect to have to think about this."

Hans sighed and shook his whole body.

"He understands," said Hunter.

"Nah, he just wants his daily treat. Excuse me again." Ulee left to fetch an apple from the trailer and gave it to Hans.

"He loves you, I can tell," said Hunter.

"It's because I give him treats every day; he's a bit spoiled."

"Is he your horse?"

"No, he's his own horse. Hans doesn't have an owner."

"But who owns this field?"

"That's Amundson property. I guess Carl owns it now."

"So I guess Carl owns Hans?"

"Unfortunately, Carl doesn't even know Hans is alive, nor does he care. If he did, he'd probably have him put down."

"What, does he hate horses or something?"

"I think he hates everything, especially himself."

"Poor guy, so does Carl own the store?"

"Yeah, he took over after his parents died."

"Why did he fire you?"

"I think he's trying to get rid of everything that reminds him of his parents."

"Why would he do that?"

"I think he feels guilty."

"Guilty for what?"

Ulee didn't answer.

"He and I never saw eye to eye. Not even when he was a little kid. He was a spoiled brat, but his parents were awesome. They were like family to me. Carl doesn't even treat us like employees. He treats us like we're disposable."

"Sounds like a jerk."

"Yeah, he is a jerk. Eff Carl!"

Yeah, eff Carl."

"Amundson's used the best place to hang out in town and have coffee. Everything changed now. I didn't want to believe it, but I'm starting to think he–" Ulee cut herself off, then continued, "Crazy how people who have everything want more."

The two sat for a moment in silence.

"Where are you from, Ulee? You don't sound like you're from California?"

"Who's from California anyway? I grew up in Detroit."

"How'd you end up out here?"

"George DeCarlo. You ever heard of him?"

"Yeah, we found one of his paintings at the A-Frame. A bee playing guitar."

"Never seen that one. Maybe George was going through his toddler art phase."

"I heard his paintings are worth a lot of money. Is that true?"

"I don't think they are, but some might think so."

Hunter attempted to sip her tea but put it down, realizing it was too hot.

"George's performance art was the coolest stuff he ever did. Can't put a price tag on that, though.

"What would he do?"

"Well, one time, he did this beach scene performance.

He filled a room full of sand and lay on a beach towel with a beach umbrella sticking out of his stomach. Blood spurted out into the sand through a pump he had set up. He lay there smiling with a Beach Boys album playing. Like a normal day at the beach. Fun in the sun."

"I would have liked to have seen that."

"George was a funny guy. You know, he really did get impaled by a flying beach umbrella at the Jersey shore?"

"That's some crazy bad luck."

"Yeah, he got sepsis, and it nearly killed him. He was a teenager when it happened."

"I'll bet it scared him away from the beach."

"I don't think it scared him from the beach. He'd be the first to jump in the ocean. I think the accident woke him to live in the present for the rest of his life. To see how something so stupid could kill you at such a young age. He realized not to take it all so seriously."

"Yeah, I get that. I think losing my mom when I was a baby had a similar effect."

"Sorry to hear about your mom. "

"It's alright. It's a long time ago, and I don't remember. I was so young." "My advice to you, Hunter, is never stop acting like a kid, even as an adult. Never say you're old because that's what you'll be. Okay?"

"I know my sister has been saying she's old since we were kids, and she acts that way, too, like an old lady at twenty-seven."

"Some people like being old. Acting old. I'm guilty of it sometimes."

"Not me; gonna stay young until I die. Like that 7 Seconds song."

"I don't know that song, but I like the idea."

"I just wanna go and see stuff. See the world over and over again."

"I wanted to go everywhere, but I ended up here."

"It's not such a bad place to end up," said Hunter.

"We followed the Kerouacian dream for a little while at least."

"What's that?" asked Hunter.

"You know, the writer, Jack Kerouac, we all wanted to live out our road fantasy."

Hunter took the comb out of her back pocket and started plucking the teeth of it with her fingers. "Well, my dad caught Hunter S. Thompsonitis. That's how I got my name."

"You sure it was your dad who named you?"

"Well, he is a fan."

"Me too," said Ulee. "What do you wanna do? I mean, really wanna do, other than just see everything?"

"I wanna live like I'm making a movie, but I want it to be interesting. Jump into scenes and change the focus of my eyeballs! I'm a camera." said Hunter. "I want my memories to be interesting to remember."

"Have you ever tried to clear away all your memories?" asked Ulee.

"Why would I wanna do that?"

"So you don't have to keep going back."

"But I wanna go back."

"I'm not talking about forgetting everything. It's just an exercise. Something to calm you down if you don't wanna keep remembering something. You put it away for a while. Like hanging up a shirt in the closet. Like the job, who cares. I'm gonna put the shirt in the closet."

"The memory shirt. Ha, I like that idea. Maybe I'll call my movie 'The Memory Shirt'"

"Think about all the poetry yet written."

The two sat silent as the breeze kicked in and the bird feeder swung on a string.

"Have you ever thought about being a Monarch butterfly? We'd never have to worry about where we were going," said Hunter.

"We'd have a built-in flight plan."

"I wanna join my genes with the butterflies and travel forever!" said Hunter.

"Maybe in the next life, sweetheart."

"You followed the temperature. Right? Isn't that why you're in California?"

Hunter smiled, and the sun shone down on the two of them.

"What happened with you and that guy, George?"

"Well, George had many partners, and so did I. Male and female. It got pretty wild after we first got here. Free love and all. We tried to push it to the limits. The only problem is that the ego got in the way."

"What, did someone feel like they weren't getting enough?"

"Everybody wants more. More hugs, more drugs, more land, more money. The problem is that everyone has got a different idea of sharing. What's fair? Who's being left out? Who deserves more? Who's taking too much? Who's not pulling their weight? Resentments. We all wanted peace, love, and understanding. We wanted something beyond rent and capitalism. Real community. It was beautiful for a while. But people got bored. People got sick. People started having kids, and it's expensive. Some people found selfishness."

"Have you ever had a child?" asked Hunter.

"Yeah," Ulee hesitated momentarily, "but I had to let her go. I couldn't afford to raise her. Especially here." She nodded over to her spot. "What kinda life would that be? I didn't wanna be married to her dad. I'm not straight. He had a wife already and kids. His wife was a friend of mine. We all agreed that they would raise the baby."

"Man, that's intense! She wasn't mad at her husband when he got you pregnant?"

"Mad? She was there! She encouraged him to do it. We were all friends back then. Friends and lovers."

"Sounds pretty wild."

"Yeah, it was."

"People are pretty hung up on sex nowadays," said Hunter.

"AIDS changed everything in the '80s. It killed a lot of our friends in the city."

"When was the last time you saw your kid?"

"Not since she was a newborn baby. I guess she's fully grown now."

"I hope someday you'll get to meet her again."

"Yeah, me too. I remember when George's daughter Aramoana showed up out of the blue. He didn't know he had a kid. She turned up in town one day. She tracked him down."

"What a surprise for George," said Hunter.

"She knocked on the trailer door looking for him, and I told her where he was. I think he got pissed off at me for telling her where he was. Then, she never left. George was the only man I've ever cared for, and I'm not into men. I tend to gravitate towards ladies if you know what I mean?"

"I totally do. I'm that way too."

"I've been celibate for many years now. Hardly any drama. I like it that way," said Ulee.

"Yeah, me too. I think I'm asexual. I've always been kind of a loner, but it gets so lonesome, doesn't it? Do you like it? To be lonesome? Like I do?"

"I'm the highest of the lonesome, honey," said Ulee

"Damn, we need some pedal steel on that line. So, is that your trailer?"

"I'm not sure if it is or not. George implied that he gave it to me but never gave me the title. Now, it's all dilapidated, and he's dead."

"My condolences, Ulee."

"It's okay. George is probably haunting his property as I speak. He always wanted to be a ghost, and now he finally got his wish. I got his teapot. I got my best friend

Hans standing over there. It'll be okay."

"Have you ever been to the place George built? I drive past it every day. It's all overgrown, like a haunted house. Spooky."

"That's what he wanted, a haunted house. I've only been there once, when he first finished it. He had a party up there. It's how I met your dad. He gave me a tour of George's place. Showed me the house and all the paintings. A big gallery room with a vaulted ceiling. He built it for Aramoana. I don't understand how he built it himself."

"I think Henry helped him."

"Yeah, and Otto too." How did my dad fit in?"

"Otto? He was the 'wizard of weed'. He taught George and Henry. They both learned everything they knew from your dad."

"That's the only time you ever went up there?"

"Yup. The last thing George said to me was, 'I gotta be alone out here if I'm ever gonna get anything done!' But then his daughter Aramoana moved in, and I didn't hear from him again. I'd see him sometimes, but he never waved or anything. I didn't mind. I didn't wanna have small talk with him. I hate small talk. "

"Why didn't you leave town?"

"I got settled in. Working at the store. It was easy. Zen, you know? Breathing and living simply. I wanted to meditate. It's been a forty-year retreat. Living for a cup of tea, you know what I mean? Living to get out of my mind. To float away from the shell. Every day, I practice."

"Meditation?"

"Yes, I haven't spoken to anybody in years. Other than the customers at the deli. I'm not speaking at all; just taking orders. Completing mundane tasks. Nobody listens to anyone anyway, but thanks for listening to me."

"I enjoy listening to you," said Hunter.

Ulee noticed how Hunter crossed her legs and held

one hand in the other. Much like herself. Exactly like Ulee would sit.

"You know George and I made a bizarre painting together?"

"Do you have it? I wanna see."

"No, it's in the gallery house. His daughter Aramoana owns all those paintings now. Since her dad passed."

"What's it look like?"

"It's the trailer, and I'm floating above it. I sketched it out for George. It's a collaboration. The painting shows me floating out of my body in a cloud above myself. He added screws to my feet, and one of my feet is screwed into the top of the trailer like I'm a balloon lady being held to it. Otherwise, I'd fly out into the sky. He knew it would be the anchor. He envisioned me in suspended animation. He could never draw like me. It made him jealous. I thought about going out there and grabbing it."

"Would Aramoana let you? Take the painting?"

"No. I asked her for it, and Aramoana wanted twenty thousand dollars! I couldn't believe it! I said it's half mine; I'll give you ten cents. She's sitting on about a million dollars worth of her dad's art. I don't think she cares about any of it."

Hans huffed at the fence line.

"I love Hans. He's always there in the same spot listening. He's the horse Buddha."

"Do you wanna come out to the BBQ at Henry's place on the 4th of July?" asked Hunter.

Ulee looked a little nervous. "You should ask your dad first."

"Why's that?"

"Just ask your dad."

DUFUR HIKES THE RIVER

Dufur packed provisions for a week in the woods. He planned to go down the river from the Dos Rios Bridge and follow it to Alderpoint. Searching for evidence of people poaching or stealing water. An ongoing summer weather pattern resulted in severe drought conditions throughout the West Coast. Most of the creeks in Northern California were dry, and the Anguilla River had gone down to a trickle at the beginning of July.

Dufur didn't give a shit if people were poaching or stealing water. The hike allowed him to set up raids on pot farms and make real cash. He and his buddy, Sheriff Rick Johnson, would assemble a task force for September and October. Sketching out plans to target farms that grew large amounts of weed, knowing these farms operated on a cash-only basis. Dufur would fabricate photographic evidence to justify the raids and ensure simple, lucrative scores.

At the start of his journey, the trail had turned to a talcum-like powder because there hadn't been rain for several months. The temperature reached 100 degrees many days, but the Anguilla River still had deep water holes along the route. He camped on a sand bar the first night. A fire ban remained until the rains returned, but Dufur enjoyed his reconnaissance mission. Getting paid by the state to steal from the hippies. He swaggered up the trail, feeling empowered by his position of authority.

Dufur always envisioned himself as a star athlete or destined for greatness but his life became a steady diet of sweet cereal and video games. A latchkey son with divorced parents, he developed a severe inferiority complex. Dufur struggled to keep his weight down, and his daily bar visits gave him a beer gut the size of a beach ball.

He went to community college and fell in love with the great outdoors. But he could never really escape himself and his impulsive behaviour. No matter how far out into the wilderness he hiked. He found his way into working for Fish and Game in California, somehow ending up in Dias Verdez. They provided him with modest housing on the outskirts of town at an affordable price. In the back of his mind, he always wanted something more. He wasn't living up to the person he envisioned himself to be. He battled depression but self-medicated with cocaine and liquor. He'd been sinking for years but didn't see a reason to try any harder. It's how he became a regular at Slingers. It's how he fell in with Rick and Carl.

Dufur hiked Lost Creek, which surprisingly still flowed. He followed it to the Schieffelbein property and scanned the creek bank. He had to stop intermittently to catch his breath. It wasn't a strenuous hike for the average person, but it was a true challenge for him. "There she is," he muttered, wheezing in the heat. He snapped a few photos of the water pipe Carl had planted months before and heard music from Henry's place. He snuck around and took some more photos to get the layout. Walked through the woods around the perimeter and photographed the gate leading out of the property on the other side of the hill. He snuck back down and followed Lost Creek back to the Anguilla River.

"Gotcha motherfuckers." he whispered gleefully.

Dufur spent a few more days hiking down the Anguilla and found another farm to shakedown off HWY 101. This could be a test run.

CAMPING WITH LUKA IN TAHOE

Henry set up a large tent near Lake Tahoe at a prime camping spot.

"Dad, how come mom can't come to camp with us?"

"She doesn't want to come. Remember, she doesn't like camping."

"I think I'm like mom."

"What? You don't like camping now?"

"I need to skate. I wanna learn this new trick."

"You can practice in the parking lot by the camp store."

Luka rolled his eyes, "I need a ramp, Dad. It's not gonna work there."

"I don't know what to tell you then. You wanna go back?" Henry looked at Luka in frustration.

"No, I wanna go swimming."

"Alright, but it's cold."

"I don't care if it's cold."

Henry walked with Luka to the lakeside, and the boy broke free and jumped off a boulder into the water.

"Come on, dad! What are you waiting for?"

Henry lit a joint and smiled.

"One second man." He pulled off his shirt and took another drag.

"Why do you always gotta smoke first? Can I have some?"

"No, bud. This is for grown-ups."

"Why is it only for grown-ups?"

"Adults have anxiety. It's medicine for anxiety."

Luka looked confused. "Why do you have anxiety? Do I have anxiety?"

"No, I don't think so. You're twelve."

"Yeah, I do. I have anxiety, Dad. Lemme have some!"

Henry made a Tarzan moan. "Here I come!" He made the leap into the freezing water. "Oh my god, it's cold!"

"Dad, it's not cold. I wanna be on your shoulders."

"Because you're cold, you wanna be on my shoulders. Okay, come here."

Henry became a tugboat, pushing through the water.

"I tell you what, Luka, if you think you have anxiety, I think ice cream will help."

"Yes, Dad! I have anxiety! Ice cream helps with anxiety. I know that for a fact!"

"Also, I think there's a skate park in South Lake Tahoe. You wanna go? Practice your trick?"

"It's a backside grind, dad."

"C'mon, Luka, aren't you still a kid?"

"Yeah, Dad, can we go there now?"

"I thought you wanted to go swimming?"

"I'm cold! Let's go skate!"

"Alright, Luka. Ice cream first?"

Luka nodded, and the two spent the rest of the afternoon at the South Lake Tahoe skatepark. Luka pulled off his first backside grind.

Later, they cooked hobo stew on the coals of the campfire.

"I was only kidding about being like mom with camping. I like camping, Dad. Wish mom liked it too."

"She used to. I remember when it was all she wanted to do."

DUFUR'S PICS

"Dufur Fleck in the flesh. What'd you just come out of a cave?" asked Sheriff Rick Johnson.

"Been in the woods hiking those creeks. I took a lot of pictures." He smiled wryly, "It was a beautiful hike," as he twirled his waxed mustache.

"Do you have any other options for us come September?"

"As a matter of fact, I do, Rick. Check out these photos."

Dufur bellied up to the bar next to Rick. The skin around his eyes remained white in the pattern of his sunglasses, and the rest of his face was sunburned, red, and bloated.

"Look here, Rick. There's a small farm near HWY 101. Easy access and does not seem to be in compliance as far as I can tell."

"I like the sound of that. Did you get aerial photos? How far back does that farm go?"

"I'm sure it stretches back for miles. I think the Duggins place has hundreds if not thousands of plants," said Dufur.

"I had no idea. You oughta to double-check on your next flight. How about a margarita? "

"Double, please. "

"Holly, please put two double margaritas on Mr. Dufur Fleck's tab?"

Dufur gave Rick an evil glance for charging the drinks to his tab.

Holly shrugged and grabbed two dirty pint glasses. She dumped a handful of limes in each and started muddling, imagining them to be Dufur and Rick.

NEW HIRE

Hunter arrived at the cabin in the Jeep and hopped out, ready for action. Another day of tending to the plants. Her father was already hard at work.

"Hi, dad. What's on the menu for today?"

"Well, let's see, I'd like you to spread a little compost on the tops of the beds. Mix in some of that molasses juice; you know the routine."

"Copy, Dad. I have a question for you."

"Go ahead."

"I've met this sweet old lady named Ulee down at the RV park, and I would like to know if it is okay to invite her to Henry's BBQ on the 4th. She told me that she knew you."

"Oh yeah, I know, Ulee. I haven't seen her in ages, how's she doing?"

"Didn't seem too good. Apparently, she just got fired from Amundson's."

"Fired? She's worked there forever!"

"You know she's staying in the trailer next to our spot. I thought it was abandoned."

"She's been there for years."

"I think she's sweet. I feel like I've known her my whole life."

Otto seemed about to say something but stopped.

"Do you like Ulee? Would you be okay with her coming to the 4th of July picnic at Henry's?"

"I don't see why not, but I thought she hated parties?"

"It's not a party; it's a picnic. I'd like for Ulee to come. We had a nice talk today."

"Cool with me; it's good to see her coming out of her shell after all these years," said Otto.

"What if we gave her some work?"

"Honestly, I haven't spoken to her since you–"

"Since what?"

"Well, I haven't spoken to her in over twenty years. "

"So, will it be weird if she comes to the BBQ?"

"It's okay. It may be awkward at first. I can handle it."

"Why would it be awkward, Dad?"

"It's a long story."

Hunter smiled and said, "Copy, Dad. What if she helps do some trimming? I could bring it to her trailer, and she could work from home."

"Let's see how the BBQ goes first."

NO REFUNDS!

Walter and Ulee always worked weekends and holidays at Amundson's. The 4th of July would be a busy day, and Carl had to work because he fired Ulee. He wasn't happy about it.

Walter approached Carl's office door and knocked lightly.

"Hang on a minute!" shouted Carl. "Come on in."

"Hey C-C-C-Carl. I-I-I-I needd-dd need to ask you?"

"Spit it out, Walter! I'm pretty busy here!"

"Ch-Ch-Ch-Chickens are pretty much rrrr-rrrrr-rrrruined. B-B-B-Billy keeps leaving them in t-t-t-too long. They all b-b-b-b-burned and dried out. I'm g-ga-ga-getting some com-com-com-complaints."

"Well, deal with it. Take 'em out if they're in too long. I'm not tossing any chickens today. Keep 'em out there."

"I-I-I-I-I had th-h-th-three refunds today. I'm t-tah-tah-tr-try—"

"Try what Walter? Come on, say it. You can do it!"

"I-I try-try-try to set up the strawb-b-b-berry shortcake display. B-B-But k-k-keep having to-to-to-do ree-reee-ree-refunds. Lotsa com-complaints."

"Refund? What the fuck are you giving a refund for? No more refunds!" Carl looked like his head was going to pop off his neck. He grabbed a sharpie from his desk drawer and hastily scribbled, "NO REFUNDS!" on a sheet of paper.

"Here! Put this sign up at the rotisserie station." Walter looked shocked. He took the paper and slowly turned towards the door. Carl found a roll of duct tape and threw it at Walter's back.

"You'll need this!" as it ricocheted off into the hallway.

Walter grimaced and bent down for the tape.

"Close the door, Walter! And knock like a man next time!"

Walter put up the sign, and Carl monitored him through security cameras.

He didn't notice when Walter said to himself, "Fa-Fa-Fa-Fuck you, Carl!" under his breath. When the task was completed, Carl switched cameras to Billy Johnson, who checked his phone behind the deli counter.

"Good boy, Billy. What's a couple of chickens anyway? I might have a little job for you. It pays well. You wanna work for me, Billy?" Carl returned to his daily masturbation ritual. When finished, he made the rounds of the grocery store. Carl walked the aisles, ignoring details but lost in thoughts of partying with Rick and Dufur. He paid no attention to the dried-up chickens on display with the sign that read,

"NO REFUNDS!"

"Hi, Billy. So, um, I'm wondering if you'd be interested in doing extra work for me?"

"Maybe, what is it?"

"I need to install a drainage pipe in my backyard. Are you interested? I'll pay you twice as much as you get working at the store."

"Wow, really? Thanks, Carl! When?"

"Anytime you're ready. You can start this week if you want?"

"Okay, well, how about I start after football. I've got a three-day football camp coming up this week."

"Sounds good, buddy. How's your dad, by the way?"

"I don't see him much, honestly. Not since mom and him divorced."

"Well, being the Sheriff of Dillitts has a lot of responsibilities. I'm sure he's got a lot of official police business to take care of. "

"Yeah, I never see him." Billy looked down sadly.

"Well, if you ever need a buddy or wanna talk, I'm here for you, Billy."

"Thanks, Carl. It means a lot to me. "

"So how about next Wednesday? After your camp?"

"Okay. But I have to ask my mom."

When Billy got off work, he stepped out of Amundson's and noticed his dad, Sheriff Rick Johnson, blazing by in his squad car at high speed. He thought there must be another emergency. He hadn't spoken to his father in months.

RED NECKLACE

Holly poured ice into the well as she prepared the bar at Slingers for the big 4th of July bash. Sheriff Rick's favorite band, Red Necklace, was scheduled to play, but the fireworks had to be canceled due to extreme fire danger.

Red Necklace was a Southern rock tribute band whose members dressed in drag with Daisy Duke cut-off jeans. Rick's squad car screeched into a handicapped parking spot, and he hurried into the bar, hoping to meet them before the show or at least catch a glimpse.

"Are they here yet?" Rick asked excitedly.

"Is who here yet?" replied Holly.

"Who do you think? Red Necklace! Are they here?"

"Not yet, Rick. They won't be here for a few hours. Will you please move your car out of the handicapped spot? I know you're mentally handicapped, but–"

"I'll move it. I just wanted to talk to the band."

Dufur Fleck slouched at the corner of the bar, nursing a Coors Light and twisting his curly mustache. Rick plopped down next to him.

"Holly, can you put a margarita on Dufur's tab for me, please?"

Dufur shook his head. "No, Rick. Not this time."

"What do you mean not this time? Red Necklace is coming tonight, and we are gonna fuckin' party, bro! I got two eightballs."

"You need to pay, Rick," stated Dufur. Finally, he put his foot down.

"I gotta pay for the little fucker's football camp, Dufur! That's what I gotta pay for. What do you mean I gotta pay? You don't have any kids. You pay! I forgot my wallet."

"Hey man, don't act like you're some kind of victim because you have a kid. You chose to have a child, man. Don't lay that trip on me!"

The comment didn't register with Rick.

"Come on, Dufur! Don't be so stingy. How 'bout I trade you this for a drink?" He reached into his pocket and pulled out a baggie full of white powder.

Dufur quickly changed his tone. "Sounds like a plan, my man."

Rick handed off the baggie like a quarterback handing off the rock for a winning touchdown.

"Holly, can you please make my friend Rick a margarita?" asked Dufur.

"No salt, Holly!" shouted Rick.

Holly grimaced and grabbed another dirty pint glass for the Sheriff.

Red Necklace arrived early, and Holly set up a makeshift backstage for the band. Full deli tray, chips, and salsa. Per the band's request, five rotisserie chickens, complements of Amundson's Grocery. Holly noticed the chickens were a little dry but set them out anyway.

The band loaded in while Dufur and Rick watched anxiously like schoolgirls waiting for the Beatles.

"I can't believe they're back. Man, they are gonna fuckin rock! Hey! Can you guys do the Molly Hatchet cover, "Flirtin' with Disaster?" A bearded man in tight shorts and lipstick loaded a Marshall cabinet onto the stage. "Flirtin' with Disaster." You guys smoke it, man!" screamed Rick, letting out a hoot, "Whoo!"

He slapped Dufur on the back. "You should take it easy on the blow, Rick."

The band filtered in with their gear, and Red Necklace's manager chatted with Holly. He complained about the chicken, "They're all burned up and dried out. The band specifically requested fresh rotisserie chicken. That's day-old chicken!"

"Sorry about that," said Holly. "I'll increase the bar tab, or I can ask Carl to bring some fresh chicken. The food was donated by Amundson's across the street. Here he is now." Holly pointed towards Carl, and the band manager frowned.

"Don't worry about the chicken. Drinks will be fine." The manager got on his phone, doing his best Albert Grossman impression.

Carl walked in, looking sad and disheveled. "Why the long face sporto?" asked Rick.

"I hate working holidays. I s'pose I shouldn't have fired Ulee until after the 4th."

"Why the hell did you fire Ulee?" said Dufur. "She's the best you got. That Walter guy is worthless. M-M-M-May I h-h-h-help you?" mocked Dufur.

Carl sneered at Rick and said, "Remember? You asked me to do you a favor and give your son a job. I had to let someone go. Why not the grumpy old bitty?"

He ignored Carl and shouted, "Red Necklace in the house! "Rick gestured to Dufur to give the baggie of cocaine back. Dufur obviously handed it to him under the bar.

"I want some," said Carl. "Then I gotta go close the store."

"Follow me, you little bitch."

Carl followed Rick to the bathroom like a puppy dog.

Rick released another "Whoot!" as they passed the band setting up their gear but stopped for a second.

"Hey! Bass dude!"

A man who looked like Hulk Hogan with lipstick perked up from the back of the stage.

"Yeah, you, bass guy!"

"What? What's up pal?" grumbled the suntanned giant.

"If you guys need anything, let me know. I mean anything! I'm the Sheriff around these parts!" Rick winked at him.

The guy let out a dismissive pphhttt! He shook his head and got back to adjusting his amplifier.

"Come on, Carl, let's go to my office," said Sheriff Rick. "You look like you need some marching powder."

The two staggered back to the bathroom for another blast.

When Carl walked by the band again, he said, "How'd you like that chicken, boys! Compliments of Amundson's Grocery! My own secret recipe! We're just across the street. Knock it out, fellas! Knock it out! Can you give it a mention on stage tonight?"

The Hulk Hogan look-alike glared at Carl, but Carl didn't get the hint to leave him alone.

"I'll be back soon, and then you're gonna fuckin' rock this house down, right motherfuckers?!" yelled Carl.

Red Necklace's manager stepped in.

"Excuse me, sir, the band is trying to set up. Please respect the stage area."

"What stage area? They're playing in the dining room. Who are you? You're not in the band." said Carl, flabbergasted.

"I'm their manager. Are you the guy who supplied the chicken?"

"That's me. My own secret recipe."

"The chicken is disgusting! It's not even edible. Red

Necklace is not happy!"

Carl looked like a kid who had his cotton candy taken away at the fair. But then he snapped into management mode.

"It's that goddamned Walter! I put him in charge of the chicken today. I'm so sorry. Gonna make it up to you guys."

"The band can't perform on empty stomachs."

"I'm gonna go across the street and whip up another batch for you personally. I'll be back in a couple hours."

"A couple hours!? They're hungry now!"

"Okay, I'll be back in a half-hour with fresh chicken."

The manager looked at Carl skeptically, "If you bring us some fresh chicken by the time the sound check is over, I'll give you a signed poster of Red Necklace."

"Are you fucking kidding me?!" Carl nearly wet his pants. He raced out the door and jumped into his monster truck. It would be impossible to cook a rotisserie chicken in half an hour, so he drove to the Safeway in Dillits.

Carl wore his sunglasses for fear of being seen with a competitor's chicken and quickly made the purchase. He hustled back to Amundson's Grocery and transferred the chicken into his trademarked "Poultry Paradise" packaging.

He returned it to Slingers, and the band's manager met him at the back door.

"You're late. I thought you said thirty minutes?"

Carl hustled the chickens to the folding table inside.

The behemoth on bass approached.

"Is it gonna be 'Poultry Paradise' or just dried up and disgusting?"

He tore off a leg quarter and bit into it like a caveman. His eyes widened with excitement.

"Mmm. Now we're talking! Hey, fellas, chicken's here!"

They all dug in.

"This is fucking good, man!" said the lead guitarist, resembling Barbara Bach with a beard.

Carl watched them devour the chicken with uneasy pride. The band manager brought him the promised poster even though he was late.

"I'm hanging this in my office immediately. Thank you!"

"Thank you! Kyle, right?" asked the band manager.

"It's Carl."

"I can see why you call this 'Poultry Paradise' thanks Kyle." The band manager got back to another important phone call.

4TH OF JULY

Hunter interrupted Ulee while she was sketching a picture of Hans. It was her first drawing in decades.

"Hey, I talked to my dad, and he's cool about you coming to the BBQ. I'm gonna head up there to Henry's place if you wanna go?"

"Do I need to bring anything?"

"Just you, Ulee. What's that a drawing of?"

"Hans, what do you think?"

"Wow, your drawing's like a photograph."

"I like doing pointillism. I call it dots, though."

"Well, it's pretty badass! Do you want to go in a little while or keep working on the drawing?

"Ready now if you are?"

"Oh, here, I found a Red-tailed hawk feather."

"Thank you! Sweetheart, It's beautiful," as she ran the feather through her fingers.

The two drove the Jeep up the gravel road into the mountains. Ulee hadn't climbed the hill for over twenty years. Flashes of the past with her and George streamed through her mind. She hadn't spoken with Otto for decades and felt nervous, remembering the party many years ago. Sitting next to Hunter, she saw the resemblance and wanted to break the news but didn't know how.

She looked into the canopy of trees, and the sunlight glistened through. A cloud of dust drifted back from the Jeep into the forest. The ruts in the road formed into berms at the hairpins. They crossed the trickling creek and entered through the gates. The grass had grown waist-high around George's house, and poison oak had overtaken the satellite dish he'd installed in the '80s. The Jeep climbed again at the fork in the road and continued up to the A-Frame where Otto stood, drinking his Arnold Palmer.

"Greetings, Ulee!" shouted Otto, but then coughed as his drink went down the wrong pipe. She didn't hear him in the noise of the Jeep doors slamming.

"Well, hello Otto!" said Ulee. "What's it been, twenty years?"

"How could it be that long?"

"Where'd all your long hair go? You used to have such pretty hair."

"Yeah, well, I've got to keep up appearances."

"Care for an Arnold Palmer ma'am?"

"I'd love one, Otto, but please never call me ma'am. "

"Sorry, one Arnold Palmer coming right up."

Otto retreated to the cabin.

"I think he likes you," said Hunter. "He's acting all nervous."

"Yeah, he always starts fumbling around. I don't get the crew cut mustache thing."

"He told me it's good cover from the cops taking weed cross country. I think he's nostalgic for his time in the service," said Hunter.

Otto appeared with Ulee's drink. "Shall we walk over to Henry's estate?" he questioned in a faux British accent.

"If the horses are not ready, I suppose it shall be,"

replied Ulee in the Queen's English. The three set off down the hill towards Henry's house.

Henry had pulled the large barrel grill down from the solar shack. A steel barrel cut in half with a hinge and a stove pipe welded to the side. It could handle large slabs of meat. He set it up at the edge of the driveway overlooking the garden. Making sure to have the grill safely on the gravel and away from anything flammable. He set up the garden hose for safety because the forest had become a tinderbox.

I sniffed at the food Henry had set out. A feast was in the works.

"You hungry, Chaos?" asked Henry.

Becca brought a large bowl of snap peas and asparagus from the garden as Taj Mahal's "Further On" played from a speaker on the floor by the door. Henry sparked a large joint and pushed the coals off to one side of the barrel with a garden hoe.

"How are you feeling, Becca? Are you enjoying your stay on the farm?"

"Feeling better every day."

"It's what it's here for."

"I feel like I can breath again."

"Remember, your only obligation is to live and breathe. Find peace. Know what I mean?"

"Yes, Henry. It's happening. I'm starting to see it. It's simple."

"It is simple," Henry smiled at the sun. Stoked by the positivity of the moment.

Aino arrived with his arms covered in scabs from his recent bout with poison oak.

"I moved the fence a little further away from the house at Schieffelbein's."

"Ahh, good news. It will give us breathing room. How's your head, my friend?"

"I've been feeling pretty steady, Henry. I can sleep

again since the poison oak scabbed up. Man, I was awake for a week. Scratching all night long!"

"Whoa, is that Skip? I thought he had left," said Becca.

"He moved his van to the top patch," said Henry. "His dogs were driving me crazy with all the barking, so I asked him to relocate."

Skip descended the hill with his two dogs on leashes. "Howdy all! Happy 4th, whatever it means." He brought the dogs to the shed and tied them up to a tree. They were surprisingly calm. He placed a large bowl of water in front of them. They lay down and fell asleep. "I gave them a little hash in their doggie treats," said Skip.

"It's fine if you wanna park the van by the house again if the dogs can stay quiet at night," said Henry.

"I'll stay at the top patch, I dig the view up there. I've been letting the dogs off the leash. They don't run off trying to get into the trash pit and chasing after Chaos. "

"More of a cross breeze at the top of the ridge. Just gotta listen to the pump motor."

"Oh, I cut it off at bedtime," said Skip.

"You wanna start getting light deprivation in order?"

"Yeah, it's about time. When we see the first star. I'd like to be out of here by mid-September. I gotta get back to Idaho, you know? "

"Yeah, I figured on the middle part of the month. We'd be ready to have you on your way."

"It's looking good. No mold, minimal parasites. The drought hasn't hurt. You're lucky you got a spring on the property. "

"It's still pushing plenty of water."

"Who else is coming to this shindig?" asked Skip.

"Well, Nate should be here any minute. He's bringing Annette and her daughter Sky. They're gonna stay a couple days to trim. Otto and his daughter Hunter. I heard Ulee is coming too. Do you know Ulee?"

"No, who's that?"

"She was a friend of George. She works at the deli at Amundson's."

"I don't go in there. The guy's a price gouger, what's his name, Carl? I do my shopping in Dillits."

Nate pulled in with Annette and Sky. The two ladies wore embroidered dresses, Nate his usual canvas slip-ons and loose trousers. He donned a green polyester shirt left over from a '70s golf outing. Upon arrival, he popped open the trunk, reached for a large watermelon, and handed it to Henry.

"Beer's in the fridge; wine's on the table. Aino, I got Calistoga's in the mini glass bottles you like. The cooler is full. Do not hesitate to help yourself."

Otto, Hunter, and Ulee appeared at the top gate. Otto wearing his USMC t-shirt tucked into the coaches' shorts. Hunter wore her cowboy outfit with turquoise jewelry, and her hair was slicked up like Elvis. Ulee wore a tie-dye, sandals, and loose-fitting cargo shorts. She sported a bandana with a Red-tailed Hawk feather Hunter had given her sticking out of the back.

Aino arrived holding his trumpet and wearing his finest Ben Davis green work pants. The ones for special occasions that had been altered at the ankles.

Annette and Sky were playing the Amish card game Blitz at the table on the deck. "Those are amazing dresses. Did you make those yourself?" asked Aino.

"Sky made them," said Annette. "Comfortable, too."

Sky was focused on the game and still wearing headphones as usual.

Otto, Ulee, Nate, Becca, Hunter, and Skip had gone to the swimming hole. Henry slathered sauce on the meat and roasted potatoes while tending to the BBQ.

"Dinner's gonna be ready at dusk, I told 'em," said Henry as Aino approached the grill.

"I haven't seen you with the horn in a while. Are you gonna blow some tunes tonight? Is your lip all healed up?"

"I think so. I'm getting the itch. I didn't think I'd ever want to play it again."

"Well, sometimes you gotta put it down for a while and let it return to you."

Aino blew a little number as Henry turned the chicken. Ba badda da da da da da da ba beed up ba beed up. "Salt peanuts…salt peanuts."

"The best trolling of an audience in history," said Henry.

Aino nodded in agreement.

"This chicken is about perfectly done." Henry stuck a meat thermometer into the center of the largest piece. "Can you get the others down at the swimming hole? Blow the trumpet for the dinner call?"

"Of course."

Four goats were munching away along the trail leading to the creek. Aino walked the pathway and heard the voices of the others through the forest. The goats were in heaven, chomping away at their favorite poison oak meal. Aino blew the riff to "Salt Peanuts."

"Is that the dinner horn?" asked Otto, treading water." I hope it's more than peanuts."

"Yup, Henry is taking the chicken off as we speak. Plenty of veggies for vegetarians," said Aino.

Nate perked up in approval, and Ulee came to life, splashing water at Otto with her foot. Hunter perched on a stone above them like an old west gunslinger standing watch. At the same time, Becca sat on a boulder, meditating. Otto put his clothes on, and they walked back to the house as a group. Ulee walked by Otto, and they were glowing with something unspoken between them.

I followed off the trail, creeping through the poison oak, hissing at the goats as I passed. I found my perch on the house and watched the others assemble near the BBQ. Chairs were set out, and the sun was nearly down.

Heat lightning flashed in the clouds on the ridge beyond. I was beginning to feel like a complete cat.

"You've cooked the perfect chicken, Henry," complimented Otto. "What did you do to it? It's like a smoky honey flavor."

"Well, I soaked those mesquite chips in brine and cayenne. Then, I poured honey all over them and added them to the coals. Shut the lid and let it smoke into the meat. "

"Remember the cowboy beans on the stove. Nate, I made a veggie version. In the crock pot. Check 'em out."

Nate walked to the kitchen and filled a bowl surrounding it with grilled asparagus and carrots.

I jumped off the roof to get a closer look. Otto saw me and said, "Come here little buddy; I got something good for you, my friend." He handed me a nice piece of thigh meat. I snatched it from him, and Otto tried to pet my back. I came around with a quick claw swipe to make a bloody scratch on his forearm.

"God dammit! You little bastard!"

"Yeah, Chaos doesn't let most people touch him. With a few exceptions," glancing towards Becca and Aino. "Sorry, Otto. I should have warned you."

"He's gotten me pretty good before; I should know better. My bad," said Otto

That's right. I don't like to be touched. And I don't like your crew cut and fuckin' mustache. Why don't you grow your hair back, Otto? Don't touch me with those greasy chicken fingers. It'll take me hours to get it out of my fur.

"Meow, Meow, Meow! That's what they all say," said Otto.

Who's they, Otto? Aramoana appeared with Luka. She held a large bowl of potato salad and wore a patch dress flowing down to her ankles. She had grown waist-long dreadlocks, and they were tied into a ponytail. I was annoyed because she must have recently gotten a facial tattoo that covered her chin in stripes and curled back to her jawline. I wish she hadn't done that. She's still my daughter, even though my life has changed into a different form. I tried to be cool about it, but I think she made a terrible choice. Who am I to say. I sound like an old man. Kid's today, right? But she's not a kid anymore. I'm supposed to be an open-minded artist, but I'm a cat now and don't like the face tattoo. Even if I were still human, I doubt I would like it. I know one day, she's gonna regret getting the tattoo on her face. She's not even Mauri! Talk about cultural appropriation! It's her body, her choice, but she's a part of me. What am I gonna do about it? Go hiss in the woods. She had Mehndi's art covering her hands, which was cool because it was temporary. Geez, Louis!

Luka held cherry pie in one hand and his skateboard in the other. He wore overalls with a San Francisco Giants baseball jersey underneath. His hair was cut into a mohawk.

"Hello, everybody. I'm Aramoana, and this is Luka."

Henry seemed surprised to see them but welcoming, nonetheless.

"Hey bud, can I get you a lemonade? How about you, Aramoana? What would you like to drink? Help yourself. There are plates over here and plenty of everything. Veggie, meat. Whatever you like. Glad you could make it. I thought you were going out of town."

"We changed our plans when you needed the goats. I wanna be around to make sure they don't get out of hand."

"Those are your babies," said Henry.

"Yes, those are my babies."

Aramoana loaded a veggie plate, and Luka piled on the ribs and chicken.

"Go easy on the meat Luka. One of each, Okay?"

He scowled and pretended not to hear.

"Hey there, kiddo," said Becca. "You like The Freak?"

"The Freak?"

"Lincecum. You like Tim Lincecum?"

"Yes! My favorite pitcher of all time."

Becca gave him a hip bump and said, "The Freak, uh huh. The Freak!" as the two giggled in Tim Lincecum solidarity.

"I don't understand the baseball obsession." Aramoana rolled her eyes.

"I appreciate you letting us have those goats for a few days," said Henry.

"Well, you better make sure you have secure fencing. They'll eat your entire crop in minutes."

"No worries. We've got the precious ladies secure."

Skip nodded reassuringly, munching on a rib.

"So, Skip, about light deprivation," Henry chimed in.

"I've got it covered, Henry. Hoop houses are ready at the patch near the wood mill. Should be able to wrap all that up by mid-September. If you want to start helping me pull the drapes, it would be a huge help, Aino?"

Aino nodded. "Anything you need, Skip. Just lemme know. Wow, your dogs are zonked out.

"Yeah, they sleep like puppies when I give them hash oil. "

Just as he said that, the two animals stirred. Still, they were sedated. Ilf lapped water from the bowl as Petrov lay motionless on his back. I sat on the roof of the woodpile house, watching them.

"What do you say we move this party inside?" said Henry as Luka did kickflips in the gravel driveway at dusk.

They all made their way into the great room of the main house. Henry got on the double bass while Aino sat in the rocking chair with his trumpet, meditating on the music, holding his instrument like a baby to his chest. Hunter improvised on piano, and Ulee nursed a small glass of brandy. Otto stood by the door, smiling and tapping his hands on the door frame. Aramoana ate a piece of the cherry pie, sitting at the trim table with Annette and Sky, who had already begun their work trimming buds. The hash ball on the table had grown to the size of a tennis ball.

I moved to the top of the refrigerator at the edge of the kitchen for a better view. Aino and Hunter took turns in the musical conversation. Luka strapped on the accordion and created an ongoing drone in the background. Otto grabbed two spoons from the kitchen drawer and kept a herky-jerky beat on his knees.

The combination of piano chords and accordion morphed into a unique-sounding dissonance. Luka couldn't make the accordion react as fast to the chords Hunter played. This created a delayed accent and lingering drone. Henry smiled, keeping the precise rhythm on the bass. He felt elated, and the jam evolved into several peaks and valleys. Even Aramoana belted out some vocal improv similar to Ella Fitzgerald, and she had the pipes to pull it off.

They put each other into a musical trance which lasted nearly several hours. Hunter's Elvis pompadour had fallen into a Misfit's devilock down the length of her face. Ulee sat with Annette and Sky at the table, sketching the scene with a pencil. The clarity of the drawing had a fantastic depth. She captured the moment in points, like a psychedelic photograph. The jam wound down, and Aino set his trumpet on the piano. Reaching for a Calistoga, he noticed the hash ball on the table.

"What if I tried a little of that?" he asked Henry.

"It's potent. Are you sure? I'm not gonna stop you. It's up to you, remember? "

"It's drawing me in. I just want a little nibble. It's a holiday."

"Suit yourself. It's not gonna make you drink, is it?"

"No, I think I'm safe here."

"I wouldn't recommend more than a tiny nibble."

Aino picked up the ball of hash from the table while Annette shook her head, like, boy you're making a huge mistake. Sky didn't pay it any mind. Aino felt the weight of the hash ball in his hands. The hash from hundreds of hours of trimming buds. The hash from the fingers of the trimmers.

"It's gotta be a few pounds!" said Aino.

He scraped off a little nibble and chased it with bubbly water, then joined the others outside to watch the heat lightning sparking in the clouds like fireworks. The sky opened, and the Big Dipper came out through the patches of clouds.

"Is it gonna rain tonight?" asked Becca.

"I doubt it. It's heat lightning," said Skip.

TWELVE PACK TO GO

Red Necklace hit the stage, and Carl had already lived up to his full drunken potential. Slurring and weaving. He waited impatiently at the end of the bar for another drink. Snapping his fingers trying to get Holly's attention.

"Clapping and snapping will get you nowhere, Carl. Can't you see I'm like three deep here? I'll get to you when I get to you."

"I'm a regular god dammit! I spent a lot of money in this shit hole!"

"Alright, what do ya want, Carl?"

"Sex on the beach."

"You want a UTI chaser? We don't serve those here. How bout a real drink, Carl?" smiled Holly.

"Well. Ah, Hmm? Let me think? What's your favorite drink to make? Surprise me," as Carl intentionally slowed

Holly down.

She poured a shot of well whiskey for him. "There you go, Carl. It's on me. My favorite drink."

The place was packed, and the musicians were nearly in tune. Five men with beards, lipstick, thick blue eyeshadow, cowboy hats, and boots. The frontman wore a silk scarf with hearts, and the drummer had a gong. Their silhouettes appeared in a haze of stage smoke and started off the set with "Hold on Loosely," a 38 Special cover.

Sheriff Rick Johnson smiled wildly from the side of the stage. His favorite song of all time. He sang along at the top of his lungs, completely coked up and ecstatic. He rocked out with them for another half a song before realizing he needed another bump of cocaine. He started feeling through his pockets, looking for the little baggie. He panicked. It wasn't there! He quickly made his way to the bathroom and started searching the urine-soaked floor in the stalls for his little lost friend. He had to find it. The band faded away from his mind. All he could think of was his little lost baggie of blow.

"Sweet Melissa" played in the background, and the crowd roared. Dufur noticed Rick had gone to the bathroom and followed him there. Rick searched behind the toilet in the stall. He found it!

"I knew you were here, baby. I just knew it!" he gloated, not noticing Dufur standing behind him. He sat on the stall floor with the door wide open, pulled a key from his pocket, took a big bump, and leaned back against the wall by the toilet. Dufur had photographed the whole thing. He snapped a final photo of the sheriff on the floor snorting the bump.

"Gotcha," he whispered and quickly put his phone away. Rick looked up after taking the blast and noticed Dufur hovering above him.

"What the fuck, Dufur. You gonna help me up?"

"Yeah, bro. You got some for me?"

"Of course. Don't do it all. Baby bumps, Dufur. Baby bumps!"

Holly had a little break behind the bar as the band reached their Grand finale.

She stretched her neck and took a deep breath. The night had reached its peak and began to trickle out.

She nodded to Hector as he left. Implying he'd sold out of all his cocaine. She smiled at him.

Carl passed out in the back corner booth. At closing time, Holly found him snoring.

"Wake up, Carl! We're closed!"

Carl wasn't moving. "Where'd your friends go, Carl? You gotta leave now. What? Did you piss yourself? Dude! Get out of here! Come on man, Wake up!"

She got a pitcher of cold water and dumped it on him.

Carl came to. "What the fuck are you doing? You bitch!"

"Get out of here, Carl! We're closed! The band has already loaded out."

"Can't I sleep here tonight?"

"Fuck no, Carl! If you're too drunk to drive, go sleep in your office across the street."

"Wait, you're not the boss of me, lady!"

"Get the hell out; we're closed!"

"What are you gonna do? Call the cops? Rick ain't gonna do shit."

"I dunno, they left a long time ago. Just leave, please!"

"Alright Holly. Gimme a twelve-pack for the road."

"No! We're closed!"

Carl went behind the bar and grabbed a twelve-pack of Coors Light.

"Get out of there, Carl!"

"Put it on my tab!" he ran out the door with it as Holly chased after for a moment but realized it wasn't worth it. She felt relieved he'd finally left and locked the door behind him.

Carl got into his truck and peeled onto HWY 101, driving in the wrong lane and heading north. He pulled off onto Lost Creek Road and popped open a beer

PLENTY OF ROOM

Nearly an hour passed, and Aino felt no effects from the hash. He snuck back inside and grabbed another little nibble about the size of a Hershey's kiss. Then he went to stretch out in the solar shed.

Ulee, Hunter, and Otto left up the driveway, and Otto shouted, "Adios and a happy 4th to you, my friends! Muchas Gracias! Until we meet again!"

Henry sat in a lawn chair on the porch, watching the Big Dipper and smiling. Nate sat beside him, enjoying the sky and the sea of stars.

Hunter walked ahead of her dad and Ulee. She left them alone, feeling they needed to talk.

"Have you told her anything about me?" asked Ulee.

"No, I haven't said a word. Hunter doesn't know a thing," said Otto.

"I thought you would have said something by now. "

"She still thinks Carolina's her mom. I'm worried she's gonna freak out."

"Well, she's gotta find out sometime. She's fully grown. We gotta tell her. I'm connecting with her, Otto."

"I know. I can see you two are hitting it off. Like mother…"

"And daughter. Exactly. I mean mother and kinda like a son."

"Yeah, she's got both goin' on. "

"She's one of a kind, Otto. I really love her."

"Yeah, me too, but I worry she's gonna hate us for not telling her."

"Hey, you two. Are you gonna take all night?" yelled Hunter from the deck of the A-Frame.

The two made it into the driveway's light and held hands.

"Wait, what's going on here? Holding hands?"

"You're welcome to stay here, Ulee. Plenty of room."

"No thanks, Otto. I can't sleep anywhere but in my own bed. I'd toss and turn all night."

"Suit yourself, but you know you're welcome. Hunter told me you might need some work. Do you wanna come to work with us? No pressure, we could use another hand, up to you."

"I would, Otto. You know I got fired from Amundson's?"

"Yeah, Hunter told me."

"I've been at the store too long. Forty years."

"Holy moly! Really?"

"I didn't think I'd ever leave."

"We have the work if you want it."

"I don't need to think about it. I'm in! Thank you, Otto. But when will you grow your hair back and stop looking like a cop?" Ulee nudged his shoulder and smiled.

"Don't you like a man with a 'stache?

"No, not really; the hair doesn't matter. At least you still got some, unlike most men your age. When could I start?"

"Tomorrow, whenever you like. Plenty to do. Always plenty to do."

"Well, Hunter? You wanna hit the road?"

"Yeah. Sure. Did you two come to an agreement? Are you gonna work with us or what?"

"Yup!"

"Wonderful!" said Hunter.

"Good night, Otto. I'll see ya tomorrow then?

"Bright and early. It'll be nice having you here."

Hunter and Ulee climbed into the Jeep and returned to the RV park, leaving Otto alone in the A-Frame. He stared at the stars while the heat lightning lit the room of redwood walls, showing the knots in the wood with each flash. Hunter and Ulee drove carefully through the canyon to the summit. Hunter pulled over, noticing another vehicle speeding up the hill from below.

"Gonna let this person pass. All the drunks coming back from the bar. I wanna give 'em plenty of room. Sorry if I drive like a granny."

A BUMPER ON THE ROAD

Ulee and Hunter were parked at the summit as Carl sped by in his monster truck. As he passed, he threw a bottle out the window, leaving them in the dust.

"Gonna kill somebody driving like that, you asshole!" yelled Hunter.

He failed to slow at the first hairpin, slammed on the brakes, and went off the road, scraping the whole side of his truck on a string of boulders. He came to a stop in the ditch.

"Fuck this shit!" he screamed and punched the roof of the truck. "BALLS!"

He slammed another beer and revved the engine, but it wouldn't move forward. Back and forth, he rocked it, cursing all the while. It broke free of the ditch in reverse and popped out onto the road. He bashed into another stone behind him, damaging the rear bumper and snapping the connecting bolt on the driver's side. It hung down to the road, scraping the gravel as he put the truck into drive again. Finally, the bumper broke free and lay blocking the middle of the road.

"Cock suckin' mother fuckin'!"

Pulling into the driveway, he popped another Coors Light, but it slipped from his hands and spilled into the crotch of his trousers. His distracted driving resulted in a collision with the weight bench, which pushed it into the garage wall, breaking the sheetrock. The weight rack bent into the form of the truck's front bumper. He passed out in the driver's seat with his head on the steering wheel and the horn honking. His own George Jones song finally came true.

GOODNIGHT ULEE

Ulee and Hunter made it safely back to the RV park. Hunter gave Ulee a big hug.

"I hope you have a good night's sleep, darling."

Ulee couldn't find the words as they embraced.

"Is there something you'd like to say?" asked Hunter.

"I'm so thankful. So thankful to know you." Tears welled up in her eyes. She couldn't say it. "Well. Will I see you in the morning for tea? Before we go to work?"

"I'll be over the first thing. Good night, Ulee."

"Good night, sweetheart."

PSYCHEDELIC SAWDUST

Aino shone his headlamp on the door of the solar shack. He entered the room and crawled inside his sleeping bag. He had built the bunk in the side room of the solar shed to look out the window before he went to sleep. It had a view of the canyon.

He found the Great Bear in the sky. Ursa Major. Tracing it with his eyes, Aino imagined it coming to life, lunging down towards him. At this point, the hash started kicking in. The sky came alive behind his eyelids as he closed them. He thought he could sleep through the night and dream the visions of the hash, but it wasn't to be.

Aino started spinning, and the stars were too bright to look at. He sat in bed, and the motion slowed to a crawl.

Like he was suspended in gelatin. A translucent dark gel that held his limbs in place. He noticed a distinct pain in his abdomen and bladder. He could pop like a tick at any moment. He'd overeaten.

Aino took a deep breath, lay back down, closed his eyes again, and tried to force himself into sleep. Images flashed through his mind. Short bits of film suspended in a dark void. He could control the images and scenes from the past. His mother smiled and held a spoon of spaghetti-o's. A goose flew at him at the creek as a child. He could stop the film and rewind it. Playing it repeatedly. The moment he broke his hand on the gym floor while playing volleyball. The white bone sticks through the skin. He homed in on the image of the bone with the blood oozing and sucking back into the wound. Then, the pictures of people he knew. Some he didn't, but still seemed familiar. The faces mixed with dogs, cats, and goats. The faces blend into one another and the animals. The image of Christ integrated into his mother's smile, then the Buddha, then Giuseppe in a boxer stance, Chaos the cat, and Muhammad Ali.

Images quickly blurred into a singular face of light. The brightest color Aino had ever seen without burning his eyes. The face of light exploded into the dark void, and the film scattered everywhere, leaving him without control of the picture. He yearned to backtrack to the simple clips of time he had control over, but it became impossible.

Aino sat up again and tried to breathe deeply but couldn't fill his lungs. The lingering stars from the explosion mingled in the void like fireflies but moved further away from the picture. Adrift in outer space and into the slots of the existing stars. Aino felt a pressure below and needed to use the bathroom.

He began the intrepid journey to the outhouse. One endless step at a time. He fell to his knees and grabbed hold of the grass for fear of being sucked out into the sky as if gravity had reversed itself. He slowly journeyed down the hill. Crawling on his hands and knees. He counted the crawling steps one by one and breathed laboriously with the pressure swelling in his bowels. He saw eyes in the poison oak. It was me, Chaos the cat, no longer George, no longer anything but watching him. Watching all of it. He knew I knew everything now.

Aino tried to crawl away faster, but I only mocked him in his clunky human form. His dull, frumpy self. His mixed-up mind. His loss of love and no purpose to living. An amoeba now, trying to find the shit house. He crawled onward toward the door. I jumped up on the translucent corrugated roof. He could see the form of me sitting above him with the moonlight full now and high in the sky. Aino sat on the seat and attempted to relieve the pressure. The pressure of a lifetime of consumption built up in his body, scraping the lining of his insides and shitting it out into the plastic bucket. All of it came out like the shedding of a snake from within.

The entire body with all of its cells shedding at once. The entirety of his memory is cleared into the plastic bucket. Aino groaned and panted as if he were giving birth. My serpentine tail wound around in the dim light of the moon above him. Aino continued to push, but nothing came out. It drained him. All of this wasted time. All of it came out as he felt it burning from his asshole to his lungs. From the inside of his skull through his fingertips and even trying to escape through his belly button. Aborting his former self and turning inside out. He felt the exposure to the nerve endings, which normally didn't feel air. The cold burn of it all. It slowly subsided and slunk back into his asshole. He sat motionless and cried. Sobbing on the pot. I jumped away and ran off into the forest. Aino found his feet. He wanted to wipe his ass, but there was nothing to wipe.

Nothing in the bucket. Only sawdust.

SUMMER FESTIVAL

Henry drove into the field a few miles north of Dias Verdez on the weekend of The Beatrice Bear Music Festival. He figured he'd visit some old friends and try to enjoy some live music. There were thousands of cars and campers. John Prine headlined the festival.

He entered the grounds, and the temperature exceeded a hundred degrees while mist sprayed from tents that lined the pathway to the stages. Old Thyme McGillicutty Swanson resonated from the Green Man stage. The up-and-coming Americana sensation.

"What's this new genre of music?" thought Henry. Then the next band came out. Bearded guys with plaid shirts and vests stomping around in the heat with banjos and mandolins. The Brine Mountain Boys played the same sounding songs as the Old Branch Picnic Party. It could have been the same band. He couldn't tell them apart. They were dressed like they'd just stepped out of the Dust Bowl.

Henry got more and more disgusted with each song. "What a pretentious load of shit!"

Henry's anxiety started to spiral out of control. He reached for his weed but had left it in the Suburban. He wanted to throw something at the stage, then scream in protest and call the art police to start writing out tickets.

"Genericana is more like it!" He muttered and walked on through the festival grounds in a huff, embracing his inner curmudgeon.

A cop on a golf cart almost ran over his foot. He was eating a jumbo turkey leg and trying to drive simultaneously.

"Sorry, partner!"

Henry tried to hang on for John Prine, but it would

be four more hours of torture. Drunk kids with glow sticks around their necks. Techno music blaring from tents. Naked elderly people painting their bodies to look like lizards. A geriatric man who could have been the real Jim Morrison returned after faking his death to proclaim. "I AM THE REAL LIZARD KING!"

Henry nearly sprinted back to the Suburban for a quick toke of weed and a beer from the cooler, but the turkey leg cop in the golf cart came racing towards him.

"What are you doing bud?"

"I'm grabbin' a beer. "

"Sorry, pal, but you can't drink beer in the parking lot. You gotta go into the festival and buy beer. "

"Are you serious?"

"Yup. Those are the rules. Thanks, buddy!"

"Who made those rules? I used to know Beatrice Bear. She's dead now, but we were friends. I put the road into this place. She wouldn't like these rules! In fact, it would've pissed her off not allowing someone to have a beer in the parking lot. It's not what Beatrice would have wanted. Do you realize that?"

"Look, man, I don't care if you knew Beatrice Bear. If you wanna give me trouble, we can go there, but I suggest you go back to the festival to buy a beer, or you can take your rig and go home. I didn't make the rules." The cop took another bite from his oversized turkey leg.

"Hey, ah, ok." Henry smiled, "Guess I'll be goin'."

ELECTRIC JACK HAMMER

"Carl! Mr. Amundson! Are you okay? "shouted Billy.

Carl snored with his head on the steering wheel. A large welt had formed on his forehead. The can of Coors Light he'd spilled into his crotch had dried onto the truck seat and mixed with his urine. His Oakley Blade sunglasses were caught up on the turning signal, and the stretch band left a line across his cheek. The battery had drained from the horn honking all night, which had stopped when Billy arrived.

"Are you okay, Mr. Amundson?"

"It's Carl. It's Carl, you fuck! I mean, call me Carl, Billy. Sorry, what are you doing here?"

"I'm here to work. Remember? Something about a drainpipe."

"Oh yeah, Shit! I forgot."

"Do you need medical attention?"

"No, no. I'm alright." Carl moaned when he looked in the rearview mirror," Ahhh, man!"

"Your truck is messed up. I think I saw your bumper on the road. What happened?"

"It's those goddamn Mexicans. They were hippies; they jumped out at me in the middle of the night. Out of nowhere! Illegals. They ran me off the road. Those fuckin' Mexican hippies!"

Billy knew he was out of his mind.

"Gimme a minute here," Carl checked the damage on his monster truck. "Oh no. What did I do?" he whispered under his breath. His identity! His truck! "I mean, what did they do!? It was them. Those Mexican hippies! Alright, Billy, your first job of the day is to go get the bumper you saw on the road and bring it back."

"Okay, Mr. Amundson."

"Call me Carl, Billy! How many fucking times do I have to tell you?"

Billy fetched the bumper from the road and returned in minutes while Carl realized his battery was drained.

"You got any beer, Billy? Oh wait, I still have some. You want one?"

"No thanks, Carl." Billy was thinking about a way to get the hell out of there.

"Hey, can you pull your truck up to mine? I gotta get a jump. I left the lights on, and it drained the battery."

"Sure, Carl. I'll pull around." Billy returned with his jumper cables.

"Let's let it charge for a while," said Carl. "Come with me, and I'll show you what I want you to do today."

The two circled the house to the backyard.

"I want you to install a drainpipe from the corner of the patio. It's been ponding up right by the house. Funneling off the roof into the corner. So, the drain will go right in the corner. You gotta chip away through the stone and bury it about a foot down. It doesn't have to be too deep. A straight line down to the tree line. Make sense? Follow me to the garage, and I'll show you where the tools are."

Carl limped his way around the house, and Billy could smell the piss and beer odor emanating from him.

"I've got this electric mini jackhammer thing. It works well for chipping stones. Have you ever used one of these?" Carl ran an extension cord from the garage. "The bits are already on it. Run a line from the corner, and it's only about ten feet. That's the hard part. The yard will be easy. Go ahead, Billy, try it out." Carl popped open another Coors Light and stood there swaying like he could pass out again any second.

Billy got to work with the jackhammer, and Carl went to bed. He popped a sleeping pill and slept until dusk. Coming to a groggy awakening as Billy had finished chipping through the stone patio.

"Wow, Billy. Good work. You're pretty strong, aren't you? You take after your dad. Wanna beer?"

Billy declined with a head shake.

"Come on, man. One beer won't kill you."

"No thanks, Carl. I'm in training, and I gotta drive."

"You need to take it easy on all that shit. Partyin's better than football."

"Well, I'm trying to get into UCLA. I can party when I get there."

"I'm just kiddin'. It's good you're not drinking. I'm proud of you. When's your first game? I wanna come and watch you as quarterback for the Dragons."

"Friday after Labor Day."

"I'll be there front and center for sure. You know, I used to be a Dragon," Carl made the claw motion with his right hand.

Billy looked at him vacantly.

"I still gotta pick up the drainpipe. Can you come back tomorrow? "

"Not 'till next week."

"Okay, next week, Billy. I'll be ready for you. Say, Billy. Lemme know if you ever wanna run through some plays. You know, I used to be a pretty good football player in high school. I know the whole playbook, man."

"Oh, really. Did you know coach Brenneman?"

"Coach, who?"

"Brenneman. I think he was around during your time. "

"Doesn't ring a bell, but like I said, I have pretty good hands if you wanna toss it around the ball and hit the weights. I could be your trainer or your partner."

There was an awkward silence.

"I like to work out at the high school."

"You know I train nearly every day, "Carl took off his shirt and flexed for Billy.

Billy felt a little weirded out by Carl's exhibition.

"I've been doin' it for years. Check out my back," Carl said as he turned to flex his back muscles for Billy.

"Well, I think I better go now, Carl. My mom's making dinner."

"Okay, Billy. I'll see you at the store next week. We have a date. Next week, work out and finish up the drain. Right? "

"Yeah, Carl. See you at the store."

Billy got in his truck and slowly pulled out of sight.

"I'll see you next week. Oh, and thanks for charging up my battery."

He waved as Billy's taillights faded down the driveway.

Carl went to the living room and extracted the videotape from the security camera he had positioned by the back patio. He poured himself a tall glass of vodka with orange juice and watched Billy break through his patio's stones.

"Instant replay! Good work, Billy. Hit it, Billy! Put your back into it! Mmm. Jackhammer time. Yeah!"

HIATUS

"I guess we're gonna be heading back to the city now," said Nate.

"Glad you guys could make it up. I hope you got some good photos," replied Henry.

"I think so. I took a few rolls of the jam session. I'll take the film to the dark room this week."

"I like the fact you're still using film. Everybody's using those digital cameras nowadays. Nothing like a real picture," said Henry.

"Speaking of," Nate pulled a manila folder from his backpack. "Here's some shots I took last harvest. Some good ones of you. I like the one of you standing atop the Corolla by the creek."

"It's like I'm floating in the darkness the way it's exposed. Cool shot! May I keep this? I wanna give it to Luka."

"Sure, man."

"Well, I think we're gonna take off. I'm gonna give Becca a ride back, too," said Nate.

"Oh, Becca's leaving? I thought she'd be staying around a while longer."

"No, I've decided to return to the city until harvest. Take a little break," she appeared, holding her backpack ready.

"You've got the garden humming, Becca. You've done a fantastic job here. I can keep up with the weeding. "

"The irrigation's on timers,"said Becca.

"I didn't know, thanks for the heads up. Well, all of a sudden, it's gonna get a little quieter around here. It's ok. I can take it, "Henry looked a little blue at the sudden departure.

"I'm gonna be back in a few weeks," said Becca.

"Yeah, me too," said Nate. "I wanna help with the light-dep harvest."

"Well, I could use a hand. Love to have ya," Henry lightened up a little.

"Thanks, Henry," said Becca.

Annette and Sky appeared at the door with their bags.

"You all set?" said Annette to Nate.

"Yup."

"How many Pablos this time?"

"Not sure how many this time around. "

"Holy moly, you gals are fast. I barely noticed you working all this time with all the festivities. Gimme a minute, and we'll settle up," said Henry.

He strolled to the garage and pulled the old refrigerator from the wall. The back side had a secret door, and he opened the hatch. Inside were large stacks of cash. He peeled off their payment and a few extra for a holiday bonus.

"Here you go, ladies, and I threw in some extra. I sincerely appreciate your work," He smiled and handed them each a roll of hundreds.

"Thank you, Henry. Much love to you, my brother," said Annette as Sky stared vacantly off to the forest.

The group departed in Nate's car, leaving only the sound of the crows cawing on the branches surrounding the compost pit. Henry had gathered the scraps of meat from the night before and presented a feast for the birds. The Ravens were even in the mix. I watched them fight for the leftovers but was too full to compete with them.

Henry placed a bowl of meat on the porch for me in the morning. It was too much to handle, but I scarfed it down anyway. I lay in the shade by the water pipe, grooming myself, and then fell asleep, waking up at dusk. A quiet stillness came down upon the farm.

Aino had only just woken up. He'd stayed in bed all day, hoping to move, but he felt paralyzed under the thumb of the hash ball. Finally, alive again, he made the walk to the main house.

PRECISE MARKSMANSHIP

Due to the intense heat, I continued hanging around the shaded parts of the house. The Schieffelbein place got a little too hot in the attic. I ditched out of there. Besides, the sound of machine gun fire became a nuisance. I went to check it out for myself, so I followed the sound up and around the mountain. The furthest I'd gone from the farm since my arrival. It's a bit risky for fear of skunks and mountain lions. A porcupine scared the crap out of me, but nothing happened between us.

I climbed into a manzanita tree within view of the gunslinger. Carl stood dressed up like a commando doing a military drill by himself. Saluting to an imaginary drill sergeant. He targeted two watermelons placed on fence posts and stood about twenty yards away.

He fired a full clip from his machine gun but failed to hit either one. This was odd because you'd think with so many bullets flying, at least one of them would have connected with the melons. He reloaded and then managed to knock out both. Carl punched at the sky in celebration.

I didn't wanna get too close because he'd already

tried to shoot me once before. At least I found out what all the racket was about.

LIGHT DEPRIVATION

Each day, Aino and Skip pulled drapes over the light-deprivation hoop houses a little earlier to mimic sunset after Solstice. They had begun harvesting the buds in late July and had already accumulated over a hundred pounds. The garage had been set up as a drying center with wires strung from each side. The Schieffelbein house was also used for drying. Dehumidifiers and fans blew on the plants suspended upside down from the cables to expedite the process. Portable gasoline generators provided the additional power needed to run these machines twenty-four-seven. They were set up behind the garage to buffer the noise.

Henry walked the rows to make the final determination as to when to harvest them and trim them down further into individual buds. The final trimming would be done later. The hot and dry dog days of summer rolled on, and the last light-deprivation plants were completed by mid-September.

Nate returned to the farm with Becca for the final push into harvest. Skip and Nate worked the upper patches. Henry, Aino, and Becca worked the lower areas and the furthest patch next to the Schieffelbein house. Aino had been noticing the airplane again. Once a week, around noon, it would swoop over the farm.

"Have you noticed the plane, Henry?" asked Aino. "I saw it once a few months ago, but it's coming back every couple days now."

"Nothing to worry about. They do it every year around this time."

"Why do they keep doing the flyovers? Who is it?"

"Fish and Game. The Police. I don't know. They work

as a team. Trying to put raids together. They take aerial photos for proof we're breaking the rules. It used to be worse. They're only going through the motions. Trying to justify their monthly budgets. We have the right amount per patch. There could be a few extras, but they can't see it from that high. We're in the ballpark. You put the permit laminates up on each patch, right? Even the top patch?" asked Henry.

"They're all posted," said Aino.

"Hey, ah, If anything ever happens, it's on me, okay. Remember, I take the heat if they decide to come up with some bullshit reason for a raid. You're a private contractor doing carpentry," said Henry. "If they arrest me, I'll be out the same day. I've got the top lawyer for this shit. "

CARL'S SMOOTHIE

Billy returned a few weeks later to complete the drainage project. Carl stacked the drainpipes behind the garage and instructed Billy to dig the trench to the tree line.

The grass surrounding the Amundson house had turned a light brown, and the soil underneath felt like stone. It took a whole day for Billy to dig to the edge of the forest. The next morning, he laid all the pipes by early afternoon.

While carrying the tools back to the shed, Billy turned to find Carl watching him from the patio.

"When's your first game? You excited?" asked Carl.

Billy shrugged and scratched his arm. Then, he held up his hand, giving the peace sign for 2 days.

"You don't seem really pumped on it, buddy. Where's your enthusiasm?"

Billy didn't answer.

"If you wanna throw the ball around a little later, I'm

game."

"Well, I need to clean up and head back. My mom's expecting me."

"Say, Billy, can you do me a quick favor before you go? I need you to spot me in the garage. I'm gonna go heavy today. Just leave the tools; I can take care of that later."

Billy kept his distance but followed him to the weight bench. Carl took off his shirt and started hyping himself up with heavy breathing and pulsing pssshhtt-pssshhhts. He checked himself in the large mirror by the bench.

"Okay, I'm fuckin' ready! Spot me, Billy."

Billy noticed the warp on the bench from the night Carl drove his truck into it.

Carl jerked the weight from the rack and dropped it down to his chest. His face turned beet red, and his veins popped from his forehead. He groaned, but he couldn't move it. Billy reached down to help him.

"Don't you fuckin' touch it! I got this, Billy!"

Billy backed off while Carl strained. The weight teetered back and forth as Carl's body began to shake. He was losing it, but Billy tried to help again, reaching for the bar to bring it back up.

"Don't touch it, I got it!" Carl spat.

The weight went sideways and crashed to the floor. One of the plates rolled out of the garage and into the yard. The bench fell sideways, sending Carl to the floor. He landed on his sunglasses and cracked the frames.

"You okay, Carl?"

"I had it, Billy! What the fuck! Help me up! God Dammit! Now my glasses are fucked! Why didn't you spot me?"

"I tried to, but you told me to stop."

"Shit! Don't you know how to spot someone?"

"Sorry. Mr. Amundson," Billy took notice of the poster on the ceiling, "What's the poster on the ceiling?"

"Judas Priest, man! Don't you know who the Priest is?"

"Why do you have it on the ceiling?"

"I use it to get pumped. You want a smoothie?"

"I guess. What kinda of smoothie?"

"Weight gainer smoothie. You gotta put some meat on your bones if you're gonna be a varsity QB. Follow me, Billy. It's too hot for this shit right now, anyway. Let's go in the house."

Carl broke out the blender in the kitchen. Smoothie time.

"I'm gonna make a mix of fruit and veggies. You like real milk, right? None of that soy shit. Protein powder. Raw honey. Chicken!"

"Chicken? I don't know about chicken in a smoothie," said Billy.

"I'm just foolin'. No chicken, Billy, protein powder. This is the magic right here. Go have a seat in the living room. Take a load off, man; you've been working hard. It's done, right?

"What's done?"

"The trench, the drain, what the fuck you think I'm talkin' 'bout?"

"Yeah, the drain's all in."

"When it cools down a little more, wanna toss the ball? Go through some plays?"

"Well, I gotta go soon, Carl. My mom's expecting me back."

"It's always your mom and dinner. Look, you're still on the clock, Billy. I'm paying you double, remember? So, relax, buddy. Why not milk the clock? Do you want to work out a trade, or would you like cash?

Billy sat on the couch below the stuffed Musk Ox Carl's dad shot in Alaska.

"Cash is good. What's this animal above me?"

"Musk Ox. I shot it on my last expedition to Alaska. Have you ever been up there?"

"No, I wish."

"Alaska's no joke, Billy. You gotta be in top form to be messing around in the woods up there. Nature has the upper hand if you know what I mean?"

"What do you mean?"

"You know I go all over the world, right?" Carl pointed to a Zebra head on the opposite wall. "I like to hunt with no clothes on."

"What?"

"Animals aren't scared of you if you have no clothes on. It's easier to track 'em if you rub mud all over your body. Ever been hunting like that, Billy?"

"No, I've never gone hunting."

"You mean your dad never took you huntin'? I've got to talk to him. I know he's a busy man, but jeez. He needs to find some time for his son. I'll take you hunting."

"I wish he had more time."

"Want me to show you?" Carl got closer.

"I should go. I gotta be back."

"Wait, Billy, hang on, bud. Have you ever shot a machine gun?"

"No, my mom doesn't want me shooting guns."

"Well, she'll think twice next time you have a home invasion. I've trained myself to pinpoint accuracy. I'm like a sniper with a machine gun. That's a deadly combo. Check out that Mule deer I shot in New Mexico."

Billy looked confused.

"It's over there. The eight-pointer. Ain't you ever seen a Mule deer?"

Carl discretely pulled a baggie of pills from the drawer and threw several into the smoothie blender while Billy checked out the taxidermy.

"That fur hide you're standing next to is from a 1200-pound Grizzly I killed on the Kenai Peninsula. I emptied a full clip from a .44 magnum, and it kept coming at me! Lucky, I sharpened my buck knife, or I'm not sure I'd be standing here today."

Even Billy didn't believe this line of bullshit, and he rolled his eyes.

"What, you don't think I'm telling you the truth?"

Carl set the blender on high and popped open a beer for himself.

"How bout a happy hour smoothie, Billy? A little reward for a hard day's workout?"

"What's in a happy hour smoothie?"

"A little shot of vanilla vodka, I won't tell your dad."

"No, Carl. I signed a contract with the coach. No drugs or alcohol. I'll get cut from the team if they find out."

"I ain't telling. It's just you and me here, buddy," Carl winked and smiled.

"I gave my word. Sorry, Carl."

"I was just testing you, kid; you're in training. Good work, you passed. Besides, I wouldn't want your dad to find out I fed you liquor. " Carl handed Billy the smoothie, "He'd put me in handcuffs, " drink up, buddy. Good job today!"

Billy slurped down the smoothie, and Carl watched him take every sip. He played a video of himself shooting his machine gun, dressed in full tactical gear.

"This is the first day I got her," Carl said. "Look, I nailed both melons on the first shot."

The video showed Carl smiling and stroking his machine gun. Then, thrusting it out at an imaginary foe, firing away instantly, blasting the melons. His belly jiggled with each round. The edit made him out to be an expert shot.

"Hell, fuck this, I'm gonna show her to you," said Carl.

"Show me what?" Billy drank another gulp of the smoothie.

"My AR-15, hang on."

Carl disappeared into the back room and returned carrying the machine gun. He had taken off all his clothes except his G-string underwear and stood posing with the gun. His beer belly hung over his banana hammock.

"What do you think of this, Billy?"

"What are you doing?"

"Getting ready to go shooting. I told you, it's better in the buff."

"Better in the buff? This is weird, Carl. I'm gonna go now."

"Life's weird, I know it. But I think I know what you need, Billy. Your shoulders must be sore. You should probably take off your shirt."

"Stop Carl." Billy slurred and then shouted, "Stop!"

"I'm gonna get another drink and let you calm down, chief! Then we're gonna go shoot this thing. It's better with no clothes on, I swear. You can feel the power."

Billy felt a tingly sensation come over him in the chair and started to fade out. Carl returned with another drink.

"Feel this gun, Billy. You wanna shoot it?" Carl held Billy's arm while he passed out. He rubbed his hand on the gun. Carl ran his fingers through Billy's hair and watched his face, ensuring he wouldn't wake up. His personal video still played, and a scene came up of himself bench-pressing after the gun sequence. He lost interest in Billy when he saw himself on the screen.

"God, look at how ripped I was. I was seventeen in this video!" Billy started snoring.

Carl took another big swig and lay in the chair, watching himself. The sequence ended, so he rewound the video. He pressed slow-mo and watched himself slowly lift the weight he had dropped that day.

"See, Billy, that's how you do it with no spot needed. Are you seeing this? Why are you passed out, fuckin' lightweight?" He watched it again and fell asleep next to Billy. He didn't wake up until sunrise and realized he'd slept through his chance.

"Fuck," he whispered. Carl poked at the sleeping boy.

"You up bud? Are you awake?"

Billy leaned back, snoring.

"How bout a nice shoulder rub, Billy? Are you sore from yesterday? All your training. How 'bout a body-on-body rub?" Carl was grinding up against Billy's face with his bulge, and Billy awoke from being zombified.

"What the fuck are you doing, Carl?" said Billy in a groggy haze.

"Don't worry, Billy. It's good to keep your mind right for sports. This helps."

"Get off me! Carl! Get off me!" Billy slurred and tried to get up.

"Billy, stay down and be calm. This feels good, doesn't it?"

"Get off of me!"

"Don't resist, you little bitch! Don't resist me!" he slapped Billy on the head.

Billy pushed him off and fell to the floor. He tried to get up but knocked over the end table lamp and fell again.

"If you broke my lamp, you'll pay, Billy!" Carl lunged at him on the floor and tried to pull his shorts down. Billy squirmed away and staggered to his feet. Found his way out the door and started running towards the woods in a delirium.

"Get back here, you little fucker! You're still on the clock! I ain't paying you if you leave like this!"

Billy reached the forest, and Carl cut his foot on a broken beer bottle in the yard. Billy ran down the steep slope towards Lost Creek Road. He had a hard time keeping his balance and fell from the cliff in a panic, tumbling through the bushes and snapping his ankle in the fall. He landed near the edge of the road and passed out again.

BROKEN ANKLE

Early the following day, Aino ran to the dump in the old Dodge truck, pulling a trailer. He came around the bend and noticed a human head sticking out of the bushes on the side of the road. He stopped the truck and got out to find Billy lying in the bushes, snoring away. At first glance, he appeared to be bleeding from his forehead, but the kid had landed in a raspberry bush. Crushed berries stained the side of his head, and he was actually bleeding badly from his ankle.

"Hey, man. You okay? "Billy didn't answer. Aino nudged him a little. "You alright, man?"

Billy's groaned, "I think my ankle's broken."

Aino helped him out of there.

"Damn, man. Lemme get you to the clinic. You're bleeding bad," Aino helped him into the truck. Billy moaned in agony, "What's your name, man?"

"Billy. B-B-Billy Johnson"

"Don't worry, man. Just hang on, bud." Billy passed out again in the passenger seat.

Aino noticed the scrapes on Billy's arms and legs, and the ankle looked like a compound fracture. It was swollen up like a grapefruit. A deep patch of blood was dripping through his sock where the bone had punctured the skin. He'd lost a lot of blood, and his shoe was soaked with it.

"Just a few more miles, my friend." He pulled into the clinic parking lot and went inside for help while Billy lay in the truck's front seat. The staff came to help with a rolling cot, and they wheeled him inside.

"Are you his father?" asked the nurse.

"No, I've never seen him before. He says his name is Billy Johnson."

"Oh, it's Billy! Sheriff Rick Johnson's boy."

"I found him passed out on the side of Lost Creek Road."

SHERIFF ESCORT

Sheriff Rick Johnson had several voice messages when he woke up with a pounding hangover. Pizza boxes and empty liquor bottles surrounded his lumpy bed. He listened to the first message and dressed into his wrinkled uniform, forgetting to zip up his fly. He raced out the door and reached the clinic in minutes.

"He told us to call you," said the nurse.

"Well, what the fuck do you expect me to do about it?" sneered Rick.

"We don't have the facilities here to deal with his ankle. He said he didn't want an ambulance. He wants you to take him. He's gonna need surgery. We've stabilized it, but he needs to be taken down to Ukiah. He's coming down from Rohypnol."

"What the hell is that?"

"It's what they call roofies," said the nurse.

"Where the hell did he get roofies? Dammit! Alright, alright, alright," He muttered, "Help me get him to the car."

The nurse wheeled him out on the gurney, and they sat him in the front seat of the squad car. He regained consciousness but was in severe pain.

"Stop moaning, you pussy!" yelled Sheriff Rick as he pulled out of the lot, squealing the tires.

"Sorry, Dad, it hurts!"

"Where'd you get roofies, Billy? Why'd you take roofies? Where's your truck? Did you wreck the truck? "Rick pulled out a little baggie of blow from his pocket and drove with his knees. He pinched some in his fingers, wiped it in his gums, and put the flashing lights on with the siren.

"Answer me, boy!"

Billy moaned again. Sheriff Rick Johnson slapped him on the forehead.

"I told you to quit your moaning boy! If this shit costs me a lot of money, I'll give you a reason to moan!"

"Stop it, Dad! It hurts."

"Don't tell me, Billy!"

"I don't care anymore! Stop it, Dad!"

Rick didn't know how to respond, "How did you get roofies, Billy?"

"I didn't do roofies, Dad."

"They said you were coming down from the roofies! Don't lie to me!"

"I'm not lying!"

"The only time I ever heard of someone doing roofies is Leif Brody. He nearly died. I'd leave that shit alone if I were you."

"I didn't do roofies, Dad."

"Who slipped 'em to you then?"

Billy didn't say anything.

In Ukiah, Billy was immediately admitted to surgery, and he spent the night in the hospital. Rick didn't stick around. He called Billy's mom to pick him up in the morning.

"Madge, he's at Ukiah General. You gotta go get him at 9:00 a.m. I don't know where his truck is. I think he wrecked it. I gotta work. Please, Madge, for once, can't you cooperate?" Then he hung up the phone. Rick sped north back to Dias Verdez. He came to a screeching halt in the handicapped spot at Slingers.

"Get me a double margarita, Holly. Put it on Dufur's tab."

"What's up with you, Rick? You look like you've been run through the ringer." Dufur smiled, twisting his waxed curly mustache.

"Someone found my dumbass son on the side of the road with a busted ankle, high on roofies. Stupid little fucker just ruined his football career. Holly! Double margarita! Please!"

"Oh, please, this time. Okay, I'll jump right to it."

"What's he doing roofies for? Is that what the kids are into nowadays?" mumbled Rick.

"I need to talk to you, Rick," said Dufur. "Have you got everything for next week? I wanna make a bust on Duggins farm. You know the place? South on HWY 101 by that Mystery Spot billboard?"

"Yeah, I know where it is, just past the entrance to the Bigfoot souvenir shop. I'm good to go. We gotta get Carl up to speed. He said he's been target practicing up in the hills. Not sure what good that's gonna do. At least we got him as a point man. He can distract the dogs while we're getting down to it."

"True that, Rick. I've taken some aerial photographs of Henry Hodkey's place." He handed Rick an envelope. "Just so you know the lay of the land. I don't see this happening until mid to late October. We should do Duggin's farm first and then let it simmer down awhile."

"Where's the photos of the Duggins farm?"

"I don't have those yet, but that's easy."

Rick slurped the double margarita down in one swallow. "One more just like it. Please, Holly. I'll make it worth your while." Holly grimaced.

Carl limped through the door and plopped up onto a seat at the bar. "Coors Light Holly and a shot of Old Overholt."

"Why the limp, Carl?" asked Dufur.

"Oh, I cut my foot chasin' a bear off my property. Four bears, actually. A whole family. Fuckers were getting in my trash, and I ran out and stepped on some broken glass. Scared the shit out of the bears."

"Wasn't my son at your place doing some work

yesterday?"

"Yeah, Rick. He's done a fine job putting the drain behind the house."

"Well, I had to pick him up from the clinic this morning and bring him to Ukiah today for surgery on a broken ankle. He was all fucked up. Did that happen at your place?"

Carl hesitated to answer. "No, he seemed fine when he left my house."

"You sure about that, Carl? He wasn't fucked up, like on roofies or something?"

"Not at all. In fact, Billy finished early and said he was gonna go for a run through the woods. He said he's training for the football game comin' up. I wondered what happened to him because he left his truck at my place and never returned."

"What time did he leave?"

"I can't remember exactly. A while before sundown. I was so hungover. I figured I'd see him on Lost Creek Road, but nope."

"Well, someone found him on the road and brought him to the clinic. He got roofied."

"You wanna come back to my place and fetch his truck for him?" asked Carl.

"I don't wanna deal with this shit," said Rick.

"Come on, help the kid out Rick, "said Dufur. "He got roofied."

"Alright, fuck it, let's do this. Billy always leaves the keys in it, so let's go. If not, I'll hotwire it."

Rick and Carl drove back up the hill to fetch Billy's truck.

"Thanks for carting me around and giving Billy some work. You didn't slip him anything, did you, Carl?"

"Why would I do that, Rick? And risk his football future? I wanna see him succeed as badly as you do. Go Dragons Bro!"

"So, he didn't seem at all fucked up yesterday?"

"Not that I could tell. I already told ya. Billy knocked the job out, and he did good work. I fell asleep. Then he ran off. I figured he wanted to get in some extreme trail running. I expected him back at my place, but he never showed up. We were gonna go through some drills and pass the football around."

Rick looked over at Carl suspiciously. Carl squirmed, looking uncomfortable in the driver's seat.

"Why did you just leave without finding out where he was, Carl?"

Carl didn't answer. They pulled into his driveway, and Rick noticed the bumper in Carl's garage.

"Man, you've torn your truck up. You shouldn't drive drunk all the time. Gonna have to give you a DUI if you don't cut it out, Carl! Why don't you try some of this?" And he pulled out the baggie of powder.

"Well, thank you kindly, Sheriff." Carl reached for the bag and a key from his pocket. "I'll meet you back at Slingers."

"Yeah, we've got details to discuss. We have a mission coming up in a few weeks. You're gonna be a point man."

Carl let out a yelp, "Whoot! "

Sheriff Rick drove Billy's truck back to town and left it in the Amundson's parking lot with the keys inside. The gears were spinning in his tiny mind. "Why would Carl drug my son?"

AUTUMN

I'M YOUR MOMMA

It was Ulee's birthday and she worked with Hunter. They spent the day thinning out the plants to allow them to ventilate and tied the heavy branches with twine to keep them suspended off the ground. They checked each plant for mold and parasites. Some of the plants were reaching heights over ten feet.

"Sorry it's not much of a birthday, Ulee. We'll have to make up for it later," said Hunter.

"No need to apologize. This is a great way to spend the day. I haven't celebrated a birthday since I don't know when."

"How old are you?" asked Hunter.

Ulee paused with a confused look on her face.

"Hmm, I don't even know. I stopped counting. How old do you think I am?"

Hunter smiled and didn't say.

"I moved here when I was twenty two and I've been here forty years."

"We don't have to talk about the number," said Hunter. "Not if you don't wanna."

"Does it really matter?"

"Not really, I suppose."

"People gotta know it, so they can put the number into the box on the form. You know what I want for my birthday?"

"What do you want, Ulee?"

"No more birthdays, no more boxes and no more forms. Just a free flow of time."

"I totally relate."

"Wanta know what I really want? I want you to understand and not be mad."

"I'm not mad, I understand you don't like birthdays and forms. How could I be mad about that?"

"I want you to understand what I'm about to tell you and not get upset. I've been struggling and I don't know how."

"Tell me what?"

"I'm your mother."

Hunter dropped her cup of tea into the gravel. "What? My Mother is Carolina."

"No, she wasn't your biological mother."

"Carolina's my mom, she died."

"No, I'm your mom. We never told you. We thought it'd be best if she raised you back in Texas with your other sisters and your dad."

Hunter crossed her arms and stared straight at her. Looking into her face, trying to make sense.

"Your dad and I got together and I got pregnant."

"A fling? I'm the result of a fling?"

"No, honey. You are far more than a fling."

"Why didn't you tell me?"

"Your dad already had kids with Carolina. We thought it would be the best way. We all agreed. Carolina, your dad, and me. I wasn't in any shape to raise a child. I'm so sorry I let you go. I had to."

Hunter withdrew into a long silence before asking,

"Did you love him?"

"Hell no! I barely knew him."

"I don't know what to say," said Hunter.

"I know how I feel."

"It feels weird but kinda natural." Hunter took a deep breath. "You know I had this feeling. When I first saw you, I knew we were connected."

"I'm so glad you're not angry."

"How could I be angry about this. Do you think maybe we should take the rest of the day off? Take a drive to the ocean?"

"Sounds like a wonderful idea."

Otto returned from his run. "Whoa! Looks like you guys got a lot done. What's left for me to do?" asked Otto.

"Relax and take it easy, dad. It's Ulee's birthday. We're gonna take the rest of the day off."

"Ah, Happy Birthday! Don't worry, I'm not gonna ask. Everything going okay?"

"Totally fine!"

"Dad, you never told me Ulee was my momma."

Otto stood with his mouth open, searching for words.

"We're gonna go now, okay, Dad? We'll see you tomorrow."

SKIP'S OUT

"Ilf! Petrov! Up!" Skip shouted and closed the sliding door on the two white furry dogs as they rubbed their noses up against the glass.

"We're gonna move down to the main house, fellas. Just for the last couple of days."

Skip maneuvered the VW van down the slope from the top patch as the dogs panted and fussed in the back. He pulled it next to the garage in the original spot he had landed. The dogs were not so agitated this time and kept quiet as he tied them to a tree near the van. Plants were drying in the garage on wires, and dehumidifiers were humming. All the light-deprivation plants were processed. Skip had to go back to Idaho for the Autumn registration. He'd take his cut early to begin the new school year. He nibbled at the ripe raspberries next to his van. The crows did, too, and cawed at him from the branches above. As if to say, "Mine! Those are mine!"

I hadn't enjoyed the summer, to be honest. The heat had been relentless. I even resorted to swimming at the waterfall. Not something I thought I'd ever do. I felt overheated, so I took the plunge. I'm not much of a swimmer, but I followed Henry to the waterfall where he had stashed his cash that day. I've noticed him burying it in several spots around the property.

"Whoa, Chaos. I thought you hated water."

Not when it's over a hundred degrees outside. I can make an exception. So, I swam around in a circle a few times, got out, and shook off like a mangy dog. Temporary relief because as soon as I got out, I felt hotter. The water on my fur heated up, but it dried quickly on the walk.

Henry made a continual loop around the farm, checking on the plants. I tried to keep up with him but opted for the coolness underneath the house. I snoozed through the day, preparing for a night on the prowl. I avoided being sprayed by a skunk at the back side of the house. It let loose some of its stink, but the stench only lasted a few days. So thankful it didn't get me.

A cold front pushed down from the Pacific Northwest, and the heat relinquished its grip within hours, dropping the temperature by forty degrees overnight. The leaves of the poison oak turned scarlet brown.

Henry returned to the main house and left the door to the great room open. I ran inside and tried to reach the loft without being touched. Nate tried to grab at me, but I swatted his hand away. Broke the skin with my right claw. The crew was playing cards at the trim table. They seemed utterly worn out and dirty in their ragged work clothes. I imagined myself as a human and how strange it would be to lick my arms and legs, cleaning them without fur.

"Hey, ah, it's gonna be a few more weeks," said Henry.

"Yeah, we don't wanna rush it," said Nate.

"If we're patient, we'll get some extra weight. Those ladies haven't given us all of it yet. I'd be surprised if we get more than a sprinkle of rain," said Henry.

Skip sat on a stool at the edge of the kitchen.

"If we do, the mold will come fast. At this point, I'm praying it doesn't rain. The top patches are doing great." said Skip.

Henry nodded as he walked by, gesturing to meet him on the porch to talk business.

Skip followed.

"So, I can pay you all in cash or Bitcoin. Half and half? What are you thinkin'? Do you know about Bitcoin?"

"Oh, you're doin' Bitcoin now. Shit Henry. Tech savvy," said Skip.

"Well, Nate clued me in about it last year, and it's been a good move so far."

"What's it at now?"

"About ninety cents a coin. So, if I paid you half in Bitcoin, I figure it would be four months at ten thousand a month. So, forty K. If you want half in Bitcoin at the current price. It's over twenty-two thousand Bitcoin. A lucky number, don't you think? I mean, it's a gamble. I put a hundred K on it last year at twenty-five cents, and I've almost quadrupled my money. Think about it, Skip," as Henry grinned behind his round glasses and floppy fishing hat.

"Alright, man. I'm a gambling man." Skip sat pondering and wringing his hands together. "Gimme a minute; I gotta make some calculations."

"No centralized bank. It's the future," said Henry.

"Shit, alright man. I'll take the twenty-two thousand

on Bitcoin and twenty K cash. Deal?"

"Deal, brother. Sit on the Bitcoin, Skip. Ride it out. Just don't touch it for a few years," said Henry. "It's what Nate suggested."

"Right on, man," said Skip.

"You gotta set up a wallet. Bitcoin Core. I'll sort you out when I go to the city. You still have the same email address?" asked Henry.

"Yup." Henry poured Skip some brandy into a Barry Bonds souvenir cup. "Too bad he fucked it all up with the steroids."

"But he had an exciting run."

Skip nodded, and Henry started plucking at the bass. Nate, Becca, and Aino played Blitz at the trim table.

"The Amish are pretty fucked up, but they knew how to make an exciting card game," said Henry as he watched the three immersed in flipping cards. I sat on the edge of the windowsill.

"The Amish are assholes. They abuse their animals," said Becca. "They work their horses to death. Treat 'em like farm tools. Fuck the Amish! Someday I wanna save all the horses from those assholes."

"BLITZ!" shouted Nate.

"You bastard," said Becca, with a grin.

DUGGINS FARM

Sheriff Rick dialed Dufur to meet up for their first mission. "Dufur, are you ready for this motherfucker?"

"Damned right Rick! I was born ready."

"That's original. Meet me at the Amundson's parking lot."

Dufur was applying some fresh wax to his curly mustache. He put on his bulletproof vest and steel-toed commando boots.

"Bring all the ammo you can and the night vision

goggles. Did you get the Jeep from Fish and Game?"

"All set. What kinda ammo do we need?"

"Bring the eight ball."

"10-4 good buddy. Carl's gonna meet us at the store."

They met at dusk, and Carl prepared a mix of snacks for the tactical team.

"Fellas, I've got Cool Ranch Doritos, beef jerky, energy bars, Coors Lite. What else do we need?"

"We're performing a tactical strike, not going on a picnic, Carl."

"Gotcha Rick. I can leave it in the Jeep for safety. In case we get stranded."

"Stranded, we're gonna be right off HWY 101. What are you talking about, stranded?" said Rick.

Carl dressed from head to toe in camouflage. He had his AR-15 slung around his shoulder with several extra ammunition clips.

Rick started off by giving Dufur and Carl a briefing for the upcoming mission.

"We're going to pull off HWY 101, just past the entrance to Duggin's farm, after the Mystery Spot billboard. There's a little logging road that follows the creek along the perimeter of the property. It's an easy in and out. Carl, as we discussed, I want you to be the point man, and I have a machete for each of us. We're gonna hack the plants down and then go through the place. We're looking for cash, guns, or other illegal substances. Who knows what these hippies have on the farm, so be careful. Oh, and here's a walkie-talkie for each of you. Channel 3. Carl, you're the point. Got it?"

"Yes, sir!" Carl stood at attention, all amped up, like he finally had a purpose in life.

"Easy, man. Why are you yelling?" said Rick.

The three set off to make their first raid of the season. They parked the Jeep by the creek, and Carl unwrapped a Snickers bar and scarfed it down.

"Ok, go, Carl. Go! Go!" said Rick.

Carl ran off toward the farmhouse alone while Rick and Dufur walked behind. There was no one at the place.

"Look at the fool run," commented Rick.

"He's goin' for it," said Dufur.

"Watch out for flying bullets," whispered Rick, thinking about the possibility that Carl had drugged his son.

They strolled to the vacant house. On the porch, a cat rolled on its back near the front door. There was a veggie garden in the yard and about a dozen marijuana plants growing behind the house. A light-deprivation hoop house sat empty.

"Dang, I thought this was a decent-sized farm, Dufur?"

"Well, it looked like it from the air. I mean from the road."

"Wait, you didn't even look at it from the air? You said it went way back."

The radio broke in with Carl's voice, "I checked the perimeter. All is good on my side of the property. Nobody's here. Over!"

"10-4 Carl. Make your way back to the storage shed, and we'll meet you there."

Dufur and Rick hacked the plants and left them on the ground. Carl waited at the storage shed.

"Carl. Go to the Jeep and get the bolt cutters."

"Roger that, Rick!" Carl ran full speed back to the Jeep, returning out of breath with the cutters.

Rick cut the lock to the shed door.

"I'm sure we'll find what we're looking for here. "

They entered the shed and found a deep freezer inside. Rick opened it up to find several venison, beef, and chicken packages. They found fishing rods and gardening tools after foraging through the entire shed.

"What the fuck?! There's nothing here?" said Rick.

"Let's go in the house," said Dufur.

"Are you sure we can go in the house? Is that legal?"

"Shut the fuck up, Carl! I'm the law around here!"

Sheriff Rick Johnson kicked in the front door, and they entered the farmhouse. "Go search upstairs, Carl!"

Carl searched through the closets but only found clothes and shoes. Same for the chest of drawers. Sheriff Rick went straight for the fridge. There was a six-pack of microbrew beer and some kombucha.

"What is this shit beer? Where's the Coors Light motherfuckers?" He grabbed one and popped the top while Dufur rifled through all the drawers.

"Nothing upstairs. Just clothes and towels," said Carl on the radio.

"Did you check under the beds? Over," asked Rick.

"Affirmative, over."

"Well damn. This is a clusterfuck! "Rick plopped down on the recliner and pulled the footrest out.

"Nothing here, Rick, Nothing at all. Sorry, man," said Dufur.

"I'm not leaving empty-handed," Rick got up and looked through the fridge again.

"Fuck this!" He stormed out to the shed. Feeling his bass boat dreams evaporating. He filled a garbage bag full of the meat from the freezer and grabbed one of the fishing rods.

"So that's it? Are we done here?" asked Carl.

"Let's get the fuck out of here," said Rick.

The three walked off back to the Jeep.

"What the fuck Dufur? I thought you vetted the place?"

"I was sure it went back further."

"Well, we're having a cookout at Carl's. Carl, you take this meat to your place."

"10-4 Rick. "

"Stop talking like we're on the radio. I'm sitting right next to you, Carl! Let's go to Slingers."

They changed out of their outfits in the parking lot and went inside for a drink.

"Carl, level with me. Did you give my boy roofies? By accident?"

"How could I do that, Rick? I've never had roofies in my life. I don't even know where to find them."

"You and Leif Brody were good buds. Remember how he ended up in the hospital from that roofie thing. How Leif crashed his truck almost head-on. You said he went to rehab in New Mexico. Then the whole family split town. I never understood that," said Sheriff Rick. "Why did they sell the place to Henry? Why didn't they sell it to your mom and dad?"

"Dunno. Leif had a drug problem. I don't know why they all left. I guess they were trying to save his life."

"It's weird how they all left Carl. Your folks and his folks were like best friends. Didn't they say anything before they split?"

"Nope." Carl sipped his beer and stared blankly at the flashing Coors Light sign.

TITLE & PAINTING

Ulee trimmed the branches into smaller, more workable sections and hung them from the wires. They cut all the harvestable buds and prepared them for the long journey across the country. Otto felt more upbeat than usual. They vacuum-packed the turkey bags full of dry buds into ten-pound packages.

"I'm relieved you told her, Ulee. She didn't even freak out. No bad vibes. I thought it would blow up in our faces."

"It's the best possible outcome," said Ulee.

"You wanna come back with us?" Otto blurted out.

"Back to Houston?"

"Yeah, why not? Why don't you come back with us?"

"What the hell am I gonna do in Houston?"

"You could relax. You can do anything. Be with us. You and Hunter. My other girls. They don't live at home anymore. Plenty of room."

"Well, what would they think about it? Bringing an old lesbian momma back to conservative Texas."

"Houston's not so conservative these days. It's just the surrounding areas. You know, I don't care about any of that stuff. You're getting along so well I figured it makes sense. Aren't you sick of being alone in the trailer?"

"I like being alone in the trailer. It's my home, but I still need to figure out if it's mine. George never signed it over to me. It's still in his name."

"Well, the title is probably in his house somewhere."

"I don't think he cared about stuff like that. He probably used it for kindling."

"Well, let's go over there and look for it. Aramoana covered all the doors with plywood, but we could pry it off."

"I guess we could. Feels like I'd be breaking in, though," said Ulee with a worried look.

"I don't think anybody cares. Nobody's been in there since he died. Unless Aramoana cleaned the place out."

The two walked to my old place, which stood partially covered in poison oak. I've tried to get in a few times but I couldn't get past the plywood gate. A gutter had fallen, and a large branch damaged the roof. It upset me to see the place going to hell. Birds flew in and out of a back window that broke from that fallen branch. It was too high for me to climb up.

Otto pried loose the plywood and pushed the front door open. A dozen birds fluttered through the window. Everything was still the way I left it. Art supplies rested on a series of folding tables. Several paintings were midway through production. I was working on a cat wearing a red sweater. Its entire body is shaved except for the fur on its feet and head. Looking at it now, I realize this is my dream cat. Was I channeling my future self? So bizarre. It lay on my easel next to a faded leather sofa I remember buying at Goodwill. There it was! The Bobcat I was working on. The last thing I remembered as a human. Branding the leather with a hot paper clip. Bobcats and mountain lions. Man, they look so real. I was a good artist! My tea kettle still sat on the burner with the gas turned up; all the propane must have drained from the tank.

"I don't think Aramoana even came in here," said Ulee.

"I don't think anyone did," replied Otto. "I heard Aramoana found him out in the yard. Behind the propane tank."

Otto noticed me in the living room, "Look who followed us in; hey, Chaos. You wanna move in here?"

I've already moved in, Otto.

"Same old story with you, meow, meow, meow," said Otto.

"You're the famous Chaos. I didn't get to meet you at the party," said Ulee.

Good to see you, Ulee. We already know each other. Don't you remember me? You don't have to answer, I understand.

"What is he trying to say?" said Ulee.

"I don't know. Most talkative cat I've ever met" replied Otto.

I always meant to give you the trailer title, Ulee, but kept forgetting. You'll find it. It's right over there; check the file cabinet.

A moldy smell filled the room from all the rain that leaked in, and the birds made a mess. My pickles still lined the shelves.

"We should take these pickles," said Otto.

A turquoise stone sat on the shelf by the kitchen

sink. Where did that come from?

"He always made the best pickles; let's check the file cabinet."

Otto looked through the top drawer and found the title immediately.

"He made it easy on us. This must be it." He pulled out a folder that read "Trailer title."

Then he found the note I left.

Hi Ulee, I figure you'll come looking for this. I signed it over to you years ago. I just never got around to giving it to you. I don't like coming to town. I think you know that. Well, here it is. The title. Isn't it weird how we obsess over these things? Titles, pink slips, pieces of paper. I want you to know I never meant anything malicious by painting those screws on your feet. It was all in jest. You know, we really don't own any of this stuff?

See you on the other side,
George

"Do you think he killed himself?" whispered Ulee.

I did not kill myself, Ulee! Why on earth would you think that?

"I thought he had a heart attack."

"Yeah, me too. But this note makes it seem like..."

"I don't think he killed himself, Ulee."

Thanks, Otto.

"Even if he did, it doesn't matter now."

"Did he really know Warhol, or was that a bunch of malarkey?" asked Otto.

"I had seen them together. They were aware of each other, at least," replied Ulee.

Bullshit, Ulee. I didn't know him, and he didn't know me! Complete bullshit!

"Why did he mention the screws in the painting?"

"That was his decision in our collaboration. I painted

most of it, and then he turned my feet into screws."

I thought you'd think it was funny, geez!

"Why does that bother you? You seem angry now," said Otto.

"It's supposed to show me escaping the body through meditation and floating above the trailer. The screws were George's way of calling bullshit on it. I'm the only one he's ever collaborated with. He never did with Warhol; that was just a ruse to sell paintings."

"Why do you want the painting so bad?"

"Because he fucked it up on purpose to get my goat. He didn't follow through with the idea we agreed on. He altered it as a mockery of meditation."

I was kidding. Damn, Ulee! I wasn't mocking.

"I remember the painting but never thought of it as a mockery."

Thanks again, Otto. See Ulee, even Otto sees it!

"He wanted control. A form of manipulation through art. He had me stuck, and he knew it. I gave up. He told me that the perfection of my art was a lie. Still, George had insecurities because his ability to paint was mediocre."

Mediocre! I hissed as the two of them left the house and started walking back to Otto's with the title in hand.

"He convinced me that I had no talent. He had the notoriety, not me. He convinced me not to try. After I told him he was average, he shut me down."

I did not shut you down! That was your choice, Ulee. You stopped. You were a brilliant artist, but you quit!

"Why didn't you leave? Go back to New York City?" asked Otto.

"What could I do back in New York? I wasn't gonna be enlightened there. Not a chance."

"Did it happen here?" asked Otto, "did you get to be enlightened?"

"I don't know. Maybe for a moment."

"Decades for a moment," whispered Otto.

"The audacity to leave me wondering about an image of an anchored balloon, not a meditational escape. George ruined the whole idea in a few quick brush strokes."

If I had known it would have affected you like this, I would never have done it. I'm sorry, Ulee. I was being childish.

"Chaos is trying to console you," said Otto.

I rubbed up against her ankles and dug my paws into her shoe.

"He likes you, Ulee!"

"Hey buddy, you wanna come live in the RV park?"

I don't want to live in the RV park, Ulee.

"So why obsess over it? Aren't you contradicting the practice of meditation by ruminating?" said Otto.

"I suppose you're right, but I can't help it. I wanna set the record straight."

"Who cares about the record? It doesn't matter. It's all rotting away. What about right now? Why don't you come with us? You can stay in the RV at the Houston house or wherever. We can pull the trailer back with the pickup and park it in the driveway next to the RV. It doesn't matter to me. It'd be nice to have you around.

"I don't know, Otto."

"Hunter goes to gay bars all the time. I'm sure she can introduce you to the community."

"Well, those are all young people, and I'm not looking for a girlfriend anymore. I don't like bars."

"Well, whatever you want–I'm telling you, I'd like it if you were with us."

Ulee looked at Hunter returning with a wheelbarrow full of plants. "She looks a lot like you, Otto. She's smart like you, too."

"Hell of a piano player."

"Yeah, takes after me for that, I suppose," said Ulee.

"We've got a baby grand in the house's great room. You could get back into it. "

"You know something, Ulee. I could talk to Aramoana and buy the painting for you?"

Ulee shook her head. "She's not gonna give it up. She's like a little girl in the sandbox, and if you start playing with a toy nobody wants, she wants to play with it, too. Keep it for herself. That's why she ended up alone."

"Well, aren't you alone too?"

Ulee and Hunter loaded up the first round of buds at sundown and brought them to the RV. They packed them in the cargo container underneath using Marine Corps waterproof duffel bags. All the luggage had to have the USMC logo on it. Otto reached his goal of growing at least two hundred pounds to return to Texas.

He went for a jog towards Lost Creek and Aramoana's house. It was a Saturday, so the lights were on. She usually spent the weekends there, so he ran up to the porch to knock. She came to the door in a long black dress and a ring of flowers around her head like a crown.

"Hey, Aramoana, I thought I'd stop by. I was taking a run and saw the car in the driveway."

"What a surprise! Come on in. When's the last time I've seen you here?"

"It's been a while, for sure. What, fifteen, twenty years? Say, I've been talking with Ulee, and we were reminiscing about George's paintings. Got to talking about the painting he did with Ulee."

"What painting with Ulee? There's no painting with Ulee!"

"Well, yeah, there is. They collaborated on that one with the trailer?"

"I'm trying to figure out which one you're talking about. My dad didn't collaborate with anyone except Warhol."

"He and Ulee had a collaboration. It's the one with the woman flying over a trailer. Can I look at the gallery?"

Aramoana looked upset and crossed her arms as if

guarding the entrance to the Louvre.

"Can I go in and have a look? I was hoping to buy it."

"None of them are for sale. My father is no longer for sale; he's dead."

"Well, I know he's dead, and my condolences. He was a friend of mine. You know that, right? Look, Aramoana, I don't mean any offense. Can I take a quick look? Just to see them again."

"Well, a quick one. I've got to go to Dillits soon. I'm gonna have to flip the breaker. Hang on." Aramoana disappeared and looked annoyed while Otto stood in the dark doorway of the gallery.

The lights illuminated the great room full of paintings. Otto stepped inside and noticed it immediately. Hanging in the center of all the others. The most prominent of the bunch. He walked up and saw Ulee's face in the image of the floating woman. The trailer has a painted horse at the fence line in the same spot. Much more detailed than the others.

"I can see why she wants it back," he mumbled.

"Ok, that's it, Otto. I gotta go now. The gallery is closed."

"Aramoana, I'd like to buy the painting. Name your price."

"It's not for sale, Otto. None of these are for sale."

Otto looked confused.

"Money would only cheapen this body of work," said Aramoana as she turned off the lights.

She got in her Subaru and drove out without saying goodbye. Otto walked up the driveway and back to his cabin. He didn't understand why she could be so opposed to selling.

A CHILL IN THE AIR

Skip drove out in the predawn hours while the dogs were still asleep. The VW slowly meandered through the hairpins to the summit, where the trees were coated in frost. He headed North on HWY 101 to Crescent City, over Grants Pass, then up to Portland and onward. He'd finished his work and had twenty K in his gym bag to prove it. Another twenty K for a long-term gamble on Bitcoin. He felt confident in his decision.

That evening, Aino spoke about Skip, "He sure didn't talk much; I think I said 'hello' and 'goodbye' to him. The man of mystery."

"Yeah, he's a loner for sure. But he knows his shit," said Henry. "I'm going down to the shack. Gonna start a fire in the wood stove."

"Feels like Fall is here," said Aino.

Henry nodded and was out the door with his headlamp on.

Nate sipped a brandy and Aino sparkling water. "You seem to have metamorphosized," said Nate.

"Feeling good, man. The work's been therapeutic. I'm becoming someone I like to be around," said Aino.

"That's amazing, brother."

"Thank you for sticking with me, Nate. I'm sorry for punching you in the car."

"You've already apologized a million times. Let it go, man!"

"I really mean it."

"This time, I think you really do, and I appreciate that."

"I do, brother."

"We all gotta stick together. Help each other down the road."

"True that," chimed Becca. "Gotta be willing to accept the help is all, I s'pose. I think this place saved my life. Honestly, it did. I'm not sure where I would be if I didn't come here. Henry is a saint, but I don't even believe in a god."

"He's got his own demons too, you know," said Nate.

"He kills them off with kindness. Such a subtle helping hand. You don't realize what he's done for you until it's well on the way," said Aino.

"Well, good night, all. If you ask me, I think we should start harvesting tomorrow. At the top of the hill and work our way down. See how things look in the morning," said Nate. "We'll see how Henry feels about it."

DELI IN A CAST

After sweeping the aisles to Al Stewart's "Year of the Cat," Walter waddled behind the deli case where Billy struggled on aluminum crutches to set up for Saturday morning.

"L- L-L-Lemme help, B-B-B-Billy."

"Thanks, Walter."

Walter brought the chickens from the walk-in cooler and arranged them on the steel tray so Billy could apply the dry rub.

"H-H-How is y-y-your leg h-h-h-healing?" asked Walter.

"Hurts, man. Throbs all night kept me awake again."

"Th-Th-Th-That sss-sssucks. Y-Y-You got hurt w-w-w-working at C-C-Carl's?"

"Yeah, Carl kinda roped me into working on his place."

"W-W-Were you w-w-working on the roo-roo-roo-roof?"

"No, I didn't take any fucking roofies!" Billy slapped a chicken onto the tray and twisted around to face Walter. "Who told you about roofies?"

"I th-th-thought you f-fell off th-the roof?"

Billy drew a deep breath and fixed his hairnet. "I didn't fall off the roof," he said. "I fell off a cliff, running away from Carl. I think he drugged me."

"L-L-Like really d-d-drugged?"

"I think Carl roofied me."

Before thinking about it, Walter said, "L-L-Like he d-d-did to Lee-Lee-Leif? Leif Bro-Brody?"

"What do you mean like he did to Leif Brody?"

Walter reached into his pocket to switch off his radio. Then, very softly, he said, "It's w-w-why L-L-Leif q-q-quit."

"Leif quit because he got roofied by Carl?"

"C-C-Carl t-t-tried to kiss him. M-M-More th-than j-just k-kiss. L-Leif p-p-passed out. So so so mad. It-It's why th-they le-left."

"The Brodys left town because of that? Because Carl roofied Leif and tried to fuck him?!" Billy pulled his hair net off and threw it on the spice rack. "That's what you're telling me?"

"I d-d-d-don't know wh-what ex-exactly hap-happened b-but it w-was s-some heav-heavy sh-sh-shit."

Billy closed his eyes and rubbed his forehead. No one had seen Carl around the store. Not since Billy's accident. He had come in after closing to do payroll and post the schedule. He probably waited at Slinger's until Billy left, which Billy didn't mind.

"Why do you still work here, Walter?"

"I-I-I can't l-l-lose th-this j-j-job. I-I-I c-c-can't aff-afff-afford it." Walter stepped behind the cooler out of range from Carl's security camera.

"H-H-He knows I-I-I know. H-He th-threatened me. H-He is fff-fff-friends with the only c-c-cop ar-around and he's c-c-crazy."

"Take it easy, Walter. I won't get you fired."

"I-I-I th-think he is e-e-evil." Walter lowered his voice even more. His hands trembled. "I think he really did kill them. His parents." said Walter crystal clear then returned to stuttering, "W-W-W-With the mmmm-mmmmush-mmmm–"

"Mushrooms?"

"Y-Y-Y-Yeah.   D-D-D-Death   C-C-Cap   M-M-Mushrooms."

Walter's head swiveled in reflex as he glanced around the store, checking for Carl.

"Stop being afraid of Carl, Walter. He's a fuckin' pussy. As soon as I can walk again, I will pummel that guy."

"Y-Y-You sh-should t-tell y-your dad. B-B-Be v-very c-careful B-B-Billy."

"My dad won't do shit," Billy said. "Besides, he'll blame me if I tell him."

LOADING THE RV

Ulee, Otto, and Hunter were in full harvest mode, and plants were hung up to dry in the A-Frame. When sufficiently dried, they were vacuum-packed and loaded into the storage compartment of the RV. At that point, they had already surpassed Otto's goal of 200 pounds.

"I can't believe the yield this year! We're already way beyond the mark," said Otto.

"This last batch is drying," said Hunter.

"We're a week ahead of schedule. Thanks to you, Ulee."

"That's it? I hoped this would last a little longer," said Ulee.

"Are you coming with us? I gotta let the campgrounds know if we will pull the trailer. Get an extra spot." said Otto.

"The trailer's been sitting there for decades. We'd

have to get new tires, and it doesn't have a plate. "

"I'll get new tires, and we can pull it with the pickup. I'll follow closely with the RV so cops can't get a look at the tag. "

Ulee looked annoyed..

"I talked with Aramoana about the painting. She said it's not for sale. Pretty adamant about it."

"Well, it's okay. I don't care if it's not for sale." She looked at Hunter as if they had already made an unspoken agreement.

That evening, Hunter pulled down Aramoana's driveway. Aramoana had returned to Dillits, and the goats were grazing on the hillside. Hunter simply walked inside the house through the unlocked door. She entered the gallery and recognized the painting in the dim light. Ulee sat in the Jeep, frozen in fear of Aramoana returning. Hunter waltzed right out with the large painting in hand.

"Happy Birthday!" Hunter smiled, presenting the painting to Ulee like one of those large Publishers Clearing House checks.

"We gotta go!" said Ulee.

Hunter propped up the painting in the rear seats of the Jeep and smoothly rolled out of the driveway, leaving the goats chomping away in the distance.

Ulee looked back at the painting, feeling apprehensive yet satisfied with the caper. Hunter turned the radio up loud. Elvis's "In the Ghetto," echoed through the canyon. They pulled into the RV lot and were the only two campers left after the tourist season. Ulee pulled the painting from the back seat and propped it up against the trailer while Hunter unloaded the rest of the weed into the RV.

"Not an exact replica of the trailer. This window isn't even here, and the lady doesn't look like me. Well, does it?" asked Ulee.

"Yeah, she looks like you. I could tell right away. And the trailer, too. It's the trailer plus one window. And Hans. Hey, look, you're in the painting," Hunter called out to Hans.

"It's not Hans. It's Hans's dad, Victor."

"You better put it inside. What if Aramoana drives by and sees it?"

"Okay, for safekeeping," said Hunter.

"First, I need to fix it."

Ulee went to the trailer and got out a small toolbox full of old paints. She placed the painting on the picnic table and quickly painted over the screws, and gave herself feet again. Hunter watched in awe at her precision adjustment to the painting.

"See, this is the idea we agreed upon. It's what we talked about!"

"You've transcended. You're flying away. I love it, Ulee! I mean, mom."

NORMAL DRUGS

Due to his ankle injury, Billy couldn't drive, so he hobbled out to Amundson's parking lot and waited for his dad to pick him up.

Sheriff Rick pulled up in his squad car.

"Get in, Billy! I'm already late enough."

Billy had barely shut the door when his dad sped away onto HWY 101.

"How much longer 'til you're outta that thing?" Rick asked. "I can't keep being your private chauffeur."

"Three more weeks, Dad. Then rehab, but I think I can drive once it comes off."

"Well, that's about two weeks too long if you ask me."

"You think I'm happy about this?"

"Fuck man, you screwed up your whole deal, didn't you?" Rick shook his head. "I thought you'd get a football scholarship. But no, you had to party and do drugs What the fuck were you thinking, Billy?"

Rick checked himself in the rearview mirror to make sure he didn't have any cocaine remnants in his nose. "I can't bring you home next Sunday. You gotta make another arrangement. I've got official police business."

"I'll ask Walter," Billy said. "It'll be fine."

"Yeah, ask Walter because it ain't gonna be me. Not Sunday."

A car approached from the other direction and honked. Rick began to flip the driver off until he realized it was just Dufur saying hello. They sped past each other.

"Isn't that your party wingman?" Billy asked.

"Look who's talking," Rick said. "So, what were you doing roofies for, anyway? Date rape drugs? Why don't you do normal drugs?"

"I didn't 'do' roofies. Why would anyone take roofies, Dad?"

"Well, they found it in you. Don't be lying to me, Billy. I'll whip your ass if you lie to me!"

"I'm not lying, Dad. I am trying to remember what happened. The last thing I remember is drinking a smoothie Carl made. I'm thinking Carl put roofies in it."

"Why would Carl spike your smoothie?" Rick really seemed stumped by the notion. "He would never do that. What are you trying to say about Carl?"

"I don't know, dad. I don't remember anything after drinking it. It was banana, strawberry, and raspberry. He put some protein powder in it. He offered me a shot of vodka, too, but I said no."

"Carl fed you a smoothie, and now you can't remember anything." Sheriff Rick Johnson contemplated this news. His jaw muscles tensed. "So, you were working at Carl's, and he invited you inside for a smoothie. What happened then?"

"Not much. I remember Carl talked about hunting

naked. He said you guys hunt naked. Is that true?"

"Fuck no, it's not true! Are you still high or something?" Rick nearly ran off the road and then swerved into the oncoming lane. "What else do you remember?"

"Some dude woke me on the road and brought me to the clinic."

"You sure the roofies didn't come from the guy who picked you up?"

"How the fuck could it be the guy that picked me up, dad?!"

"Don't curse at me! Who the hell do you think you are?" Sheriff Rick tried to slap Billy with the back of his hand. Billy grabbed his father's forearm and stopped him mid-swing. Rick tried to pull away, but Billy waited a second before letting go.

"That is going to stop now, Dad!"

Sheriff Rick Johnson looked stunned.

"Stop the car! I'm getting out!" Billy said.

The Sheriff pulled over. "I could bash your skull in, boy!"

"Go ahead then!"

The Sheriff watched Billy lift himself out of the squad car and reach for his crutches.

"Why don't you leave now?" Billy said calmly as he propped himself up on the shoulder of the road. Sheriff Rick sat idling, searching for words. "I don't need a ride from you."

"Suit yourself, you little prick!"

The Sheriff peeled out, spraying gravel, but Billy didn't flinch. Instead, he put his thumb out, and the next car pulled over and gave him a ride back to Dillits

THE WIND

The dry wind blew heat from the valley funneled up through the canyon. It became a steady flow of air with wind gusts over 50 mph. The dried leaves blew from the trees and formed little swirling clouds of brown, sucking up into the ravine and around the craggy cliffs. Dead branches from the eucalyptus and manzanitas snapped off in random cracking sounds like lightning muffled by the wind. A bobcat ran the gravel road with a grouse in its mouth as I looked on with envy from the water pipe.

I certainly didn't wanna tangle with another bobcat, so I made myself small as it passed, and luckily I was downwind from it. The water pipe still trickled. I'd been fending for myself for most of the week and recently had caught a jackrabbit almost the same size as me. I left half of it for Henry, but he threw it in the compost pit, and those damned ravens ate it up.

They harvested most of the plants and dried them in various spots. I made the rounds from place to place. It felt more accessible to run the farm without those dogs around anymore. I went everywhere. Found the remnants of some sardine cans Skip left behind. The plants hung below the lean to's and inside the Schieffelbein house. When it finally got cold, I spent a night in the attic. In the solar shack, wires were strung in rows to dry the plants. The same happened at the main house; several rows were set up in Henry's shack. I liked laying on top of the refrigerator in the garage with the fans blowing on me. Henry had the doors open on both sides to let the air flow through. The weed dried rapidly in the crisp Autumn air. The crew approached the finish line.

"Gonna run to the city on Saturday this week. I'm bringing a big haul for three dispensaries. I just picked up a couple more clients in Oakland," said Henry. "So you're on your own through Tuesday."

"No worries, Henry, we've got this. We'll probably be finished by Saturday, and I'm gonna chill 'til you get back," said Nate. "Try to get some photos."

"You wanna jar up some of those cucumbers? Make

some pickles and roasted pumpkin seeds? Maybe make some raspberry jam?" asked Becca.

"Hell yeah!" said Aino.

"Plenty of greens in the garden we need to try and gobble down. Give some of 'em to those goats. I'm sure they'd love it. Whatever we can't finish up. I know there's a lot left," said Henry.

"So, all of you are getting the same. I can do the same deal with you if you want? Pay part in Bitcoin and part in cash. If you want it all in cash, it's fine too," said Henry. He figured paying them in Bitcoin was better since it was pretty much free money for him at that point.

"I think I want mine in cash, Henry. I don't know enough about that stuff," said Becca.

"I second that," said Aino. "I'll take cash."

"I'll go half and half," stated Nate firmly.

The others looked at him with surprise. Not knowing he had convinced Henry to get involved the year before, it paid off.

"I'll stick with cold hard cash," said Aino.

"Suit yourself. Whatever works for you is cool with me. So, Becca and Aino. I still owe you both fourteen and a half thousand. Gonna round it up to an even fifteen K. Sound fair?"

"Absolutely," nodded Becca and Aino in agreement. Aino had been paid before the four-month summer and hadn't drawn any money since. They were all stoked to complete the season and collect a stack of cash.

Aino considered hanging around but wasn't sure. He picked up his trumpet and blew a little random ditty. His mouth still wasn't right from the bottle cut a few months back. Henry plucked the bass, and Becca started playing chords on the piano. Nate popped open a bottle of wine.

"It's that Merlot, my friend in Cloverdale, made," said Nate.

Henry obliged and said, "I know that guy," while

Becca and Aino abstained. "Yeah, ah, we're mutual friends."

Nate snapped photos with an old 35 mm camera, and the night became an extended jam party.

Henry took a stroll to the garage and pulled the refrigerator away from the wall when the music died down. He opened the trap door on the backside of the fridge. His headlamp illuminated the contents, and he pulled out a stack of bills, counting the payments to his employees and friends. Hundred-dollar bills in rolls of five thousand. Three rolls per envelope for Becca and Aino. Seventy-five hundred for Nate, and he'd settle the rest when he got to the city. He went to leave but turned around to repeat the process. He pulled out an extra three K and added a thousand more to each of their stacks to show his gratitude. A bonus.

A stack of five thousand went directly to his house in the East Bay for upkeep and stocking the pantry. It was a communal house where he rented rooms to artists for half of the market value. It was an affordable spot forever as far as he was concerned. Never raising the rent. Ever! I followed Henry back into the great room where the others were now enjoying Dizzy Gillespie's At Newport album.

"Here you go, Becca and Aino, this is for you." Handing them both a manila envelope with a string tie. "I put a little extra bonus in there for ya, and Nate, this is yours, plus the Bitcoin coming soon. Everybody cool?"

They all nodded in agreement, and the album played on through bedtime. Becca stashed the cash under her bed in the loft, and Aino placed it on the shelf with all the records in the solar shack. Nate stashed the money in the glovebox of his car.

Henry loaded fifty pounds of pot into the Suburban and took off early the following day.

THE FINAL RAID

Sheriff Rick Johnson, Dufur Fleck, and Carl met at the parking lot of Amundson's on Sunday night. Dufur had the Fish and Game Jeep, and Carl had his monster truck. The three decided to BBQ some of the meat they'd confiscated on the last bust.

"We need a good meal if we're gonna pull this one off correctly," said Rick to Carl. "I'll ride with you."

Rick jumped into the truck, and they followed Dufur up the hill to Carl's place.

"Man, you need a step ladder to get in this rig. Why do you drive this goddamned thing, Carl?"

"I need it for the clearance. I couldn't make it up these roads in a little pussy truck. "

"Well, I can make it up there in my squad car. Crown Victoria has no problem with these roads. "

"So what do you think? Fifty K each on this one. I know they've got cash money. I can smell it from my house," said Carl.

"We might do better than that. Much better," replied Sheriff Rick.

"Oh, hell. Why do we have to wait? Why can't we do it now and eat later?"

"We need fuel, Carl. I can't do it on an empty stomach."

"I suppose you're right, Rick. You're always right. I guess it's why you're the sheriff, and I'm not."

Rick stared at Carl from the passenger seat. Noticing how flustered he was.

"Something wrong, Carl? You look nervous."

"I'm not nervous, Rick, I'm excited!"

"Why are you all sweaty? You look terrified."

"Oh man, it's nothing. This is what we've been building up for. I'm a little nervous. I worry they might come out blasting or something. What if they're all on meth like the guy who picked up your son."

"My son. What methed out guy?"

"I heard some dude on meth picked up your son and brought him to the clinic."

"What else did you hear, Carl?"

"I heard he was pretty fucked up, is all. He broke his ankle, and the meth head from Henry's farm picked him up. I heard he gave him some drugs. Tried to rob him. It's the word on the street."

"Well, he was leaving your place, Carl. You should know the word on the street. You know what I heard the word on the street was?"

Carl didn't reply.

"Do you know what I heard, Carl? From my son?"

"Well, here we are. Man, I am starving," said Carl. "I'm gonna stoke up the grill."

Rick watched him hustle to the house, almost running away from him. The winds were howling up the canyon as the day approached the golden hour.

Dufur parked the Fish and Game Jeep, pointing toward the narrow gravel footpath leading to Henry's farm.

"I suppose a BBQ will do just fine on such a lovely day," said Dufur, twisting his mustache.

"Why do you always gotta twist the thing every time you speak, Dufur? What do you think you're in a movie or something? Why don't you shave that goddamned thing? Whenever I hang out with you, it's all about your mustache. Your goddamned mustache!"

"Well, you got one too, Rick. What crept up your asshole today?"

"I don't continuously play with mine and try to make it the topic of conversation like you do."

"Rick, whatever's got you agitated, let's calm down. You're getting a little hangry. Low blood sugar."

"Shut up Dufur!"

"Carl, we gotta get the Sheriff a candy bar or something. He's getting cranky. Hasn't had his snack yet."

"You keep talking, and I'm gonna knock that curly mustache into the back of your throat, Dufur."

"Okay, okay, boys. Settle down. I know this is a big day. To think I'd be telling you guys to settle down. Look, I've got some T-bones and some chicken cooking. Who wants a rum and Coke? Rum and Coke Dufur? Rick?"

Both nodded in approval. Rick put on his bullet proof vest and slugged down the rum and Coke like chugging a Gatorade. He pulled the small baggie from the front pocket of his sheriff shirt and took a quick bump. "Anybody need some medicine?"

"Medic! Please help me medic!" shouted Dufur reaching out for the baggie. "Carl?"

"Oh lovely." Carl grabbed it and took a big blast. He poked at the chicken with a large buck knife. "I think this shit's done," as he stabbed each piece and put them on a plate. "Dig in fellas."

The three ate with their fingers and scarfed the meat down like rabid hyenas. The sun dipped out of sight and the stars filled the sky once again while Sheriff Rick Johnson wiped the BBQ sauce from his hands onto his pants and took another bump of cocaine. He seemed to forget the boiling anger he had inside over what Carl had done to his son.

"You sure you wanna do this? I'm feeling good just chilling out here."

"Fuck you, Carl! we're doing this."

"Well, give me another blast of that fine powder then."

"Save a little for us, Carl, what the fuck?!" shouted Rick.

"Okay, okay." Carl put his bulletproof vest on to complete his commando gear outfit. "Anybody want a smoothie for the road?"

"Smoothie? No thanks, Carl. I know all about your smoothies," grumbled Rick.

"We should go now if we're gonna go. What do you think, Rick, Dufur?"

"Let's do it! "They said in unison.

They piled in the Jeep and slowly descended the stony pathway behind the Schieffelbein house and the outermost patch through the creek. The plants had all been harvested, but the main stalks were left behind.

"Man, these plants must have been fifteen feet tall!" said Dufur.

They rolled through the other patches on the property, looking for plants still in the ground. They were all gone. Only stalks remained.

The Sheriff walked behind Carl and poked him in the back with a stick. "Did you feed my son a spiked smoothie, Carl?"

"What? What do you mean, Rick?"

"Did you feed Billy a spiked smoothie when he was working up at your house?" Sheriff Rick jabbed him again with the stick.

"Hell no, I didn't feed him a spiked smoothie! You're crazy, Rick!"

The wind drowned out their conversation, and Dufur couldn't hear what they were talking about.

"You spiked my kid's smoothie, didn't you? I know exactly what you did, Carl!"

"What are you saying? I can't hear."

A quail fluttered out of the bushes, and Carl accidentally fired a round from his gun.

"Holy shit!" Dufur exclaimed. "Why do you have your finger on the trigger, you idiot!"

"Don't call me an idiot, Dufur!" said Carl. "I gotta be ready to defend myself at a moment's notice."

"You are an idiot," hissed Rick. "Make sure everybody's

on channel one on your walkie-talkies."

"10-4, Roger that!"

They approached the Schieffelbein house, and the front door was slightly open. Carl kicked it in, and It thwacked against the wall inside. Wires were strung in rows, but no plants remained. The house was vacant. They checked the upper floors, and Sheriff Rick cursed. "What's this shit? Skunked again! Let's move, boys!"

They made their way up the hill to the wood mill and the remnants of the light deprivation hoop houses. Nothing! They could see the light coming from Henry's house and heard music playing.

PICKLES, PUMPKIN SEEDS & RASPBERRY JAM

The kitchen bustled with four projects. Pumpkin carving, roasting the seeds, making raspberry jam, and jarring pickles. Becca, Nate, and Aino had already filled several cases with mason jars full of pickles, forming a chaotic assembly line. Five pumpkins lined the chopping block, and a pile of pumpkin guts and seeds globbed behind them on the cutting board. Nate and Becca spread the seeds on cookie sheets and toasted them while adding various spices.

"I like a little Chesapeake seasoning on mine," said Aino.

"You like that on everything," Becca quipped.

"My short time in Maryland. They brainwashed me. Not the worst habit, I s'pose."

"We got a case of raspberry preserves for all three of us and one for Henry. Skip loses out, but I can mail him some."

"Yeah, we need to mail Skip a care package.

Chesapeake seasoned pumpkin seeds from California "

"I second that motion," agreed Becca.

They continued working on their jarring and pickling while Aino spun the Dead Kennedys Plastic Surgery Disasters.

"What better music for a pickling and pumpkin carving party," said Nate.

All three of them sang along in unison. Aino chugged sparkling water like chugging a beer.

"Go easy. All those bubbles will go to your head," said Becca.

"But I'm partying, Becca! It's almost Halloween. I'm gonna shotgun two more."

"Better not. Your stomach will explode."

I grabbed a piece of pumpkin and ran up to the loft. Nate stepped out onto the back porch, and heard a single gunshot. He noticed some lights coming from the ridge above. Three headlamps. Slowly walking down towards the house. Something wasn't right!

"Why would Otto and crew be coming from that side? It's not Otto!" He heard some radio static from Carl's walkie-talkie. He had it cranked up at total volume. Nate's heart raced because he knew immediately what it meant.

"You guys. We gotta get out of here!"

"Why, what's going on?" asked Becca.

"I saw three lights coming down the hill. They're coming from the Schieffelbein place."

They stepped out on the porch together.

"Did you hear the gunshot?"

"I didn't hear it,"said Becca."But the stereo's pretty loud."

"We should get outta here! Just leave it. Turn off the stove." All three bolted out the door and ran for the woods below the house.

The song "Winnebago Warrior" ended, and "Riot"

by the Dead Kennedys began. Rick, Dufur, and Carl approached the house.

"Ok, Carl, you go first. Dufur, check the garage, and I'll stand watch out here."

"Roger that, Rick," said Carl.

Carl snuck up to the porch with the open door. All the lights were on, and it smelled amazing. Again, he kicked the already open door and entered the kitchen, noticing the freshly roasted pumpkin seeds on the tray by the stove. He took his tactical gloves off and grabbed a handful.

"Mmm, Chesapeake seasoning." He whispered to himself but didn't realize his radio was still on.

"What do you mean Chesapeake!?" shouted Rick. "Over!"

"Oh– Sorry Rick. They got pumpkin seeds. Roasted pumpkin seeds. Over."

"What the hell are you talking about? I'm coming in, Over."

Rick appeared in the doorway holding his assault rifle.

"Pumpkin seeds. They're fucking good, Rick! Try em."

"Search the house, you imbecile. Check the insides of books. They like to stash cash in books!"

"10-4 Rick." Carl made his way to the loft where Becca slept. He went through her belongings. He found a bundle of sage held together with twine, which was burned at the end for incense. He found "The Bhagavad Gita" on the bedstand and started flipping through the pages. "What the fuck is this? Must be some kinda satanic shit." None of the books had anything stashed except her journal, which had some pressed flowers. He checked under the bed and pulled out a small hand-carved wooden box. He opened it, and three rolls of hundred-dollar bills were stashed inside.

"Jackpot!"

"Can I get a status on the garage, Dufur? Over," asked Sheriff Rick Johnson.

"Still searching. Over."

"Copy that." Rick checked the fridge in the kitchen and found a Sierra Nevada beer. He popped it open and took a seat in the great room. Pot plants were still hanging from the wires, and raspberry jam was neatly packed in cases of twelve in vacuum-sealed mason jars.

Dufur searched the garage, and there were dozens of industrial garbage bags full of pot. He noticed the fridge on the wall. The dehumidifiers were still buzzing, and the fans circulated the air. He checked the refrigerator that was taped shut, so he pulled it away from the wall. The back hatch came loose and opened up. He pulled it further from the wall and shined his headlamp at the opening.

"What the fuck?" he said to himself, then whispered, "Holy shit…"

Dufur peered inside and saw countless stacks of large bills in zip-lock baggies. He closed the hatch and pushed the refrigerator back against the wall.

"This is my jackpot!"

He searched around a little more and hatched another plan. A plan that didn't include Rick or Carl. He walked up to the main house and saw Sheriff Rick Johnson sitting in the rocking chair in the great room.

"Find anything, Rick? Other than a bottle of beer?" asked Dufur.

"Not personally, but Carl scored some cash upstairs. Fifteen K. It's not a bad start. Can you turn whatever that shit is off now? Christ! I'll do it!" Sheriff Rick Johnson approached the turntable and smashed it with the butt of his gun. "That's not music." Then Rick swung his weapon at the upright bass and smashed it in."

"What'd you do that for, Rick? I wanted it," said Carl.

"You don't play bass, Carl! What are you gonna do,

haul that big ass thing through the woods? I'm going out to check the vehicles." Rick waltzed out the door and started going through Nate's car. He rifled through the glove box.

"Score!" He found the envelope with Nate's pay inside. He quickly looked through the envelope and pocketed some of it for himself before bringing the rest back to the others.

He brought it into the house and counted out another five K. Dufur checked the shack where Aino slept and found fifteen K.

"Man, there's cash all over this place. Let's check the shack down below."

The three men walked together down the hill as Aino, Nate, and Becca looked on from the forest's darkness. They foraged Henry's belongings but found no more cash, only Harry Potter CDs.

"Man, this guy really loves Harry Potter, "said Rick.

"Gimme those," snapped Carl. "I like Harry Potter," he stashed the discs in a pillowcase he took from Henry's bed. Henry had a 22 rifle in the shack, and they took that, too. Sheriff Rick Johnson made a list of confiscated items. The gun, the DVDs, the scale, the snipping scissors, ninety-three industrial-sized trash bags full of marijuana buds. There were three more bags of pot Sheriff Rick Johnson didn't put on the list. They took all the brandy, three bags of pot, and the cash but did not put them on the confiscation list.

"I'm not burning all the pot. It's too dry out here. I ain't causing no forest fire over this shit." said Rick.

"This is a good run. Where the hell did they go?" asked Dufur.

"Well, I'm not going after 'em," said Rick. "I aint chasin' no crazed hippies through the woods. I wanna go to Slingers and celebrate! You got the blow, Carl?"

"No, I don't have any more."

"What?! You fuckin' did it all?" asked Dufur.

"It's cool. Hector's at Slingers, we can get more. Let's go to Slingers! Hector's there, I'm sure. He owes me!" said Rick.

"Yeah, let's get the fuck outta here. We got what we came for."

"Nothing in the garage? No cash in the garage?" asked Rick. "Are you sure?"

"I'm sure Rick, I checked it top to bottom," said Dufur.

"C'mon, let's move. "The three disappeared back up the hill, and their headlamps faded into the night

WHAT HAPPENED?

"Jesus Fuck!" yelled Nate. "They took it all." He sat in the driver's seat of his car and wrung his hands together.

Aino and Becca were already inside the house. Becca came out to the back porch wrapped in her blanket.

Nate sat on the counter in the kitchen with his head down.

"Well, at least they didn't torch the weed," said Aino after checking the garage. "We should give Otto a heads up. We've got to go to town and call Henry."

The three drove up the gravel road towards Otto's place. As they approached the front door, they could hear him snoring inside.

"No wonder Hunter stays at the RV park," said Nate.

"No doubt. Otto's gonna snore the house down," said Becca.

They rapped on the door, but no answer. "Otto, wake up! Otto!"

A light came on, and the door slowly opened. Otto stood naked in the doorway. USMC in giant letters tattooed across his chest. "What's up? Sorry, I was sawing logs."

"Yeah, we heard." smiled Becca.

"We got raided, Otto! Three of 'em came and trashed the place. Took all our cash."

"Oh fuck! Did they burn all the weed?"

"No, but they took three big bags," said Nate.

"Motherfuckers!"

"Wanted to give you a heads up. Are you alright here?"

"Yup. I'm fully loaded. Another run tomorrow, and we'll be gone. Heading back to Tejas."

"Looks like you're in the clear."

"Any idea who it was?"

"Nope. they didn't leave anything. We're gonna go to the summit to call Henry."

"Well, sorry about your misfortune. Y'all be careful."

The three continued to Lost Creek and drove to the top of the hill for cell phone reception. At the summit, Nate called Henry.

"Henry, we got raided."

"You ok? Are you in jail? "

"No, no. We hid in the woods. They trashed the place.

""Did you get a look at 'em?"

"I couldn't tell who they were, but there were three. They smashed your turntable and bass. Took all our money."

Henry was silent for a moment. "Not the double bass! God! I'm coming back. I'll be there in the morning. Did they burn what's in the garage?"

"Nope, but they took three bags."

"Shit! They'll be back. Can you do me a giant favor?"

"Anything, man."

"Get the Dodge truck and trailer. Load all those bags and bring 'em down to Aramoana's place in Dillits."

"Not a problem."

"You guys alright?"

"Yeah, we're fine other than losing all our money for the season."

"Don't worry, I'll make you whole again. I'll see you

in the morning," and Henry hung up.

"What'd he say?" asked Becca.

"He wants us to get all the weed and bring it to Dillits."

"Were those guys federal cops?" asked Aino.

"I don't know, man," said Nate.

"I knew the plane was a bad sign."

"What plane?" asked Nate.

"The surveillance plane. It's been swooping over all summer."

"I never saw it. Henry thinks they'll be back to get the weed; we gotta move it."

COUNTING THE LOOT

The posse arrived back at Carl's place and dragged the bags of pot into his living room.

Carl let out a rebel yell and fired off an entire clip from his machine gun into the night sky.

"Who wants a piña colada?"

"Piña colada? I need a beer and a shot," said Rick.

"Piña colada. It's my celebration drink. Don't you guys wanna celebrate?"

"What are we gonna do with all this pot?" asked Dufur.

"We're gonna sell it at Slingers," said Carl.

"Man, I'm not gonna peddle pot at the bar. We need to sell all of it in one lump sum."

"We'll sell it at your store, Carl. We gotta go back and get the rest of it!"

"Hell no, we won't!" said Carl.

"In the produce department. Have a special with the chicken," said Sheriff Rick.

Carl glared at him.

"Well, we've got a decent score here, fellas, but it's not as much as I expected," said Rick. "Almost 10k each ain't gonna cut it. We need to move on that Otto dude." Dufur and Carl didn't notice the wad of cash Rick stashed in his front pocket.

"The marine?" asked Dufur. "I don't know if I wanna mess with that guy. Isn't there another option?"

"Well, he's the next closest farm down the line. I suppose we could try the other side of the valley up by Spyrock. But those rednecks up there will be packing heat. I don't wanna fuck with biker dudes. We'll get shot for sure," said Rick.

"That marine dude will shoot us, Rick!"

Carl cranked up the blender in the kitchen and made his frozen piña colada. Sheriff Rick Johnson remembered once again what had happened to his son. He took a chug of beer and approached Carl in the kitchen.

"Is that your infamous smoothie blender? Is this the scene of the crime?" whispered Rick.

Carl looked nervous. "I don't have smoothie fixings at the house, but you're welcome to one of these."

"I told you I want a shot."

"Well, sure, Rick, anything. Anything you want, brother."

"Did you feed my son a spiked smoothie?"

Carl prematurely pulled the lid off the blender, spraying the contents out the top. Spattering himself and the Sheriff.

"Dammit, Carl! Put the lid back on!" yelled Rick.

"You sure you don't want some of this?" Carl pretended to be distracted from the question.

Rick approached a moment of clarity, but quickly dissolved into his need for more cocaine.

"Let's get out of here, Dufur. We gotta get to Slingers before Hector leaves!"

"I'm with ya man."

Rick and Dufur walked out, leaving Carl holding the dripping blender.

"Wait up guys, I wanna go too." He watched as the

Jeep's taillights disappeared down the driveway. Carl took a big swig from the blender.

Dufur drove slowly through the hairpins.

"I wanted to talk to you about Carl," said Sheriff Rick.

"I was hoping you would say that."

"Are we thinking the same thing?" asked Rick.

"Well, what are you thinking?"

"I think Carl is guilty of stealing money from the farm. You and I will get another couple thousand each; it's what I'm thinking. I think Carl spiked my son's smoothie, and now he must pay a penalty."

"We're on the same page here, Rick. Say, you wanna go get an eight ball?"

"Surely, my friend."

The two rolled to Slingers. Carl changed clothes and sped down the mountain back to town. He caught up to them at HWY 101 and flashed the high beams to let them know he had caught up.

"Oh shit! He's followed us."

"What'd you expect? He's a coke fiend like you," said Dufur.

"Yeah, well, he's paying."

"Damned right he is," said Dufur.

They changed out of their tactical gear in the Slingers parking lot and went inside for drinks.

A small crowd had gathered to watch the 49ers game.

"Drinks are on us tonight. Everybody! Drinks are on us!" Shouted Sheriff Rick. "Holly put all the drinks on Carl's tab." He gestured to Hector to meet him out back. The two met outside for a cig.

"We need another eight-ball man."

"I can't give you another for free, Rick. I gotta pay for another shipment."

"Carl's gonna pay when he gets here, but give it to me, ok?"

Hector reluctantly handed him the eight-ball.

"Don't give me that look, Hector! You know Carl's gonna pay you!"

Carl burst through the door. "Why didn't you wait for me?"

"You knew where we were going. C'mon Carl, let's celebrate; you gotta pay Hector for this!" Sheriff Rick held up the baggie and gestured for the men's room.

"Absolutely! Hang on, Hector. I need a blast first!"

"Right here, Carl. Here you go!"

"No problem, Rick. I gotcha."

"Mmmm. Thanks bud. So, tell me about the smoothie," as Rick took a bump off his key and started to needle Carl again.

"I don't know nothin' about no smoothie," said Carl. "I told you! Why do you keep bringing that up, Rick? C'mon man. Let's party tonight! Why are you getting all serious?"

"You're lucky I don't jack you up right here."

Carl turned and left the Sheriff in silence, holding the bag of coke.

DAMMIT! THEY TOOK MY HARRY POTTER

Nate, Aino, and Becca drove back to Henry's and immediately got the Dodge pickup and the trailer. It didn't take long to load the bags into the truck. Nate covered the cargo with a tarp, and it looked like just another dump run. Aino drove the cargo down to Dillits at dawn. Nate followed in his car with Becca. He parked the truck behind Aramoana's place in downtown Dillits, and she gave them a bag of homemade donuts. They left the truck and rode back to Dias Verdez in Nate's car.

"You know I've got another turntable in the solar shack," said Henry. "It's one of those old tube ones with the built-in speaker. Sounds cool, but it's a little wobbly."

"I'll go get it," said Aino.

"The bass is the hardest part of this. Why would the cops attack my bass? Jeez, these guys are criminals. And they drank my Sierra." said Henry.

"There's nothing we can do?" said Becca.

"Nope. I have a feeling it was Sheriff Rick and Dufur. I know it was them. I guess my number was up," said Henry. "Don't worry though. I'm gonna pay you guys. I'll make you whole again. "

"Henry, thank you," said Becca.

"So, you want half in Bitcoin this time?"

Aino returned carrying the old turntable. "What's this about half in Bitcoin?"

Henry smiled. "It's another day, my friends. It's now and onward. Thanks for taking the load down to Dillits. Did Aramoana give you donuts?"

"Delicious donuts. Speaking of delicious, try these pumpkin seeds." Becca handed a baggy to Henry.

"Chesapeake pumpkin seeds. I love it!"

Henry went out to the garage to inspect the damage. Surprisingly, there was none. He pulled the refrigerator out from the wall and withdrew more money to pay everybody again.

"We're back to paid in full. Are you guys still taking off? You're welcome to stay. I wouldn't mind if you did. I like the company."

"Becca and I are heading back to the city in a few days, but I still wanna shoot some more photos here."

"I'm gonna go to Kauai until February, but I'll be back if you'll have me?" said Aino.

"It's a plan, my friend. Kauai, I should come for a visit," said Henry.

"You should, I think it would do you good."

They enjoyed another great feast together and continued like nothing ever happened. Henry strolled down to his shack.

"Dammit. They took my Harry Potter. Bastards!"

He lay on the mat on the floor, cursing them.

OFF THE SCHEDULE

Carl sat at the desk in his office, watching the monitors, and slowly counted out the money he had taken from the farm the night before. He placed the new schedule above the time clock in the hallway. Billy Johnson wasn't on it.

"Can I speak to Billy, please?"

"Hello. This is Billy."

"Billy. Uh, hey, this is Carl. How's it going? How's your ankle?"

A suspicious pause came from the other end of the line. "Uh, I guess it's healing up ok."

"That's why I'm calling Billy. I've decided to take you off the schedule. I've been hearing from people around town about drug use. I can't afford to take the risk in my store."

"Are you fucking kidding me, Carl? You spiked my smoothie, you bastard!"

"Look, I didn't spike anything, and I can't afford to have a drug addict working in my store spreading rumors like that. You're fired, Billy!"

Billy was stunned and didn't know what to say.

Carl hung up and started searching through his stack of applications.

"Here it is," he mumbled. "Gary Zublinsky. Hello, is this Gary? Gary, good to reach you. I'm wondering if you're still interested in working at Amundson's. Oh, excellent! Well, how about tomorrow about 10:00 a.m.? Perfect. I'll see you tomorrow then."

He hung up the phone and put his feet on the desk, watching Walter check out a customer. He quickly leaned over and turned off the monitor.

Sheriff Rick Johnson pulled into Amundson's parking lot, and it was nearly dark outside.

"Walter, where's Carl?" he blurted out as he walked in the door.

Walter pointed towards the back. "C-C-Can I help you, Sh-Sh-Sheriff?"

Rick stopped for a second to stare Walter down. He put his index finger to his lips and said, "Shhhh-Shhhheriff needs to talk to Carl," mocking Walter's stutter. He walked back and tapped on Carl's door with his nightstick.

"Come on in!" The door opened slowly, and Sheriff Rick Johnson stood, giving him the stink eye.

"What's up, Rick? You look angry."

Sheriff Rick looked up at the security camera above Carl's desk. "I'm gonna have to place you under arrest, Carl! I hate to do this, but we have reports that you robbed a farm last night and ransacked it. You also drugged my son, you motherfucker! Anything you say can and will be used against you in court." Rick smiled for the camera.

"Fuck you, Rick! The raid was your idea."

Sheriff Rick realized he was on camera and caught up in a Hollywood moment. Lost in the thought that people might eventually see this bust video and see him as the hero. Carl bolted out the door and got behind the wheel of his monster truck in seconds. He peeled out of the parking lot. Sheriff Rick Johnson didn't rush. He knew precisely where Carl was going. He calmly walked back through the store and pulled a case of Coors Light from the cooler.

"This one's on Carl's tab," he said to Walter and walked out. He popped a beer while starting up the squad car and slowly made his way towards Slingers.

"Hey, Holly, gimme a Long Island iced tea and put it on Dufur's tab."

"Dufur's not here right now."

"Where the hell is he?"

"I don't fucking know. I don't keep up with Dufur's schedule." Holly scowled and grabbed a dirty pint glass for Sheriff Rick Johnson. He quickly chugged it down.

"Hold the attitude next time, remember who I am, Holly."

She rolled her eyes.

BACK FOR MORE

Dufur twisted his mustache into a perfect curl and drove past the gate of Henry's place. He was dressed all in black. A supermoon lit up the forest, and he followed the creek up the canyon to the spot below Henry's shack. He crept around the edge of the property and back to the garage in silence. Everyone at the farm slept while the fans blew on the few remaining plants in the garage.

He approached the refrigerator and pulled it away from the wall. The secret door fell open, and he whispered, "Jackpot!" Stacks of cash were loaded into a sack. Dufur was so excited he couldn't contain himself. He was about to pull it off.

A fully packed bowl of ganja fell from the top of the fridge when he pushed it back into place.

"Don't mind if I do," he pulled a lighter from his pocket to spark up the pipe. He took a giant drag and held the smoke in his lungs.

I jumped up behind him and startled him.

"What the fuck! Who's there?"

I hid behind a gas can.

He took another drag from the pipe. Suddenly, the shelf I gave way, and the gas can fell. He dropped the pipe, and the glowing ember landed in the leaves, igniting the fuel. The fans blew the flame into a swirl and reached the ceiling in seconds.

"Oh shit! Goddamnit, you fuckin' cat!"

I ran out the door and under the main house.

The flames from the patch of leaves quickly grew into a blaze and spread out the back of the garage into the trees. Dufur escaped with the loot sack, stumbling down the hill into the ravine leading to Lost Creek.

BLUEBERRY PIÑA COLADA

Carl whistled "Margaritaville," as he straightened up the yard tools. When he strolled back inside the house, he went to the top drawer in the kitchen and pulled out a clip of bullets. He kept calm, inserted the clip into his AR-15, and placed the weapon on the countertop. Then he foraged through the freezer and found a little baggie hidden inside a sack of frozen peas and carrots. A ziplock baggie was full of Death Cap mushrooms.

"You've lived up to your name, my little babies." He began to chop vegetables and made a salad in a small mixing bowl. He warmed the zip lock baggie with his hands to thaw the mushrooms within, then carefully sprinkled them into the salad.

"And now, ladies and gentlemen! For my final course of the night, I present Carl's Famous Death Cap Salad. Who will be the first to try it? Mom, I know you love it, but you're biased. How 'bout you, daddy?" Carl brought the salad to the family portrait and held up the bowl to his father's mouth in the painting. "What, not hungry anymore? Well, I know who's hungry. Rick's always hungry, isn't he? Or maybe I should eat it myself."

Rick's car pulled up in the driveway.

"Just in time for dinner," whispered Carl as he licked his lips.

Carl went back to the blender and turned it on.

Standing at the island in the kitchen, he had one hand on the AR-15, waiting for his esteemed guest.

Outside, Sheriff Rick left his squad car and popped open another Coors Light. He took a few seconds to down the whole can and then composed himself. He planned to arrest Carl and pin the heist on him, but first, he had to secure the money Carl had stashed from the crime.

He entered through the sliding glass door and found Carl in the kitchen, staring at the blender.

"Hey, Sport-o!" Rick shouted.

Carl didn't respond. He kept staring at the blender as it swirled. Rick stood watching him from the entrance to the kitchen.

"Man, that looks pretty good, Carl. What did you put in that?"

"Blueberries, man! Blueberries."

"Wow, I might have to try that."

"You want a blueberry piña colada, Rick? I made it special for you. For my boy in blue. Are you my boy in blue?"

Rick noticed Carl's AR-15 on the counter. Carl had one hand on it.

"What are you fucked up or something? Where's the money, Carl?"

Carl kept running the blender while he moved his other hand to the gun's trigger.

"I think that thing's blended enough, Carl!"

"What's that, Rick?"

"It's blended enough. Where'd you stash the cash?" Rick demanded. "I need it back, official police business. I've got to count it all. Is it in your truck?"

"Isn't it beautiful with blueberries, Rick?"

Rick came closer, but Carl pointed the gun at him. Still, with one hand on the puree button and the other on the trigger.

"Stop blending it, Carl. It's fucking done!"

"No, it's not. Only when it's nice and frothy. I know how you like it, Rick. Say, I made a salad for you. It's right there on the counter. Dig in, buddy! You're a ranch-dressing guy, aren't you?"

"Stop it, Carl. Enough!"

"Come on, man, I made it just for you, Rick. Why do you gotta be so rude to me?"

"Turn off the blender, you idiot!"

"Don't call me an idiot, Rick."

Without lifting the gun from the counter, Carl squeezed the trigger. Three or four rounds hit Rick in the crotch and lower abdomen.

"What the fuck, Carl!" Rick's eyes opened wide. He fell to the floor.

Carl finally stopped running the blender. He detached the pitcher and took a swig from it. "Mmm, Rick. Are you sure you don't want some of this? Let me give you some salad."

Rick writhed on the floor. Blood pooled around him.

"To my best blue boy! Sheriff Rick!" He raised up the pitcher. "A toast to you, Rick. To Sheriff Rick Johnson!"

The sheriff moaned in pain.

"I'm point man, Rick. How am I doing at this point, man? You get the first bullet tonight, though. Bullet points for you!"

Carl picked up the salad bowl and squatted beside Rick on the floor. "You gotta eat your veggies, Rick, if you wanna grow up to be a nice strong man." Carl stuffed a clump of lettuce and mushrooms into the sheriff's mouth using his fingers.

"Did you get that eight ball I ordered?" Carl asked as if Rick could answer. "I paid the tab at Slingers. We've got a clean slate now."

Sheriff Rick Johnson stopped breathing. His eyes had rolled back behind his eyelids.

"You look like you need a drink." Carl picked up the

pitcher from the counter and poured some blue slush into Rick's mouth. It dripped down the dying man's cheek. "Are we wasted? You're wasted, aren't you, Rick? Now we're really partyin', bro."

Carl stood up to pour himself a glass and carried it to the deck. He thought he smelled smoke but didn't pay any attention to it.

"I'd like to send a toast out to my parents. Thank you both for your support through all these years. I'd like to thank Sheriff Rick Johnson. Thank you, Rick, for being so sexy all the time in your policeman's uniform! And I want to thank Leif Brody. Thanks for nothing, Leif. Thanks for squealing on me and ruining my life. Also, thanks to your cowardly parents for selling off their place to that hippie Henry instead of me. Thanks, assholes. You made my parents try to cut me out of their will! Cheers to you all!"

Carl returned to the kitchen. He leaned down to caress Rick's lifeless face. Carl massaged the piña colada into the dead man's skin as if he were giving him a facial. Then he licked his own fingers. "Mmm. Tastes even better now. You look so healthy, Rick. You look vibrant."

Something flickered in the kitchen window. Carl stood upright and saw flames approaching quickly from the valley below. Yes, he had smelled smoke. The wind must have just shifted.

"You wanna go watch the fire with me, Rick? It'll be beautiful." Carl removed all his clothes and stood with the pitcher of piña colada and his gun.

TRICKLING WATER

Henry noticed the flickering lights coming from the hillside above.

"Oh shit!" He ran to the main house and woke the

others.

"Fire! We gotta go now! Everybody up!" The blaze was spreading to engulf the entire clump of trees across the driveway from the house. The wind blew the flames away from the house and up the hill towards the Shieffelbein place. Aino had already run to the main house to alert the others. The fire flared over the road, forming an up-flow vacuum, eventually engulfing the area.

"Come on, let's go to the swimming hole." They ran the trail to the tree line and down the rocky slope to the creek. Aino had grabbed his trumpet and was running with it. Having reached the pond's edge, they sat listening to the freight train roar of the fire above them. It blew like a beast up the mountain and engulfed the Schieffelbein house. Everything burned within minutes as the winds whipped and stoked the fires up through the trees at the edge of the Amundson estate.

They sat in the pool by the trickling waterfall. Ash fell like snow, but the wind began to die down. The firestorm had passed and gone up the mountain. They were safe.

"Has anyone seen Chaos?" asked Henry in a panic.

"I haven't seen him since yesterday." CHAOS! WHERE ARE YOU?!" yelled Aino.

I hid in the cave behind the waterfall.

MAGICAL FIRE

Carl watched from his stone patio as the firestorm approached.

"Wow, Rick, it's magical!"

Rick lay comatose in a pool of blood. The fire towered over the tree line, and Carl felt the intense heat from a hundred yards away. He noticed sparks behind him popping out of the newly installed drain in the corner of the patio. The sparks formed a spout, and soon, the flames became a geyser of molten plastic that reached up to the edge of the roof. Carl looked back and smiled as the house ignited.

"Well, let's go to Slingers. What do you say, Rick? I still got that eight ball." Carl was nude, and he picked up Sheriff Rick Johnson from the kitchen floor and carried him out to the monster truck. He placed him in the passenger seat.

"Better buckle up, Rick. Click it or ticket. Safety first." The Sheriff lay zombified. "Oh, hold on, Rick. Do you want one for the road? I know I do."

Carl returned inside for the rest of the piña colada and came back with the pitcher. He cranked up the truck. "You good, bro? Hey man, can I have a blast before we go?" He reached over and pulled the little baggie from the front pocket of the sheriff's uniform. He took a big snort and put the truck into gear.

"Thanks, Rick!"

The flames engulfed the backside of the house as he slowly made his way down the driveway.

The wind had separated the fire into several limbs flowing toward the summit. Carl drove up through the hairpins as the flames swept across the road in front of the truck. Eventually, he came to a calm spot on the road surrounded by the inferno.

"Remember that time you took all the things out of my locker and filled it with horseshit? That was a good one, Rick. I always remember that. Is there something wrong? Hey man! Is it something I said? Want another shot of my blueberry piña colada?"

He stopped momentarily and laughed like a maniac, staring at Rick in the passenger seat.

"Blueberry for my blue boy." He took another swig from the blender, which went down the wrong pipe with his laughter. He coughed and shouted, "Now we're fuckin' partying Rick! Don't you know how to party anymore, you pussy? Don't be harshing my mellow bro. Oh shit, hang on, man, I gotta piss."

Carl stopped the truck. He got out and stood in the middle of the road, facing the flames. "Are you sick, Rick? You look pale."

The fire grew more intense as it surrounded them. Carl let loose his bladder and got back into the truck. "It's all taken care of, man. No more fire." Carl started whistling again with tears running down his cheeks. "Did you do it all, you selfish motherfucker?"

The front tire exploded, and he kept driving on the rims. Eventually, the truck stalled in the intense heat, but Carl kept singing and laughing.

"Rick, you wanna party, bro? Come on, don't hold back on me now. Remember how we partied on spring break in Lake Havasu? LET'S FUCKIN' PARTY BRO!" He screamed as the flames overtook him, and the truck was completely swallowed up. "Rick! We're fucking partying!"

The Amundson estate was swept away in the fire and reduced to ash. The two men were burned beyond recognition in the firestorm, leaving only skeletons behind. The metal blender lay in the smoldering remains of Carl's skeleton.

RUN FOR THE ANGUILLA

Flames had already swallowed Otto's truck at the edge of the driveway. He put on his running shoes and sprinted down the canyon, escaping the path of the fire. His house eventually burned to the ground. Otto ran to the Anguilla River, where it intersected HWY 101, several miles south of Dias Verdez. He ran back to town while the fire raged up the mountain, reaching the RV park where Hunter and Ulee slept.

"Hunter, wake up!" The light flicked on, and Hunter came out.

"The A-Frame's gone. Wildfire! It's gone, all of it! We gotta go!"

"Holy moly!"

Ulee emerged as ash fell from the sky, collecting in her hair.

An eerie glow appeared from the other side of the mountains to the east.

"I think it's moving north. I don't think it can cross HWY 101, but you never know if the wind will turn," said Otto.

A helicopter flew over.

CalFire trucks drove north past them at full speed with lights flashing. Farmers from the hills fled to Dias Verdez and found respite for the night in the parking lot of the Amundson Grocery.

DUFUR'S BAG

Dufur returned to the Fish and Game truck with his bag of loot. He drove alongside the creek to the logging road and decided to follow it to the end. He wanted to stash the cash, not realizing how massive the fire had become up the canyon behind him. It burned in the opposite direction he traveled. He drove slowly to the dead end and parked by the railroad bridge, counting the rolls of hundred-dollar bills in the cab of the truck. It amounted to nearly one hundred thirty thousand dollars.

"Holy Shit!" he whispered. "Yes! Yes! Yes!"

Dufur packed the cash in his bag and hiked upstream along the Anguilla River past the old train trestle. He went to the defunct electrical station. Fish and Game had a storage locker at the facility, and Dufur had the key. He kept his fishing gear there. The padlock rusted shut, so he smashed it with a stone, knocking the latch from the rotten wooden frame.

Dufur's tackle box was inside the locker. It had a

sticker that read Norcal Bass Anglers Challenge 1999, with a drawing of a robot reeling in a fish. He transferred the money into the bottom of the box and covered it with a rain poncho. He would come back for it later. His mind spun with the excitement of his score, and he'd forgotten about the hills glowing behind him.

He returned to the truck and tried to celebrate with a small flask of whiskey he found resting in the glove box. He gulped it down but nearly threw it back up. Coughing uncontrollably. When he collected himself, the sleepiness overtook him. He hunched over with his head against the window. Eventually, he stretched out on the truck's bench seat and fell asleep.

In the morning, he awoke to thick smoke and a layer of ash as if it had snowed the night before. His eyes were burning, and his asthma kicked in. Realizing that he had started the fire, he felt a panic coming on for fear of being found out. He began hyperventilating and stood by the truck, leaning over with his hands on his knees. He knew he had to get out of there. He could hardly breathe. He made his way back up the canyon, driving fast. The further up he got, the thicker the smoke. The trees on the side of the road were scorched and still smoldering from the night before. He closed the windows of the truck, but it didn't help. He came upon a burned vehicle on the road at the hairpins.

"Oh my god!" The truck was blocking the way, and the tires were still smoldering. He recognized the truck's plate, NORCAL 1. It was Carl's truck. Gutted by the flames. He stopped and got out. He could barely breathe while approaching the truck. There were two skeletons inside.

"Oh my god! NO! Fuck! What have I done? Oh my god!"

He coughed and gasped at the sight. Crying and screaming, "FUCK!" The forest continued to crackle with the heat. As if it was laughing at him.

Dufur returned to the truck and drove past the charred vehicle while reaching for his empty flask. Something, anything, to calm the chaos in his brain. Further up the canyon, he arrived at the summit wheezing and almost blacked out from the smoke. He drove faster to escape it but lost control on the other side of the mountain. It was too thick to see, and he went over the edge. The truck flipped down the hill and lodged in a ravine surrounded by poison oak and manzanita trees. He hit his head on the steering wheel and passed out. He died in the cab from smoke inhalation. They didn't find the body until more than a month later. He'd gone over the edge and was out of sight from the road. The body was severely decomposed when they found it. His mustache was the only identifiable feature. Still waxed to perfection into a curl on both sides of his rotting mouth.

WEATHER THE STORM

Henry, Becca, Aino, and Nate spent the night at the swimming hole. They soaked for hours in the creek, which started heating up from the fire above. The fire swept north from its starting point, and they were spared from direct flames. Ash fell around them and accumulated on the rocks at the creek's edge. The green algae turned gray around the pond as they weathered the firestorm in the water. At dawn, I popped out of the cave behind the trickling waterfall.

"Chaos, you've made it!" said Henry.

I had a nightmare about Aino. In the dream the river raged, and the water boiled. Aino awoke and arose from the river. The boulders were cracking like giant pieces of popcorn. He emerged from the water surrounded by flames as he reached for the trumpet, Red hot and on the verge of melting. When he went to grab the horn, it stuck to his hand and burned the skin. The trumpet sizzled in his fingers, but he couldn't let it go. It didn't bother him. He put the trumpet to his lips and started to blow a note. It sounded like a freight train. The skin from his lips came off around the mouthpiece. Unfazed, he blew a long note and screamed!

"Chaos! Where are you!" That's when I woke up in the cave behind the waterfall. I said, "I'm right here. I've been here the whole time."

I pop my head out, and there he is, asleep on the moss, and everything is okay. What a crazy dream for a cat!

"Oh my god, I hope everybody's alright. The fire went towards Otto's place," said Henry as Aino sat rocking with his feet in the creek. Downstream, Nate washed his face.

"Is it safe to go up there now?" asked Becca.

"I don't know. Those trees are brittle after they burn. You guys wanna take a chance?" asked Henry.

"We should. What if Otto needs some help? Was Aramoana at her house?"

"No she's in Dillits. But Otto was at his place. His last night before leaving. Fuckin' hell!"

The four made their way up the trail back to the house. I followed along as the forest floor was still hot from the fire. It burned my paws, but I didn't think about the pain. Henry's shack stood unscathed, and so did the main house. The garage had burned completely. The forest below the house survived untouched. The forest above the garage burned to cinders, and the wood mill burned with a few vehicles. Aino's truck and the Suburban were spared along with the solar shed.

"We've got to get to Otto's," said Henry.

The four of them piled into the Suburban, and I jumped in. I wanted out of the smoke. They drove up the road and checked on Aramoana's house. It burned completely to the ground. The gallery and the paintings were smoldering in a pile of cinders. I figured that would happen one day. I would've liked to have seen the one Ulee and I made one last time. The goats were down in the ravine near the creek. Smart enough to escape. My old house burned as well. The metal satellite dish remained, but all the poison oak had burned away and was now scorched black. Warped into the shape of a taco.

They made the turn to Otto's cabin and found a smoldering foundation. Otto's truck was gutted and resting on metal rims, still smoldering at the edge of the property. They surveyed the area but found no sign of him.

"Do you think he got out?" asked Becca.

Henry sat silent as Aino began to weep. Nate put his arm around him.

"I don't think he's here," said Henry. "We should try to make it to town. I don't know if the fire's gonna loop back around or what. Let's wait a little while and let the smoke clear."

Eventually, they made it up the hill. They stopped briefly at the hairpins to examine the burned-up truck with the skeletons inside.

"Do you know whose truck that is?"

"I think it's Carl's," said Henry.

At the summit, Henry searched for cell service but to no avail. He slowly drove back down the hill and into Dias Verdez. A crowd of people had gathered at the Amundson's parking lot. They stopped at the RV park. There was no sign of Otto, Hunter, or Ulee.

Henry dialed Otto's phone, as the signal returned. Otto picked up right away.

"Holy crap! Where you at, Otto?"

"I'm down in Dillits. I got out by the skin of my teeth l"We were just at your place," said Henry.

"Tell me it's alright," gasped Otto.

Nope. It's gone, man. Nothing left."

"Oh, fuck I knew it! Flames were heading right at me. Everybody alright on your end?"

"We're all fine. We saw a truck all burned up on Lost Creek Road. Two skeletons inside. Not sure who they were, but they were burned to bones. I think it's Carl's truck. CalFire has a bunch of people heading up that way. What did you do to get outta there?"

"I ran to the Anguilla River and kept running to the 101. At the Safeway now."

"Oh man, what a relief," said Henry.

"Well, don't fear my brother. We are all doing alright. Ulee's gonna come back to Houston with us. I think we're gonna get the hell outta here."

"I don't blame you brother. Well, will I see you next year?"

"Of course you will! Hey, we left Ulee's trailer at the RV park. You're welcome to stay there if you need a place. Ulee is giving me the nod right now."

"No, we're good. My house was spared. It started in my garage; I'm not sure how."

"Fuck, are you kidding me? Ahh, man."

"It could have been the dehumidifier or a fan short-circuiting. I don't know. I'm sorry, Otto."

"It's not your fault, man. You didn't make it happen. The wind. The drought. All this shit. It's not your fault, man."

"Well take it easy brother. I'll see you next year."

"Right on man. Be safe."

AFTERMATH

Otto and the crew hit the road, camping at the Pendleton Marine Base for a few nights to regroup. They returned to Houston but took their time, stopping at the Grand Canyon and Big Bend National Park. Ulee realized her home needed to be in Dias Verdez and soon returned but would spend the coming summers with Otto and Hunter. She'd also travel to Houston to visit a couple times a year.

Henry made everybody whole again. The remaining money in the fridge in the garage burned, but the stashes at the waterfall and various other hiding spots survived. Aino took the flight to Kauai and would return the following year. Becca also returned but put her money down on some acreage that sold for cheap after the fire. She went on to run a successful farm of her own. Nate kept investing his cash into dispensaries in San Francisco and now runs a company selling medicinal marijuana patches for body aches. Nobody heard from Skip again, but it's rumored he held onto his Bitcoin and is now a billionaire living in South America.

The FBI had been monitoring Sheriff Rick Johnson and Dufur Fleck for several years. Dufur was linked to the fire, which caused millions of dollars' worth of damage. If the two had survived they would have been charged with a string of crimes.

Billy ended up fully recovering from his ankle injury but lost his scholarship to UCLA. He was a walk-on for the team at Fresno State and became a starting wide receiver. He went on to play indoor football for the Omaha Beef.

Holly's plan to purchase Slingers came to fruition. She and Hector got out of the cocaine business once and for all. Hector learned to code and created a successful gaming app. He helped fix up the bar and started his own brewery. They changed the name to Honna & Hector's and added some motel rooms. Turning it into a legitimate roadhouse.

The Amundson family will stated that if Carl Amundson died, the entire Amundson estate would go to Ulee Winooski. Ulee would obtain full ownership of the Amundson grocery store and family property along with any assets, stocks, and vehicles associated with the business. Ulee returned from Houston to set up the store again as a communal co-op. This ensured the employees would share equally in the profits of the store. When Ulee returned the following summer, she appointed Walter as General Manager and gave him a huge raise. The first order of business was to disassemble the rotisserie chicken machine and throw it into the dumpster.

They replaced the area of the deli with a coffee roaster. They started roasting their own beans, servicing much of Mendocino County. Ulee built an event space at the back of the store with a sitting area where they hosted music shows, movie nights, and poetry readings. The back parking lot was converted into a community garden. They opened one of the walls for a picture window with a full view of the mountains. Ulee removed the banner for Carl's Poultry Paradise, revealing the nature mural she'd finished in the mid-'70s.

Ulee created the George DeCarlo collaborative art gallery. That's cool, but she put our last surviving painting inside a small broom closet near the coffee area. Our collaboration hung behind the door of a closet with a single lightbulb dangling from a wire inside. I get the joke, Ulee, but I can't help but feel slighted. I still have a little pride left, even as a cat. She could have put the painting in a more prominent spot, but why do I care? Honestly, geez!

Otto and Hunter rebuilt the A-Frame and another house alongside it called "The Bud and Breakfast." This accommodated tourists much like California wine country, but only for weed.

Henry rebuilt the garage with lumber from the property. Some burned trees were salvaged, and he bought a new Wood Mizer lumber mill. I stayed in town, near where I was born. I jumped out of the Suburban the night of the fire and never returned to the farm again.

Ulee kept the trailer I initially bought, and I moved in with her again. Talk about coming full circle. Well, not precisely in with her, but I sleep underneath the trailer. It's her home now, and she's okay with me staying underneath as long as I piss away from the trailer. As I got older, I found being in town much easier, especially with all the sympathetic tourists coming through the RV Park. There were plenty of snacks, so my hunting days were over. Hans stopped coming to the fence one day, and we all knew what that meant. Henry would come by to say hello every now and again. Aino and Becca, too. Those two are an item now.

I saw the Wizard guy dressed in the monk's robe. He had his Border Collie with him and carried that same wooden staff. The dog barked at me from the road, but it was more like a farewell bark. The Wizard guy held his thumb out to hitch a ride. He was carrying a tackle box with a sticker of a robot reeling in a fish. Still don't know what his deal was. He waved and yelled, "Bye Bye, Chaos!" I don't know where he got that from; my name is George, George DeCarlo.

Lost Creek
Anguilla River

Remembering Sherman

ACKNOWLEDGEMENTS

Thank you, Natalie, for all the love and support. I appreciate the much-needed criticism and I probably wouldn't have followed through if it wasn't for you. I can't believe how patient you are. You've taught me so much. I'm lucky to have you in my life, I love you!

Thanks to several friends who read this book and helped with editing, specifically Sean Gould and Tate Swindell.

Thank you, Peter Orr, for mentoring me through this process.

Thanks to the Shepski family for giving me a haven through the pandemic and becoming a second family.

Thanks to Bill McCanless for his friendship, encouragement and support through decades..
Much love to the Interzone Coffee Shop Corvallis, OR.
Amazing coffee and the best waffle on the planet.

Thanks to Matt Gee for letting me stay with him in Sanibel Island, Florida. I wrote much of this at the Sanibel Island Public Library.

Thanks to Dan & Shannon for your love and friendship.

Thanks to Mishka Shubaly's writing tips and encouragement.

Thanks to Jason Burge for going through the roughest early draft and offering his feedback.

Thanks to Mom & Pop for always being in my corner. I love and appreciate you both.

Finally, Thank you to anyone reading this. I appreciate you taking the time out of your day. I hope you like it.

Kindly, David Dondero

About the author

David Dondero, born on June 24, 1969, in Duluth, Minnesota, is an acclaimed singer-songwriter with a career spanning 11 albums and 25 years. His compositions weave intricate tales of personal experiences, societal observations, and the complexities of human emotion, earning him recognition as a masterful storyteller. Dondero's ability to convey genuine emotion through his lyrics has solidified his place in the indie folk scene, making him a respected and influential figure in contemporary songwriting.

Chaos the Cat is Dondero's first novel.
He currently resides in Pensacola, Florida.